GONE THE SUN

GONE THE SUN

A NOVEL BY

JEFF LAFFEL

AND

MICHAEL KLEPPER

iUniverse, Inc.
Bloomington

Gone the Sun
A Novel

Cover Art by Richard Harrison

iUniverse books may be ordered through booksellers or by contacting:

iUniverse
1663 Liberty Drive
Bloomington, IN 47403
www.iuniverse.com
1-800-Authors (1-800-288-4677)

ISBN: 978-1-4502-7166-0 (sc)
ISBN: 978-1-4502-7165-3 (dj)
ISBN: 978-1-4502-7164-6 (ebk)

Library of Congress Control Number: 2010916857

Printed in the United States of America

iUniverse rev. date: 11/09/2010

(there was)…"a village called Kanuga that many years ago stood at the fork of the Pigeon River. It is long since gone and no trace remains other than potsherds that people sometimes find…"
Charles Frazier, COLD MOUNTAIN

Martha: Truth and illusion…you don't know the difference.
George: No; but we must carry on as though we did.
Edward Albee, WHO'S AFRAID OF VIRGINIA WOOLF?

"Day is done, gone the sun,
From the hills, from the lake from the skies,
All is well, safely rest,
God is nigh."
TAPS

DEDICATIONS

Jeff

This book is dedicated to my father, Robert (Rube) Laffel, who always believed in me and who taught me the meaning of unconditional love.

Michael

This book is dedicated to my mother, Rose Klepper, who told me "you will succeed in everything you do, no matter what."

THANKS

Thanks to Jonathan Bialek, Joyce Laffel, Joan D'Avanzo and Richard Harrison for always being there.

And, mainly, thanks to Bob Karmon, a great playwright and friend, whose incisive suggestions and faith in what we were doing kept us moving on.

IN APPRECIATION

of Ed Lehrer, Sam Laffel, Marty Gelobter, Sam Stein, Bob Berman, Herb Levy, Hal Ruby, Sam Greitzer, Hy Finerman, Sam Laster, Sam Schindleheim, Clive Davis, Lee Terrel, George Ross, Eddie Joachim, Mike Treib, Howard Portnoy, and, especially, the beloved Henny Goldman, who, along with all the others from a different time and a different camp, filled Jeff and Mike's summer world with never to be forgotten memories.

AFTER THE SCREENING – 1

"So?"

Henry Sturtz got up from the plush seat he had been sitting in for the past two hours and looked into the darkness of his private screening room. Three people sat there, not speaking, not moving still staring at the screen as the final credits rolled. "They're not looking to see who did the catering," he thought, "they just don't know what to say." Good. The film had obviously knocked them on their ass, that seemed clear, but he needed to hear it from them.

"No comments? Nothing?"

As the film played out and the lights came up, Sturtz looked at the three middle- aged people sitting in the seats in front of him, still staring, now at a blank screen, and wondered who they were. He had known them as kids of course, all those summers ago at camp, but thirty- five years had made them old, strangers to him. He knew *he* still looked good. In his business you had to. A little snip here, a little lift there, but the others! He looked over at where Andrew sat slumped in his seat. His face had lengthened through the years, the round, rosy cheeks that had once given him the nickname of "Apple" were gone. His hair was thinner, his stomach a bit fuller. And Nicki. Though it didn't look as though she had gained a pound since he had seen her last, there was a lot of gray in her hair now and her eyes looked tired, sad. Gavin had changed the least, still tall, rangy and boyishly handsome despite the port wine birthmark on his cheek, his hair full with only a touch of gray.

They were his friends and they were strangers and they had been invited to see the movie he had made about them and now he *had* to know.

"Damn it all, come on, what did you think?"

"For me, I think it's hot in here."

Sturtz shook his head. "That's not what I asked, Andrew."

"Well, it is. For God's sake, with all your money you could at least put on the A.C."

"The A.C. is on, Andrew." Sturtz's voice took on an edge. "Screw the A.C. What about the movie?"

"The movie?" Andrew waved it away. "It's a fairy tale. I know you meant it to be us, but it wasn't." He gestured to the dark screen. *They*, those made up characters, aren't. And the storyline," he harrumphed, "*some* fact, I'll give you that, but mostly fiction. It's not what happened, Henry."

"What's not what happened?"

Andrew shrugged. "*It*. The whole thing! It's not what happened."

Henry Sturtz grunted. "It's a movie, Apple, it's not real."

Andrew Brookman realized he hadn't been called Apple for years and he wasn't sure he liked it anymore. He pointed to the screen. "*That* wasn't supposed to be *real*? Bullshit. That was the story of us at Camp Kanuga in 1975, and you know it."

Henry Sturtz smiled and relit his cigar. "Prove it", he said.

Andrew just looked at him in disgust.

"The film itself was beautiful, Henry."

Sturtz looked at Nicki and smiled. "I thought *you* would enjoy it. Of all of us, you were always the one who had the best taste." He chuckled. "Except when you married Apple, of course."

Nicki shook her head. "I didn't say that I enjoyed it. You know that I didn't, that I couldn't. I was just saying that it was well made."

Sturtz bowed to her. "Thank you, Nicki. I'll take whatever I can get from what is starting to look like a very hostile audience."

Gavin Stewart felt nauseated. He had always had a slight touch of claustrophobia and now, sitting in the close confines of the insulated screening room in Sturtz's townhouse, the smell of Henry's cigar taking the oxygen from the room, he began to feel the walls closing in.

"Forget how good or bad the movie itself was," Andrew continued. "That's not the point."

"And the point is?"

Andrew, Apple to his friends all those years ago, took a Kleenex from his shirt pocket and wiped his forehead. "It's just," and he searched for the word, "different." His voice rose. "I mean, yes, every*thing* was the same, the setting, the time and place, you caught that. That was real, I'll give you that, but the story, most of the story anyway, was bullshit. And I'll say it again. That was supposed to be *us*?" He shook his head. "No. No way."

Sturtz nodded and then looked over at the lanky man sitting at the side of the room, still staring at the empty screen. "Gavin, you?"

Gavin Stewart, feeling the gorge rise in his throat, simply shook his head and said nothing. Nicki, sitting beside him, took his hand.

Sturtz sighed. "Oh well, at least I gave you a chance to see it before the general public. You wanted me to, and I did. You have to give me that."

"Eat shit, Henry."

Sturtz laughed. "Always a master with words, Apple. You should have been a writer." Andrew glared at him. Sturtz snapped his fingers. "Oh, that's right, you *did* write a book. I had forgotten. Whatever happened to it, Apple? Get lost amongst your lesson plans?"

"Stop it, Henry."

Sturtz held up his hands to Nicki in mock supplication. "Okay. Okay. I give." No one spoke. "Well," Sturtz said, "since I don't suppose any of you would like to see it *again*...." He looked up at the projection booth and made a cutting movement across his neck. A disembodied electronic voice said, "Thank you, Mr. Sturtz," and there was a click and then total silence. Sturtz looked at Apple. "You *don't* want to see it again, do you?"

Andrew looked up at him, his face set. "*I* don't, but I'm sure that our lawyers will."

"My ass, your lawyers will." Sturtz pulled on his cigar, the gray, pungent smoke rising above his head. "Your lawyers! What lawyers, and why lawyers? I reiterate. There is nothing in this movie about you. Nada. Zip."

Andrew snorted. "Oh, come on, Henry. You changed the names but it was *all* about us. Every one of us! Anyone who was there that year will know."

Nicki's voice was thin, hardly audible. "All those things about Gavin. You shouldn't have, Henry. You had no right. And York! For God's sake, why York?" She squeezed Gavin's hand. He covered it with his. "You made it look like York committed suicide."

"All persons depicted in this photoplay are fictional. Any resemblance between them and anyone living or dead is purely coincidental."

"Screw you." Andrew Brookman stood and started to say something else, then stopped, shook his head and looked at his watch.

"I must say," Sturtz sighed, ignoring Andrew, "that all in all Lennie did a very good job with the script. I wasn't sure if the putz could pull it off, but he really did. May even win him a few awards." He chuckled. "Certainly made him more money than he'd ever seen before, that's for sure." He snickered. "You should have seen him when....."

Gavin Stewart took a deep breath and spoke for the first time. "Where is the prick?"

"Ah," Sturtz chuckled, "the dead awaken. I told you before he'll be here.

He didn't want to be at the actual screening. Thought it might influence your reactions."

Andrew shook his head, "I'll bet he did", and Gavin said, "He's even more full of crap than you are, Henry." He glared at Sturtz, who responded by grinning at him. "You know, this was the third time I've seen this little gem and it just keeps getting better and better. I smell awarrr-ds." No one spoke. "Looooook", he dragged out the word, "boys and girls," Sturtz cajoled, "lighten up. Okay, so we need to talk, I'll give you that, but we should wait until Lennie gets here. In the meantime, there's food and drink in the outside reception area. Let's wait for him out there. We'll relax, we'll reminisce; we'll schmooze."

Gavin stood up, shaking his head. "I've gotta get out of here. I can't breathe?" He looked at Andrew. "I'm sorry, man, I tried, but I can't do this." He gently pushed past his friend. "I'm going home."

"You are such a pathetic baby, Gavin." Sturtz walked the few feet to where his boyhood friend had stopped and got between him and the door. "You always were and you always will be."

"And you are still an A number one prick, Henry." With one swift motion, Gavin pushed him aside and started out.

Sturtz stopped him. "What's your problem, Gav? You're seriously gonna tell me that Lennie got it wrong, about you, about you and, well, your proliclivities. Huh? Not true? And all of those things about York; not true either?"

Andrew barked a laugh. "So much for not being about anyone living or dead."

Gavin's tone was threatening. "Forget me. I can deal, but what do you mean 'those things about York?' What does that mean? What *about* York, huh, Hank, what about him?"

Sturtz threw up his hands. "Temper, temper, big guy. A little defensive are we? Look, I'm just saying that he got it right, Dorff. Though he was quick to show him in a good light, he pinpointed his failings, York's."

"His what?"

Nicki got up and put her hand on Sturtz's arm. "Henry, stop."

Sturtz glanced at Nicki and went on. "It's just that there has been so much *crap* about him. The sainted York! I finally wanted to show him the way that he really was."

"Why?"

Sturtz smiled at Nicki. "Why not?"

Gavin's voice was hardly audible. "He wasn't the way you and Dorff portrayed him."

"No? Then what was he, Gavin, huh, what was he? A god? A superman?"

"He was my *brother.*"

"Not that anyone could see you from behind his shadow."

Gavin took a step toward Sturtz and Andrew quickly moved in, making sure he was safely between them. "You're right, Gavin," he said. "This is fucking ridiculous. I'm with you and we are both outta here." He touched his friend's arm. "I'm sorry for talking you into coming in the first place. It was a mistake." He held out his hand. "Nicki?"

"What was a mistake? What's wrong?"

They all turned. Leonard Dorff stood in the doorway, his frightened eyes going from person to person, finally stopping at Sturtz. "They didn't like it?"

"Didn't like it!" Andrew snorted. "There's an understatement."

"It seems that Gavin here is a little……."

"Shut up, Sturtz." Gavin's voice was measured and strangely calm as he looked at the tall, slightly stooped man standing in front of the door.

After all this time, finally, Leonard Dorff! *He* was certainly older, his hair, what there was of it, gray and thinning, but as soon as he spoke, there was no question that it was the same Dorff that had set everything in motion, that had changed their lives forever. Gavin stared at him and when he spoke his voice was flat and tight. "Where the hell did you get the right? Huh, Lennie? Where did you get the fucking right?"

"Gavin," Dorff muttered, backing away, "it's the way I saw it. It's the way everyone saw it."

"He's right," Sturtz said. "It's the way it was."

This time Nicki's voice was hard. "Not all of it was like that, Lennie. Not all."

Sturtz laughed. "All? You don't know what all there was, Nicki. Not all of it? Uh- uh. Not by a long shot. This was the nice version. There were a few choice things we left out."

Nicki ignored him and looked hard at Dorff. "*None* of it was like that. It was only the way *you* saw it."

"And always from the outside, Lennie," Andrew said. "You always saw us from the outside looking in."

"Apple," Dorff said to Andrew, his voice shaking, "no. That's wrong. I was there. I was part of it all. I was your friend."

"Pathetic," Gavin said.

"I was, Gavin. Everything that happened back then was all a mistake. If we had only talked then……"

Andrew cut him off. "You should have talked to Gavin years ago, before it all happened."

"I tried, Apple. I did everything I could, but he wouldn't listen. It was all a terrible misunderstanding and…."

Andrew pressed on. "And now with this", he cocked his head toward the screen, "you should have consulted with all of us before you started, Lennie." His hand swept across the screening room. "This…what you did was wrong."

"Lennie's got a pretty good track record of doing things wrong, haven't you, Len?" Gavin didn't wait for a reply. "Let me tell a truth here, not something that is arguable, a truth. Something that we all can agree on."

"Finally," Sturtz smiled, "common ground."

Gavin stared hard at Dorff. "Simple truth? Okay?" His voice took on an edge. "You are a miserable piece of shit, Lennie, you know that? You are now, you were then and you always will be, period. But I don't think that comes as any great surprise to you." Dorff backed further away, but Gavin went on. "We tried, man, oh, how we tried, *I* tried, you remember how I tried, but you weren't happy with that and so you fucked us." Gavin's voice grew louder. "You fucked us all that summer, but somehow even that wasn't good enough, so you had to do it all over again," and Gavin pointed to the screen, "with that!

"Gavin, I…….."

But Gavin wasn't listening. "You had to bring back all the pain you caused, you had to bring it back to life again, now, after all this time in a fucking movie."

Leonard Dorff gulped. "It was Henry's idea, Gavin. I swear. He wanted to make it into a movie. He called me. He talked me into it. I didn't want to. Think about it, why *would* I want to?"

Sturtz chuckled. "Right in character. Oh, Lennie. Once a coward, always a coward! Things don't change, do they?"

"You could have said no, Lennie. You could have stopped yourself. What did you do it for now Len, the thirty pieces of silver? Back then it was self preservation, but what was it for now."

"Gavin, I…."

"But that's something that you could never do, isn't it, stopping yourself?

Maybe if you had been able to stop yourself that day at camp none of this would have happened and we wouldn't have ended up here."

Dorff, his mouth dry, looked from Gavin to Sturtz and then to Andrew and realized he was on his own. He looked at Nicki. "Please."

"Gavin," Nicki said, her voice tired. "Leave him alone. He's not worth it. Let's just go."

But Gavin Stewart was not listening. His voice was hoarse as it grew louder. "You are a God damned miserable piece of shit, Lennie, you know that? A piece of shit."

"Gavin don't."

"A God damned, miserable piece of shit who twisted and manipulated things, manipulated *us*, until there was no going back. You ruined it, Lennie. You ruined all of it. Us."

Dorff was frightened. "Gavin, no, really I......"

"YOU ARE A FUCKING MISERABLE PIECE OF SHIT."

Gavin's movement was so sudden that there was no way anyone could have stopped it. One moment he was standing next to Lennie Dorff, the next he was standing over him as Dorff writhed on the floor his hand to his face. "He hit me," he mewled, "Gavin hit me." Apple and Nicki pulled their friend away as Dorff struggled to his feet. "HIT YOU? *YOU'RE LUCKY I DIDN'T HAVE A GUN, LENNIE,"* Gavin screamed as he thrashed to get free, *"BECAUSE I SWEAR TO GOD, IF I HAD I WOULD HAVE FUCKING KILLED YOU."*

"Gavin!"

"I WOULD HAVE FUCKING KILLED YOU THE SAME AS YOU KILLED MY BROTHER. YOU HEAR THAT, LENNIE, THE SAME AS YOU KILLED MY BROTHER AND YOU KILLED MY WHOLE FUCKING LIFE."

At that moment, the projectionist's voice crackled from the booth. "Will you want anything else, Mister Sturtz?"

Sturtz looked at the people frozen before him in tableau. "No," he said, "I think we're good."

PART ONE:
THE FILM OF TIME

CHAPTER ONE:

POV: Lennie Dorff:

I grew up in hand-me-downs.
When we *had* to buy new, which was seldom, we headed for Woolworths.
Jeans for instance. Woolworths. Woolworths' brand, never Levis or Lees or even Wrangler! Woolworths. The kind of jeans that had red flannel on the inside pant leg so that when you rolled them up…well, you remember. But that was when we bought new. Most of my stuff, almost everything I owned, came from things that people outgrew or no longer wanted. My father was an expert schnurer, always getting something for nothing, somehow always there when someone was cleaning out a closet, moving or simply throwing out the old and bringing in the new. Because of this, and added to the fact that my father never knew how to make enough money to support his family, bits and pieces of other people's lives were given to me. That in itself may not be earth shaking to you, but then you didn't live my life, and, most of all, you didn't go to Kanuga.

How can I describe the Jews that went to that camp without sounding at once awe struck and at the same time anti-Semitic? It isn't easy. My father used to say that there was nothing worse than a self- loathing Jew. I can think of lots of things, the first being my father.

But, I get ahead of myself. To understand me, and I would like to believe that you would, you first have to understand the Dorff lineage.

My paternal grandfather Isaaz came from Tallinn, in Estonia. His real name was Isaac, but the man at Ellis Island inadvertently changed the 'c' to a 'z' on his entrance papers. Sadly, my grandpa was easily convinced by some landsmen "Yankees" who were already old timers for having having been in America for a few months, that if he changed the incorrect letter he would be instantly deported. He was Isaaz ever after. When he would introduce himself, people always thought he was Iranian. He lived, and finally died, tending his pushcart on Rivington Street, being spoken to in two tongues, Farsi and English, neither of which he understood.

My father's name was, Schmoil.

He called himself Larry.

Schmoil quickly realized that in order to succeed in America one had to become assimilated, hence the Larry. He read books on entrepreneurship and soon, thereafter, with great fanfare in the family, bought a second and larger pushcart. Since my Old World Grandfather sold strictly Jewish items like talisman and tiffilin and came home with next to nothing, my Yankee Doodle father, using what he had gleaned from his books and with a surety of his brilliance that could not be swayed, sold crockery with pictures of Jesus and the Holy Family on them. He was soon forced into bankruptcy, never figuring out that the Jews who shopped on Rivington Street were not much interested in the face of Jesus on plates, even if His eyes *did* follow you when you moved. He had always been a bitter man, my father, but this setback made him absolutely acrid. He ended up waiting on tables at Ratner's, and, when *they* closed, at an assortment of Jewish Restaurants around the city. So much for my father's side!

My mother's side of the family, the Mendelsohns came from Minsk. They loved their homeland, but the climate for Jews in Russia in the early 1900's had become extremely "pogramatic" and they were forced to pack up and head for New York.

Mother's father, Leonard, was a Cantor who sang flat. He sang with such passion, however, that no one in his congregation on the Lower East Side of New York had the heart to tell him, much less fire him. Even if they would have wanted to, they were too poor a congregation to hire anyone better, so there Leonard remained until he dropped dead during services one Saturday morning after going for a rather ill advised high C, which to everyone's amazement, I am told, was crystal clear and dead on key.

Leonard, and Sadie his wife, had three children, one of whom, Ruthie, died in childbirth. The other two, Howard and Dora, the latter being my mother, thrived.

My mother was, and is, a gentle soul with a heart far larger than her brain. Not that she is stupid. Far from it! But mother's intelligence is innate. Though she never got past tenth grade she soon became the one to whom people came with their problems. Had she been smart enough to hang up a shingle, we would have been loaded. Instead, she dispensed her comfort and advice for free, enriching all who came to her, while she did her shopping at, well, Woolworths. As mother would say, "Nobody ever said life was easy." That line might well have been a self- fulfilling prophecy, for soon after she met Schmoil at a Henry Street Settlement House social, she married him. It was not too long after that, I am led to understand, that she developed the soft pitying sigh that endeared her to all who came to her for comfort and made my father grind his teeth, even in his sleep.

But it was Howard who was the great success in the family.

Uncle Howard was a high school science teacher. That meant that along with the respect the title brought, he was bringing home a steady salary at a time when money for many others was tight.

Howard may have been a success in our family, but not, alas, in his. One day when he came home from teaching, he found a letter of farewell from his wife, Hannah, who had taken off with her fox trot instructor, along with anything of value they owned.

Howard grieved for the loss of his Hannah. My mother consoled her beloved and successful brother. My father snickered behind Howard's back that, "Mr. Bigshot" finally had been brought down a peg or two.

At any rate, after Hannah left, Uncle Howard became a fixture at my home. At one point my mother had actually convinced him to move in with us, but my father nixed that in a hurry. There was a major fight, complete with soft pitying sighs and grinding teeth, but this time, my father prevailed. Howard, hurt and resentful, stopped coming by, except for shabbos dinners at which he would whisper to my mother who sighed, wrung her hands, clucked her tongue, shook her head and ignored my father.

Shabbos dinners at our house were, forever after, even years later when I came along, something to be avoided at all costs.

But Uncle Howard was made of strong stuff. He soon met and married a blonde, blue- eyed woman called Phyllis whom he had met through friends. The fact that Aunt Phyllis was a gentile shocked my mother and delighted my father. That she was a rather masculine girl's Phys Ed teacher delighted my father even more, and to all who would listen he would always speak of his new sister- in -law as 'Gorgeous George.' Soon afterward, Howard went into partnership with Moe Feingold, a Math teacher who taught with him, and bought CAMP KANUGA.

And that's when Uncle Howard really hit pay dirt.

To understand this, I offer a short history lesson.

In 1948 when Howard and Moe became partners, the country was experiencing a post war boom. Things that had been rationed were now easily accessible and every American wanted the best for himself and his family.

The Jewish population of America was even more determined than their Christian counterparts to find ways to be living the good life. Indeed, after the shock of seeing just how tenuous life was through the deaths of so many of their family members in Europe, American Jews decided to live, and live well. So while the gentiles were still sitting around the piano in the parlor singing songs that extolled fellowship, many Jews were working their ass off amassing small fortunes.

And when the money was made, the fun began.

But there was a problem. Money or no money, Jews were persona non grata at exclusive Anglo Saxon bastions. Ever pragmatic, when restricted country clubs kept the wealthy Jews out, they built their own. "Restricted" country clubs, Jewish country clubs! Restricted private schools, Jewish private schools!

And so it was with summer camps.

Though many Jewish summer camps had been built prior to the war, after 1945 they really took off. If young Jewish boys and girls were not considered good enough to go to "goyem" camps, the enterprising Jews said, "Screw 'em," and built more of their own. No more discrimination for the Jews!

And the camps prospered.

But there was an irony to all this for in order to go to one of these camps, you had to have money, and plenty of it! No ordinary Jew need apply.

So much for no more discrimination!

Every summer on the first of July, buses would pull into designated meeting places in Westchester, Long Island, and the wealthier areas of Brooklyn and Queens, and pull out filled to capacity with the noisy and excited children of the Jewish elite.

Summer camp became a status symbol and Uncle Howard thrived.

He had found a year round handy man and caretaker named Ike Hayes who did all the dirty work, so all that was left to him was enticing the kids to come. He spent the off months doing that. His partner, Moe, ordered the food.

So that, as they say in Hollywood, is the "back story."

Enter me.

My maternal grandmother once described me as "not much to look at, but a wonderful boy."

Unfortunately, Grandma was not entirely right.

I *was* not much to look at. "Wonderful," however, according to those who knew me, was also up for discussion.

As a kid I was a triple threat. I wasn't good looking, I didn't have money and I couldn't play ball. Every boy's dream of a best friend and every maiden's prayer I wasn't. But what I *could* do, ah, what I *could* do, was write!

From the time I was a little kid I had a way with words. Low grades in Math and Science perhaps, but the highest in English.

My mother qvelled, and my father, who was never satisfied under any circumstances, wanted to know why I didn't do better in the 'important' subjects.

I wrote everything. Plays, stories, poems, essays; I was a natural. This, you might say, was *my* pushcart. I say this because I soon became so adept at writing that many of my school friends began to ask me to do important papers for them.

But let me clarify something before moving on to the meat of this narrative. When I mentioned school friends a moment ago, I lied. I didn't *have* any friends. Well one, Teddy Moskowitz, but since I was embarrassed to have *him* as my friend, you can imagine how many friends *he* had! To be fair, I *had* had one really good friend when I was eight, Billy Rothenberg. He had been part of a popular clique in school but was dumped for some infraction of their unwritten rules. We started talking from opposite sides of a long and empty table at lunch one day and then, for the next few months, we were inseparable. But Billy's father was transferred to Lincoln, Nebraska, and my entire social life thereafter became one of doing favors for others. I was a chip off my mother's block as it were, but without the sighs. I knew I was being used by people who, under other circumstances, wouldn't have given me the time of day, but strangely, or possibly perversely, I didn't mind. Though I never charged for my services, I still would cadge scraps from those I helped. If there were a party coming up, for instance, I would hint for an invitation. Since most of the people I wrote for were embarrassed that they couldn't do an assignment by themselves, and grateful that I never said a word about my part in their subsequent 'A's," an invitation to one of those parties was usually forthcoming.

Not that I liked going. I hated it. But it kept my parents off my back and it gave me a chance to see first hand all that I was missing.

And there was plenty.

Huge homes with finished basements! Girls with straight hair and bobbed noses! Maids! Cooks! Older brothers who went away to school! Beer. Cigarettes. Indeed, these *were* the things that dreams were made of! Many were the times that I jerked off thinking of one or a combination of all of the above. These people were my peers but existed in a different sphere. I loved them as deeply as I hated them.

At this point we had saved just enough to move out of the lower East Side and to a railroad apartment on the Van Wyck Expressway in Queens, halfway, as it were, between two very distinct worlds.

And then Uncle Howard changed my life forever.

Howard had found a way to repay my mother's kindness while at the same time rubbing my father's nose in all he didn't have.

He would, he said grandly at a long remembered shabbos dinner, send me to his camp, all expenses paid.

My mother sobbed in gratitude, my father ground his teeth, and I trembled. If the kids at school were the beautiful people, the kids at camp would be gods. I was both thrilled and terrified.

Of course there was no possibility of saying no. That would break my mother's heart while at the same time aligning me with my father. Neither was an option. From the moment Howard offered his largesse I knew I was heading, inexorably, to the world of Camp Kanuga, but what I didn't know, was that it was a world that would consume me forevermore.

CHAPTER TWO

POV: Andrew (AKA Apple)

That summer, the summer York died, was the seventh the Stewart twins and I had spent at Camp Kanuga. We had all arrived at camp at the same time, as upper sophomores, babies, and by the time the season of '75 rolled around, we were Upper Seniors, what we perceived to be the "men" of the camp.

We were not alone in the bunk. Henry Sturtz, a really rich kid from the West Side had joined our group in Lower Junior year, Dickie Klinger a year later. There had been others who came and went over those years, but only Lennie Dorff, the nephew of one of the camp's owners who had joined us just the year before, remained.

And we were a mixed bag. From the finest of athletes, York, Gavin and Sturtz, to the average, Klinger and me, to the piss poor, Dorff, and from the very rich Sturtz, to the comfortable Klinger, me and the Stewarts, to the poor Dorff: we were Bunk 33 in 1975.

It is that "we", the "we" that was, that has ruled my life for the past thirty some odd years. So many years ago and I can still see each of us as though we were still "we," clear as day, sprawled around the bunk during a never-ending rest hour of the mind, still young, still happy… still sixteen.

Henry Sturtz, lying on his bed, an ever present Baby Ruth in his hand, regaling the rest of us with stories of his life during the other ten months of the year, of the private school he went to, of his achievements and, of course, his sexual conquests. All of us thought he was full of shit, though

**no one told him, for although Henry could be "hale fellow, well met",
when he chose to be, he could also destroy someone with just a look or a
word, and we all knew it.**

Not only was Sturtz rich, he was also the street -wise kid in our group. An
only child, he and his father lived in a lavish pre-war apartment on West End
Avenue. He wore only the most expensive clothes, went to the best school,
knew all of the best people, and with all that, when we would meet for lunch and
a movie in the city, he never reached for a check. When it came to an argument
he was unbeatable; when he was right he was insufferable and when he was
wrong he would get on his high horse and fight as though he *were* right.

To Sturtz, nothing was simple. Everything was, as they say, 'the art of
the deal.' Feeling really good to Henry usually meant that he had used his
wit to demolish someone so that he could purr in the afterglow. Though he
smiled a lot, Sturtz was dangerous, and everyone knew it. Now saying that,
we, most of the guys in the bunk that is, could ride his ass and get away with
it, but if anyone else said something he didn't like or crossed him in any way,
there would be trouble. A terrific athlete, maybe a rung or two below York
in talent, Sturtz delighted in breaking rules and in seeing what he could get
away with. And get away with things he did. To say that he was mercurial
would be an understatement and that his *episodes manique* were sudden
and brutal purely stating a fact.

Like the time with the wig!

Sturtz, York, Gavin, Klinger and I had met just before camp and were
walking down a street in the West Village when we spotted a middle- aged
woman walking toward us from the opposite direction. There was nothing
exceptional about her, in fact she was rather non-descript; thin, pale face,
woolen coat, pocketbook, heavy black shoes, old world looking, topped off
by a rather obvious wig that sat slightly askew on her head. I think we all
noticed it at the same time. I can remember thinking in that moment, that
she might be undergoing chemotherapy. York said later that he thought
she might have been a very religious Jew. At any rate we reached the point
where we were about to pass her, when Sturtz pulled away from us, strode
up to her and in a second that I will remember forever put his face in hers
and screamed, "You can't bullshit me with that fucked up wig, bitch." For an
awful moment I had the horrible thought that Henry might actually pull the
wig from the woman's head, but York grabbed him and pushed him forward.
We all began to walk faster and faster until we were running, the sound of
Klinger's high- pitched laughter accompanying us. A few blocks later, when

we had run out of breath, we stopped, and looked at Sturtz. He stared back at us. "What?," he said. "Why?" York asked. Sturtz shrugged. "She was ugly. I didn't like her."

Though York, Gavin and I were quiet, with Klinger constantly slapping him on the back, Henry spent the rest of the day as though nothing untoward had happened.

And he got away with it. In fact, Henry Sturtz, it was said, could get away with anything.

(His bed was the first on the left as you walked into the bunk, his shoe cubby the one nearest to the door. His father's name was Milton. No one knew what had happened to his mother.)

And with all that, I don't have a clue what we had for dinner last night! And that, you see, is my curse.

Gavin Stewart curled up fetus like, his spare gray blanket pulled up over him, fast asleep.

Gavin seemed to need more sleep than anyone else, and every day, once we were back in the bunk after lunch, he was out like a light. Gavin was York's fraternal twin. Not as handsome as his brother, nor as talented, a wine red birthmark covering the best part of one cheek, he was the quintessential good guy. Always ready for a game of hoops or taking someone's clean up job at a moment's notice, Gavin was, well, Gavin! On the playing field, Gavin was all competitiveness and desire. While York scored his points on the basketball court from the outside with smooth, fluid arcing jump shots, Gavin scored from the inside, out muscling, out hustling, out rebounding his competitors for "garbage points." What he lacked in style, Gavin made up for with tenacity. Off the court, while York was outgoing and loquacious, Gavin was more withdrawn and quiet. He said little, content to let his brother take the spotlight and speak for both of them.

Once, when York was off to Princeton for a debate championship, I called Gavin to see if he wanted to get together in the city for a movie. I was surprised when he said he did as he seldom did anything without York being there, and even more surprised when he talked me into going to a small art theater on 8th Street in the Village to see a revival double bill of *Wild Strawberries* and *La Strada*. They have remained two of my all time favorite films.

I called him York three times that day.

Dickie Klinger, sitting up on his bed, Buddha-like, nodding his head at anything Sturtz said.

Dickie was a follower. What I remember about him, and to be honest I remember less about him than any of the others, was the way he idolized Sturtz, while at the same time being terrified of him. Dickie was only so-so as an athlete, but people grudgingly gave him the benefit of the doubt because of his willingness to try. Sturtz wouldn't and broke Klinger's chops at the slightest infraction of what Sturtz thought was to be expected. Klinger thrived on it. Hell, at least someone was noticing him. I think of Klinger, I think of Sturtz, two for the price of one.

Lennie Dorff lies on his bed, his ever- present clipboard resting on his knees up in front of him.

Lennie. Oh, Lennie!

Most people had a nickname at camp. Mine was "Apple." It was York who, that first summer, had given me that nickname and it stuck. One day, kidding around as he so often did, he pinched my rather round, red cheeks, and laughingly said, "Apples." I was Apple thereafter. Andy I was to my friends at school, Andrew to my parents and Nicki, and always Apple to the guys at Kanuga.

Leonard Dorff's nickname was "Pulitzer." Sturtz dubbed him that, and it was a name not given out of affection. Henry didn't like Dorff from day one, and we all knew it, Lennie included. Whether it was because Lennie's uncle was one of the owners of the camp, that Lennie was really poor or, most probably, because Dorff was better with words than he, Dorff was always on Sturtz's shit list. Lennie ran the camp's newspaper, hence the "Pulitzer." The rest of us came to call Dorff that affectionately. When Sturtz called him that there was venom.

Lennie tried to be a ballplayer, but he simply didn't have it in him. Gavin, York and I accepted and down played it. Sturtz didn't. One day, after an extremely close baseball game that we lost because of Dorff's errors, Gavin, Dorff and I were picking up the equipment to bring back to the H.Q. Sturtz walked up to us and smiled at Dorff. We held our breath. "Pulitzer," Sturtz said, shaking his head, and still smiling, "you are an expert in failure." Dorff stared at him for a moment, then picked up a chest protector, and walked down the hill to the bunk, stumbling under the weight of his burden. I think it may have been one of the most awful things I have ever heard one human being say to another. Though we should have said something, Gavin and I weren't York and we remained silent.

And that was Bunk 33, Anno Domini 1975, except, of course, for me. Not a whole lot to tell there. We, the Brookmans, Mom, Dad and I, lived on the "wrong side" of Union Turnpike in Queens. The "right side", East Egg if you will (I teach English Lit), was called Jamaica Estates, and indeed, the houses *were* large and opulent. My side of the street made up of small, boxy, two story houses built as a development by an insurance company just before W.W.II, was called at different times Jamaica Estates North, which we all knew was a crock of shit, Fresh Meadows South, which was probably what it was, and finally, in the wisdom of the Postal Service, Flushing. The jokes I was subjected to at camp because of that name are, I believe, self- evident!

My father had a mid level job in advertising and as a kid, when none of my friends understood what he actually did for a living I told them that he had designed the giant red "K" on the Kellogg's box. Most of them probably still believe he did. Dad was a good guy who loved his family and gave most all of his paycheck to my mother. He didn't make a great deal of money, but he wanted what he considered to be the best for me, and I was sent to Kanuga as a matter of course. He and York used to discuss politics when York and Gavin came to our house to sleep over. My father told me once that even though York was just a kid he had a mind better than most adults he knew. I didn't disagree. My father looked forward to those discussions with York, and I loved listening to them.

Dad died of a heart attack in either 1985 or 1986.

I can never remember which.

Mom was and is a housewife. She is a good lady, a simple quiet person who always has a good word for everyone.

She adored York.

But, back to Bunk 33 and Kanuga in 1975! We had a faucet on the sink that read hot for cold, our counselor was Bobby Milburn, our waiter was Jimmy Springer who was a sophomore at Yale, the laundry was collected on Fridays, Sturtz subscribed to the New York Times, weekly *and* Sunday, Gavin's combination was 4 right, 7 left, 9 right, the co-ed musical that year was *Carousel,* Sue Barnett got pissed at me during the carnival, Klinger had a steel gray Sony boom box that someone stole, the DJ at the co-ed Cabaret was a waiter named Ralph Sanchez, mail call was at 4:30 p.m., during the inter-camp game with Lackawaxen, Klinger was beaned by a badly pitched ball, York invented "Roof Ball", and I got laid for the second time in my life.

1975.

And then there was York, and when York died that summer, all summers from then on, were called on account of darkness.

CHAPTER THREE:

POV: Gavin:

I was five on the day I grew up.

Mother had taken us shopping, and we were at our last stop before we headed home. It had been a wonderful morning and the afternoon, with the promise of a big lunch and then a movie, looked to be even better. "Just let Mommy pay for these things and we'll be on our way," my mother said.

We almost made it.

We were waiting for the clerk to ring up mother's purchase, York and I standing hand in hand next to her as we had been taught to do. I heard a giggle come from behind me and then felt someone tapping me first on one shoulder, and then, as I turned that way, on the other. Someone wanted to play! As I turned, I saw a boy, maybe a year or so younger than we, who stood with *his* mother who also was waiting to be checked out. He was smiling as I turned, but when he looked at me, he sucked in his breath and took a step backward. Then with a seriousness that still cuts into me all these years later, he tugged at his mother's arm. "Mommy," he said breathlessly, pressing his body to hers, his eyes holding me at arms length, "Mommy, look at that boy's face. There's grape juice on it. Is his face sick?"

There was dead silence for a moment then chaos. York dropped my hand and immediately punched the little boy who, in turn, started to cry. His mother pulled her son into her arms and yelled at my mother over his yowls. My mother pulling York away, yelled at *her* as the salesman nervously looked around, going, "Shush, shush, shush." Others came from all over the floor to see what was happening while I, very quietly and without anyone noticing, moved away from them all. It wasn't that the little boy had told me something I already did not know. Hell, as long as I could remember people stared and kids laughed and pointed, but that day, as the others yelled, cried and "shushed," I stared into the three way mirror in front of me, looked at the port wine birthmark that covered half the right side of my face, and knew, for the first time, how it set me apart, how it made me different. Somehow it had never really sunk in it until that day when I stood amongst the new, clean smelling clothes and stared at myself in that mirror.

And that was it. An epiphany at age five in an up-scale clothing store on the Manhasset Miracle Mile.

The moment, quite obviously, has stayed with me.

True, as I got older I hardly noticed the stares. I had grown to expect them. Yet every now again the little boy's frightened face would appear in my mind's eye, and I would almost have to physically shake myself to get rid of it. So "the blot" stayed with me and surprisingly, when I got into high school, it actually took on proportions I would never have had expected.

It became a chick magnet!

For whatever reason, and my mother called it maternalism, York said it was fascination, and Sturtz labeled it perverse curiosity, for *whatever* reason, girls became enamored of my birthmark. They would pass me in the halls at school, not all, but some, and cup my cheek with their hands. Some girl I didn't know at all, at a party in someone's basement, tried to kiss me on it, almost as though her kiss could make it better. (When I later told Sturtz, he said he was surprised it didn't turn me into a frog, but then he laughed and said that since I already *was* a frog the kiss should have turned me into a boy. Freakin' Sturtz!) Anyway, the girl, Tina I think her name was, kissed it and kissed it, and though she got more and more into it, her breath hot on my cheek, she couldn't make what was there disappear. It wasn't a decal and it wasn't put there by a pissed off witch. It was just what it was, what it is and what it always will be, a cosmic joke that I didn't ask for, but that I can live with. That night, Tina got turned on and I felt nothing.

Period. No lie.

First and foremost, you see, I am a realist, and I guess *that* all started on the "grape juice" day. I have a pretty good imagination, but when it comes to the everyday routines of life, I *do* see things as they are. Or, I guess, as *I* think they are, for after all, aren't all perceptions very subjective? But that's grist for another mill!

You may have noticed by the words I use and the way that I speak, that I'm pretty bright. High I.Q. I looked at my confidential record over my teacher's shoulder once. We are talking *high* IQ here. Not Mensa, but up there.

No brag. Fact.

So, I've got a birthmark on my face and a high IQ. Two givens, neither very earth shattering. But here's something that might surprise you. I have been told, and I do believe that it is true, that I am very good looking, despite the blot. No false modesty, just a silent nod to Dr. Kransdorf, a shrink my folks sent me to until I was twelve, for his amazing curative powers. I have good, strong features and what they call a swimmer's build: wide shoulders, big chest and a narrow waist. But if I am good looking, my brother York was better looking still, handsome. Gavin, me: good looking, average Joe, York: breathtaking, "something special" Adonis. No resentment on my part, and you *have* to believe Kransdorf worked his ass off to see if I wasn't sublimating sibling loathing on that one, just calling it as it is. Fact. Look, even without my mark, modeling agencies would still not be breaking down my door; too average. But York, York could be on the cover of a magazine in a heartbeat. No lie.

So if it's not the birthmark and it's not that I'm dumb, what makes me tremble at the mention of social interaction?

What I think it may be is what Kransdorf calls "social discomfort." Translation: I just don't like big groups of people. I'm pretty good talking one on one with someone, but put me in a room with a lot of people, even people that I know well, and I am really at a loss for something to say. The IQ drops like a rock when I am confronted with three or more people at the same time. And if the people are female, it gets even worse. Not Nicki, of course, but with any other girl my lips get dry, my tongue feels huge, my voice cracks and my pits start to drip. Kransdorf says that it stems from being a twin, but York blossoms at social gatherings, and he's really good with girls.

"So then what the hell is it?" anyone interested might ask, and until that summer at Kanuga, the summer of Ralph Sanchez and, well, you know, it beat the hell out of me.

But it *was* that summer and there were, as there are every summer, dances. And man, how I hated dances. And there was no dance bigger at Camp Kanuga than the annual senior cabaret. And that year, 1975, we *were* seniors and the dance was ours.

The cabaret. The night I met Ralph Sanchez and the night that led to my part in the death of my brother.

Jesus!

No lie!

CHAPTER FOUR:

POV: APPLE

I teach 12th grade English Lit and Drama. I like the kids and I have every reason to believe that the kids like me. I listen patiently when they stay after class to discuss problems at home or with the latest boy or girlfriend. But while I listen to them or while I teach Shakespeare, Williams, Albee and all the others, every word resonates with memories of the summer of '75, the summer that York died.

York.

I am obsessed with him, with that summer, hell, with all the summers I was at Kanuga, but unlike the characters who parade through the pages of the books in my classroom, I am on to myself. I know what's going on. I understand that I am more comfortable with Blanche, Hamlet and George and Martha than I am with anyone I might find on page one of the Times or Page Six of the Post. They, along with the boys who made up Bunk 33 are more real, more immediate, than almost anything else in my life.

Kanuga, in 1975!

What did that kid say in that movie? *"I see dead people."* Nope. That's far too easy.

I see color war plaques.

"Where, my Lord Hamlet?

"In my mind's eyes, Horatio. In my mind's eye!"

They are there, row after row, hanging side by side on the walls of Hayes Hall, those glossy shellacked reminders of the winners and losers of Color Wars since the camp began. Given the time I can tell you the final scores and the names of the chiefs and Upper Senior Basketball captains from 1943 on, or at least until 1974! Many of the people on those lists are probably dead or, if still alive and sensible human beings, have forgotten that they ever went to Kanuga, that there ever *was* a Kanuga. Yet I know their names, stats and every other thing there is to know about them. To me they are both legend and reality. They are, idiotically and completely, everything.

Look, there are guys that are much older than I, collectors who are obsessed with baseball cards, and to me, *that* isn't normal. To me memorizing the faces and stats on those cards is childish, irrelevant, and the guys who do it are out of touch with the world in which they live. Yet, and I hang my head in shame while I deride their juvenile fancies, I have made an obsession out of Camp Kanuga.

"Hey Andrew, a hundred that you can't tell me what Carl Yastremski did on July 7th, 1978."

"Screw 1978. On July 7th, 1975 we had an inter-camp game with Canawanda where Dickie Klinger got the first home run of his life, and Howie Pincus broke Aaron Field's 1949 record of most runs earned in a single game during a regular season, Color War not included."

I *know* it's nuts but I can't do anything about it!

And of course, when I think about Kanuga, first and foremost is *that* summer, and in many ways *that* summer, of course, means York.

"Horatio, the potent poison quite o'ercrows my spirit."

And it all started so normally. There was no warning that anyone or anything could disturb the quiet and peace of our lives.

But, as my grandmother would say, "Who knew?"

And York is still everywhere.

Someone humming something on the street; instant York!

A certain smell on a cool morning.

York.

Just the other day, in the faculty lunch -room at school, I overheard two colleagues at a neighboring table talking about the symbolism inherent in horror stories of the nineteenth century. While others scoffed at them, I nodded to myself, took a bite of my sandwich, and suddenly, while their conversation whirled around me, I was back at Kanuga, taps long gone, tucked safely under the covers, while York, sitting up in his bed, his flashlight shining up under his chin, gave us his version of *The Monkey's Paw*, his voice croaking and shaking in terror as he spoke.

It was early July 1975.

"**Knock! Knock! Knock!** Someone, some*thing* was pounding slowly on the front door." York paused for dramatic effect as the rest of us lay blankets pulled up to our chins, our eyes closed, making fantastic mind pictures of what he was saying.

"The old woman rushed to the door. 'My son,' she cried, 'my son is back. Get out of my way,' but her husband, looking out of the window saw not the strong, healthy body of their beloved son, but rather the reality of what he had become after falling into the threshing machine and having been dead for two weeks, brought back to life only by their wishing on the paw. 'Don't open the door,' the old man screamed, his voice filled with terror and dread, but his wife pushed him aside and began fumbling with the locks."

Here York summoned a voice that to this day gives me shivers when I think of it.

"'Muuuuuuuuuthhhhhhhherrrrrrrrrrr,' a voice on the other side of the door wailed. 'Where are you Muuuuuuuuutttthhhhherrrrrr?' The son's dead, rotting fist hit the door again."

Booooom! Boooooom! Boooom!

'MUUUUUUUTTTTHHHHERRRRRRRRRRRRR!'

'I'm coming my son,' the old woman cried, 'mother is coming."

BOOOOOM! BOOOOOOOM! BOOOOM!

"The old woman's shaking hand finally undid the last lock even as her husband struggled to pull her away, and she threw open the door. There in front of her stood not the handsome young son whom she loved, but a grotesque, gory, slime coated, putrefied mass of blood and guts, eyeballs hanging from their sockets, worms creeping over its face, slowly moving toward her, a hideous smile on what used to be his lips, his arms outstretched, reaching for her. 'Muuthhhhhhher. Mutthhhherrr. Come kiss me muthhhherrrr.'

The old woman thought her heart would stop in horror, but instead she opened her mouth and...."

At that moment, without any warning, York leapt from his bed and let loose the most blood curdling scream I had ever heard.

"AHHHHHHHHHHHHHHHHHHHHHHHHHHHHHHHHH":

Our screams of real terror joined with his as we all jumped out of our beds, howling and racing about, scared out of our minds!

We, of course, woke the camp and ended up being docked from evening activity for a few days, but God it was worth it! For the next two weeks we all went around the camp going, "Muthhhhhhher, mutthhhhhher" until Henry Sturtz finally killed it by putting a long "fuckkkkkkker" at the end of it. As usual, Sturtz had brought us back to reality.

Who could have known that years later, the first time *I* would tell a ghost story, *this* story, it would be about York?

Yet I need no monkey's paw to bring York back. He has never left. I was *there,* when he died, I saw him die, and the moment will haunt me for the rest of my life.

I think of him as I do a lesson plan for WHO'S AFRAID OF VIRGINIA WOOLF?

"Which is it George, truth or illusion?
You can't tell the difference, Martha."

Amazingly, it's been over thirty years since I drove away from Kanuga for the last time, yet every day of that summer is as clear to me now as it was to me then. It fills my life. Nicki says that it *is* my life. My friends, the games, the very feel of the place, though dead and gone, are still more real to me today than today.

The irony, of course, is that no matter how obsessed I know I am, I have never, nor will I ever, set foot on the grounds of that place again.

So as I think of York, I think of Kanuga and know that as much as I love it, it is cursed to me forever.

A while ago, for instance, out of nowhere, in the middle of preparing a lesson on a comparison of truth and illusion in *Hamlet,* (I seemed obsessed with that theme), *A Streetcar Named Desire,* and, *Who's Afraid of Virginia Woolf?* I zoned out and was a million miles away at a different time in a different place. There is no way that I will be able to blame my students if they do the same.

In my dreams, everything plays out on the backdrop of Kanuga, the camp acting as a giant stage set with new actors coming and going all the time. People from then, people from now, it doesn't matter who populates it, or what the situation, the background of each dream is Kanuga.

And one actor stars in every scenario.

"Appearing nightly, York Stewart!"

York!

Picture the best- looking kid you have ever seen and you've got him. We used to tell him that he was like a walking commercial for some teen age product, skin, hair, clothes it didn't matter, York would be the spokesman. He would laugh and wave us away, but he truly was everyone's ideal boy.

Sometimes, before sleep comes, *if* sleep comes, I close my eyes and see a slide show, a Technicolor montage of York as I remember him. Perfect in every way. (One of the many shrinks I have gone to over the years asked if indeed I had homoerotic feelings for York and if I had been sublimating my feelings over the years. No, no and no. We were both straight, and would have been appalled if anyone had suggested otherwise.) We were just two young guys who were best friends with all the intensity that implies, yet, saying all that, my montage runs the same way as those cheesy love story movies that York and would see and hoot off the screen.

It was so long ago, yet it never fades.

And there is York, his long, golden hair flopping in his face going gracefully up for a lay-up. York, moving smoothly, his muscles loose and fluid, his eye on the ball as he returns his brother's strong backhand. York, as he pulled back a bow, then letting go and watching while the arrow sped to its target. York sitting at the old upright in the social hall, his friends around him, the sleeves of his blue boat-neck sweater tied around his neck over a crisp white shirt, his head thrown back, laughing at something that is lost to memory. York reaching across the space between our beds and shaking my hand goodnight, something we had done since our first summer together, and then always falling asleep first, "the sleep of the innocent," as he jokingly called it, sleeping as I stare at him, his mouth open slightly, his face serene.

York, his future so rich and vital spread out before him.

TRAGEDY AT CAMP IN THE POCONOS!
(Story on Page Three)

I know that the whole idea of a "golden boy" has turned into a major cliché over the years like that kid in *A SEPARATE PEACE*, but there is no other way to describe York. He *was* the golden boy, and, to quote his obituary in The New York Times, "beloved by all."

Yes, beloved. Though no one was more competitive than he, no one was more compassionate. On July 12, 1973, for example, just after he had pitched an unheard of no-hitter, instead of accepting the accolades that were being thrown at him, he went over to Paul Binger, a fat, non athletic kid on the other team, who had popped up twice and walked once in the same game, and told him how much better he thought he was playing. Binger was speechless, and I never forgot it.

"Lost. Everything lost."

And once, during our Upper Intermediate year, while playing a crucial color war tennis match, York stopped play and corrected a call a judge had made *in his favor*! His honesty gave the game, set, match and, subsequently, color war to the other team. If anyone else had done it, he would have been crucified by his team members, but since it was *York,* it was unquestionably right.

"But hell, that's blood under the bridge."

I said before that we were not lovers, and no, I am not protesting too much. But it is true that I did love him. God, how I loved him! I can say that now, but how impossible it was to tell him that then! We were boys, and boys don't tell their friends they love them for if they do, they will soon be looking for new friends! I think York knew, and I think he loved me too, but that will have to remain, forever conjecture. Since boys aren't allowed to express their feelings to their friends, then or now, three simple words that could have healed and comforted me for years afterwards were never spoken. You simply can't tell someone you love them, that you see the goodness in them and you exult in it, when you're a child. It is not done, and the words not spoken are replaced by a silence that will, if nothing else prevents it, metastasize into emptiness so vast that it destroys anything good and positive in its way.

Three fucking words!

All I I know is that I loved him more than I have ever loved anyone except for my daughter Jessica, but as he was *York,* she is *Jessica,* perfect in my eyes.

I know that I wasn't York's only friend. York was *everyone's* friend. Others felt the loss of his death too, but I was his *best* friend and when he died there was simply nothing and no one else to take his place.

Before *that day* I used to have friends too, a lot of them. Not anymore. Since I lost York, I have never, it seems, cared to depend on the kindness of strangers.

For you see, as much as I loved York Stewart, that day in 1975, I wasn't there for him when he needed me most.

CHAPTER FIVE:

POV: Lennie

amp Kanuga was all I had expected and worse. Built in the early twenties as a gentile camp, it was still crisp and clean and freshly mown, things with which I had no frame of reference.

The boys, of course, were from privileged homes. Their clothes were from the finest stores, and even the name -tapes sewn into them seemed to be high class. The trunks that the boys unpacked were all black and shiny and new. Their toiletries were name brands. After their showers the cabin smelled of Dial Soap. I would take my showers when no one was around, rubbing my body with a hard white bar from John's Bargain Store. And I actually shoved my generic toothpaste and deodorant to the back of my cubby, hiding them with the notebooks filled with my writings that I had brought along with me.

My fellow campers' haircuts looked as if they had all gone to the same stylist. And some of that hair was blond! I don't think I had ever seen a blond Jew before my first summer at Kanuga.

But it wasn't only the material things and the visible things that set these young men apart. They all seemed, somehow to have a certain ease, a certain knowledge that they were the best and that all that came to them, whatever it happened to be, they deserved. I had read GATSBY when I was twelve and immediately thought that if the original settlers of East Egg had been Jewish, these would have been their grandchildren. And though many of them proved to be dull and vapid or cruel, I instantly overlooked that because of whom they were. These were Jews who could be taken for Gentiles.

They were dazzling, and I was entranced.

Making my way at Kanuga was probably the hardest thing I had ever done in my life. My expertise was meant for a classroom, not for a playing field, and I was awake for the first two nights, long after the others slept their dreamless sleeps, worrying, planning and, I am embarrassed to admit, grinding my teeth like my father.

I was fifteen that first summer, almost sixteen. Since being Bar Mitzvah two years before, technically I was a man, but standing at assembly every morning and evening at the back of the line of boys that made up my bunk, I felt like an infant. Unprepared and inept, I longed to be at home surrounded by my books.

Then, once again, Uncle Howard stepped in.

Howard and Phyllis had their own cabin at the top of the steep hill that rose from the front campus. Placed snugly at the side of the Victorian Guest House that had been built in the late 1920's to accommodate visiting parents, this was the place where Uncle Howard could retreat from the pressures of the camp and find solace in the well- muscled arms of Aunt Phyllis.

It was to this cabin that I was summoned on the third morning of camp while the others in my bunk had clean up.

"So, Lennilah," Uncle Howard said, staring into a mirror as he ran a straight razor across his face, "how do you like Kanuga?"

He was looking at a reflection of me, standing behind him as he shaved and I knew that if I lied he would be able to see it in my eyes. He *was* my mother's brother after all.

"Pretty good, Uncle Howard," I said. "It's a little hard to fit in. Being a new boy, I mean."

"New, schmoo," he said, evening out his sideburns. "Leonard, you are my nephew, my sister's son, and I want you to have fun. Two months in the sunlight away from the schmutz of the city. This should be a happy time for you. Not 'pretty good'."

I fidgeted in the wicker chair I was sitting in. "Well, you know that I was never good in sports and," I said with a weak smile, "this *is* a sports camp."

"But no one likes a quitter, Leonard." Phyllis's booming voice startled me. I turned to see her walking into the cabin, letting the screen door slam behind her. She was wearing a white tee shirt with the camp's name on it, plaid Bermuda shorts and sneakers. Her thin blonde hair was tied back in a ponytail held in place with a rubber band. "If you're having trouble with sports, you have to plug harder." She put the bunch of flowers she was carrying on the table next to me. "We've all had to do that from time to time. Even me. You embrace that which is difficult. That's the sign of a man." She tousled my head as she walked over to Howard. She pointed to his jaw. "You missed a spot." Uncle Howard pulled his face with one hand and ran the razor over his jaw with the other. "Tell him Howard," she said. "Nobody likes a quitter."

Howard rinsed his face with cold water and turned to look at me. "Leonard is not a quitter, are you Leonard?" I shook my head. "But time it will take. Most of the boys started here when they were seven or eight. They've had time to build friendships, to get to know how the camp runs. You, you're coming in late."

And that's when he said the words that would level the playing field for me.

"So I had an idea. A way to get you to know the camp and the boys." He paused and looked at me. "How would you like to start a camp newspaper?"

My mouth dropped open, and he laughed.

"Let me explain. When Moe and I bought the camp in 1948 we started a newspaper that came out every week. The KANUGA INQUIRER, we called it. News, reviews, gossip...things like that. After a few years it fell apart mainly because we could never find a camper who could hold it together. You're right, Leonard, this *is* an athletic camp and writing is not a priority to most of the boys. But seeing their names in print is."

For the first time in two days I felt myself breathing. Yes, I could do this. I could do this very well. It would be the camp counterpart to what I did in school. It would be my passport to tacit acceptance. That was all I wanted. I didn't need more.

"Yes," I said.

"Yes? Just like that? You don't need to know more?"

"No. I mean yes, I don't need to know anything more. And yes, I would really like to run the newspaper." I was grinning idiotically.

Phyllis looked at me from over the flowers she was placing in a vase. "You realize, of course, that you will still have to take part in activities," she said.

I nodded.

"No special privileges."

I nodded again and smiled. I was back in control of my life.

I almost danced back down the hill.

"Hey Pulitzer!"

Everyone had a name for me, each one having to do my being associated with the weekly two- page paper known as THE KANUGA INQUIRER, but that was the one that stuck. Pulitzer.

Did I say I was *associated* with the paper? As editor, writer, reporter, printer and distributor of the mimeographed journal, I *was* the INQUIRER. For the first time in my life I began to enjoy a type of status and privilege, and I liked the feeling very much.

First of all, I had the run of the camp. While the other kids were restricted to their beds during the rest hour, I was free to roam the campus from bunk to bunk in search of material. Nuggets. Stories. Usable items. Everything boosted my stock.

Also, and most important, I had the inside scoop on everything that was going on in Kanuga.

But it took a bit of time to get to that point. At first the Inquirer and I were a joke. I was compared to the A/V guy at school and found myself the brunt of a lot of mean comments and even some pranks. But I persevered and little by little, as the camp enjoyed my good- natured gossip and my humorous way with words, I was granted a grudging respect.

And, even, by some, friendship.

Now when the Umpire called strike three on me, former jeers became good- natured putdowns. I was finally in on the joke instead of *being* the joke.

"Hey Winchell," a camper would yell, "put this in the INQUIRER. Sussman has a hard on for Susan Miller."

"Hey, Spinmeister," a counselor might ask, "what have you heard about bonuses this year?"

"Leonard," Uncle Howard would whisper, "is it true that some of the counselors are smoking marijuana on their nights out?"

And as I answered their questions, seemingly telling them everything, I made sure to tell them nothing. I never gave away a confidence, I never played management against labor and I never ratted out anyone. I told enough to be provocative and no more. And little by little, when everyone knew I could be trusted, everyone began confiding in me.

I felt like my mother, albeit in baggy shorts that, of course, came from Woolworths.

I briefly alluded to the boys in my bunk before, and now is probably a good time to tell you about them as they too played a large part in my being accepted at Kanuga, and, in fact, with the rest of my life.

It happens, I learned, that when parents signed their child up for camp, they had the right to request he be placed with certain bunkmates. Most of the time the boys knew each other and the requests were easy. Sometimes though, no one wanted a certain boy as a bunkmate, and that's when trouble began.

Henry Sturtz, Andrew Brookman and the Stewart twins, York and Gavin, had been bunkmates seemingly forever. Gary Klinger had joined them the year before. There had been two other members of their clique, but that summer, the summer I first came to Kanuga, one had moved to California and the other's family had fallen on hard times and couldn't afford to send their son to camp.

Two openings in Bunk 29!

The first opening was filled with Marty Posner, a red- headed, loud-mouthed fat boy whom no one else in the camp would even consider for his bunk. Howard and Moe were desperate. When Howard heard that Posner's father was a financial advisor, he turned to Henry Sturtz' father, *his* financial advisor, for help. No one knows what happened, but one night in mid June, Mr.Sturtz, Mr. Posner and Uncle Howard met at a restaurant in Manhattan, and a deal was made. I heard later that Mr.Sturtz had spoken to Henry, Henry had spoken to his friends, and soon after, Marty Posner became a member of Bunk 29. When asked for the details of what happened in that restaurant, Henry Sturtz just smiled. "It all comes down to business," he said.

I filled the second opening.

Posner being in 29 could not have worked out better for me, for next to him only Hitler, *maybe*, could have been more disliked. Next to Posner I was a golden boy.

What I was, actually, was innocuous. I didn't try to insinuate myself into the proscribed order of things. I stayed out of people's way and helped out around the bunk. I was at first tolerated, and then, slowly, accepted as an adjunct to the almost inseparable quartet. I say quartet for Klinger had close friends in Bunk 21 and spent much of his time with them. A major plus for me was that the Stewarts, and Brookman all liked Uncle Howard, and from that there came a 'give the nephew a chance' kind of thing. And then, when Posner started screaming in his sleep one night at the start of the second week of camp, and couldn't be quieted until he was given some kind of shot, we held our collective breaths. Sure enough, later that day Posner was packed off home, and all of us breathed a sigh of relief and went on with our lives, Sturtz adding cryptically something about "real value for money."

We had a good summer that summer, and when the trunks were once more loaded onto trucks and then dropped off in front of the bunks for airing out before being packed for their return to the city, something wonderful and totally unexpected happened. The "four" took me aside and asked me if I'd like to be in their bunk again the following year. I was so taken aback that all I could do was grin and nod my head.

"It's mainly so that we're sure that we won't get another real loser like Posner."

Gavin punched Sturtz in the arm. "Shut up Henry." He turned to me. "We want you because we want you. Case closed."

That was one of the most wonderful moments of my life.

Of course I didn't know then if I would be coming back, but just to be asked made everything else superfluous. As it turned out, Uncle Howard's delight in my success with THE INQUIRER, along with his perverse delight in annoying my father, prompted him to extend his largesse for the next year. Schmoil grudgingly agreed for, after all, it *was* something for nothing.

I thought about them, the others in the bunk, all during the months I wasn't with them. Gangly, good- natured Gavin, rosy cheeked "Apple," which is what we all called Brookman, wise guy, ascerbic Sturtz, and most of all York.

York was everything I had always dreamed of being, but knew I could never become. His ease with people, his self- deprecating sense of humor, his athletic ability…everything. Sturtz worked at being popular, and he succeeded, but he was not York. And Sturtz had a nasty streak. He pulled a cruel joke on me the winter between camp that he thought hilarious, but hurt like hell. It isn't important what. Suffice it to say it really hurt. Yet Sturtz could be charming when he wanted to be and had many, many friends.

York, on the other hand, was popular without even wanting to be. He was admired by his peers, treated as an equal by his counselors, and revered by the younger campers who always flocked to him asking for his advice with their jump shots or backhands. Though Sturtz was almost as good an athlete as York, he didn't have what York had. York was special.

And, what's more, he was nice to me.

Then came the next summer.

Upper senior year! We were finally in Bunk 33, the last cabin in the quadrangle, symbolically marking our last year as campers. Though we could come back the next year as junior counselors, this was the last year without responsibility.

And, as with all camps, everything major had to do with the senior group. Who would be the upper senior color war chiefs? Who would start in the upper senior basketball game? Who would get "All Around Camper," at the end of the summer? And first, who would be elected senior group president?

And that's where all the trouble began, with the damned presidency of the senior group, the thing that, in a roundabout way, led to my part in the death of York Stewart.

CHAPTER SIX:

POV: Nicki

It takes a lot to surprise me. It didn't used to.

An example. One day, when I was little, my father took off with the maid before I got home from school.

Okay, *that* surprised me and I cried for a week.

Then my grandmother died in a car accident and I was so stunned that I stopped speaking for over a month.

Some weeks after that, I made it home from school only to find my mother in bed with the tennis pro from our club who seemed to me was closer to my age than hers. I was twelve.

What really surprised me about that one was that I *wasn't* surprised. A kind of "Who Cares?" feeling took over, so that from then on, any *look* of surprise on my face was pure Acting 101.

"A man is walking on the moon Nicki."

Eyes wide. Hands clasped in front of open mouth. "Oh wow, Mom, that's really amazing."

"And you'll always remember where you were when you saw it, honey."

Yes, I certainly would. I was sitting on the floor in front of Mom and Lance, (the tennis pro had, amazingly, lasted through the spring into summer), in our knotty pine basement in Jericho, Long Island. Though it was late at night, Mom and Lance were still in their tennis shorts, still dressed to play. Since they were behind me they felt safe in quietly fooling around, having no idea that I could see them just by glancing at the mirror on the sidewall. And so, on that hot July night, I sat watching Neil Armstrong bounce up and down on the moon in front of me, and Mom and Lance bounce up and down on the sofa behind me. One small step for mankind, and one major grope for my mother.

Summer, 1969. Memorable, perhaps, but no surprise.

By the summer of '70 Mom had been through Lance, Todd, Biff (really), John and about five others all of whose ages and IQ's, probably added up to less than the date. None of it surprised me except possibly why Mom had not yet been arrested for endangering the morals of minors. I watched the ebb and flow from a safe distance, picking up lots of interesting stuff, none of which I could use for show and tell.

By the time 1970 did roll around, Mom suddenly announced that she thought a full facelift was indicated. What precipitated this decision was that Mom and Rick, the guy from the bowling alley, had gone to a bar in Manhattan, she dressed like an aging Lolita, her hair in pig tails, her skirt way above her knees, hoping to pass for years less than her age, and *he*, at twenty two had been carded! Though Rick had tried to convince her that the bartender had been myopic, my forty five year old mother took to her bed, and stayed there for a week sobbing into her pillow. That on its own might not have amounted to much, but combined with the stares that she and Tony, the pizza guy, had been getting as they made out at the local drive in, with or without their top down, my mother was starting to feel her age. She finally emerged from her bedroom, red eyed, still teary, and determined to do her best to push back the clock. A facelift it would be for Mom that summer, and because she would recuperate incognito at an exclusive spa in Cape Cod, a stay at a summer camp suddenly loomed in my future.

Mother threw herself into finding an "appropriate" camp for me as she did everything. "Ask your friends," she told me on her way out the door to Studio 54 with Trace, the aspiring rock star.

I did.

All weekend, that weekend, I talked to my friends about the camps they went to. All were eager for me to join them.

Tina Schwartz spoke highly of the arts and crafts program her camp was known for and I immediately scratched it off my list. Joan Lichenfeld loved her camp because it was extremely Orthodox. Scratch. Marge Rubin went on and on about the drama program at her camp, Lori Wagner the food at hers while Fanny Waxman could not stop extolling the virtues of her counselor, a weight lifter named Charlene, who was headed for the Olympics.

Let it suffice to say that I drew a line through all of the above.

As she drove me to school the following Monday morning mother furrowed her brow and warmly showed her concern.

"Please find a camp by this afternoon, Nicki," she sighed. "I want this over and done with! It's making Mummy very stressed." She blew me an air kiss as I got out of the car. "Have a good day. Mummy loves you."

I set my twelve year old jaw, determined to find the perfect camp by the end of the day or to die trying. All this was getting little Nicki stressed too.

The school morning dragged on as it always did, and just before the lunch bell rang Miss Young, my science teacher, asked me to run a note down to the principal's office for her. I did, and after waiting half an hour to bring back a reply, I ended up being late for lunch. By the time I arrived at the cafeteria, ordered some food and sat down to gobble it down, the period was almost over. My friends, long finished with their lunches had gone outside to the courtyard and were making funny faces at me through the windows. Just as I was sucking in my last bit of milk, Millie Collucci pressed her tongue against the window and licked it as though she were making passionate love. I laughed so hard that I started to choke and the milk came poring out of my nose.

"I hear you're looking for a camp."

As I sputtered and wheezed, I looked up to see a tall, good- looking boy with a purple birthmark on his face staring down at me trying not to laugh.

"Hi," he said smiling as he reached down and handed me a napkin. "I'm Gavin Stewart. We just moved in across from Marge Rubin. She told me you were in the market for a camp, but," and here he laughed out loud, "I'm not sure this is the right time."

Through watery eyes I checked out Marge's new neighbor! She had told me about the people who had moved in next- door and how handsome the young son was. Gavin *was* good looking, but from the way Marge had talked I had thought he would have been a god.

"Hi. I'm York. Gavin's brother."

There are times that you say to yourself, "If this were a movie, I wouldn't believe it." This was one of those times.

York Stewart stood, his hand out to me, framed by the sunlight that streamed through the windows. There was a glow around him that made it hard to see his features. Had there been violins and a choir I wouldn't have been at all surprised. What did come as a pleasant jolt was that by just touching York's hand I suddenly knew where I was going to spend July and August!

Mother was delighted to hear that I had found a camp I wanted to go to. She called the Stewarts, got the pertinent phone numbers and then, a week later, wasted an entire hour getting dressed to the nines to meet with the camp owners who, being in their fifties, were far too old for her. Brochures were shown, papers were signed, hands were shaken and I was signed up and name-taped way before it was time to turn the clocks ahead for daylight savings.

Mom was in a hurry to get young. After meeting York Stewart I was in a hurry to get through puberty.

For me to say that at the ripe old age of twelve I was in love seems absurd to say the least, especially given my mother's track record, but you didn't know York. From the moment I saw him standing over me smiling kindly as the milk dribbled out of my nose and my friends outside the window screamed with delight at my embarrassment, I knew I had found someone to love. Something clicked. Can you have chemistry at twelve? If you can, we did. And, as he told me on more than one occasion, at that moment, York had felt the same way. It was a match made not, as we used to joke later, in heaven, but rather in a very smelly lunch- room, with a grinning Gavin looking on.

Now, one could say that meeting York the way I did could be chalked up as a surprise, but no, it wasn't. It felt right, right from the beginning.

We were an item from that first day, as much as you can be an item in seventh grade, and I knew I loved him and that he loved me. When we weren't with our friends we were together, when we weren't together, we were talking on the phone. I can still recall the many times I made a tent with my blanket and sat under it whispering to York on the other end of the line late into the night. Sometimes our conversations were so good that we kept talking even after I heard my mother turn off Johnny Carson and giggle as her partner for the evening made a tent of *their* covers. Our phone bills must have been astronomical, but my father, wherever he was, was paying hefty alimony, so mother couldn't be bothered with the small stuff. York's parents just said nothing.

And then summer and camp.

And as with York, it was love at first sight. The rolling hills, the white clapboard bunks, the instant camaraderie with the other girls, here was what I had been looking for all my life. Mother, her lovers and her rejuvenation were all at once put far behind me as the joy of being at Camp Kiunga, swept over me.

Of course another and very important plus was being only a short walk away from York and Gavin at Kanuga, Kiunga's brother camp. Though we didn't see the boys often, the times that we did get together were all the more special, as was the fact that we three now had yet another frame of reference to draw us close together.

"Nicki and who?," the kids in the other bunks used to yell, "Nicki and who? Nicki and Yoooooooork, thaaaaaaaat's who!" And the girls who were happy for me would cheer and the ones who were jealous would stare, and the counselors would grin and it was the happiest time of my life. I loved York and I loved Kiunga. "What," as, my friend Sue Barnett once said, "could be bad?"

And if York was my love, Gavin became my family.

I had always wanted a brother, other than the gang that Mom dated of course, and Gavin was the one. He was sweet, lovable, slightly awkward, goofy, handsome, well, Gavin. And though he was terribly shy with girls, we were easy with each other from the first day. After only a few weeks we had secret looks together that even York couldn't decipher. We would giggle over things that no one else thought funny. We would spend hours trying to find a home for a stray cat or dog, not giving up till the animal had been placed. I told him my problems and he helped fix them. I helped him in Science and he helped me in English. We traded 45's. Next to York, there was no one in the world I loved more than Gavin.

Talk about lucky.

Or so it seemed then.

CHAPTER SEVEN:

POV: Gavin

Davy Eisner once told me that he was so terrified of deep water that he would get a sick stomach every time the bugle blew announcing swim period. "But you have to go." I said, "How do you deal with it?" He shook his head. "I sit in the john until I'm all shit out." He paused and shrugged, "And then I go swimming."

I loved that answer.

The camp socials, and especially the yearly formal dance, the "cabaret," were my swim periods. I dreaded them. I had a serious case of butterflies, spent some serious time in the john...and then I went dancing.

Now the first thing you will assume is that my fear of socials probably stems from my being self conscious about the large, purple birthmark I have on my face.

Maybe, but I don't think so. I just hated dances.

But there was no avoiding them. So every Friday night throughout the summer the seniors had a dance at the girl's camp after taps. No biggie, just a dance. We guys would get dressed up in our white longs and crisp white Kanuga tee shirts and trudge down the road to Kiunga, the girls camp, where the girls, dressed in their best Bermudas and *Kiunga* tee shirts would be waiting. Cherry punch, frenzied gyrating for an hour, an ancient scratched "78" of "Goodnight Sweetheart" that, we are told, was being played when our folks were campers, still played for tradition, then back to camp and sleep, able to relax for one more week. No biggie, kind of tolerable yet certainly not pleasant. Call it merely only a two- dump event.

Cabaret was different. To begin with, it was the highlight of the Kanuga/ Kiunga social season. Almost everyone, except me of course, waited for it to come, like a swim period on a hot summer's day. It was, after all, *the* big dance, the reason the girls had packed their "good" dresses and the guys had dragged up their blazers and dress pants. "Hot stuff," Howard Mendellsohn called it. It was the last dance of the season, the last social get together before the intense competition of color war. And I dreaded it. Four visits to the john and at least a few slugs of Pepto Bismol. Like swimming the lake back and forth, eh Davey?

And the cabaret was exclusive! Upper seniors only, thank you. And for the only time of the summer, the dance was held on the boy's turf, in Hayes Hall. Here couples sat at tables dragged in from the boy's dining room, which were covered with starched white tablecloths. Hot food was available from a buffet table, and music played through speakers all over the hall. Every year the senior group tried to make the cabaret the classiest of events and this year, 1975, was no different. We had been working on it for weeks, led by an indefatigable Dorff, and now the dreaded day was here.

That night, the night of cabaret, dinner was over, free play had begun, and the senior group, most of us without shirts and sweating in the August heat, started moving tables down the short distance between the Mess Hall and Hayes. Most of the decorations had been put up earlier in the afternoon in a social hall that, for the only time in the summer, was off limits to any camper except for seniors for any reason. Since we had to wait for the dinner dishes to be cleared before we could move the heavy tables, time was now of the essence. York was on a table with Apple, Dorff with Klinger and Sturtz, of course, as there was work to be done, was nowhere to be seen. I pulled off my tee shirt, shoved it into my back pocket, squared my shoulders and started yanking one of the heavy metal tables toward the door by myself.

"Gavin," Sam Schneider, the head of food services called. "Don't pull it. You're going to scratch the floor. Wait till someone comes back."

"Here Gavin, let me give you a hand."

I stopped pulling the table.

"You're gonna give yourself a hernia, man." Ralph Sanchez smiled as he walked up to me. "Sam's right. You shouldn't be pulling that thing yourself. But screw the floor. You're gonna hurt *yourself*. Come on. On my call, one, two...three!" We both lifted at the same time and both holding it, the heavy table suddenly seemed to have no weight at all.

We made our way slowly down the stairs, and across the road toward Hayes.

Ralph Sanchez. How can I describe Ralph Sanchez? The girls, Nicki told me, thought of him as gorgeous, and I guess some people would say that he was. To me he was simply Ralph, a standoffish member of the kitchen staff with whom I had shot a few hoops in early July. Except for nodding at each other in the mess hall, I had seldom seen him anywhere on campus again. I looked at him straining across the table from me. He was a few inches shorter than I, and very Latin looking. Copper skin, black hair and deep brown eyes, with lips so dark that they were almost purple. His skin was *so* golden brown that his white tee shirt seemed to actually glow on him. Sometimes he wore glasses, especially when he was waiting on tables in the mess hall. Sometimes he wore contacts that made his dark eyes even darker, even deeper. (In retrospect, I guess I had noticed him more than just once or twice.) "Hold it a minute," he said, and we both lowered the table to the ground. He pulled off his shirt, stuffed it into his back pocket so that part of it hung over his cut offs and grabbed the other end of the table again. His body was bronze and the sweat on his chest defined his cut pecs and abs. He caught me looking at him and smiled. "Hot," he said. I gulped and nodded. He called "One- two-three," we lifted the table, and kept walking.

As I said, I hadn't seen much of Ralph over the summer except in the mess hall. No one had. Once down at the dock, I saw him pulling in a canoe with another kitchen guy. They were laughing about something. I don't think Ralph saw me at all. Ralph was part of a special group of guys who came to camp each summer, courtesy of Howard, who belonged to an organization called "S.E.E.K: Sponsoring Equal Education for Kids." In a sort of Big Brother program each adult in S.E.E.K. took an inner city kid under his wing and helped him or her get into and through college. Each summer Howard would invite some of the S.E.E.K kids to camp, offering them summer jobs and a chance to get away from the hot, steamy city. Sturtz always said that Howard was merely using his S.E.E.K connection as a way of hiring cheap help to do the jobs no one else wanted like washing dishes, waiting tables or doing grounds work, but that was Sturtz. It seemed like a good program to the rest of us. At any rate, Ralph Sanchez was a "Seeker."

"You have one helluva lay-up shot," he said as we maneuvered the bulky table toward the Hall.

I was pleased that he remembered. The day before he had been standing in one of the doorways to Hayes watching me shoot hoops while the others were at the Carnival. He had applauded when I made a tough shot, I had smiled over at him, and he had nodded. No biggie. "Wanna play?," I had shouted and he had shaken his head. "Wish I could. Need to get set up for dinner. Some other time though." We had waved and that was that. That had been weird enough, but this! What surprised me was that now, halfway through the camp season, Ralph Sanchez, who had never said a word to me nor to anyone else I knew for that matter, and who didn't even wait my table, had spoken to me one day and was praising me while helping me move a table the next. Most amazing of all was that he had actually known my name. York I could see, but me? I was surprised and kind of flattered.

"Thanks, man," I said. "It was a lucky shot."

He knit his brows and shook his head. "Don't put yourself down, Gavin. It was a good shot. Scientific even. You play good B -Ball. You play like they play in the projects. Smart, tough ball."

"No big deal. Just messin'. Just one shot," I said, "hardly...."

Ralph cut me off. "There you go again. Not just one shot. You're a good player. I've watched you before, other times."

He had? Other times? How many other times? I didn't know what to say.

As though reading my mind, he smiled the most dazzling smile. "Now you say, 'Thank you, Ralph.'"

I laughed and nodded. "Thank you, Ralph."

He tilted his head to the side and winked. "Por nada."

"Over here would be good," I said as we brought the table into the social hall. We put it down and Ralph looked around. "Man," he said, "this place looks dynamite."

I smiled. It did look good. In fact it looked great. Dorff's famous crepe paper, which I had been sure would look tacky, looked magical strung across the huge room. Colored paper covered the backboards and paper lanterns hung everywhere. The prismed ball that Klinger and Dorff had worked on for so long hung in the place of honor in the center of the room waiting for the lights to shine on it so that its sparks of light could cover everyone and everything with its magic.

Ralph nodded and smiled. "A real good job, Gavin. A real good job."

I smiled back. "Gracias." Ralph didn't say anything. Just stared at me, a small smile on his lips.

"Shit," I thought, "was that a stupid thing to say? Why is he smiling? Did I sound like an idiot, condescending in some way?" I had to break the silence. "The theme is STUDIO 75, you know, like a........"

"...like a take off on STUDIO 54. I get it." Ralph smiled. "I been there once." He surveyed the room again. "This works. It looks somethin' like 54. Of course you don't have the big coke spoon hangin' in the center of the floor. But thas good because you wouldn't want to give Howard a heart attack."

I shook my head and laughed. "No, we would not want to do that!"

No," he laughed, "that would not be a good idea."

"I wish you were gonna be there," I said, before I even knew what I was saying, and then added, "but it's just for Upper Seniors."

Ralph's face broke into a wide grin. "Thanks Gavin. Thanks for saying that. I 'preciate it. But man, if the Upper Seniors want to dance, they need records to dance to, and records are just no good witout a fine D.J." His grin turned to a smile as he swept his arms open.

"You? You're going to be the D.J.?" I laughed, for some reason happier than I had been in weeks. "That's fucking amazing!"

Ralph winked at me. "I done it a coupla times at a little club in the Bronx that you never heard of. I told Howard and he asked me to do it." He adopted a tough guy swagger. "Tonight," he said, his eyes filled with life, "I'm gonna bring the hood to the lake."

Klinger yelled something to me from across the hall.

"You're busy, man," Ralph said, "and I have got to get myself lookin' gooood for tonight! So I'll see you later, okay, bro?"

I nodded and watched as he turned and walked toward the door. Just before he left he turned back to me. "Lookin' good," he said, "looking real good!" He pointed at me and was gone.

Ralph had brought my spirits up and I joked with the others as I helped cover tables and put the finishing touches on the hall before going back to the bunk. By the time I was done, only Sidney Thaner and I remained, and the place looked great.

That night the Upper Seniors were excused from evening activity so that we could get ourselves ready for the dance. The bunk was a madhouse when I walked in, so I turned right around and walked out onto the porch. I could wait.

The rest of the camp was spread out on front campus in front of me watching a movie projected on a huge sheet hung on the side of the arts and crafts shack. *Rebel Without A Cause.* As I waited for the shower and the sinks to be free, I sat on one of the bunk's lawn chairs watching James Dean put his red satin jacket over a sleeping Sal Mineo.

"Gav," York yelled, "sink and shower are free."

I got up and opened the screen door looking back over my shoulder wanting, yet really not wanting to see Mineo get gunned down. It always made me cry.

I walked into chaos.

"Can I borrow your blue blazer?"

"What's that funny smell?"

"It's musk, you ass hole."

"Well, it smells like ass hole, you musk!"

"You're not gonna wear *that* shirt?"

"Gav, you got another shirt I could borrow?"

"Klinger you have so much deodorant on, your armpits are gonna sag!"

"Dorff, seriously, *you* have a date?"

"Gentlemen, gentlemen, gentlemen. Take it down a notch."

"Have you seen my black penny loafers?"

"Hey Apple, you and Barnett gonna sneak off again?"

"Dorff, you sure the suds'll be cold enough?"

"What suds?"

"Nothing Bobby. Nothing."

"Can I borrow your gold chain?"

"Who the fuck took my Right Guard?"

"Klinger. He fuckin ate it!"

"Speaking of eating, Hank, are you gonna eat Mimi Horowitz on the football field?"

"No, I'm gonna eat her in the pussy, and don't call me Hank!"

"Who blew one?"

"Fuck off."

"Fuck you!"

"Eat me!"

"In your dreams."

"Dickhead."

"Hey Dorff, did you buy me the scumbags?

"Sturtz, you *are* a scumbag!"

"Gavin, I took some of your Aramis."

When everyone finally cleared out of the back of the bunk, I stood in front of the mirror, looking at myself, preparing to shave for one of the very few times in my life. I wished as I always did that I had a razor that could do the impossible, that could shave off the grape juice stain so that I could wash it down the chipped white porcelain sink and be done with it forever. Not that I minded it, just........

Then all at once something hit me and I started to grin, a funny feeling making my breathing ragged. In that moment all thoughts of destroying the stain were forgotten. "Holy shit," I thought as I started to put on the shaving cream, covering the blotch. "Lookin good," Ralph had said, "Lookin' real good."

And in that moment I realized that he had not been speaking about the decorations.

CHAPTER EIGHT:

POV: Apple

I should have known. There were hints, but at sixteen you do not swim against the tide. And the funny thing was that the summer of '75 almost didn't happen. But it did. Oh yes, it did.

That summer, the summer I turned sixteen, I lost two things, my appendix and my best friend. Thirty something years later, the scars from each are still visible, the emptiness the latter brought still overwhelming.

My appendix, however, blew at 10:00 o'clock on the morning of June 21,1975, totally unexpected and right in the middle of a choose-up basketball game in the schoolyard of P.S. 26, in Fresh Meadows, Queens. I went up for the ball and came down in a heap. I thought I had never known such pain.

Such pain! Ah, the arrogance of youth!

"Perfect timing, Brookman," my friend Jimmy Coyne said. Another friend, Jordan Behr had rushed to a pay phone and called 911, and now as he scanned 73rd Avenue looking for the ambulance, Jimmy knelt down next to me, while the members of both teams, all friends of mine, concern apparent on their faces, milled about behind him.

"The day *after* school lets out! Andrew, you are such an asshole! An appendix is good for at least three to four weeks of missed classes."

"Jimmy," I whispered between clenched teeth, "This wasn't *planned*!"

He shook his head. "Be that as it may, my friend. You're timing sucks." He smiled over at me as I struggled not to pass out. "In any case," he said, "you really are a loser."

Needless to say, Jimmy Coyne was *not* the friend I have been mourning for over a quarter of a century! Today, though, I hear, he is a well- known motivational speaker on the West Coast, like the guy with all the teeth. Then he was just an asshole.

We all were.

We were sixteen.

Coyne shook his head. "Either way, Andy, you have a major problem. From where I stand it looks to me like you can say good-bye to your summer."

I think back to those words constantly.

"From where I stand, you can say good-bye to your summer."

Now, I doubt that Jimmy Coyne was prescient, but man did he call that one. Oh, I went to camp as planned all right, though for a few days after the offending organ was removed there was some question as to whether I would, but that wasn't the point. I *did* say good-bye to summer that year and, as it turned out, to all my summers to come.

For that was the summer of '75!

But, the appendix came out, I got sewed up and through cajoling, whining and a very liberal doctor, when the bus pulled away from Cunningham Park, on June 30th, I was on it, joining my friends on the raucous four hour ride to Pennsylvania, swapping new comics and catching up on the secrets and lies of the past ten months. Limited activities and no swim for the first two weeks to be sure, but I was on my way to Camp Kanuga once again.

The bus bounced a lot and I winced in pain at the bumps in the road.

Pain!

I had no idea.

Sometimes I wonder what my life would have been like if I *had* missed that summer. Would the events that played out have played out differently without me? Would York still be alive, or would he have died in some other way? Was it just simply his time?

Time!

Time. The word and the concept are meaningless. Today is yesterday, yesterday today. No difference, no matter, for every day, either way, I think of York.

Everything reminds me, from, I am sure, the song of the same name.

York and I did everything together, went everywhere. Many times York's twin Gavin *would* join us, but most of the time it was just the two of us. Don't get me wrong, Gavin was terrific, and we were great friends, but the days I spent alone with York were magic, unbelievable. With him, everything was good. Everything made sense.

An example.

The fall before senior year at Kanuga, Henry Sturtz called us with a proposition. If we wanted to get laid, he could set us up. As soon as I got off the phone with him, I dialed York and Gavin.

"I'm in," I said.

"It wouldn't be fair to Nicki," York said, and Gavin, on the extension in their house, agreed.

I thought fast. "Look, York," I said, "it'll be a positive thing for you and for Nicki too. For both of you."

"Positive? Trust you Apple. Okay, so tell me how it would be a positive thing."

I leaned back on my bed. "Easy," I said. "You're a virgin, Nicki's a virgin... or at least I think she is........"

"Apple!," York warned.

I laughed. "Only kidding, bro. Major joking going on here." I heard him quietly "harumph," and went on. "You go to this hooker and you learn how to fit Tab A into Slot B. Then, when you and Nicki are ready, it'll be a night to remember, with no misfires, so to speak."

I could hear Gavin breathing on the line.

"York?" Silence. "Apple to York. Come in."

"Nicki wants our first time to be together."

"So she'll *think* it's your first time," I said. "You'll *tell* her it's your first time and when you perform like the world's number one stud, she will think you're a genius in the love department."

Twenty minutes later I had him. Gavin went along with it as I knew he would.

So it was that on a Saturday afternoon in early November I subway-ed to Penn Station, my stomach shivering with butterflies. I went to the Long Island Railroad area and stood waiting for York, Gavin and Sturtz next to the Information window as planned.

Only York showed.

"Where's Gavin?"

"Home in bed with a fever."

"Bullshit."

"Hundred and two."

"That pussy!"

"He's really bummed that he couldn't make it."

I grunted. "He probably held the thermometer up to a light- bulb. You want to put it off till he can come too?"

We were still too young to see the joke in what I had just said.

York shook his head. "I asked him that. He said he'd go the next time, and that we should have fun."

I nodded. "Where's Sturtz?"

"He's not coming either."

"What!" The butterflies flew off, and I felt a wave of relief sweep over me.

"He called just before I left. Said something had come up and that he was really sorry."

"I'll bet."

York shrugged. "Just telling you what he said."

"So what do we do?" I asked, my voice so much brighter that even I could notice it. "Movie?"

York's face broke into a smile. "Or we go do the deed on our own."

The butterflies returned and they brought friends. "Sure," I stammered, "but we don't know who, what or where?"

York grinned and pulled a piece of paper from his pocket. "Sturtz gave me all the info. You in?"

"*Murder on The Orient Express* is playing at the Coronet."

"Pussy."

I sighed. "Let's go."

We taxied up to 126th Street and Amsterdam Avenue, got some strange looks as we wandered around, and finally found the place, part of an old attached row house that had seen better days. We climbed the stairs and rang the bell. A woman's voice crackled over the intercom and told us to wait.

And as we stood on the chipped plaster stairway that led to the front door I was afraid that I might have to make a quick trip to the bathroom. I was frightened enough to feel myself shivering even though the day was warm. If York noticed, he didn't say. I looked at him standing confidently in front of me, casually looking up and down the block, and knew that there was no way to tell him how truly terrified I was.

I didn't have to.

York looked over at me and smiled.

"Hey Bro," he said, "you as scared as I am?"

God, I loved him!

I nodded. "Probably more."

"Doubt it."

"Scale of one to ten?"

And then the front door opened and we were led inside and soon we had no time left to think.

York went first.

When it was my turn, the girl was not very attractive, the sex was clumsy but, as we went down the same plaster steps less than forty minutes later, we were, for all intents and purposes, men.

"Jesus," I said, as we walked toward the subway, "that was it?"

York nodded. "That was it. I'm guessing that with the right girl it will be better."

"The right girl? *Any* girl! My God," I said shuddering, "I still got the skeeves. I can't wait to get into the shower. Talk about ugly!"

"She wasn't that bad."

I stopped. "What are you talking about, she was repulsive. Her room was repulsive. The fucking bed was repulsive."

York smiled. "She had nice eyes."

I laughed. "Nice eyes? Who the hell was looking at her eyes?"

York put his hand on my shoulder. "I was."

To celebrate the occasion, we bought cigars at a corner store, took a few puffs, laughed, and threw them away. Then, because I wanted to, we went to the movies.

York.

That people spoke of us in the same breath made me proud. I knew that I was always referred to as "York's friend, Apple", never the other way around. I knew that and I didn't care. Nicki Polis, who was the most popular girl at Kiunga from the moment she stepped off the bus, became almost mythic because she and York were a couple. York had the power to do that with his eyes closed. Everyone loved him, and I was his best friend and when he died the world came to a screeching halt.

He was so fucking *good*! So fucking kind. He was the first to praise and encourage and the last to put down or ridicule. That was left to Sturtz.

When I dream of Kanuga I usually wake up in a cold sweat. Those are the easy times. The hard times are when I dream about Kanuga and I am not asleep.

I rub my eyes, put down my pen, stretch the fingers of my writing hand, sip my tea, and Browning by way of Tennessee Williams is back.

"And if God should wish it, I will love you even more after death."

I admit I have a major problem. I have been to a number of shrinks about it, and I have spent hours in bed with Nicki going over and over it. I have put her to sleep, and the shrinks into catatonic states, but even as I hear them shuffling their papers behind me, or watch as her eyes slowly close and her breasts rise and fall to the cadence of my words, Kanuga and York are always there, ghosts that will not go away.

And though I try to explain it, no one can see them but me.

"You have seen the King, my Lord? Where?"

"In my mind's eye Horatio."

And sure it's nuts. Look, people are starving in third world countries and dying of every disease known to man, and I am losing it because I am a middle aged asshole merging lines from an English 12 reading list, with memories of a time that is over a quarter of a century ago.

"Jacket doctor?"

Shit!

Nicki reminds me of something that happened last week and I can only vaguely remember it, while I can remember anything to do with Kanuga with a clarity, a brightness equal only to that such as an epileptic knows just before a seizure.

There is simply, and oh, *not* simply, no room in my life for anything else.

CHAPTER NINE:

POV: Dorff

N ow being president of a camp group might sound pretty lame to those who have never *been* to camp, but those who *have* been there know just how important it is. Though in the long run the position might bring only fond memories, in the short run, the present, it offered recognition, status, and, from many of the younger campers, adoration.

Tradition had it that on the first Monday in July three senior boys would be nominated. Sturtz and York were shoo ins, but the last spot was a question mark. I knew that Gavin didn't want to run against his brother, and sure enough, when he was nominated at the senior group meeting held under the huge Oak Tree at the foot of the campus, he declined. Gavin then nominated Apple, who said that his vote was going to York and, therefore, he wasn't interested.

Then York raised his hand.

"I nominate Lenny Dorff," he said, sending me into a state of shock and provoking a few titters from some of the lower seniors. "Lenny's a good man. He proved that last summer. And he has his finger on the pulse of the camp. He could get more done in one minute than Sturtz or I could do in a few days. And besides," he smiled, "he's got the INQUIRER on his side." The group laughed warmly. "So my nomination goes to Dorff. What do you say Pulitzer?"

Before I could say anything, boys began applauding and I hoped that I wouldn't be called on to speak, because there was a huge lump right in the middle of my throat. I was in heaven, just to know that York thought enough about me to nominate me, but one look at the scowl on Henry Sturtz' face brought me back to earth in a hurry.

Bob Milburn, our group leader and counselor, held up his hands. "Hang on a minute." He looked at York. "You realize that you can't drop out! Rules state that it has to be a three man race."

York shrugged. "Okay then. I'm still in." He winked at me and whispered, "But you've got my vote, Lennie."

I nodded, in my mind finally having a best friend and a brother combined. "Thanks."

The election process, as also stated God know where, took a week, and the campaign was energetic and vocal. It was as close as you could come to a real campaign, with slogans, speeches, placards, the works. Howard and Moe wanted it that way. They said it was a good teaching device for the little kids and that it promoted good citizenship as well.

Sturtz and I didn't care about all that. We just wanted to win.

During meals in the mess hall the entire camp joined in the campaign. Though they knew that only the seniors would end up voting for one of the candidates, every group, every bunk, every camper, had a favorite. And with most of them it was York.

"Bang bang bangbang, York!" The pounding on the table and the calling of a favorite candidate's name would rise from one bunk, only to be answered by another. "Bang bang bangbang, Sturtz!" There was bedlam for them, but after the first day of the campaign the cheers for me still were not forthcoming.

Starting with breakfast of the second day, each candidate was expected to make a speech in the mess hall, and here, I figured, I might have a chance. I just needed to find a hook, a slogan that would set me apart from the other two.

After breakfast, Sturtz led off. He got up on his chair to great applause and said, "If I'm elected, I will do my best to have the bunks inspected for cleanliness only every *other* day." And the kids cheered and Ed Lasker, the head counselor, and my uncle at the head table smiled benignly, knowing, as the campers did, that the speeches were all for show, and that none of their promises could be kept.

And after that day's lunch, York stood up and shouted, "If I am elected, I will stamp out inspection altogether!" And the boys all cheered louder, and happy camper's hands slapped York's back, as Howard and Ed nodded and applauded.

And then it was dinner and my turn. As I got up on my chair and the mess shall quieted -down, I prayed that I wouldn't shake and that my voice wouldn't crack.

And I still had no idea what it was I was going to say. I knew I had to say something that would top both York and Sturtz, but what? All day I had thought of promises I could make, and all of them seemed lame. Childish. Longer swim periods? They were already almost an hour. How much longer could they be? Better food? Kanuga was known for the quality of its food, and besides, to mention this would be to insult to Moe. More dances? Jesus, how many could we have, one a day? And the frustrating part was that whatever I came up with was only make believe anyway. Maybe that was it. Maybe say something that was totally outrageous; something that would let everyone know that I was in on the joke. I needed something quick and memorable. I needed a joke, something that they would laugh with me for and not at me. A joke? Me? And I remembered *Rebel Without A Cause* when James Dean wanted to fit in and went, "Moooo," at the Planetarium. "Moo?," the in-crowd said, "Moo?" And Dean looked like the biggest loser of all time.

What in hell was I going to say?

I took a deep breath. "If I am elected," I began, and at that precise moment, a waiter going into the kitchen dropped his tray. There was loud crash, broken glasses and plates flying everywhere. The mess hall cheered as Ed Lasker stood up, looked at the damage and scowled. "Well," I said off the top of my head, "the first thing I'll do as president is to get that guy's job back!" And the place went wild! Everyone roared his approval, with even the waiters joining in.

I had them.

"And the very next thing, and probably the most important," and here I paused for dramatic emphasis, " I promise to stamp out virginity!"

It had come out of nowhere and for a moment my words hung in dead silence. Oh Christ, was this going to be my "moo?"

And then the place erupted. I had never heard such a noise.

Hands reached up to me, and I was lifted onto the shoulders of some of the lower seniors. And the roar turned into, "DORFF! DORFF! DORFF! DORFF!"

Howard looked bewildered and Ed was frowning. Screw that. I had topped Sturtz and York.

I looked down at my bunk. Gavin was laughing and slamming Klinger on the back. Sturtz was shaking his head, his mouth screwed into a petulant purse. Just below me, York looked up, winked and gave me a "thumbs up".

I thought I would explode with happiness.

From that night on, the election went into high gear.

Sturtz made up cards that read, "Win with Sturtz," so I went into the arts and crafts shack and printed up some cards that read, "Lose it with Dorff!" Mine were the hit of the campus. The phrase became my campaign slogan, and even the smallest kids, totally unaware of what they were saying, chanted it wherever they went.

The tide had definitely turned. Because of a clumsy waiter and an impromptu slogan, all at once I was the front- runner.

Even Howard, who at first asked me to change my slogan, because, he said, Aunt Phyllis was less than amused by it, backed off and seemed pleased. "I don't want it to look like I'm playing favorites," he said as we sat on the porch of his cabin after dinner of the third night, watching the campers at 'free play' below, "and I hope you know I'm not." I nodded. "But," he said, pulling a straw hat from behind his rocker. "I got a few extras for this year's carnival. I thought you might make good use of it." He glanced furtively over his shoulder. "Just don't tell Phyllis where you got it!" He handed the hat to me. "Use it well."

And I did. I had my slogan printed on a ribbon that covered the hat-band, and I wore it everywhere I went.

And then, just two days before the vote, something weird happened.

York started to campaign.

Small things at first, mock leading a cheer for himself at line up, taking a free period to walk the campus shaking hands. And then a sign nailed to the front of our bunk. "Get into the New *York* state of mind!"

"It's only to make things more interesting," he told me as we walked to line up the day before the voting. "Build the tension. That kind of thing."

But at dinner that night I noticed that the cheers for the three of us were just about even, and that York was playing the candidate for all it was worth.

And as York campaigned, I fought even harder to win. I knew instinctively that this was my one chance to make a statement about myself: to show that I was worthy, capable, and, wonder of wonders, even likable. It was the only arena in which I could take on the York Stewarts and Henry Sturtz's of the world and possibly have an outside chance to win.

But I knew it was a long -shot. Sturtz had started with a strong voting base that was still in place, and after a full week my clever slogan and cool straw hat had paled and were fast being replaced by the magic that was York Stewart.

And then, after a week that was both the shortest and the longest of my life, Election Day arrived.

During clean up that day Bob Milburn went around to all the senior bunks carrying a batting helmet into which each senior dropped a piece of paper on which they had written the name of their candidate. The symbolism of the hat was not lost on me. Even in elections Kanuga was still an athletic camp. There were forty- five ballots, and there were forty- four jocks and then there was me. Even I, who sucked in Math couldn't miss the probable outcome. My chances, once bright began to dim. I watched as the folded pieces of paper were dropped into the hat, hardly able to breathe.

"Meeting under the tree," Milburn yelled as Klinger dropped in the last ballot. "On the double. Let's go."

Even Sturtz moved quickly and in only a few minutes the entire senior group was sitting under the large oak tree near the H.Q.

"Gentlemen, the ballots will now be opened and read. Larry has been kind enough to keep a running count." Larry Caboy, the head lifeguard, grunted and lifted his clipboard for all to see. "So now," Bob went on, "let's begin."

I looked over at Sturtz. His face was grim and he was biting his lower lip. York, on the other hand, was nodding at something that Apple was saying to him. He laughed and turned as Milburn said, "York."

"Yes?"

Gavin smacked his brother on the head. "He wasn't calling you. He called your name. You got a vote numb nuts."

"Yessss!" York said, jerking his hand in a Jewish version of the black -panther salute. "I'm in the lead!"

Everyone but Sturtz laughed.

Milburn reached into the hat. "York."

York punched the air again in a gesture of victory.

"Sturtz."

A burst of applause from Bunk 29!

"Dorff."

"Okay, Pulitzer!," Gavin yelled, and I smiled over at him.

Bob went on. "York."

No noise this time, but silence.

"York."

"Dorff."

"Dorff."

"Sturtz."

"York."

And as the ballots were pulled out of the hat and the name on it read aloud, the silence and the tension grew.

And then, finally, the last name was called.

"Sturtz."

Milburn turned the hat over and shook it to show that it was indeed empty.

We all looked over at Larry Caboy. He was very quiet as he checked his addition, and then he looked up at Bob. "You want to read this or should I?"

Bob nodded at him. "You go ahead."

Larry cleared his throat and looked at us sitting before him. "Gentlemen, we have a three way tie."

There were some whistles of surprise and Sturtz said, "Oh come on!" but Larry shrugged. "That's it."

Bob Milburn nodded. "Well," he said, "there's gonna have to be a recount."

Everyone whispered to the boy sitting next to him as the ballots were put back in the hat. This time Larry drew them out one by one, calling out the names, as Bob kept the tally.

The loudspeaker crackled, and a few of the boys focusing on the count actually jumped. "Ten minutes before first activity. At the bugle, freshman to nature, sophomores to the hall...", and as Ed's voice droned on we all tuned him out, mesmerized as Bob and Larry counted the votes again.

Finally, Bob looked up. "No mistake. It's a tie."

"Shit." Sturtz looked over at Bob. "Bobby, can we miss activity and do the damn vote again now? I mean, this is so lame!"

"That would have to be a decision made by the entire group. You've got baseball this morning. If you want to miss part of the period, fine with me. Or we could have the recount during rest hour." He looked at the group. "What do you say?"

"Bob?"

Milburn glanced over at York.

"I agree with Henry. This *is* foolish. But there's another way around it."

"Go on."

"I'm dropping out and I'm throwing my votes to Pulitzer."

Time stopped. No one moved.

"You're what?"

I don't think I had ever seen Sturtz as angry as he was at that moment. York smiled at him. "Oh, come on Henry, you don't need this. I don't need it! We've got enough on our plates already. Dorff'll do a better job than either of us would. You know that in your gut, the way I know it. Why not just throw your votes his way and make it unanimous."

"Bullshit." Sturtz stood up and turned to Milburn. "I want a revote, Bobby. York's idea is bullshit."

Milburn shook his head. "No can do, Henry. If York wants to give his votes to Lennie there's nothing I can do to about it."

"But that can't be fair."

York stood and moved in close to Sturtz. "Sure it is, Henry. They were mine, now they're his. No big deal."

"No big deal?" Sturtz' face was beet red. He glared at York standing next to him. "For chrissake, I worked my ass off for this, York. It's not a fucking toy that you can play with. It means something to me."

Milburn's voice was soft yet firm. "Easy, Henry."

"No! I mean this is so freaking typical. Whatever York wants, York gets." He turned to me, pointing a finger. "And *you*. You probably had a hand in all this."

York's voice sounded weary. "Oh for God's sake, Henry. He had nothing to do with anything. It's my decision."

And while this was going on, I felt an emptiness that was rare even for me. The way they were talking about me as if I wasn't there, as if my feelings meant nothing, that I *felt* nothing, that I *was* nothing! All at once I didn't care if I became president or not. I just wanted this humiliation to be over.

"Lennie." I looked up at Milburn. "What's your opinion about this?"

Sturtz snorted. "Oh, shit, Bobby, what's he gonna say? He wants to be president so bad that he'll be happy to take York's votes."

"No, Henry I don't....," I never had a chance to finish.

"Bullshit," Sturtz snapped and turned away from me.

"Oh, okay." York's voice was calm and he smiled at Henry Sturtz and then at me. "If it means that much, let's have the revote."

I never had the chance to say anything. Once again, everything was out of my hands.

Sturtz stared at York for a moment and then, mollified, nodded at Milburn. "All right, and let's do it now."

Paper and pencils were brought and the batting helmet filled once again. No surprise.

I won by ten votes.

The group applauded. Sturtz glared at York, growled "Fuck you!" and stalked off.

York smiled, looked over at me, nodded at the retreating Sturtz and shrugged. He opened his mouth. "Pul-it-zer. Pul-it-zer," he said, and the others joined in. "Pul-it-zer," they chanted, and as the sound of my nickname grew to a shout, boys from the lower bunks jammed their porches to see what was going on under 'the tree.'

York stood apart, beaming. That's when I started to cry. Some of the seniors laughed good-naturedly and slapped me on the back, pleased to see that my happiness had actually brought tears, but that was not why I was crying. They had no way of knowing that the tears were not for a win, but rather for a loss.

I had come so close to achieving something on my own this time, something new, something that was mine and no one else's. Whether he had meant to or not, York had taken that away from me. It wouldn't have mattered if I had won or lost, either way, the outcome would have been mine, and not a hand me down, something that York no longer needed or wanted, something that he thought would fit me better than he.

And I cried because I would never know if I could have made it on my own.

The meeting broke up and we all went back to our bunks. The others got their gloves and cleats, and I picked up my clipboard, ready to spend the period on the bleachers writing the INQUIRER. No one expected me to play. It was expected that I wouldn't. No one questioned it. No one cared.

Another given.

Bob Milburn paused at the screen door and looked at me sitting on my bed. "You coming? I'll walk with you."

I shook my head. At any other time in the summer, in *any* summer, I would have given anything to walk and talk with Bob Milburn, but not today.

"Need to hit the head," I said. "Too much excitement or something."

Bob laughed. "See you up there then." He looked back as he went through the doorway and smiled. "Congratulations, Mr. President."

I waved to him. "Thanks Bob."

The door slammed and except for me, the bunk was empty.

Thanks?

Thanks for what?

Don't thank me," I thought "thank York.

I had nothing to do with anything.

I looked down at the loose-leaf pages on the clipboard in my lap and I realized that everything I had written so far this summer, anything that I had accomplished at Kanuga, that everything I had ever done, in one morning had turned to shit.

I sat on my bed in the gloom of the empty cabin and stared. A broken shoelace lay on the floor but, other than that, everything was perfect. Dappled sunlight coming in through the screened windows, the tightly made beds with their rough wool blankets tucked into hospital corners, the extra blanket folded over just so on each end. The pillows covered by crisp white pillowcases. The stacks of comic books piled neatly at the side of Sturtz' bed. York and Apple's tennis rackets hanging side by side on the wall! Gavin's forgotten baseball cap on a nail over his bed!

Neatness.

Cleanliness.

Everything in its place, everyone safe in the knowledge he belonged.

The incredible order of Bunk 33!

I took a deep breath. Old Spice, Aramis, the ever- lingering smell of Dial Soap! The overpowering freshness of privileged youth!

I got up and moved to York's bed. I lifted his pillow and pressed my face to it. Again, the wild impulse to cry! The clean, fresh smell of York; he who could give and take away! He who could bestow!

He who had the greatest gift of all!

Perfection.

Only one available!

One of a kind!

No more to be had at any price.

My heart pounded in my chest. I wanted to laugh, to cry, to explode, to be, all at once, all of this, and, at the same time, to be no more. To exist as York was the ideal; to exist as Lenny Dorff was a sentence.

And yet, I realized, as glorious as York was, what he had done was unforgivable, and maybe that hurt me most of all. If he had done it out of charity, it was cruel. If he had done it out of vanity it was worse, unthinkable, for then York Stewart was no longer perfect. And if *he* wasn't, who or what was?

And I climbed onto York's bed and lay with his pillow under my head.

I closed my eyes and behind the closed lids, in my mind's eye, we were playing in the Upper Senior basketball game.

I could actually hear the squeak of sneakers, smell the sweet smell of sweat, and in front of me, York Stewart, in the open, dribbling effortlessly down the court. He has an easy shot, one that he could make with his eyes closed, but he slows, smiles, feints, and passes the ball to me.

Me!

"Shoot, Lennie, shoot."

And I don't know how.

No one has taught me to play this game. I shouldn't even be playing on the same team as York, but he has passed the ball to me anyway. I stand there frozen, the ball in my hands, while the crowd roars my name.

"Dorff. Dorff. Dorff."

Hands pat me on the back! The crowd roars my name! Hands lift me onto shoulders! And I still hold the ball. I have not moved. I am congratulated for doing nothing, for being nothing.

And then there is only one voice, and it repeats and repeats and repeats, and I pull York's pillow so that it covers my ears so that I do not have to hear it. But it is everywhere, and I curl up, my knees against my chest and the words crash in my brain.

"Congratulations," they say. "Congratulations, Mr. President."

CHAPTER TEN:

POV: Gavin

James Dean wept over the dead body of Sal Mineo, the lower campers picked up their blankets and moved to their bunks, and the seniors started moving toward the social hall.

"I can't wait," Klinger said.

I could!

And, as always, our bunk arrived first.

We stood in the center doorway and looked at our handiwork.

"So?" Dorff asked, gesturing around the room.

"Great," York said, and patted him on the back.

"Fair," Sturtz said, "where are the suds?"

"Jesus, Henry," Dorff said. "For the tenth time, they are under the stage with the vodka and the gin." He looked at me. "You think it looks nice, Gav?"

"Most excellent, Lennie. Most excellent indeed."

"Thanks Gav," he said. "Thanks a lot."

Sturtz persisted. "Pulitzer, you're sure Milburn won't see us with the booze? Don't forget, if I get shit from him, you get shit from me."

Dorff sounded exasperated. "Yes, Henry, he will *not* see us. There's an access door backstage that no one has used in years. I'll go in there, crawl to the front and drag the booze with me."

"Anyway, Milburn's cool." Klinger said. "He knows what's up."

York shook his head. "Don't put Milburn is harm's way. Anyone finds out he knows anything about the booze, he loses his job."

Sturtz waved him away. "Don't worry about Milburn. Worry about the libations."

"I don't know why having booze at the cabaret is so important anyway," Dorff grumbled. "The dance should be enough."

"Maybe to you, Numbnuts," Sturtz sneered, "but not to the rest of mankind. And you will notice that I stress *'man*kind!'"

"Lighten up, Sturtz," Apple said. "If it weren't for Lennie there would be no booze at all, so cut him a break. The booze did not get here by magic!"

Apple was right. But if there *was* magic involved in this slight of hand, the prize had to be shared; Sturtz was the sorcerer and Dorff his apprentice.

Long before cabaret, Sturtz had started haranguing, cajoling and generally keeping on Dorff's ass about getting beer and booze for the night of nights even though it was weeks and weeks away. Dorff, of course, was a natural for this as he had access to both his uncle's cabin, (a bottle of Stoley and a half bottle of schnapps appeared from there), and, because of being Senior group president, his frequent trips to neighboring towns. Sturtz made up a list of what he thought we needed and supplied a fake ID that was supplied by a friend of his from home. Soon after the Fourth of July weekend, Dorff, ostensibly on "official camp business," started treking into town, buying six packs of beer and putting them on the bottom of cartons filled with dance decorations and 45's. Though Dorff was the main supplier, our cache grew too from the generosity of a few former campers, now parents, who "remembered what it was like to be a senior", who dropped in with a few 40's, and from one disgruntled waiter who had been fired and was on his way home. He supplied three jugs of Gallo red for twenty-five bucks. (I had also heard a rumor that our one bottle of Gordon's gin, had actually been supplied by "The Luggage King." Doubtful, but thought provoking nonetheless).

So, the decorations were in place and the booze was ready and Cabaret 1975 was waiting to begin.

And then we heard the girls coming down the road, their voices raised in their camp song.

"Camp Kiunga, fight, fight, fight,
Hear your daughters singing,
Through the darkest night, night, night,
Fighting round the clock

We are in the right, right, right,
Noble voices ringing....."

We started singing at the top of our lungs, finishing their song as we always did.

"Camp Kiunga, bite, bite, bite,
Honey, suck my cock!"

We were still high fiving each other when the girls started coming through the social hall doors. They 'ooohed and ahhed' at the decorations and when I glanced over at Dorff, I saw that he was beaming. He caught my eye and I gave him a thumbs -up. He smiled at me and nodded.

We searched the faces of the girls as they entered walking up to our dates and giving them welcome pecks on the cheeks.

York saw Nicki and waved to her from across the room. I waited for a minute until they had embraced and walked up behind her. "Hey, Little Poop," I said. She turned, a big grin on her face and threw her arms around me. "Hey, Brother In Law, how's it going?" I held her tight. She and York were an item, but next to York Nicki was my closest friend. "I am good," I said. "And after seeing you I am even better." York laughed and pulled Nicki away. "Who writes your material, Bro? It's got Oscar written all over it. Go find Ellen and get your ass over to the table. We'll save two places." Nicki kissed me on the cheek and I stood smiling as I watched York lead her to the table that we had reserved.

I looked back to the door of the hall. Apple had his arm around his summer steady Sue Barrett, and Sturtz had his hand on Carol Kaplan's ass. She made a half- hearted attempt to get it off, and then cuddled into the crook of his arm and giggled instead. Mimi Horowitz had her arm around Klinger's waist and was looking up into his eyes with slavish devotion, while a girl whose name I thought was Elie something had Dorff in, from where I was standing, what looked very much like a headlock.

Two small hands over my eyes! A whiff of Heaven Scent perfume mixed with a hint of Ban.

"Guess who!"

My stomach did a flip-flop and for a moment I thought I might have to get back to the john. But, as Davy Eisner had put it, I was all cleaned out and it was time to swim.

"Ann-Margaret."

"Close."

"Elizabeth Taylor."

"Closer."

The hands slipped then tightened over my eyes.

"Well, if it's a combination of Ann-Margaret and Elizabeth Taylor, it can only be one person."

The hands over my eyes were sweaty. The voice giggled. "Who?"

"Lennie Dorff!"

The hands left my eyes and started pummeling me playfully. "Very funny...not," Ellen Marcus said laughing.

Ellen Marcus was my mother's best friend's, friend's sister's daughter. Really. No lie. Physically she was what is called petite. Her head came up to the middle of my chest and after dancing with her for a few years I would know the smell of her hair anywhere. She was feisty and cute and we liked each other.

"How are you, kiddo?" she said.

"I am just fine, kiddo. Let's go sit down."

Ellen wrapped her arm around my waist and I led her over to our table. We were just about to sit down when a voice, amplified almost to non-recognition blared out of the speakers.

"Are there any party people in the house?"

I looked over to the front of the stage as Ellen sat down.

Ralph Sanchez, a microphone in his hand, stood in front of the stage and called out again. "I said, 'Are there any party people in the house?'"

"Yeah," came the tepid response from a few of the tables.

In one leap, Ralph was on the stage. He was wearing a white shirt open down the front, tight white jeans and white shoes.

He looked amazing.

"I can't hear you people! If you are ready to party say 'yes.'

More of a response!

"What was that? Ralph shouted.

"Yes!"

"What?"

"YES!"

"WHAT?"

"YES!"

He had them by the balls and, as I stood beaming, he caught my eye and winked at me.

"Okay you mothers and assorted sisters, get ready to blow the spot up. Throw your hands in the air and let me hear you scream. Come on everybody, let's party!!!" And with that Ralph ripped off his shirt and let the music play.

And the place went wild.

So it began. The senior cabaret of 1975! Studio 75. And, amazingly, for some reason that I could not explain then, there was no place in the entire world that I would rather be.

Ralph opened with K.C. and the Sunshine Band's "That's the Way I Like It!" People were on their feet moving to the beat and howling 'Uh-Huh, uh-huh,' and laughing as they did.

Ellen got up, quickly grabbed my hand and whisked me onto the dance floor. She may have been a serious girl with a million liberal causes during the rest of the year, but at that moment she had only one, getting me to dance. She loved to dance and was truly great at it. York might well have had just about everything I didn't have, but Ellen Marcus was the best dancer at both camps, and she was my date.

I, on the other hand, was a clod. A lump. A lox. I stood off to the side of Ellen, grinning like a fool and faking a few steps while she gyrated. Ellen's body moved in planes and angles that defied the boundaries of human motion. Though there was no way in the world that I could even think of keeping up with her on the dance floor, I basked in the glow of being associated with someone special, someone who stood out from the crowd... in a good way.

Though the social hall doors and windows were all opened wide the heat and humidity closed in on the whirling dancers. The music was torrid and soon sports jackets and ties were discarded. Hair became damp and flattened, the smell of wet hair spray everywhere.

With an instinct that was right on target, Ralph called out, "Okay people, it's grindin' time. Time to slow jam." He played 'Falling In Love Again,' with Hamilton, Joe Frank and Reyne, and sweaty couples held each other close and danced as many of their parents had in the same hall decades before.

As Ellen went back to the table to wipe her streaming face and to re arrange her makeup, Sturtz sidled up to me and handed me a lily cup. "Have some water," he said. "But slug it fast." I put the waxy cup to my lips, tilted it back, and felt the gin burn as I swallowed. "Jesus," I said.

"Yes, my son," Sturtz said with a smirk, as he handed me a can of beer wrapped with a napkin. "More holy water." The beer felt good after the gin.

I took a few more gulps and handed the almost empty can back to Sturtz. "Thanks Henry."

He nodded. "Avec plaisir. If you want more, find either Pulitzer or me. There's plenty more where that came from." He disappeared amongst the swaying dancers.

"Baby, baby, falling in love,
I'm fallin' in love again."

I felt good. No, I felt wonderful. The gin and the beer provided an immediate buzz and I actually felt myself moving slowly to the song as I looked up at the figure of Ralph Sanchez on the stage in front of me.

"You and me for eternity.
This love will always be,
Young and sweet and naturally,
The way it's got to be."

I looked over at the dancers around me and I was happy and mellow. Mellower maybe than I had ever felt before.

"Baby, baby, falling in love
I'm falling in love again."

"See," Ellen said, coming up beside me, "you can dance. You just need the right partner."

I put my arms around her and we moved to the music, my head, as always, in her hair.

After a few more songs, Ralph announced that it was break time. "Time to feed up, chow down and suck dem ribs." He laughed. "Ooops. Wrong crowd. What I meant to say is 'suck dem *beef* ribs!" People laughed and applauded. Ralph was a smash and for some weird reason it somehow transferred over to me. We ambled over to the buffet table to the sounds of America singing Sister Golden Hair Surprise. York and Apple were already there, filling their plates while arguing over the merits of Johnny Bench and Carlton Fisk.

The food was good, and the beer, still wrapped in napkins, seemed unending. Good work Sturtz and Dorff! Ellen finally smelled it and demanded a few sips. I felt warmer toward her than I ever had to any girl before as she drank from the lake-water cooled can.

The music started again and York mouthed, "Time to get lost," at me. He and Nicki headed for the dance floor and then, so that no one could see them, slipped out of the stage door of Hayes. York and Nicki followed soon after.

Ellen looked at me. "Shall we?"

I nodded, and for the first time of the evening I felt the old familiar pain in my stomach, the butterflies running amok. As Ellen led me past the stage I looked over at Ralph. He was still shirtless and covered in sweat. Four girls were standing around him. One was giggling. From the looks of it, he was enjoying his new found celebrity very much.

Ellen squeezed my hand and we slipped out the back door.

We walked down the small embankment in back of the social hall, across the highway that ran by the camp, and down into the shrubs that surrounded the guest's dock.

Though the moon was hazy and I could see my brother and Nicki standing under a tree close to the lake. His hand was under Nicki's blouse and she had pulled his shirt out of his pants and was stroking his bare- back. I quickly looked away. Apple and Sue Barrett were nowhere to be seen.

"Over here," Ellen said, leading me to a small copse of trees. There was one large, red garbage can for the whole guest dock area and this was the spot Ellen had led me to.

"Right next to a garbage can?"

Ellen giggled. "The others have taken the prime places. I'm with the guy I want to be with so anyplace will be fine."

We sat down on the cool grass and Ellen put her head on my chest. "This is nice," she said.

I looked over at York and Nicki but couldn't see them from where we were. Good.

Ellen's small hands pulled my head down and she pressed her mouth to mine. Strawberry flavored lipstick and beer! It tasted nice. Warm. Welcoming. I returned her kiss gently touching her lips with mine.

I looked at Ellen's face in the moonlight. Her eyes were closed and she was breathing heavily. Her arms moved, wrapped around me and, suddenly, her tongue was between my lips, searching for a way into my mouth. I was surprised and pulled back a bit.

Ellen took her lips away.

"I'm sorry," I muttered, "I just..."

She smiled. "No problem. And I'm the one who should be sorry. Just got carried away by the night."

I felt like a fool. "No," I lied, "it was nice." I opened my mouth and we kissed again. This time Ellen pulled back.

"You're not into this, are you Gav?" she said, and I was relieved to se that she wasn't angry.

"It's just that York is the social one in the family, you know? I'm the one who'd rather play ball or watch T.V. I guess that sounds kinda weird." I snickered. "I know it does to me. I just haven't been........"

The pounding bass line from Hayes started again and I stopped talking. I could hear Nicki whispering something to York nearby and strained to hear what Ralph was saying over the pounding music. I couldn't make out what it was, but brought a sudden cheer from those in the hall.

"Want to go back?" Ellen held my hand in hers and gave it a little squeeze.

I shook my head. "No," I said, turning back to her. "No. I want to be here with you." I took her in my arms as I had seen so many leading men do to so many leading ladies in the movies that I loved, and I pressed my open mouth to hers. I tried to be James Dean to Ellen's Natalie Wood, but it wasn't happening. Ellen returned my kiss and though her mouth felt warm and nice, I knew she felt my discomfort.

A few feet away, Nicki cried out and then was still.

Ellen pulled back. I could see her smile, warm and reassuring in the soft moonlight. "It's okay. Really." I started to say something but she put one of her little hands over my mouth. "Ssshh," she said, "trust me. It's okay. If it's going to work it has to be with someone you want to be with."

"But I want to be with *you*," I mumbled, staring to feel a desperation grow in me that I had never known before. "It's probably just the booze and that I'm really tired and all. We've been working our ass off to get this thing in shape for tonight."

Ellen smiled and shook her head. "No," she said quietly, "There's no need for excuses. Nothing is wrong. It's just not the right time and place. I wish it was but things don't always work out the way you want them to. Maybe some other time." She reached up, put her hands over my ears and brought my face down to hers. She brushed my mouth lightly with hers, leaving the waxy residue of her lipstick on my lips, then moved away. "Time to join the others, Kiddo," she said, getting up. "Cabaret won't last forever, and Gavin my boy, I want to dance! Let's get back."

I held her hand as we retraced our path and entered the social hall. The lights were so bright that we stood near the stage for a moment to let our eyes adjust. Ralph was just starting to read some dedications.

"This one's for Apple from Susan," he read from an index card in his hand, " a return engagement by KC and the Sunshine Band and 'Get Down Tonight.'"

Laughter.

Music.

Dancing.

"To York from Nicki, 'This Will Be an Everlasting Love,'"

Ahhhs and Ohhhs.

Dancing.

Music.

Me, half- heartedly trying to keep up with Ellen!

Then, for the first time in the evening silence! No music. Nothing. All eyes turned to the stage.

Ralph, drenched in sweat and glowing in his success looked over at Ellen and me. Though he stood totally still it somehow seemed that he was still moving, still throwing off the power and energy he had been giving off all night. And he was looking at me.

"Gavin, my man, if it's okay with her, would you mind if I danced with your lovely lady? I saw her on the floor before and she is really awesome." Gasps as people turned to look at me.

I can't explain what I felt in that moment that followed for I don't truly know myself. Helpless, lost, proud, jealous, weaker, stronger than I had ever felt before.

Ellen looked up at me. "Do you mind?" she asked me. "I don't have to."

"But you'd like to!" It was hard to get the words out. Ellen nodded.

I lifted her onto the stage, and for the second time that night, the place went wild. Everyone knew that Ellen was the best dancer in the hall, and Ralph, well Ralph was a force of nature chained up long enough for one evening. Ralph put on Elton John's "Philadelphia Freedom," took Ellen's hand, led her to the center of the stage and they began to dance.

I stood below them watching, feeling so weak that I thought I might fall down. Dorff came up and pressed a cup in my hand and I downed whatever it was, knowing only that it burned.

Ralph and Ellen danced as though they had been dancing together all of their lives. Ralph's movements were lithe and graceful, yet filled with muscle and power. He looked over at me and smiled. Ellen was dancing as she had never danced before, following Ralph's moves with ease. I had never seen her smile the way she was smiling at him. They instinctively knew what the other was going to do, twisting, turning, bodies almost brushing bodies and both camps were watching, and clapping and calling out and whistling and someone handed me another drink and I slugged it down, and the music seemed louder and the dancing continued more intense and passionate and someone slapped me on the back and said, "Good man, Gav," and I saw York staring at me from the door, worry in his eyes and I wanted to laugh and cry and disappear into the lake that stretched in the dark below us.

Ralph was everything that I wanted to be, graceful, powerful and totally in charge. The smile he was smiling radiated pure joy, pure freedom: pure confidence. He had all the things I knew I could never have, that only he and York had, that no one else but they in the camp had. They were special, my brother and Ralph and they were powerful and they were beautiful and they were the same and I loved them and hated them so completely that I thought I might explode.

And then, suddenly, the song was over and the applause was deafening.

As everyone congratulated Ralph and Ellen, I drifted over to Dorff's secret door and grabbed a half empty bottle of gin. I took two large swigs and then moved back into the hall.

The things that happened after that are fragmented, like the pieces of light that flew out of Dorff's crystal ball that twirled above the social hall or the crazy prisms that threw color everywhere in the Arts and Crafts shack.

I remember York telling me not to drink so much.

I remember Ellen telling me that she loved me and that there was no one greater in the world than I.

I remember Nicki Polis kissing me and saying, "Goodnight, 'Big -Poop.'"

I remember more plastic cups.

But most of all I remember what happened afterward, when the girls had left and the music stopped.

Some of the guys collected all the discarded empty plates and cups. Others were already sweeping the torn decorations from the floor.

Someone handed me a chair and told me to bring it back to the mess hall.

I was a little wobbly but I navigated the small rise toward my destination. Ralph was standing there, in almost the same spot we had stood in hours earlier as we carried the table to Hayes, his shirt stuffed into his back pocket accepting everyone's congratulations for being such a great D J.

I made three trips back and forth and when I started back to the social hall for another chair, the lights suddenly went out and I realized that there was nothing left for me to do, no place left for me to go.

I remember trying to find my way in the dark, my hands out in front of me like FRANKENSTEIN, and stumbling over the exposed root of the old oak that stood beside the social hall.

I remember a hard, bare arm stopping my fall.

I remember Ralph Sanchez smiling at me.

I remember his telling me to follow him.

I remember his taking me to the costume closet back stage.

I remember the musty smell of the costumes almost as in a dream.

I remember his sure hands taking off my shirt.

I remember my warm chest pressing against Ralph's.

I remember a voice in my ear. "I was dancing wit you, Gavin. I was dancing wit *you*."

I remember a hot mouth on mine, and then a hand undoing my belt, the top of my pants.

I remember Ralph's hands and voice becoming my world.

I remember pain mixed with euphoria and the sensation of exploding into a million pieces.

I remember fear mixed with elation.

I remember how wet from the dew my shoes got as I walked back to the bunk.

I remember wondering what I was going to tell Bob Milburn when he asked me where I had been.

I remember how scared I was that York would find out, all the while knowing that somehow York already knew and would understand.

I remember wanting, for the first time in my life, to be sure of who I was.

But most of all, I remember how the smell of Ralph's cologne and sweat lingered in my nostrils and on my body, and how I knew with a clarity I had never known before that my life would never be the same again.

Fact.

No lie.

CHAPTER ELEVEN: LOVERS AND LOSERS

POV: Nicki:

I was sitting at Athenaeum. Years before, someone, an obviously well read someone, had given the hidden cove on the lake between Kanuga and Kiunga that, to all intents and purposes, somewhat pretentious name. In the dictionary Athenaeum is described as a temple in Athens where writers and scholars met. Whether the person who named this place, intelligent as she was, knew what she was talking about is doubtful because the girls who gathered here through the years were far from being writers or scholars. I must admit that there were some pretty good stories told here, some pretty good *hot* stories told here, but writers and scholars, not really. Actually, the place was mainly a gathering spot for we older girls and some of the counselors who would sit on the ground, sprawl on blankets, or just lean against the huge trees that dominated the area, smoke a cigarette and dish the dirt. Athenaeum was a perfect spot for getting away from it all as it wasn't visible from Kiunga and could only be accessed by using a brush covered hidden path that led between it and Kanuga. "Nancy Drew and the Hidden Cove," someone once jokingly called it. For me, when there was no one else around, it was the perfect place to sit and think for a while.

Today was 'Lazy Day' at both camps; a day on which there were no scheduled activities and reveille was forty minutes later than usual. There were two such days every summer: this one, after the Cabaret, and the one that followed the last day of color war. This one gave the upper seniors a chance to regroup after the cabaret the night before. By tradition, "Lazy Day was nicknamed "Loser's Day," at the boy's camp, and "Lover's Day" at ours. All we had to do was lounge about as we, recovering slowly, reviewed the events of the night before and gossiped to our hearts content. At Kanuga on 'Loser's Day,' the boys, we heard, shot hoops. We, as Sue Barnett so genteely put it, shot the shit

Ellen, Mimi Horowitz, Sue and I had drifted down to Athenaeum during rest hour. We re-hashed the night before, waded and lolled the afternoon away. When the bugle sounded for swim, the others decided to go while I, leaning up against a giant oak, closed my eyes, delighting in the solitude. There were many times in my life when there was nothing I enjoyed doing more than just sitting by myself and listening to the quiet. Knowing my home life, I am sure you can understand.

This was one of those times.

"Don't be late for line up," Ellen had called over her shoulder, and I waved as she and the others walked back to campus.

I glanced at my watch. Three thirty. I had plenty of time to do nothing. I leaned back into the oak, took a deep breath and let it out slowly. I loved this spot, this oak. I leaned back and looked at it soaring above me. My God, how old was this tree? How many girls had sat as I was sitting, looking at the massive roots that ran deeper than I could even imagine. And before the girls, who? Farmers? Settlers? Indians? And before them, and before and before and before, and the tree still stood oblivious to all that had gone on around it. How many hundreds of years, how many people, how many lives? "And," I thought to myself as I closed my eyes, put my face into the dappled sunlight and let myself drift, "isn't it amazing that each one of the people who sat beneath this tree thought her life was the most important one in the world! And yet we are all so puny. 'Full of sound and fury signifying nothing.'" I smiled. Mr. McLoughlin's English class *did* pay off. My mind began to wander as I listened to the water lap up against the pebbles on the shore. I felt sleep coming and I welcomed it.

The thoughts whirled behind my closed eyes. I owed my mother a letter. But then again, when was the last time *she* wrote? Where was she now, Monaco? Pago Pago? Please! God, York looked handsome last night. It was a magic night. His lips. His hands. His gentleness. His caring. His unselfishness.

Not like Apple. I had heard him grunting in the bushes last night. York was so gentle; so beautiful.

"Are you cold, Nicki?" he asked me.

"Is this okay?"

"Am I hurting you?"

"Don't do anything you don't want to."

And his just having said that had made me do anything he wanted to, and yes I wanted to.

The sun covered and warmed me and it was York and I slept.

POV: Gavin:

For the first time in my life, I did not want to play basketball.

We had slept late, and awakened groggy with hangovers that had to be kept hidden from Bob Milburn. Klinger, who had been sick all during the night, threw up a few more times and we explained it away as pigging out on the food at the cabaret. Milburn looked skeptical but said nothing. We all thought he knew but being a good guy was saying nothing. Apple chugged down a handful of aspirin, and even York looked a little green. Only Sturtz was perky.

"Great fucking night," he shouted again and again between choruses of "Oh, What A beautiful Morning," as he soaped himself in the shower.

"If he doesn't shut up I am going to fucking kill him," Klinger groaned as he headed for the john. "Him *and* his bright golden haze on the fucking meadow."

We picked at our breakfasts and napped through what usually was clean up period. Around nine thirty Ed Lasker dropped in to talk to Milburn. He walked into the shambles that was our bunk and shook his head.

"Look at this place! It's a pigsty!"

"It's Loser's Day," Apple muttered and Lasker nodded. "And looking at you, Apple, I know where the name came from!"

Apple gave him a sickly grin and turned his face to the wall.

"Where's Dorff?" Ed yelled.

"On the pot!" came a voice from the back of the bunk.

"Great job, Pulitzer. Great job."

"Thanks Ed." The sound of toilet paper being pulled off the roll, and we all smiled.

Ed Lasker looked over at Sturtz who was lying on his bed, walked over and sat down next to him. Sturtz put down his Batman comic book. "Sturtzy," Ed said, patting Sturtz' leg, "you done good! A helluva party! Big success."

I could see that Sturtz was pleased. "It rocked didn't it, Ed?"

"Not the words I might have used, but yes, I guess it did!" The head counselor got up and walked to the door. "Milburn come talk to me on the porch," he said pulling open the screen door.

A voice came from the back of the bunk, followed by a toilet flushing. "Hey Ed. It's color war, isn't it? You're gonna talk color war."

Lasker shook his head. "No, Pulitzer, we are not gonna talk color war, so turn off your tape recorder. I just don't want to have to talk about anything in this freakin' pigsty, *if* that is okay with you!"

"It's okay. Sorry Ed."

"And don't forget to wash your hands, ya pig ya."

Lasker and Milburn walked out of the bunk as Dorff came through from the toilet. "They *are* going to talk color war!"

"Who gives a flying fuck," Klinger groaned, pulling his pillow over his head, "I just want to die!"

And Sturtz said, "Jesus, Lennie, you didn't wash your hands!"

And so the morning went. By ten thirty most of us were feeling a bit better so when Kenny Levine came in from Bunk 32 carrying a game of SORRY, York, Apple, Dorff and I gathered around York's bed as Kenny set up the board.

"Sturtz?"

"Only if it's MONOPOLY. I have my standards."

"Screw you, and screw your standards," Apple said, waving him away. "SORRY is way cool. Hey," he said as Kenny set up the men in front of each player, "*I* wanted red."

Kenny shook his head. "Sorry, Andrew. I called Red."

"When? When did you call it? Did any of you other guys hear this asshole call Red?"

Dorff and York said, "Yes," at the same time as Apple sat down grumbling behind his blue man. "Well at least Dorff has green. I really hate green."

I looked over at Klinger. He was curled up in a fetal position fast asleep.

"Gav," York said. "You want to play? I'll play winners if you do. We've got yellow."

I shook my head. "No, I'm good. I'll kibitz."

The die was rolled and Apple went first. "Well, that's something anyway," he grumbled, and York smacked him playfully on the back of the head.

I noticed that Klinger was shivering so I got up and covered him with his bedroll.

I caught Sturtz' eye as I walked back to where the others were playing.

"Touching, Gavin. Downright touching," he whispered.

"Screw you Sturtz!"

"Nah," he said, smiling at me. "Not my scene."

Now this is important. Did this ever happen to you? Let's say something bad happens and you try to put it out of your mind, so you go to a movie or something. And it works. You're lost in the movie. Then all of a sudden something triggers something in your head and you remember what you were trying to forget? Is that the most awful feeling in the world, or what? Like waking up feeling great on a beautiful morning and then, bam, you remember you have a dentist appointment after school. You get butterflies in your stomach, and you feel a little shaky too. And once that bit of reality sneaks back in, you can't fool yourself into forgetting anymore. It's always with you no matter what you do.

That's a really long way around to describe how I felt when Sturtz smiled and said, "It's not my scene."

All morning long I had tried to put what had happened the night before away from me. Holding Klinger's head when he puked helped, talking with York and Apple, stuff like that, but it was always lurking just out of sight ready to go 'boo!' when I least expected it.

And Sturtz had just gone 'boo!'

Had he been there? Had he seen? Was he just being Sturtz when he said it or was there something else? What the hell did that smile mean? He *must* know. He *had* to know. But where could he have been? We were well away from everyone else. Was he hiding somewhere? Why would he be hiding?

And then the sane part of my brain kicked in. You're making a mountain out of a molehill. There is no way he could have seen. But let's say he *had* seen. There is no way that Sturtz would have kept it to himself even this long. I mean, it's freaking *Sturtz* for God's sake! He would have blurted it out when we got back to the bunk last night. Gone on the loud speaker in Ed's bunk and broadcast it to the world. But wait a minute, he was *in* the bunk when I got back so there's no way that he could have been there. Oh Yeah? He could have seen and not stayed around for the main event. He might have been so turned off that he took one look and left. But that would mean that he still knew. But if he knows what the hell is he waiting for? Why doesn't he *say* something? But maybe he just did. Maybe, 'It's not my scene,' *was* his way of saying something. But this is nuts. The horses are running away with the cart. Sturtz knows nothing. No one knows anything. I mean if Sturtz *did* know, what was he saving it for, to have Dorff put it in the INQUIRER?

Cold sweat. Hands clammy. Oh Christ, what if Dorff *does* put it in the INQUIRER. Then *everyone* will know. Know, know what? That you're gay, asshole! But being with Ralph doesn't mean that I'm necessarily gay. Maybe I'm bi. Screw that! I'm neither! I'm straight! Look, I had a lot to drink last night and Ralph was all over me. I can hardly remember anything that happened.

You fucking liar, you remember everything. His chest warm against yours! His mouth on yours, his hands unbuckling your belt and undoing your pants! *No!* It didn't happen that way! Oh yeah, then why is your dick getting hard while you're thinking about it? Oh shit man, *shit!*

The SORRY game went on until lunch.

When I got to play, I lost.

The noise level in the mess hall was noticeably lower than it had been on previous days and when the sophomores started a color war cheer, the upper camp shouted them down. Loser's Day was a lazy day and all we wanted was quiet!

I tried hard not to look for Ralph as we stood for the prayer, but I looked for him everywhere, and he was nowhere to be seen. I was relieved and uneasy at the same time.

Ed Lasker stood on his chair.

"Hold it down. Hold it down." The rumble of noise subsided. "Today the prayer will be said by..."

"Oh God," I thought, "not me. Don't let it be me!" If I have to say the prayer and Sturtz looks at me, everyone will know. They'll all know."

"*Look Mommy. Look at that boy's face.*"

"...the two men who made last night's Senior cabaret the great success that it was. Lennie Dorff and Henry Sturtz."

Bang! Bang! BangBang! LEN-NIE. Bang! Bang! Bang Bang! HEN-RY!" The cheer rose as Lennie and Sturtz stood up and covered their heads with their hands. The mess hall grew silent.

"Baruch atoi Adonai, elhuhenu melech cho ulum, A motzie lechchem minoretz. Blessed art thou, oh Lord our God, King of the Universe who bringeth forth bread from the earth. Amen."

Sturtz and Dorff sat down, the noise level began to rise and the waiters began serving.

"Thank you God," I whispered. "Thank you."

But where was Ralph? There was another waiter at his station. Where was *he*?

And then I started to shake. Oh Christ, someone saw, someone told Howard and Ralph was fired. Oh my God, oh my God, oh my dear God.

I looked over at Sturtz but he was leaning over to Bobby Milburn passing the water pitcher. He never once even glanced over at me. But maybe that's just the way he's playing it. Make you feel self-confident and then, bam, he tells everyone.

But if Ralph *was* fired, then the pressure's off you. I mean it would be Sturtz' word against yours and no one believes Sturtz about anything, much less this. And if Ralph was fired and Sturtz *didn't* see then I am home free. Free. Free.

And for some reason I thought of THE THIEF OF BAGHDAD as the genie leaves Sabu stranded, lost and alone in an unfamiliar world. "Free," he cries, as he flies away. "Free, Little Master. Free!"

My stomach turned over. What kind of a dick are you? You would want Ralph fired so that no one would find out about you? Talk about low! Talk about shitty people.

But I *don't* want that!

Then what the hell do you want you self-indulgent asshole?

And then I knew.

I wanted to see Nicki. I *had* to see Nicki.

After lunch and a rest hour that seemed never to end, while the others went to the hall to play basketball, I made some lame excuse and left the bunk, only Dorff and Milburn remaining. Careful that no one was watching, I headed down the long road to the waterfront. Technically the lake was off limits, even on Loser's Day, so there were no counselors or campers on the road. As I got to the lake three waiters, one of whom I knew slightly, were leaving.

"Hey Gavin man, what's happening?"

His name was Tony Elsner and he had been our waiter the year before.

"Nothing much, Tone," I said. "How's the water?"

"Unbelievable. Bathwater. Really beautiful."

"Is Caboy down there?"

"Actually, he just left, I think." Tony said, squinting into the sun. "But what's this about your girl dancing with Ralphie Sanchez last night?"

Bingo!

Be cool Gavin. For God's sake be cool.

"No problema," I said, smiling. "Ellen's a great dancer. I'm glad she found someone who was as good as she is."

"I wasn't there last night," Tony said, "but I hang out with Ralph in the city sometimes and man you ought to see him at the clubs. He is the man! He's got girls all over him. The guy screws everything that moves."

Ralph screwed girls, lots of them, so he wasn't gay. But if that was true, then what did he want with me? My stomach flipped over. Because all the girls up here are either virgins or getting it from their boyfriends, that's why! No! That couldn't have been the reason. There had to be more, or else Ralph would be the world's biggest son of a bitch. But if he was such a son of a bitch, why had hearing that Ralph hung out with Tony in the city made me so jealous? Why? What did *they* do? Had Ralph and Tony been together the way Ralph and I had been last night? And most improbable, most hard to believe, Ralph actually had a life before last night, before he met me. It was somehow incomprehensible. *I* wanted to hang out with Ralph, to go to clubs with him, to spend the night at his home. *I* wanted to be a part of his life.

"But just a few minutes ago you were hoping that he had been fired so that the heat would be off of you," I thought. "What the fuck do you want, Gavin? What?"

And at that moment I knew that I couldn't lie anymore. I wanted to be with Ralph Sanchez more than I had ever wanted to be anyone else in my entire life.

"I didn't see Ralph today," I said as nonchalantly as possible.

"He's hiding from you," one of the other waiters said with a smirk.

My heart stopped beating. "What?"

Tony smiled. "Yeah, he's afraid you're gonna kick his ass for dancing with your girl."

The other waiters laughed, and I breathed again.

"No, really," Tony said, "Howard gave him an extra day off for doing the DJ thing last night. I think he went into town to catch a movie." He did a bad imitation of Jimmy Cagney. "Want I should tell him you're after him?"

"No," I laughed, "I want to take him by surprise."

"That's cool. Later, Gav, " Tony said, slapping my hand and the three continued on their way.

The waterfront was deserted when I got there and I immediately went over to the boat dock, righted a canoe on the slide, grabbed a paddle and pushed the boat into the lake. I hopped in and started paddling toward the girl's camp.

"And just where do you think you're going?"

I turned to see Larry Caboy coming out of the boathouse. "Jesus, Gav, you know better than taking a boat without asking."

I took a deep breath. "Really sorry, Lar, but it's kind of an emergency."

He stood in front of me on the dock, hands on his hips. Somehow all I could focus on was the Red Cross emblem on his red trunks. "I'm listening."

I lied easily. "I had a little girl trouble last night. I really have to make it right so I thought I'd paddle over to their dock and leave a message."

"The girl who danced with the Puerto Rican guy."

I nodded.

"She seemed to be having a good time with him."

"Well, that's just it, Lar," I mumbled, "I kinda got on her case for dancing like that and I really want to make it right." I hated lying to him but I really needed to see Nicki.

I looked at Larry's face. I wasn't sure if he was buying it, and even if he were, if he would let me go out in the canoe. "You wearing trunks?" I stood up a bit and showed him that I was.

He thought for a moment. "You passed your lake test? I don't want to have you drowning out there over a girl dancing with some guy."" I nodded. "Actually, I did the test back and forth. I'm a strong swimmer, Lar. I'll be okay. Promise."

He looked doubtful. The waterfront was Larry's domain and he didn't want anything to go wrong down there.

"And if I let you go there'll be no fooling around. Just get the message sent and come back?"

"Unless she's at the dock, and if she is maybe I'll be a little longer so I can talk to her, okay?"

Another pause. Larry nodded. "Okay," he said, "but you have this canoe back by swim period. Deal?"

I grinned at him. "Deal!"

"Okay. Get out of here, before I change my mind. Be careful."

"You bet." I paddled quickly away. "Thanks Lar."

"Good luck." He waved and walked back towards the deep water swimming area.

Half way across the lake I stripped off my tee shirt. The hot afternoon sun felt great on my body. The fear and tension of the morning began to fade as I got further and further away from camp. I guided the canoe swiftly toward the girls dock. As I was passing Athenaeum, almost on a whim, I turned and headed into the small cove. As I got nearer to land I could see someone lying up against the tree, fast asleep. When I saw who it was, I smiled.

I looked up into the blazing blue sky. "Thanks again," I said aloud. Thank you God." It was Nicki.

Until I had met her a number of years before, I had shared everything with York. Now when there were things that I couldn't discuss with him, I had Nicki. She was in love with my brother and he loved her and they were perfect and I loved them both more than anyone or anything in the world. If there was anyone who would understand what I was going through it was Nicki.

And then my stomach knotted and I stopped paddling. But what if she *didn't* understand. What if what I was going to tell her disgusted her and she stopped loving me? What if she told York?

What had I been thinking?

I began turning the canoe back towards Kanuga when I heard a voice.

"Hey you Big Poop. What are you doing here?"

I took a deep breath, forced a smile, turned the canoe and started heading slowly into shore.

CHAPTER TWELVE:

G avin Stewart paddled slowly until he felt the gravel on the bottom of his canoe. Nicki Polis walked to the water's edge, and as Gavin jumped out of the boat, she helped pull it up onto the shore. She reached up and threw her arms around his neck.

"What a great surprise!" She pecked his cheek. 'And how did you manage a canoe?"

"Stole it."

"You're not going to get into trouble, are you?"

"Nope. I'm joking." Gavin managed a smile. "I checked it out with Larry. I'm cool."

"Not that I'm complaining, but what brings you here? I am so surprised!"

"Wanted to see my best bud."

"You're looking at her. So, what's happening brother in law?" She looked over his shoulder. "And where is my main man?" Before Gavin could answer, Nicki held up her hand. "Don't tell me. He's shooting hoops with Apple!"

Gavin smiled. "And Sturtz."

"Apple and Sturtz! Well that would make anyone grab the nearest canoe and split!" She laughed but furrowed her brow when she saw that Gavin wasn't laughing with her. "What?"

"What, what?"

"Listen you Big Poop, who knows you better than anyone in the world?"

Gavin smiled. "Your mother!"

"Tell me she came on to you and I will kill her."

Gavin laughed and for a moment he almost forgot the gnawing fear in the pit of his stomach. "Relax," he said, "I'm sixteen. Far too old for her!"

They both laughed.

"Come. Sit. We're at Athenaeum. Tell me stories," Nicki said as she plopped back down against the oak. Gavin leaned against the tree looking out onto the lake, and said nothing.

"Okay. Now you're starting to scare me. What's the matter, Gav?"

Gavin shook his head. "Beautiful spot. Beautiful day."

"Yeah, right. Zip a dee doo dah! Gavin, what's the matter?" Again, a shake of the head! "Are you and York at each other again?"

"No."

"What then? Come on Gav, tell."

"It's nothing like that."

"Ellen then?"

Gavin looked down at Nicki, nodding almost imperceptibly. "Yeah."

"Oh boy," Nicki said. "You *were* jealous of her dancing with Ralph Sanchez!"

Gavin's laugh was bitter. "That's for sure but....." He squatted down next to Nicki. "No. Don't listen to me. Of course I wasn't jealous. Not really. They looked great together. I kind of enjoyed watching them."

Nicki nodded. "You and everybody else. They were better than AMERICAN BANDSTAND and SOUL TRAIN combined."

Gavin nodded. "What did you make of Ralph? Did you like him?"

"Ralph? What's not to like? I loved him. Most of the girl's loved him. We were just talking before you got here, all of us wondering where he had been all summer."

Gavin laughed softly.

Nicki looked at him. "What?"

"Nothing."

"Sue Barnett said that she wanted to take him home with her."

"What about Apple?"

Nicki grinned. "You are so literal. She was just kidding. Lighten up, you Big Poop. And why all this interest in Ralph all of a sudden? Gavin, you *are* jealous!"

Gavin shook his head. "No. Forget Ralph. Ralph and Ellen are no problem. Trust me."

"I always do. Ralph and Ellen are not a problem. Boom. Forgotten."

Gavin rubbed the back of his neck and looked down at his feet, idly kicking a clump of dirt. Nicki smiled. "I like your Jimmy Stewart imitation, but if you say 'shucks' I'll brain you."

"Nicki."

"Gavin."

"Nicki, what do you think of me? I mean how do you see me?"

"Now there's loaded question!"

Gavin shook his head. "No jokes. Not now. Please. I'm really serious."

Nicki's smile faded. "Damn, did I just sound like Apple? I had better be careful." Gavin didn't smile. "You *are* serious aren't you?"

Gavin nodded. "Please answer my question. It's important to me."

"Okay, Gavs, if it means that much, I'll give it a try." She looked at the water for a moment. "How do I see you? Okay. I see you as one of the best people I have ever known and if I didn't love your brother so much that I can hardly breathe, I probably would have snagged you a long time ago. As it is though, you are my best friend and the one person who probably knows more about me than anyone else."

"Go on."

"More? Okay. You're really smart. You're handsome. You're really funny. More?"

"Not just the good stuff."

Nicki laughed. "But all I think about when I think of you is the good stuff."

"No bad? No bad at all?"

"Gav, I am not a shrink and I don't know what it is you want to hear? I'm kinda flying blind here, you know?"

"Just go on. Say anything that you feel."

"Okay. Let me think. All right. Something bad. Well, not really bad. Okay. I think you're too insecure in who you are."

Gavin looked startled. "Who I am?"

Nicki nodded.

Gavin's mouth was dry. "What do you mean by that?"

"I mean that you don't see yourself as others see you."

Gavin's body relaxed. "Oh that!"

"Yes, that! What did you think I was going to say?"

Gavin shook his head. "Nothing. Go on. Please."

"I will." Nicki smiled at her friend. "Gavs, people love you." Gavin looked away and Nicki reached over and pulled his face back to hers. "You asked me, now listen." Gavin nodded. "Gavs, I love it when I hear the girls talking about you and calling you the strong silent type, when I know the sweet pussycat you really are."

Gavin snorted and looked, embarrassed, down at the ground. "Jesus."

"Listen to me, you're the kind of guy who can be sexy without saying much. All the girls at Kiunga think that you are the biggest dish and Ellen is pretty much in love with you, but you, you big poop, you don't see it." As Nicki looked at him, Gavin brought his hand to his face and covered his birthmark. "Oh Gav, no! You can't be worrying about that! Most of the girls think that it adds a touch of mystery."

"Nicki."

Although she was starting to feel uneasy, Nicki Polis smiled and played the way they always did. "Gavin."

Gavin cleared his throat and looked away from his friend. "Thank you for saying all that, but that doesn't..." He looked back at Nicki and she was startled to see that there were tears in his eyes. "Oh shit. I have got to tell you. Nic, you *were* right about my being jealous of Ralph and Ellen."

Nicki took his hand. "Oh honey, no. I just told you. Ellen is crazy about you. She just told me again a little while ago. There's no reason for you to be jealous of Ralph, Gavs. Ellen just wanted to dance with the best dancer in....."

Gavin took Nicki's hand with both of his and shook his head. "Aw, Nic, that's not it." He took a deep breath. "I wasn't jealous of Ralph."

CHAPTER THIRTEEN:

NICKI

A nd I wasn't surprised.
Somehow, sitting beneath the massive oak, I knew that I had always known. And sure, I know that's easy to say after the fact, but I knew. I knew from the moment Gavin introduced himself as the milk ran out of my nose and down my face. I knew. I knew all the times that I had worried about him being alone without a girlfriend. I knew.

But if I had known, others hadn't, others like York and Ellen. In the split second after the words left Gavin's mouth, the ramifications of what he had said hit me like a ton of bricks. And I panicked for him as if he had told me that he had a cancer growing in him for I knew that his saying the words he had just said marked the beginning of his life, with all the pitfalls that I knew were inherent in it. And I thought of York and I thought of Ellen and I thought of an uncharted road that I could not understand. And in that moment everything changed though nothing changed and I reached over and held Gav's hand.

Gavin

Boom. A minute before the words were inside me and, in an instant they were no longer mine alone. And as with my feelings for Ralph I was torn in half once again. It felt amazing to unleash words that I guess I had always known had one day to be said. Sure, I had gone through "a stage," I just never remembered really coming out of it. I liked girls and I didn't lust after guys, but "the stage" had never ended. It was always there ready to make its re-appearance, and I guess though I could deny it up and down, I always knew it would be back. And it was, and now Nicki knew.

And that was the other part of the feeling, the terror that things would no longer be the same. The toothpaste was out of the tube and there was no way it was ever going back.

And I couldn't look at Nicki. What if the look of complete love I had always known from her was no longer there. What if in its place was anger, or hatred, or, most horrible of all, pity?

Oh my dear God, what have I done?

And then I felt Nicki take my hand.

CHAPTER FOURTEEN:

Gavin's voice was husky. "I had to tell someone. I had to tell *you*. And if you don't understand it's okay because *I* don't understand and if you want me to go, I'll go and I'll understand that."

Nicki pulled Gavin down to her and put her arms around him. "Oh Gavs," she said, "oh, honey. 'If I want you to go?' What are you talking about? You're my best friend, my brother in law, you big poop. I love you, dopey, and there is nothing you could ever do that could change that." She pulled back and looked in her friend's eyes. "Do you understand that, Gavin? Nothing." And Gavin smiled weakly and nodded. "But what's most important is are you okay? I mean honey, you and Ralph. Now excuse me if I am a little slow. Is it that you *want* to be with him or...."

Gavin shook his head.

Nicki shook her head as if trying to clear away cobwebs. "You and Ralph Sanchez were together!"

Gavin nodded.

"How? What? I mean when did all this start?"

"Just last night, Nic. That's what I'm trying to tell you. I had been drinking and after everyone had gone back to the bunk he and I went backstage at Hayes Hall."

Nicki looked at him. "Do you think it might have been *because* of the drinking that you...?"

Gavin shook his head. "No. I thought maybe at first, but Nicki I can't stop thinking about him. All I can think about is being with him again."

"Have you spoken to him about it today?"

Gavin flicked a pebble with his thumb. "Howard gave him an extra day off. I haven't seen him since last night."

"Well," Nicki said, taking Gavin's big hand in hers, "I guess the most important thing is how you feel about all of this."

Gavin shook his head. "I feel like I may be going crazy because I have no idea *how* I feel. I don't know. One minute I'm scared to death and I don't ever want to see him again, and the next minute I'm missing him so much I want to die. And I'm scared. Shit, Nicki, I am so fucking scared." Nicki tightened her grip on Gavin's hand as he went on. "Like I thought Sturtz knew about it before and I got totally paranoid. I was terrified that people were going to find out, yet, and this is why it's so messed up, at the same time, I want to get on the P.A. and shout it out to the whole camp. I am so totally screwed up Nic."

"What about York?"

"What about him?

"Does he know?"

Gavin shook his head. "No. You're the only one I've told, the only one who knows."

"You have to tell him, Gav."

Gavin shook his head. "Uh uh! No way. No. Things have been a bit weird between us already this summer.This would totally freak him out."

"Gavs, he's York. He loves you."

"I don't think he'll be able to deal with this. No."

"Gavin....."

Gavin's voice shook. "Nicki if this freaks *me* out, how is *he* gonna deal with it?"

Nicki patted Gavin's hand. "But honey, you have to respect him enough to tell him. If it freaks him out, and I really don't think it will, well, then that's his problem and he'll get over it. But Gavs, he has to know."

Gavin shook his head. "Maybe later, maybe when we're back home, but not here. Not when we're in the bunk with Apple and Sturtz and the others. I can't lay that on him. I just can't."

Nicki nodded. "Okay, I can see where you're coming from, but let me ask you this. What if the situation was reversed? What if York had this happen? Wouldn't you want to know?"

Gavin looked away. "That would be different."

"How? I don't see that. Explain it to me."

"It just would!"

Nicki screwed up her face. "Oh real intelligent answer, Gavs. I'm surprised you didn't end that sentence with 'so there.'"

"Nicki......"

"Gavin.....York is your brother, your twin, the other half of you for God's sake. He has to know."

Gavin's voice was firm. "No. Not now. And you have to be with me on this, Nics. You can't tell him. You can't even tell him that we had this conversation. Promise me.

"Gavs I...."

"Promise me."

Nicki didn't answer for a moment, but finally nodded. "Okay, I promise. It's not my place to tell him anyway, and I know that. But you know how sometimes you just know things?" Gavin nodded. "Well, I just know that *you* have to tell him, and soon. If you don't, you'll be messing things up." She looked down. "And to be selfish, the longer you wait the harder you'll be making it on York and me. It concerns all of us now. We have to be able to confront it and talk about and put it into perspective.

"But you promised."

Nicki nodded and looked up at him. "And I won't break that promise. You have my word. Have I ever broken my word to you? Gavin shook his head and Nicki went on. "No, I haven't, and I never will. But Gavs, you know, if you take a step back from all this, and I don't want to sound unfeeling here, but if you take a step back, it isn't all that much of a big deal."

Gavin looked shocked. "Jesus, Nicki, I just told you that I was gay and that's not such a big deal!"

"Gavin, no it's not. To be honest, I really wish you weren't, only because life would be easier for you, but honey this is 1975! What intelligent person could care less if a person's gay or not?"

"What about the majority that are not so intelligent?"

Nicki smiled. "To quote Sue again, 'Fuck 'em, and the horse they rode in on."

"All right, you mentioned Sue. What about her? I mean, what would Sue say if she knew?"

Nicki shook her head. "Probably something stupid and crude."

"See."

"But Gavin, what do you *care*? When have you ever cared about anything Sue said since you've known her? Sue is fun, but a major intellect she is not! Hell, she's dating Apple, for God's sake."

Gavin groaned. "Apple! Can you imagine the jokes...."

"But Gavin, *he's* a joke! All he *does* is joke. I don't think he has ever taken anything seriously in his life. Are you going to start giving credence to every idiot there is because you're gay? You're an intelligent guy. Where's the logic in that?"

Gavin smiled. "How'd you get so smart?"

"From raising my mother." They both chuckled. "Hey," Nicki said, "progress. You actually laughed."

"I chuckled," Gavin said, smiling at his friend. "I did not laugh."

"Well maybe you *should* laugh. Maybe if you did you'd see that you are making this thing far too serious. Jesus Gav, lighten up. Come on...gimme a smile."

Gavin pursed his lips. "Now you're being silly."

"Being silly could be a good thing. Gimme a smile Gavs."

"Quit it Nicki," Gavin said, frowning. "This is not funny. This is no laughing matter. You think I wanted this to happen? You think I needed this aggravation? I never expected this, Nicki. I never asked for this. It just, well, came."

The two of them looked at each other for a moment as they realized what Gavin had just said, and then exploded with laughter. And the laughter grew and every time they tried to stop laughing, they simply laughed louder.

After a few minutes Nicki held up her hand and tried to catch her breath. "Nuh, nuh," she gasped. "No more. No more."

And slowly the laughter subsided, and the two friends sat side by side, looking at each other, knowing they had shared something that would cement their friendship forever.

"You okay?" Nicki asked quietly.

"Yeah, I am now I think. How do I say thanks, Nic?"

"I think you just did."

The two friends sat quietly for a moment and then Nicki shook her head. "Wow," she said. "I can't get over it. All the girls are salivating for Ralph Sanchez, and you *do* it with him!" She paused. "You and Ralph Sanchez! That blows my mind!" Nicki covered her mouth with her hand. "Oh God. Talk about a bad choice of words. It just came out the wrong way."

And Gavin Stewart started to laugh again and Nicki Polis laughed with him and they held each other and they laughed again until they cried. And when the laughter stopped and Gavin did *not* stop crying, Nicki held him and rocked him and whispered, "I love you Gavs. You're my dear, dear friend and I will always be here for you and you being gay means nothing to me. Nothing. Nothing has changed except maybe I love you even more now than I did before. It's okay, baby. I love you. Nicki loves you. And unless you want me to, I promise I won't tell York. I won't tell anybody. I swear that to you. You have my word."

And Nicki held him and kissed him, and they both sat clinging together, unaware of someone listening to them on the path between the two camps.

CHAPTER FIFTEEN:

L eonard Dorff lay on his bed, his clipboard propped against his legs. He had work to do and Losers Day gave him plenty of time to get it done. The others had gone off in many directions and Leonard was in his element, alone.

Now that Cabaret was over, he had to focus on the editing of his piece on the Carnival of the weekend before, but with the warmth of the day and the quiet in the bunk, his eyes betrayed him and they closed without his knowing it.

The praise for the Cabaret had been more than he had believed possible. The crystal ball still sent its reflected prisms across the crowded social hall of his mind, the echoes of the pounding music.

His eyes snapped open. No! There was work to be done. He looked down at the clipboard, at the banner for his lead article,

CARNIVAL COMES TO KANUGA

Good alliteration though no one would get it. He sighed and willing his eyes stay open he read what he had written.

The scorching hot day was awash in color!

Good. Good grabber.

Crepe paper was everywhere; wrapped tightly on the porches, festooned on the large red garbage pails that dotted the area, and held by small boys who swooped like dive bombing planes, bright red and white paper streaming out behind them. Navy surplus signal flags, strung from telephone poles, crisscrossed and intertwined high above the campus. Counselors dressed as clowns wandered up and down, honking rubber horns and squirting the unsuspecting with water pistols.

Carnival Day had finally arrived!

Kanuga had been decorated, the booths set up and the girls of Kiunga were there. All was in readiness.

Ed Lasker's voice boomed over the loud speakers.

"Welcome visiting parents! Welcome to the lovely ladies of Kiunga!" Around the campus, there were isolated cheers, mainly from the younger girls, and a few of the older boys. "We couldn't have asked for a more beautiful day," Ed echoed, "so have fun, eat, drink, and play, and just remember that everything you spend will go to a truly wonderful cause, the underprivileged kids at Camp Essex." A few more half hearted cheers. "So if you are ready." He paused. "If you are ready." Another pause. "Well, ARE YOU READY?" The entire campus exploded with a loud "YES!" "I couldn't hear you," Ed said, a grin clear in his voice. "YES!" screamed both camps. "Well then," Ed continued, "in that case, without further ado, with no further hesitation....."

"Come on Ed," the campers yelled, as they always did when he played this game. (Note to Ed: We're on to you!)

This time Ed did laugh. "I hereby proclaim Carnival Day of 1975, officially begun!" Over the cheers of all those on campus, the sound of a needle on a record and the start of the tinny music that would continue for the rest of the day took the place of Ed's voice as the booths opened for business.

This bunk sold hot dogs, that one ice cream; this bunk sold sandwiches, that one hamburgers. Huge aluminum vats held bottles of sodas that bobbed up and down amid great chunks of floating ice. A few of the bunks served solely as rest rooms: this one for the boys, that one for girls.

Cries of, "Step right up and try your luck," filled the air, as counselors in straw hats clicked bamboo canes on the porches of their bunks, trying to get those passing to play.

One bunk offered ring toss, another guess your weight, fling the pie at the clown, fun poker, turtle races and, the most popular of all, "Dunk 'Em." Long lines of campers stood waiting to take a chance on throwing a softball at a bucket of water, under which sat Ed Lasker, Howard or Mo dressed in loud, baggy

Hawaiian swimming trunks waiting to have pails of water fall on them. (Note to LD: Redundant. Change later.)

One bunk offered pony rides to the younger kids, while others sold tee shirts, costume jewelry or records, all of which were donated by parents who were "in the business."

And though positive he was awake, Lennie Dorff slept, his clipboard fallen to the side of his bed.

And now he dreamed of someone else; Elie, her hair in his face, smelling of Aqua Net and perfume.

"Goodnight sweetheart, till we meet tomorrow."

Leonard Dorff slept, snoring softly, his mouth open, the sounds of the day droning about him.

He had been everywhere at the Carnival, seen everything. Henry Sturtz conning a young counselor out of two Allman Brothers albums at the "Bunk 21 RECORD EMPORIUM," and, a few minutes later, selling them to one of the younger boys for five dollars a piece.

And he had written everything he had seen on his ever- present clipboard.

Notes for "Just Asking": What entrepreneurial (note: check spelling!) Upper Senior was seen entering the record business during Carnival? Could Arista Records be far behind? Look out Clive Davis!

York buying a pin for Nicki in the shape of a butterfly!

Notes for "Just Asking":

What very popular Upper Senior Boy presented his lady with a beautiful piece of jewelry on Carnival Day? No social "butterfly," he! (Too cutesy? Vague?)

Gavin, walking alone, in back of the sophomore bunks, a basketball in his hand, heading for the Social Hall!

Notes for "Just Asking":

What upper senior spent Carnival day practicing his "lay-up" without his girlfriend?

(Note for "Just Asking": Should the item about Gavin not doing the Carnival with Ellen be stronger? More pointed? Or dump it altogether? Consider.)

Apple and Sue fighting over something as she stalked away from him and into the bunk marked, "Girls."

Notes for "Just Asking":
What Upper Senior was seen chasing his girlfriend across campus during Carnival, begging her to not be angry with him. Hmmm? I guess the apple does fall far from the tree! (Clever, but what does it mean? Re-think.)
And then there was Elie. All at once there was Elie!

"Whatcha writing?"

"Huh?" Lennie Dorff looked up at the girl standing next to him.

Elie Pincus craned her neck to try to see what Lennie had scribbled on his pad, but he was already flipping it closed and tucking it back into his back pocket.

"Nothing. Just some background color for the Carnival issue of the *Inquirer.*"

Elie nodded. "You do such a great job with that paper, er, Lennie, right?" He nodded. She smiled. "So much better than Felice does with the *Chronicle* at our camp."

"It's always nice to get a compliment. Thanks." He quickly rummaged through the filing cabinets of his mind, and smiled when he found what he was looking for. "Elie, right?"

Pleased, Elie Pincus nodded.

A fly buzzed onto Leonard Dorff's cheek and without waking he carelessly brushed it away.

In his sleep, Lennie Dorff looked at the girl standing in front of him. He vaguely remembered dancing a few dances with her at socials over the past two years, but as the music stopped, so had Dorff. He had always seen her as just another of the "not so pretty/just slightly overweight" girls in Kiunga tee shirts that seemed to gravitate to him. And this was the quandary that Lennie Dorff found himself in. The girls he wanted, the really pretty girls like Nicki Polis or Anna Etkin, were far out of his reach, while the plain ones, like Elie Pincus, all seemed to lust after him. And though Dorff knew that he himself was no more than average in the looks department, he couldn't help but want someone prettier and more popular than the girl who stood before him.

Elie, he noted, was a bit chunkier this year. Love handles were clearly obvious through the tee shirt that was tucked into the elastic on her shorts. At least her mustache was gone, but her kinky auburn hair, pulled tight into a pony- tail, seemed almost too sparse to cover her large round head.

But as Lennie was about to excuse himself and slip away into the crowd he noticed Elie's eyes.

Her eyes!

Lennie thought that he had never seen eyes quite the color of Elie's. Why had he never before noticed Elie Pincus's eyes? They were the clearest blue he had ever seen, and though he knew words to identify many things, Lennie was at a loss when he tried to pinpoint their exact color. Without the color of her eyes, Elie Pincus would have been less than ordinary: with them, Leonard Dorff noted, from the right angle and not up too close, she was almost beautiful. Why had he never noticed her before?

"You doing the Carnival with anybody?"

"No," Lennie said, "just trying to formulate an article; sights, sounds, who was seen with whom. You know."

Elie nodded. "If you want, I have something that you might use in *Just Asking*."

"Sure. I can always use something interesting. Who's it about?"

"Carol Toobin. You know her?"

Lennie nodded. "I think so. Tall, kinda gawky."

"Bunk 31."

"What's it about?"

Though they were standing alone with no one near them, Elie leaned in close and whispered. She smelled clean, of Lifebouy soap and Jean Nate. Elie's lips were so close that they tickled Dorff's ear. Dorff felt his groin tingle. "Carol's father went bankrupt and she's only up here because her uncle loaned her father money so that they could send her. No one knows but me and Nicki Polis." Elie's breath was warm and smelled of Clorets. Dorff's penis twitched.

"She told the two of you?"

For a moment Elie looked uncomfortable. "Well, not exactly. She actually told Nicki and I happened to overhear them." Dorff raised an eyebrow. "No really. I swear. She even made Nicki promise not to tell."

"Sounds usable," Dorff said, pulling out his notebook and starting to write.

"You won't mention that it was me who told you."

Leonard shook his head. "I never disclose my sources. That's a matter of editorial integrity that means a lot to me."

Dorff finished writing.

"Can I see?"

"Lennie shook his head, stopping himself before he corrected her with a 'may.' "Sorry. Its kind of a superstition I have that I don't show anyone what I've written until it's published. I figure that it's bad luck if I do."

Elie smiled at him and once again Dorff could ntake his eyes fro hers. "I don't believe in luck, good or bad," she said. "My father says that you make your own luck."

"In most cases I agree with your father." Dorff said, stuffing the notebook back in his pocket. "But in this case...." He didn't finish his sentence.

"No, don't get me wrong," Elie said, reaching over and touching him, her fingers cool on the warm skin of his upper arm. "Just because I don't believe in something doesn't mean that I don't respect another person's right to believe what he or she likes. I come from a very liberal family."

"Really!"

"Mmmm. My maternal great grandmother, my mother's mother mother...?"

Dorff smiled slightly and nodded.

"Well, she died in the Triangle Shirtwaist fire." Elie paused, as if waiting for Dorff to say something, and when he didn't, she went on. "My parents are very interested in better wages and equality in the workplace for men *and* women."

"I think that..."

"My father gives to many worthy causes. He's deeply involved in the ACLU."

"I'm sure if..."

"But one has to draw the line somewhere when it comes to being liberal, don't you think? I mean, you can't be liberal with *everything*. Now I for one cannot see marrying outside the faith. I know that many of those who call themselves liberal think that it's okay, but I have to draw the line there. When I get married I want a good Jewish boy. My parents are *very* religious."

"My grandfather was a........"

"We were once conservative but my father went searching for his roots and we ended up orthodox. Are you orthodox or conservative?"

"Actually I'm......"

"For a woman conservative is better, more liberal, but then, if you want liberal, become a reform. Though I am *not* in favor of that. I believe in traditional family values. Not like those who are totally liberal! Reform!" She snorted. "'Reform, my tuchas', my father says. It's like being a gentile. But," and she sighed, "I guess if you really want liberal, you might as well go all the way." She giggled. "No pun intended." She snaked her arm through his. "And here we are back to liberal again. Back to where we started. I love when that happens."

Leonard Dorff looked at the girl holding on to him and for a second didn't know whether he was charmed or repulsed. Her non-stop talking! Her ridiculous views! Her not letting him get a word in! And then he looked at her eyes and he smiled.

"*You* doing the Carnival with anybody?"

Elie blushed and shook her head, holding his arm more tightly.

He smelled the Jean Nate again. It made him hard.

They threw rings at nails driven into boards, shot water pistols at balloons and shared a hot dog and a coke. Lenny glowed with pride when York passed them at the House of Horrors and gave him a "thumbs up" as he nodded at Ellie. Then, with more than an hour and a half left before the Carnival was scheduled to end, Sturtz and Elie Pincus had run out of things to do.

"Are you sure you don't want to throw a ball at the pail and soak Howard? I throw well for a girl."

Leonard Dorff shook his head, knowing that he did not want Elie to see the way *he* threw. "No," he said, "Howard's my uncle. I wouldn't feel...."

Elie tightened the grip on his arm. "Of, how dumb of me! Of course he is. No, you're right, you really shouldn't." She looked over the campus. "But I think we've done everything there is to do." She paused. "Unless *you* have some ideas."

And Leonard Dorff didn't know what to say!

In all of his sixteen years he had never had a girl come on to him, and now, standing at the edge of the campus near the Freshman bunks with Elie Pincus's hand in his, he wasn't quite sure if she had. "Unless you have some ideas," she had said, and that surely *sounded* like an open invitation, but what if he was misinterpreting her meaning; what if she was just being friendly, being one of the guys, just wondering about something else to do.

But she had stressed "you." "Unless *you* have some ideas." Wasn't that throwing the ball into his court? If she had stressed "ideas!" well then he would have known without a doubt. Then he would have known for sure. "Unless you have some *ideas*!" That was a clear invitation. But was "*you*?"

'Unless *you* have some ideas." And what if she had put the emphasis on 'unless." "*Unless* you have some....... "Think!" he thought with desperation, "think!"

Though his mind raced through a file catalog of lines from movies and songs, he came up with nothing to help him. All he could think of was the song the buxom blonde band singer had sung at his bar mitzvah as he danced with his mother, all the while staring into the singer's laughing blue eyes. "...*for goodness sake, How long has this been going on?*"

"Christ, don't let my voice crack," he thought and taking a deep breath he said, "We could go for a walk, er, behind the bunks...around the diamonds...I mean we're not supposed to, but I could always say that I was doing some research for the Carnival Issue if someone says anything."

Elie Pincus pressed her body against his. "I'd like that," she whispered, and even though she hadn't stressed any of the words, he knew for sure what she meant.

Hand in hand they drifted between the freshman bunks and walked up the slight incline leading to the baseball diamonds. Their hands were sweaty and Dorff's mouth was dry. His mind raced and whirled. "Is this it? Am I going to finally get laid?" And he thought he might shit his pants.

They walked in silence until Elie stopped and said, "My goodness, what's that?"

Dorff looked where she was pointing and saw colors dancing like the Aurora Borealis in the middle of a hot summer afternoon. For a minute he stood not comprehending then he laughed. "Prisms."

"Excuse me."

"Prisms. Uncle Howard bought them cheap from some guy who was looking to unload them. He's keeping them in the shop until he figures out what to do with them. They're nothing particularly special, but I think he was dazzled by the color. They're the talk of the camp." He paused for a moment. "I guess you could say that Kanuga is a prism camp."

She looked at him for a moment not comprehending and then exploded in laughter. It was a loud braying laugh that shot out of her, unexpected and, he thought, strangely inappropriate. His joke, Apple's joke actually, was funny, yes, but hardly deserving of this response.

She barked a laugh, caught her breath and barked again. Then, as suddenly as it had come, the laughter stopped. "Oh, shit," Elie said, holding up her hand. "Don't move."

Dorff was totally confused. "What's wrong?"

Elie looked down at the yellowing grass. "I dropped my lens." She looked up at him, and Dorff took a step back. One of her eyes still shone crystal blue, while the other was a non-descript gray. Her face seemed lopsided, out of kilter.

"I said don't *move!*"

"I didn't. I......"

"Yes, you did. You did. Just stand still." Her voice was no longer sweet, but angry and shrill. "This pair is all I've got." Slowly Elie dropped to her knees, her face inches from the ground.

"Are you sure that I can't....."

"NO! Just stand where you are."

And Lennie Dorff no longer wanted Elie Pincus. "Who the hell is she talking to me like that?" he thought. "Fuck her. She'll find the lens or she won't and either way I'm taking her back to camp and ditching her." He stood, resolute, glaring at her as she combed the short leaves of grass. "She pulled a fast one with those contacts," he thought. "Damn good thing she popped one."

And as Elie sifted through the grass, she began to shift her body slowly, until all at once her large behind was squarely in front of Lennie Dorff.

And he felt the stirring in his groin again. The large, full ass, the cheeks clearly defined as the thin white fabric stretched over them, the outline of her panties, all of it was making Lennie hard. The bare leg, somewhat stubbly but still soft and plump, emerging from the tight white shorts and ending in white sweat socks was to Lennie one of the most erotic things he had ever seen. And she *wanted* him! He could *have* her! Was he some kind of fool? Why dump her right away? Why not get what he could and then bring her back to campus, say goodbye and never see her again. Other guys did it all the time. Why not him?

"Oh shit, oh shit, oh shit," Elie was murmuring as she sifted, and her words only got Dorff more aroused.

And then Lennie saw it.

"Elie......"

"Shush, I'm concentrating."

"But I see it."

"Huh?" She froze in place. "Where?"

The blue piece of glass, picking up the colors of the prisms, was winking at him just near her right hand.

"Look a little past your right hand. No, to the right of your right hand."

"Where? I don't......oh thank God! My mother would have killed me. You know what these things cost?"

Elie looked at him as she put her index finger in her mouth and sucked it. He closed his eyes and took a deep breath. When he opened them he watched as she gently touched the lens with her wet finger and lifted it slowly to her other hand. She looked up at him and smiled, her demeanor changing again. "My hero," she said, as Lennie moved in and helped her up. "Gimme a minute." Elie put the lens in her mouth and swished it around. Dorff stood close enough so that his face was only inches from her hair. Again, he was overwhelmed with the sensuous odor of her Aqua Net. He wanted nothing more than to bury his face in her round ass, to bite it, to lick it, while his fingers felt the softness of the hair under that which hadn't been stiffened by the hair spray. As she rolled her eye back up into her head, gently jabbing it with her finger on which the lens was perched, Dorff took a deep breath and kissed her on the neck. "Gimme a *minute*," Elie said again, shrugging him away, but this time with what could almost pass as a giggle. She blinked. "It's in!"

Elie turned to Dorff, taking his face in her hands. "Thank you," she whispered and rubbed her lips along his.

Lennie Dorff thought he might cum in his pants.

Elie squeezed his hand. "Come on. Show me the prisms. I want to see the colors up close."

They walked past the hardball diamond and the handball courts and up to the front door of the shop, the colored lights from the prisms dancing over their white clothing.

Lennie Dorff was shaking as he reached for the doorknob. "It's probably locked."

"Try it anyway," she said coquettishly. "You never know."

The doorknob turned in his hand and the door swung open.

"See," she said as she led him into the darkness of the room. "You never know unless you give it a shot."

Elie shut the door behind them and turned to Dorff. Before he could make a move, her arms were around him, her mouth pressed against his. Her tongue pushed at his lips until his mouth opened and then it entered, warm and thick and wet, and Dorff thought that he might explode. Her arms still around him she pulled him down to the floor, rolled over on top of him, and undid his belt and the top button of his shorts. Dorff moved his hands down to help her, but she pushed them away. "Let me," she whispered, and in a moment Dorff was naked from the waist down.

Elie looked down and chuckled. "And look who's happy to see me!" And as gingerly as she had taken the lens, she took Dorff into her mouth.

And Leonard Dorff's mind raced as the soft, wet O of Elie's mouth encircled him. "Oh my God. Oh my God. Oh good God, yes! Jesus, it feels wonderful. She's done this before. She couldn't know how to do this unless she's done it before…..ohhhh, God! And she wants me. Me! Fuck you Sturtz, Fuck you, York, fuck you." Elie's mouth was a soft, sweet suction, pulling and pulling. Dorff's hand moved tenderly to her hair and she slapped it away. He lay back, his hands at his sides and let her continue. "I've never been this hard. Never. It can't get much harder." He pushed his hips up so that he moved even deeper into Elie's throat. She made a soft noise but didn't stop. Her hand moved under his scrotum, and slick and warm and wet, amid the vises, the screwdrivers, the hammers and the pliers, Elie sucked and pulled until with a cry, and an explosion of color, Dorff erupted.

"Oh Jesus," he gasped. "Oh fucking Jesus." He felt the hard wood floors against his naked ass as he bucked, and then he lay still. "Oh my God. Oh fuck. Oh Jesus fuck."

Elie Pincus smiled down at him. "Good?" Dorff nodded, dumbly, his cock still spasming. "Well," Elie said, brushing her salty lips against his, "there's more where that came from." She began flicking her hands over his balls and cock; her feathery touch making him groan.

"Like that, Lennie?"

Again Dorff nodded.

"We can have lots and lots of good times like this. Yes?"

Dorff nodded.

"Starting at the Cabaret tomorrow night? Sound good?"

Dorff groaned as his dick started to grow again.

"Was that a yes?"

"Yes," he whispered.

"Yes?"

"Yes."

"Good. That's very, very good." And her mouth once again replaced her hands.

As Elie manipulated him, Dorff thought, "So I take her to the Cabaret. No harm in that. Maybe we can sneak out back and I can get some more of this. I'll dump her the next day. I have nothing to lose and everything to gain. That's what Sturtz would do. Hell, that's what they all would do." And with that decided, Dorff was able to hold back as he savored the sensation of Elie's mouth and tongue. "Oh God that feels so good," he thought, "so amazingly good."

And in a flick of his mind, he found a way to make it even better.

He had always lusted for movie star Jacqueline Bisset, and now, in his fantasy, Jackie Bisset's head had taken the place of Elie's. Her hot mouth manipulated him. His cock thickened. "Oh, good God, Miss Bisset," he thought, "Jackie. You are so amazing. So amazing." She was perfect, almost Jackie Kennedy- like in appearance; clean, sophisticated, yet with a mouth that sucked, and hands that were everywhere. He opened his eyes for a moment and saw teased hair over his belly and colored lights dancing around the room. And he closed his eyes again, and it didn't matter who was down there because it felt so damned good.

And as Elie sucked she smiled. "What Upper Senior boy and Upper Senior girl are the newest item in camp?", she thought. She laughed to herself. "Just asking."

And as Dorff came again, his eyes tightly shut, Elie Pincus held his cock firmly in her hands.

"And she wants to see me today!"

Dorff woke irritable. The memory of Elie's mouth on him though still erotic, made him nervous and cranky. As his mind adjusted to the quiet bunk, his counselor Bob Milburn snoring softly on his bed across the room, all he could focus on was Elie Pincus. Elie whom he was sure he would dump at the end of the Cabaret who had told him to find a way to see her during Loser's Day, and that day was almost over, and Dorff wasn't sure he wanted to go. She hadn't told him, he thought, she had ordered him! "Make sure you get over to see me tomorrow, Lennie." Sure the dance with her was good, but ordering? No. Enough was enough. In the first place she was no prize and in the second place…... Dorff looked at his bedside clock. Three fifteen. He felt a strange mixture of annoyance and relief as he swung his legs onto the floor, picking up his clipboard and placing it under his pillow. "There's still an hour and a half before we have to get ready for dinner. I can still make it to Kiunga, see Elie and get back in time."

And as Leonard Dorff crept quietly out of the bunk he wondered where he get Elie alone and have her give him a blow job again.

Hell, he could always dump her tomorrow.

He knew that the fastest way to get to the girl's camp was by boat, but he also knew that there was no way that Larry Caboy would let him have one without supervision. Dorff sighed. "Overland," he thought. Creeping surreptitiously between the space between the lower senior bunks, onto the main road and then through the vast expanse of trees that bordered the perimeter of Kanuga, Dorff wended his way.

So it was that ten minutes after he had left Kanuga behind him, the young editor of the Inquirer stood frozen, his heart racing in his chest, halfway between two camps at the shaded back of Atheneaum, listening to Gavin Stewart tell Nicki Polis something that he knew he could never publish.

Just asking.....................................

And Leonard Dorff, something like a small smile forming on his lips, found that he could hardly breathe. For the first time in his life, in a world of Sturtzes, Apples and Yorks, he was no longer the only outsider.

CHAPTER SIXTEEN:

POV: APPLE

A nd with all that, with all my admiration for him and, I admit it, the hero worship, there was just one moment, one unguarded moment that stays with me, that eats at me though I try in vain to shake it off. It was so different from who he was, so totally unexpected, that from that day to this it becomes an unwanted part of my lexicon of York. At the time it hit me like a sledge hammer because I never saw it coming, and though it was only a few words said to someone else, the memory of that moment, sickens me when I think of it now as it did then, shames me somehow, weakens me with an overwhelming feeling of impotence.

That night in July, the night of the Senior hayride, the bunk had, as usual, been an explosion of activity. The shower had been on full blast from the moment we had come back from dinner, clean clothes were laid out on everyone's bed, the air smelled of cologne and talc and Bob Milburn, our counselor, had just done one hundred and twenty six one arm push ups much to the delight of Klinger who, declaring a new world's record, dressed quickly and sped out of the bunk to spread the word.

Dorff took me aside to tell me that he would have a bottle of vodka with him if I wanted some. I thanked him for the offer, but said no. "Okay," he said, "but just ask and it's yours."

Then it was my turn at the shower. I stripped down and hopped in hoping that the hot water wouldn't run out before I was through. I must have been taking my time because before I knew it I heard Milburn yelling, "You still in the shower, Apple?"

"Coupla more minutes, Bobby," I said, soap all over my face, "Just a few."

"Well hurry up. I need my shower. I smell like a dead muskrat."

I laughed. "No problem. I'll be on time."

Milburn paused. "You know what? I'll take mine in 32. Just hurry." I heard the squeak of the screen door and, then Milburn yelled back to me again. "And while we're on the subject of fuck ups, where's Gavin?"

"Haven't seen him. Sorry, Bobby," I called soaping my pits for the third time. Milburn yelled to Dorff who was combing his hair at the sink. "Lennie, you're finished dressing. Go find Gavin."

"But Bobby I......."

"Go!" I heard the reverberation of the screen door as it slammed shut. Over the sound of the shower I heard Dorff mumble, "York and Sturtz are ready. Why don't you ask them?" so I pulled the shower curtain open and stuck my head through. "Don't let him bust your chops, Lennie." Dorff grunted in answer. "But if you do find Gavin, tell him to get his ass back here or he'll be docked." Dorff sighed, stuck his head around the corner so I could see him, and waved to me. "Will do," he said and walked out onto the campus.

Since I was the last one for the shower, I took longer with it than usual. I was excited. I had been looking forward to this night for a long time. I would be with Sue, and since Bob had asked me to bring my guitar, I would have a captive audience on the hayride leading to the barbeque. Tonight was definitely going to be my night.

I squeezed the shampoo bottle and nothing came out. "Shit."

I heard Sturtz laugh from the other room. "And now for the cologne. I say screw the cologne behind your ears," he said. "There's only one really important spot to put it." I didn't have to see him to know where he was splashing it. "You never know when you're going to get lucky."

Leaving the shower running at full blast I padded quietly over to York's toiletries shelf and picked up what felt to be an almost new tube of Prell. Skittering back to the shower, I passed the open doorway leading to the main part of the bunk. "And now for the piece de resistance!" I stopped and looked in, a bemused smile on my face, wondering what aphrodisiac musk oil Sturtz might produce. Instead, he pulled an old hardcover copy of THE COLLECTED WORKS OF SHAKESPEARE from the beat up locker next to his bed.

Though I couldn't see him, I heard York say, "If you're taking that with you, you're never going to get lucky."

Sturtz looked furtively around, saw that they were alone, and called York over. As York came into view through the mirror something made me pull back and press against the wall, not wanting either of them to see me.

"I have never shown this to anyone else, my friend, but tonight I am feeling magnanimous. Ready for some magic? Then…. abra cadabra!"

I peered around the corner to see Sturtz open the book and hold it out to York.

York hooted. "You son of a bitch," he said, with a certain admiration in his voice. Then, "Jesus, Henry, are you out of your mind? There's not even a lock on that cubby."

"And that's the beauty of keeping my summer stash in a hollowed out copy of Shakespeare. Oh there are thieves up here, my friend. But trust me, no one is going to steal a volume of Bill. It's genius. Pure genius."

York chuckled. "What the hell have you got in there?"

"Joints, pills, a few small tabs of instant 2001: A Space Odyssey, and the like." Sturtz popped something into his mouth and swallowed it. "What the hell was that?", York asked.

"That," Sturtz said, "is my ticket to Oz. I would offer you one, but I assume it would be turned down, and besides, they cost a fucking fortune."

I heard Gavin yell something I couldn't understand to someone outside the bunk. As he came onto the porch, I heard him say, "I was playing basketball. I didn't hear the bugle." I heard Milburn's muffled voice from down the line and then Gavin calling back, "So I'm docked. Okay. Fine. I'm docked."

In a swift, practiced motion, Sturtz closed the book and put it under a pile of others in his cubby. He smiled at York. "There's something to be said for a summer reading list, yes?"

Gavin slammed into the bunk, shirtless and dripping with sweat. "I can't believe you got yourself docked," York said.

"B.F.D." Gavin said, and though he sounded angry when he turned to where only I could see him, he had a big grin on his face.

The bugle blew. "Shall we?" Sturtz said heading for the door.

"Where's Apple?" I hopped back into the shower as he called my name. "Almost finished," I yelled, lathering my hair. Still got five. Don't wait for me. I'll meet you outside."

"Primp pretty, Andrew," Sturtz called in a fruity voice.

"Fuck you, Sturtzie," I called. "You are *so* lame."

I emerged from the shower as Gavin came into the back of the bunk. He shook his head. "Milburn docked me."

I nodded, drying. "Bad break. Anything you want me to tell Ellen?"

Gavin shrugged. "Just that I'm sorry." As I quickly toweled my head I heard the needle scratching the record for line up. "Oh, shit! Gavin," I yelled, "out of the way. I have three minutes to make myself irresistible."

"You couldn't do that in three years."

The way Gavin was laughing I knew he didn't give a rat's ass about not going on the hayride. As I rushed around like a nut case, I remember thinking I should ask him about it tomorrow.

Somehow I never got around to it.

"All right, Apple!"

"Beauty baby, beauty!"

The sound of the clapping and cheering echoed across the mountains, and I wondered what the people living in the farmhouses dotting the area, their lights already out for the night, were thinking.

"Sing another one Apple, please."

I shook my head, and York punched me in the arm saying, "Now don't start playing hard to get, Andrew. Sing us another one." He was sitting alone, leaning against the wood sides of the wagon. At the last minute Nicki had had to go to infirmary with a stomach bug. "Really," York said, "it looks like you are going to be my only entertainment tonight, so serenade us, Apple, serenade us!"

I grinned at him. "I don't know many more. Really."

"Well sing something that you do know really," Iris Blackman, Bobby's girlfriend said. She poked him in the ribs. "You're his counselor, Bobby. Tell him to sing."

Milburn looked at me and shrugged. "My lady wants another, Brookman," he said. "Give us one more."

"And *your* lady wants another one too," Sue said, slipping her arm over my shoulder.

"Well," I said coyly, "if you *all* want another one....."

And everyone applauded and yelled, "Yeah," as I knew they would, and York smiled and mouthed, "You fucker," and Sturtz called out, "Milk it

Brookman, milk it," and I nodded, picked up my guitar, and began to sing once again.

There's a line in a movie that has stuck with me over the years. One character asks another if she is happy and the answer comes back, "There should be a new word for happy." That's the only way I explain how I felt at that moment. That night I was the star and I knew it. Something had clicked into place and instead of being Brookman the clown, and Brookman everybody's best friend, I was now Brookman the singer, and believe me, I was loving every minute of it. I knew I wasn't anybody's idea of Sinatra so I don't know why or what, but something had happened and this was my night. For the first time that I could remember I was the center of attention, I was special, the golden boy, the one everyone wanted to be or to be with, while both Sturtz and York, were relegated to supporting player status. It felt amazing.

"Oh I tried to make it Sunday," I sang.

Some people started singing along with me, some hummed, some kissed and Sue snuggled her head onto my chest. Iris Blackman, leaning up against Milburn, stared at me and smiled.

It was like one of those lame teen age musicals from the forties I had seen on T.V. and it was amazing.

Damn, what an amazing night!

The hayride part of the hayride itself was, well, a hayride. Uncomfortable to the extreme, crowded and all arms and legs, yet somehow all of that became part of the magic of that moment. Everyone was crammed in on every one, all trying to find a soft spot with heads finally finding resting places on any convenient lap, tit or ass. I was propped up against the wooden slats on one side of the wagon with Sue shoved up against me, her boobs pressed firmly against my chest. This, of course, was fine with me even though Bern Condon's right ass cheek had somehow found its way onto my other shoulder. Since he couldn't move because of the headlock Joyce Moskowitz had on him, we stayed that way for the duration of the trip, with me praying that Condon would not give forth with one of the explosive farts for which he was notorious.

There were three wagons making their way down the two-lane country road that night, with Bunk 31 and their girls in one along with half of thirty two and theirs, and us and the other half of thirty two in another. The third wagon held all the supplies for the cookout to come. Every now and then a car would move slowly past us in the other direction, it's lights picking up our faces staring out from inside the wagons. Other than that and the brilliant stars that shone above us, all was black.

Almost everyone had a date except for Ellen Marcus, who sat pouting because Gavin had been docked, and three single non-descript girls who huddled to one side of the wagon, one of whom, a chunky, rather unattractive girl, kept staring at Dorff.

I finished the song and again there were cheers for more.

"I swear to God," I said, "I don't know any more."

"Do a Dylan."

"I did the only ones I know."

Carol Kaplan yelled, "Play 'Jessica,'" and Sturtz shook his head. "You've got to be kidding. He's barely able to play chords."

"No, Henry, you're being mean." I heard Carol say, "He's good. You're good, Andrew."

"Thanks Carol," I said and, as I looked over at her, I noticed that Sturtz was frowning. I couldn't have been happier.

"Do a Weaver's song," Linda Karmon, whose father was involved in the ACLU, called out.

"I already did the only one I knew."

"Well shit, Apple," Sturtz yelled, "sing *something*! Don't be a damned vocal cock tease."

Iris brayed a short laugh, but Milburn sat up straight and pointed at Sturtz. "Watch your mouth, Henry."

Sturtz growled. "Oh, please," and then "Lighten up, Bobby," which made Iris laugh all the more. I wondered if she was on something. I knew that Sturtz was.

"Okay, okay" I said, "not believing I was so in demand. "I do know one more, but it's not a rock song or anything. It's an old one. It's a song my grandmother taught me. It was her favorite."

"Oh shit, spare us," Sturtz yelled.

"Shut *up*, Henry." That from Carol! "Sing it Andrew."

"I don't know," I said. "It's really old fashioned....."

"So are you," Sturtz snickered.

"Sing it Apple," York said.

I nodded. "It's from an old movie. It was her, my grandmother's, favorite."

"You said that already," Sturtz groaned. "Sing the freaking song already!"

I strummed a few chords and then sang softly:

"There's a story the gypsies know is true,
That if your love wears golden earrings,
Love will come to you."

I heard Sturtz giggle and saw Milburn smack him on the back of his head.

"Pay no attention," Sue said as she snuggled in closer. "It's pretty. Go on."

And as I did I realized that everyone had gone silent, even, for the moment, Sturtz, and I wondered if I had stayed too long at the fair, bringing everyone down with a song that only I loved. "No matter what," I thought taking a deep breath for the long note that came next, "I started this and I am going to finish." The note was right on, smooth and clear and Susie pressed her lips to the top of my head as I sang on. Iris Blackman, still staring at me even as Milburn was busy kissing her neck, blew me a silent kiss.

I finished the song, my voice soft, hushed.

"So be my gypsy,
Make love your guiding light,
And let this pair of golden earrings,
Cast their spell tonight."

I strummed a few more chords to finish the song and then held the fret so that there was total silence.

I looked around the wagon. Many of the couples were intertwined. Those who had come alone, looked down or off into the night, and I think I heard Dorff whisper, "That was beautiful, Apple."

"Most excellent, Apple, really, most excellent." I smiled back at York, basking in the warmth of his approval.

As I turned to Susie, I happened to look over at Ike Hayes the camp handyman who was driving the wagon. He had turned his head to me and as I looked at him he nodded and winked. I smiled back.

And then Susie's mouth was on mine, he body pressed hard against me. And at that moment, on that night, her kiss was the most perfect it had ever been, slower, warmer and more sensuous than ever before. I wrapped my arms around her as we kissed, and one hand found her breast and even though all I could manage was the skin on top of her bra, and then the firm breast through the silky material, it was perfect.

We rode in silence for a while and then we were there.

And that's when it happened, the thing I have always remembered.

I had hopped down on one side of the wagon, helping Susie down after me. We had walked a few feet when she called to Ellen Marcus and ran to tell her something. I turned and saw Sturtz and York getting down from the other side. I started to join them when I heard Sturtz say to York, "I don't want to offend your compadre or anything, but GOLDEN EARRINGS? What kind of bullshit song was that?" I stopped, still out of their line of vision. At that moment moment, Dorff walked by carrying his ever present clipboard. Once he had gone past, York whispered, "And he was so into it too. I had to pinch myself from busting out laughing. '*So beeeee my gypsy,*'" he sang, and then, both laughing, he and Sturtz joined the others.

I am told that the barbeque was a roaring success.

Thanks to Dorff and his bottle, I was too drunk to notice.

CHAPTER SEVENTEEN:

POV: Gavin

It took me over a week to finally get Ralph Sanchez alone.

I looked for him everywhere. I was obsessed. During one important intramural game in the hall, I missed an easy lay up when I thought I saw him standing in the doorway. I fumbled balls in the outfield as I stood searching the road that ran past the diamond, and once I actually got banged in the groin with a thrown bat when I thought I heard his voice behind me.

Nothing mattered but Ralph and it was beginning to show.

York asked me what was up. I made some lame excuse that got him off my back and he seemed to be okay with it. Sturtz, on the other hand, kept smirking at every fumble and error I made. The paranoid side of me still thought it was because he knew, but the rational side, the side that had grown stronger since my meeting with Nicki, chalked it up to Sturtz being Sturtz. Amazingly it was Dorff of everyone who seemed more caring about my feelings than he ever had been before. One day he actually volunteered to do my clean up job after telling me I looked tired. I didn't let him, but I appreciated the offer all the same. I actually felt guilty about not being as good a friend to him as I could have been and determined that that would change.

But first, where was Ralph, and how could I get a hold of him? Of course I would see him in the mess hall, but there he was working so conversation was impossible. He would speed by, balancing his tray with one hand on the way to or from the kitchen and I would smile, wanting to say something, but always, before I could, he would be gone. Twice I saw him going up to the

112

waiter's cottage behind the hotel, but once I was stuck on second base and the other time he was walking with some guy I had never seen before. The first time he half waved, the second time he seemed to be so interested in what the other guy was saying that he didn't see me at all. That nearly drove me crazy! Who *was* that guy, and what was his relationship to Ralph? What made the situation even more frustrating was there was no one at Kanuga that I could ask.

Near the end of the week I saw Ralph coming back from the handball courts with Tony Elsner and even then we exchanged nothing more than a casual 'hey.' He didn't instigate a conversation, and with Tony there I was too tongue tied to say anything.

And when I wasn't thinking about Ralph, I was thinking about Ralph! The craziest thoughts kept running through my mind, and I was helpless to stop them.

Ralph and I getting together in New York!

His parents would be away and we would meet at Penn Station and spend an amazing day together. Maybe we'd hit the Village and browse through record stores or bookstores; hours at the Strand. Then lunch somewhere and sitting in Washington Square Park and talking about the things that we liked, things that we had in common. Then we'd have dinner, take in a movie, maybe hit a club and then back to his apartment for the night.

Ralph and I at college!

We would be at Columbia or NYU and we would be roommates. We would have the same classes and we would be up all night talking and studying. Laughing. Smiling at each other over leftover pizza.

Ralph and I seeing Europe together!

Ralph and I getting a dog and walking it through Central Park!

It was beginning to be a lot like those Sandra Dee movies that York and I would goof on, and as sappy and saccharine as each of those films were, my fantasies were right up there with them.

And with that came the fear that even Nicki couldn't brush away. Was I going to start to look and act gay? Was I going to get flitty all of a sudden? I remembered Sturtz telling all of us about a story he had read called "A Thirsty Evil," or something, where this guy starts out straight as an arrow but gets faggier and faggier as he gets deeper and deeper into doing gay stuff. Sturtz swore that it could happen while Dorff said it was impossible. Apple had made a joke and York hadn't said anything. I would look at myself in the bathroom mirror when no one was around to see if I was looking gayer, but I seemed to look pretty much the same as I had before. I still thought I looked straight, but I couldn't tell.

And through all of this, the frustration of not connecting with Ralph was getting me hornier than I had ever thought possible. All at once, it was if my dick had a mind of it's own. Once sleepy and rather indifferent, it now flew to attention at the slightest provocation. Underwear a little too tight...wood! A shirtless guy in one of Sturtz' comic books...hard! They showed a pirate movie in Hayes Hall, and when the young hero swung across the masts of the pirate ship, his sweaty muscles etched and glistening, I barely made it back to the bunk. This had never happened before. I used to look beyond those things, not pay attention to them, and now they were everywhere!

And speaking of making it back to the bunk, I found more excuses to get back there alone than I had thought possible. Headache on the baseball diamond..."Go back to the bunk, Gav, and take a nap." Cramp down at the lake..."Go back to the bunk, Gav, and jump into a hot shower." I went back to the bunk all right, but not to nap or to shower! And I have to say that it was a weird feeling sitting in the can, totally alone, with my shorts down around my ankles, my hand working overtime as I conjured images in my mind that startled me by their intensity. Each time I shut my eyes, the movie theater in my mind would unreel its latest fantasy. And the images were clear and in intense color and soon passion would take over. If one scenario didn't work, I instantly changed it, breathing harder and harder until my breath and my heart kept time with each other. And sometimes, before I reached a climax, I would stop dead as I strained to hear if someone was coming in the bunk. Every creak of a floorboard, every slammed locker somewhere on campus, every voice going by on the path would make me stop and listen for danger like some pathetic forest creature, ready at a moment's notice to cram it back in and zipper up. And then, when the danger had passed, I would quickly restart the movie, building myself to orgasm again while stifling any sound in case someone might be around. I had become paranoid, feeding on my lust while always on the lookout for someone finding out. I knew very well that every other guy over the age of puberty beat his meat, but I was sure if anyone saw me doing it he would know that my fantasy did not include a girl. And on top of that, what seemed so totally bizarre was that all the while the rest of the camp, unknowing and at play, went on around me as if nothing was different, as if nothing had changed.

And on every one of these furtive excursions back to the deserted bunk, I thought only of Ralph. Ralph, Ralph, Ralph. And here's something weird; as many times as I fantasized about Ralph Sanchez, I never once fantasized about anyone else at camp! I mean here were some of the best looking young guys in the world in one place, walking around with almost nothing on, and the thought of being with any of them totally turned me off, actually sickened me. They were out of bounds. Somehow the fantasy wasn't there, the excitement, and without that I simply wasn't interested. I guess I also loved the 'forbidden fruit' aspect of Ralph, no pun intended. He was different, exotic and the most exciting person I had ever met. My fellow campers and counselors: no excitement, no interest. Hell, to me they were sexless. My God, they were my friends!

The day I finally got to Ralph was a hot one. The temperature had been rising all week, and by Friday afternoon it had reached the high nineties. Ed Lasker had instructed the infirmary to dispense salt pills to any boy who felt dehydrated, quartered oranges appeared at every outdoor activity and those periods were cut by twenty minutes so that the 'all camp swims' could be longer. We were going through a typical early August hot spell in Pennsylvania, which was made worse by a heavy humidity that had everyone uncomfortable. You would be drenched with sweat before a shower and five minutes after finishing one you were drenched again. The few electric fans on campus, those that one or two counselors were smart enough to bring up with them, were on all day and night, adding nothing more than a trickle of breeze to the sweltering bunks.

And with the heat and humidity my desire to see Ralph Sanchez increased.

That Friday afternoon the upper seniors had touch football, and, after a few minutes, I was ready to head back to the bunk for another session in the john. This time my excuse was nausea from the heat, and the on duty counselor sent me back to campus to rest.

"You are becoming such a pussy," Sturtz hissed at me as I passed him and picked up my shirt from the sidelines. I flipped him the bird and heard him snicker as I made my way down the hill to the bunk.

As I walked onto the porch someone called my name.

"Gavin?"

I looked down at HQ. Ed Lasker was waving me over. I sighed, threw my shirt on the porch, put on a smile and trotted over to where he was standing.

"Hey Ed."

"How come you're not at activity?"

I shook my head. "Felt a little dizzy, nauseous. The heat and all."

He nodded. "You want to go to the infirmary?"

I shook my head. "No," I said. "I'm good. I just don't do well with heat I guess. I'm fine really. I'll just stretch out in the bunk."

"You sure?"

I smiled and patted him on the shoulder. "Don't be such a mother hen, Ed," I said. "I really am good."

"Mother hen, my ass," he said shaking his head. "You stupid kids don't know how to take care of yourselves. Always want to be such freakin' heroes, such tough guys. Remember this, Gavin. The most macho guy is the one who doesn't seem macho, who doesn't have to show it off to be it. Get me?"

I nodded. I thought I did, but I wasn't sure.

"Got an idea," Ed said. "You up for a cold soda?" Before I could say anything either way, he fished into his pocket and came up with some quarters. "Run down to the machine at the guest dock and get yourself one. And bring back a coke for me, ya bum ya."

Though all I wanted was a quick release to my tension, the offer of a cold drink did sound good, so I thanked Ed and started sprinting across campus. Lasker yelled after me. "Jesus, take your time Gavin. I don't want you falling over with heat stroke." I waved to him over my shoulder and slowed my pace to a walk. As soon as I was behind the bunks that made up the eastern edge of the quad, I broke into a trot again. Maybe I could get the cokes and still make it back to the bunk for a session before the bugle blew for the end of the activity period.

I raced down the road, skidded across the highway that ran below the camp and trotted down to the guest dock. The coke machine was on the outside of the boathouse, and as I opened the long red door the icy mist that poured from it hit my chest. I stood that way for a long moment enjoying it's cold, then inserted the quarters Ed had given me. I pulled two bottles from the steel bars that held them, and held one up to my forehead.

"You gonna heat it up you keep doin' that."

I turned to see Ralph Sanchez approaching from the road. He wore an electric blue Speedo and had a white towel over his shoulders.

He smiled at me and I couldn't breathe.

"You gonna open that thing or just keep rubbin' yourself with it?"

"Open it," I managed. My hand shook so as I tried to get the cap off on the bottle opener that after three tries I still couldn't do it. Ralph laughed, took the bottle from me, popped it open with one swipe and put it to his lips. He bent his head back and I watched mesmerized as the amber liquid drained into his throat. He took a second swig and then handed it to me. "Drink," he said. I put the bottle to my lips and tasted Ralph. My God, Ralph!

Ralph winked at me. "Good, huh?"

I nodded. "Very good."

Ralph started onto the dock. "I only have half an hour before I have to set up," he said over his shoulder. "I want to work on my tan."

Work on his tan? He was already perfect. What was left to do?

Though he didn't ask me, I followed him onto the dock's chipped white wooden planks and watched as he spread his beach towel. He stretched out with his hands behind his head, groaned as the full strength of the sun hit his body, and closed his eyes. I didn't know if he even knew I was still there.

The guest dock was deserted except for a man lying on a chaise lounge across from where Ralph lay. He was on his side facing me, and I could easily see that it was the man everyone called The Luggage King, an old man who spent his summers at the camp's hotel. There were many stories about him, he had lost his son, a former camper in the war, he was a silent partner, he was a relative of one of the owners, he had made a fortune in luggage before the Nazis forced him out; everyone knew everything and nothing about him. Now he lay, his eyes closed, a dead cigar clutched between his lips.

I turned back to Ralph. His body was already covered with sweat, his Speedo wet with perspiration.

On the dock in the full fury of the sun, I started to shake. My teeth were actually chattering. I had fantasized about him so much since Cabaret night that now, seeing Ralph lying in front of me, I couldn't move. I knew I should get back to front campus because Ed Lasker was waiting for me, but I didn't care. I had made contact with Ralph again and I wasn't going anywhere.

My mouth was dry. "Ralph."

He turned his head, shielded his eyes from the sun and looked up at me. "Hey," he said. "I thought you had gone." I shook my head. "No," I croaked stupidly, "I'm still here." He smiled. "Well I can see that." He smiled and reached up to me and I thought my heart would explode. Here, in the light of day where everyone could see, Ralph Sanchez was openly reaching up to me. I moved nearer, my own hand out, not caring who saw, ready to lie down at his side, Luggage King or no Luggage King. As my hand was about to touch his, he wagged his hand at me again. "How about another pull of that Coke?" I stopped dead and closed my eyes. What he wanted was a drink, not me. But after all, we *were* in broad daylight and there *was* someone else around. Of course he had to be careful. We both did. I handed him the bottle. He raised himself up on his elbows and took another deep swig. He handed the bottle back to me and I saw that it was almost empty.

"Ralph," I said.

"Yep?"

"I haven't seen you since...well you know...."

"Yeah," he grunted, "they been working my ass off. But I did see you when you were playing ball. I waved to you."

"No," I stammered, "I mean I haven't *seen* you."

"Like I said," he said into the sun, "I been busy."

"I thought that maybe you'd have sent me a note or something."

His voice seemed somewhat surprised. "About what?," he muttered, his eyes closed.

Conscious of the Luggage King only a few feet away, I kneeled down next to Ralph and whispered. "I thought, well, I hoped, that maybe we could find some time to get together again."

"Sure," he said, still not looking at me. "Maybe we could shoot a few hoops. I'll play you one on one."

"No," I said, "I mean, sure, that would be great too, but maybe we could find some time to be *alone* again, like before."

Ralph didn't say anything for a moment and then he sighed and sat up, putting his full weight on his elbow. He looked at me and shook his head. "I don't think that would be such a good idea man," he said. "Lotta people, lotta eyes. You understand."

"But maybe...."

"Look, Gavin," he said, "no. I mean we had a good time that night, and I think that should be it."

I couldn't believe what he was saying and figured he hadn't understood what I was getting at.

"No," I whispered. "No, it wasn't just a good time, it was great. It was wonderful. I really want to be with you again. Maybe I'm not as experienced as some of the people you've been with, but I'll learn. You can show me."

Another sigh and, "Gavin, man. You're a good kid. A really good kid, but it just wouldn't work out, you know. It was fun that night, fun, but let's just leave it at that."

But I couldn't just leave it. I had to make Ralph understand.

"Okay," I said, hearing the desperation creeping into my own voice and hating it, "maybe you're right. Maybe it's too dangerous here at camp, but camp will be over soon, maybe in the city. I could take a train in and we could get together in the city. It's only a coupla weeks till......."

"Gavin, man, look. I'm telling you it wouldn't work out, ya know? I think we should leave it at that. Hoops would be great though or maybe some handball. You understand?"

I shook my head. "No. No, I don't understand."

"Shit." Ralph stood up and yanked his towel up from the dock. "I was 'fraid of this. Shit." He slipped his sandals on and started off the guest dock with me right behind him.

"Hey Ralph, wait. What did I say? I'm sorry. Please, don't go. I won't say anything more about it." The butterflies in my stomach were going wild, and I was more frightened at that moment than maybe at any other time of my life.

Ralph stopped just short of the garbage can Ellen and I had been next to the night of the cabaret. He turned to me. "What are you, fucking stupid? I said no and that means no."

"But the other night," I began, but my voice was shaking and I was terrified that I might actually cry.

"The other night, the other night," he mimicked. "What the hell do you need, a tree to fall on you? The other night was just one time you get it, one time. No more. Nada. Finished. What the fuck, I fool around wit you for a few minutes and you think I'm in love? Hell, I was horny and there were no chicks I could touch. The other night was to get my rocks off. Shit, what kinda asshole are you anyway?"

Now there *were* tears in my eyes.

"Oh fuck," Ralph spat, "you're not fuckin' crying are you? Jesus H. Christ, man. I knew I shouldn't have fooled witchyou. I shoulda known that you were too fucking naive. But I thought you were more of a man than that. Shit, you're nothing more than a pussy, a stinkin' maricone. Now just get the hell away from me."

He took a few steps and I grabbed his arm, once again feeling the warm skin and the hard muscle beneath it.

He shook my hand off and pointed a finger at me. "Don't fuck with me maricone. I'm warning you."

"Okay, but don't go Ralph. Please. Let's talk about it."

"It, *it*," he mimicked. "There is no 'it.' There is no it and there is no 'me and you'. There is nothing. There never was anything. You understand that or are you too fuckin stupid?"

He started away, and again I took him by the arm. "Just don't go Ralph, please." I knew that if he walked away now there would be no chance for us ever again. My voice was shaking. "Please don't go."

Ralph's eyes were narrowed and when he spoke spittle came from his lips. "Do not mess with me, asshole. I am warning you for the last time. Do not mess with me. I don't want to mess you up but I will. So do not fuck with me unless you want the other side of your face marked too."

And I snapped.

All the emotion I had been holding in for the past week erupted and without being able to stop myself I punched the face I had been fantasizing about since cabaret night. It was the first time I had ever hit another human being with the intent to hurt but now I wanted nothing more than to hurt him the way he had hurt me, to destroy him, to make him disappear and to take with him the life he had left me with. My punch connected and Ralph staggered back, a startled look on his face. I was almost as surprised as he was and I stood for a second not knowing what to do next. Ralph knew. In less than a moment he had regained his balance and charged me.

"You mutherfucker," he grunted. "You are fucking dead." His head smashed into my stomach and the two of us went down. We toppled onto the grass and rolled around, his fists pummeling my chest and arms, my arm wrapped around his neck. His punches were quick and hard and as they landed on my chest and stomach I tried to fight back but was too stunned and overwhelmed to do much more than to hold on to him around the neck. At one point, he brought his knee up hard, but it missed its target and smacked into my thigh. We were both grunting, the sweat poring off of us, our bodies covered with dirt and pieces of grass. I wasn't sure if I was trying to hurt him, to protect myself or, at least for a few moments to feel contact with the body of the person I still wanted more than anything. Ralph was strong, and since all I was doing was grunting and tugging at his neck, in a few minutes I was flat on my back, his knees on my arms holding me down. I made a half-hearted effort to get up but he held me easily.

"You bastard," I cried, struggling to free myself of him. "Why me? Why did you have to pick me?"

He smirked as he watched me writhe under him. "Because I seen the way you been lookin' at me and I knew you were ripe. And don' tell me that you didn't want it."

And God forgive me, I *still* wanted it. Ralph lifted his knees from my arms and held me down by the wrists. He sat on me and I could feel the heat from his Speedo burning into my naked stomach, and all at once I was in the midst of a fantasy I hadn't ever dreamed of.

I had no control and I was less than nothing and I wanted to die.

"I should fuckin' beat the livin' shit outta you, but you are so fuckin pathetic that I don't think I want to embarrass myself. I wish I had never started anything witchyou. If I had any idea what a weak, pansyass loser you was, believe me I wouldn'ta."

I tried to push him off but he wouldn't budge. "Get off me." My voice was hoarse and so low that I wasn't even sure he had heard me. I saw that the spot on his cheek that I had punched was turning a deep red.

"Or what," he said. "You gonna tell my boss? Gonna tell Moe what a bad boy I am?"

"Please. I won't tell anyone anything. Just let me up."

"Why, maricone? From the boner you're throwing I think you like me sittin' on you."

And he was right, and the anger I had felt a few minutes before came flooding back. I had to get him off of me, to end this shame, this humiliation. I pushed Ralph back hard and almost threw him off, but with a laugh he forced me down again. He pulled up my head with both hands and slammed it back onto the ground. I grunted, and as I struggled to get up, Ralph smiled and slowly drooled a mouthful of spit on me. It was hot as it ran down my face. My humiliation was complete and I went limp.

"Get off him, son."

The Luggage King was standing above us, his cigar, now lit, clenched in his teeth. "Get off him."

Ralph glared down at me as he spoke to the old man.

"Fuck you. Mind your own fuckin' business."

"Excuse me? I don't think I heard you? You said what to me?"

"You heard me," Ralph snarled, "I said to mind your fuckin' business.

And then the small man's hands were on Ralph's arms pulling him off, and even through my anger and sadness, I was amazed at how strong he was.

The Luggage King pushed Ralph away from where I lay as I started to get up. "Now cool down, young man," he said softly. "Cool down."

But Ralph was furious and I didn't know if it was because of me or because of the old man whose hand was pressed firmly against his chest keeping him from me. It would have been an amazing sight to anyone happening by. This tiny, wizened man, in a baggy black bathing suit, with a barrel chest covered in white hair, standing on two birdlike legs, a cigar seemingly bigger than his head stuck in his mouth, holding off a furious young man who towered over him.

"Fuck off, old man," Ralph snarled and pushed against the hand that pressed against him.

"Stop it!," the Luggage King shouted, and Ralph took a step backward.

The old man looked at Ralph. "You are a waiter, yes?" Ralph glared at me as he nodded. "Then," said the old man, "I think it would be a good idea for you to get back and get ready to do your job. This incident is over."

"Fuck you." Ralph's eyes blazed as he stared at the small man who stood before him.

"That's the third time you've said that to me," the Luggage King said, "and it is the last."

And before I knew what was happening, Ralph was sprawled on the ground next to me. The Luggage King's move had been so fast, so unexpected that I had seen only a blur, but there was Ralph, stretched out in the dirt, his mouth open in surprise.

"Now," the old man said softly, "I will repeat. I think it would be a good idea for you to get ready for work."

Ralph stood up slowly and brushed some of the dirt from his hair. He took a step backward, gauging how far he could go with the old man. The Luggage King stood still and stared him down. Ralph shook his head. "Fuckin' pansyass needs an old man to protect him." I felt so sick I thought I might throw up. Ralph pointed an index finger at me. "This isn't over."

The Luggage King smiled. "Of course it is," he said, "because if anything else happens to this young man, you will be on this road hitching your way back to where you came from, without a penny of your pay. I think you have done enough damage already. Do I make myself clear?"

"You can't..."

"Oh, but I can." The old man pointed to the road. "Now I think its time for you to be on your way."

Ralph jerked up his towel that had fallen during our fight and made us way up the slight embankment to the main road. He stalked across it and, after a few moments, was lost to sight behind Hayes Hall.

"Are you all right?", the Luggage King asked me. As he spoke I realized that up until that morning I had never heard his voice before. I had of course seen him wandering around camp for years, but had never known what he sounded like. His voice was guttural, with the clear remnants of a European accent, but, strangely, there was a softness to it that I would never have had expected.

I nodded as I picked myself off the ground. "I'm fine."

The old man laughed. "You're fine like I'm sixteen!"

And at that moment, I was exhausted and all I wanted to do was sleep. I wanted to close my eyes and not see the Luggage King standing in front of me, to not see the pathetic fool that he obviously saw in me. He had seen me lose. He had seen my humiliation. I was sad and I was tired and I wanted to escape into the blackness of sleep.

And through all that, I needed to make a stab at getting my dignity back. "Maybe you didn't see," I said. It wasn't his fault. I started the fight."

He shook his head. "You may have started the fight, but it was his fault."

"I don't understand," I said.

He smiled. "Yes, you do."

Before I had a chance to say anything he held up his hand. "Wipe your face." I used the back of my hand to clean Ralph's spit away. The old man pointed back to the dock. "You're hot and you're filthy. Go take a dip. You'll feel better."

I shook my head. "I've been away from campus too long already. Ed Lasker's waiting for me."

"So he'll wait a few minutes more. And if you get into trouble I will talk to him for you. Trust me, my young friend. Go get wet."

I was drenched in sweat and covered with dirt, grass and leaves. There was no way I could go up to front campus like that. I kicked off my sneakers, walked to the side of the dock and dove in.

The water was icy cold on my hot body and for a moment I couldn't breathe. I came up for air, gasping, took a deep breath and then upended and forced myself down towards the dark bottom of the lake.

It was all over. It was *over*. *Ralph* was over. *I* was over. I was in a panic? What had I done? I was immersed in water, and yet I felt filthy. I wanted to throw up and then when there was nothing left in me, to open my mouth wide and take in all the water of the lake. I wanted to explode, to disappear. To never have been.

What had I been thinking? Was I an idiot? Didn't I see that it had to end this way? What was I expecting, a love like York and Nicki's?

You poor stupid faggot! You pathetic loser!

"Mama, that boy has grape juice on his face."

124   *Jeff Laffel and Michael Klepper*

And I pushed myself deeper down into the water.

And what about Ralph? He was going to tell everyone. Everyone. And everyone will be laughing at the pathetic, loser faggot? And what happens when York hears about it? How am I going to face York? But York would understand. Nicki said that York would understand, and I tried to believe her as I pushed down, down, down to where the truly cold water began.

But would Ralph even tell? Maybe not, not now anyway; why would he? Why would the big lady's man want everyone to know what had happened? He could fake it. He didn't have to say that he came on to me. He could say that I came on to him. And *then* what would York say? Oh Jesus. Oh, fuck what am I going to do?

But if he didn't tell now, maybe Ralph would wait until after camp, until after he got his pay and the Luggage King couldn't hurt him. He would tell Elsner and by next summer everyone would know and I wouldn't be able to come back as a counselor. It was over for me at Kanuga. And how was I go going to explain that to my parents and York?

My God, what the hell had happened? In just those few minutes after the Cabaret my life had changed forever. And I thought that it was all going to be worth it because Ralph felt the way I did. I had been going to see him in the city, for Crissake! My dream. My pathetic stupid, fucking dream! Always having Ralph at my side. Meeting his friends. Going to clubs with him. My God, what the hell was wrong with me?

That's easy, you're a pathetic faggot, and soon everyone is going to know.

And I went deeper still.

But why did it have to happen? Oh shit, why? Why couldn't it never have happened?

And all the good feelings I had after speaking to Nicki were gone, and I was back to where I had started.

And I had reached the bottom.

I pushed my hands into the cold mud and actually started digging, my hands cut on the pebbles and silt, digging myself a hole to hide in, to die in, to disappear in.

I opened my mouth and screamed and only bubbles came out, and I continued to scream until I had no breath left to scream anymore.

I pulled my hands out of the mucky bottom and rose upward into the blazing sun. I broke the water and I began to shiver. I climbed up the ladder, my hands bleeding with tiny cuts, and held myself as I shivered.

The Luggage King was back on his chaise lounge. He reached down, picked up a large white bath towel, and threw it over to me. I draped it around my shoulders and almost immediately the shivering began to stop.

"Feel better?," the old man asked. I nodded. "I have to get back," I said straining the water from my hair with my fingers. "Really."

"Really you should sit down over here for a minute and pull yourself together."

I walked over and sat on the wooden chair next to him.

"That boy, that waiter boy hurt you." I didn't answer. "I'm sorry, boychick, but I wasn't sleeping. I try, but I don't sleep well. In my whole life I never slept well, too much on my mind, but now it's even worse. But that is not what is important. Let it suffice to say that I heard you talking." I started to say something but the Luggage King shook his head and waved me away. "Don't be foolish. A person's business is a person's business. I did not get to where I am by betraying people. Others do, I never!" He paused and drew in on his cigar. "But he hurt you." I looked down at the dock, praying not to cry, and nodded. "I'm sorry, boychick. It's hard to be hurt always, but to be hurt like this so young is a pity. But who knows, maybe this is the last time it will hurt you so much, or maybe, and I think this is more likely, that it is the first of many times, like the rest of us. All that is sure is that no one gets through this life without being hurt."

From above us on campus came the scratchy sound of a recorded bugle.

"That's recall," I said, getting up. "I have to get back." The Luggage King nodded. "You're all right?" he asked. "Yeah," I said forcing a smile.

The Luggage King smiled back at me, and it was a kind smile. "The water helped?"

I nodded, and at that moment with the sun blazing down and the old man sitting in front of me, I had never known a feeling of such emptiness before in my life. I wasn't hurt, I wasn't sad, I wasn't angry; I simply wasn't anything. My body felt hollow, unattached.

I looked back at the Luggage King and gave him a small wave as I walked off the guest dock.

"Gavin," he called after me, and I was surprised that he knew my name. I turned back to him. He pulled on his cigar and then took it out of his mouth and pointed it at me. "Remember my young friend," he said, "what is, is."

I nodded, up the unopened coke that had been dropped on the grass as I fought with Ralph, and started up the hill to the road. I turned to look back at the Luggage King as I waited for a few cars to whiz by, but the sun was in my eyes and I couldn't see him at all.

I walked back across the road and as I came up behind Hayes Hall I stopped and for a moment I thought I might fall down. There was the tree where Ralph had held me before we moved off to a place where no one could see us. And everything had changed, and nothing had changed and I thought I might be losing my mind.

The entire camp was back from activity period and on front campus as I came across the quad. Lockers slammed, stiff sun dried bathing suits were taken off clotheslines, towels were snapped and impatient kids stood waiting for the bugle call that would take them to the lake.

Ed Lasker was in the HQ and I handed him the coke.

"Where the hell have you been?"

My throat was dry. "Down at the lake."

"I can see that by your wet hair. Since when do you go swimming at the guest dock? You know that area is out of bounds."

"I'm sorry Ed," I said. "It was hot."

"About as hot as this coke," Ed said putting it on the table. "And I thought you weren't feeling well. I sent Dorff to look for you and he came back and said he couldn't find you. How come?"

Dorff was there? No way! I would have seen him. "Ed," I managed, "I don't know. I didn't see him. But I'm really sorry. I didn't......."

Ed waved me away as he placed the needle on the bugle call record. "You know Gavin, you've been acting a little strange lately and I'm not crazy about it."

"Ed I......"

"So I think a swim period alone in your bunk will do you some good. You're docked, Gav. Go back to the bunk, grab a shower and just get back to normal. Now get outta here."

The sound of the bugle came through the speakers on the poles around the camp as I went through the screen door back onto the campus.

With laughter and yells, the entire camp moved slowly down toward the path that led to the lake as I moved through them in the opposite direction, heading back to my bunk. I saw York and the others walking down the Senior Path, but they didn't see me.

By the time I reached Bunk 33 the campus was empty and silent. I walked into the deserted bunk that less than an hour before would have given me a chance to be alone with my dreams of Ralph. Now I would just have forty minutes alone.

I lay down on my bed, closed my eyes and for the first time in weeks I did not dream of Ralph. A few days later I heard that he had gone. I assumed it was The Luggage King, and, as hurt as I was, I felt sorry for him. But that morning, alone in the bunk, as I worked to try to find another movie behind my eyes, all that I could see was darkness.

"What is is!"

And I started to cry.

CHAPTER EIGHTEEN

MYSTERY WALK: 1 (August 9, 1975)
-----------1:45 p.m.

Ike Hayes stood on one of the flatbed trucks, wiped the sweat off his face with a red bandana, and looked down at the boys gathered on the side of the road below. To those looking up at him, Hayes, who stood well over six foot four, and whose body was as muscled as a weight lifter's, seemed larger than life. Everyone had seen Ike Hayes around camp, and everyone had heard stories about him, but, as far as the boys knew, very few campers had ever said more than a few words to him, making him, along with The Luggage King, one of the great mysteries of Kanuga.

Hayes had been there seemingly forever, yet he looked to be no older than his mid forties. His father, or grandfather, no one knew which, had built the social hall that was named after the family. Ike, as far as anyone knew, had never been married, but was known to have two grown children who lived nearby, grandchildren even. His hair was jet black because, rumor had it, he was a pure bred Mohican, yet his eyes were almost azure blue. Lasker had told the boys that Ike had won the silver- star for bravery in Korea, yet there was a prominent peace symbol on the fender of his truck. He lived, the boys were told, in an old farmhouse a few miles from the camp, though no one, the story went, had ever seen it.

"Is Ike Boo Radley, or what!" a boy had once said, and, for most of the boys, Boo Radley he was from then on.

Nothing about Ike Hayes fit except his job, and with that there was no one better at what he did.

Hayes was the camp's handy man, and it seemed, there was nothing he was incapable of doing. Toilet backed up? Call Ike. Branches need cutting? Ike. Stranger seen on the premises; Ike will take care of it. Electronics? Automotive? An extra man for a minion; Ike Hayes could do, and did, anything.

He was shirtless now, and the boys looked up in awe at a muscular torso that was covered almost completely with tattoos.

Two huge American flags, one with thirteen stars, one with forty -eight, crisscrossed his entire chest. A flaring cobra made its way up his side and around his neck to just below his chin. His arms were filled with the likenesses of birds, and on his back a snarling leopard, its claws open and on the ready.

"You guys remember to pack the life vests?"

The boys looked at one another. No one had mentioned packing life vests.

Hayes shook his head and gave what passed for a smile. "No problem. I packed them myself. Just jokin' with ya. Gotta plan ahead though, gentlemen. Life won't always plan itself for ya."

"Ahyuck. Ahyuck. Ahyuck," Sturtz mimicked softly, and York kicked him squarely in the pants. "Shut up," he whispered, "he's a good guy."

Sturtz snorted. "Yeah, right. Freakin' Boo Radley."

"You don't know him."

"Right, and you do? Bullshit."

Ike swung down from the flatbed and stood among the boys. "Okay. Four trucks, four bunks. Most of you will sit on the flatbed along with the canoes; one will ride in the cab with the driver. Your counselors will drive three of the vehicles, I will drive the fourth because as you know, Milburn won't be coming because he's still sick in the infirmary." He pointed. "Bunk 30, there, 31, 32, over there. I'll take 33. Let's go gentlemen."

Klinger was the first to hop up onto the flatbed of the Bunk 33 truck, with Dorff right behind him. Dorff tried to hop up, but his foot slipped. "Jesus, Lennie," Klinger said as he reached down to give him a hand up, "can't you do anything right?"

"I'll need a push too," Dorff grunted. Sturtz groaned behind him. "What a spaz," he said. "York. Some help here." Together he and York pushed as Klinger pulled, until the puffing Dorff finally flopped onto the truck with a soft 'oof.' York and Sturtz hopped up right behind him.

"Oh boys," Sturtz said, looking down at Gavin and Apple who still stood on the road, "whoever is last to get on gets to sit up front with Boo Radley." Apple and Gavin looked at each other and pushing each other out of the way, tried scrabbling up onto the back of the truck with Gavin getting there first. "You don't mind, do you Apple?," Gavin said, sitting down. "I'm really not in the mood to have to make conversation with Ike? Kinda want to be quiet. Okay?" Apple nodded and turned away. Gavin had been acting weird since the Cabaret and now wasn't the time to give him grief.

Sturtz yelled to Apple. "Too bad, Scout. You ride with Boo!"

"Fuck you, Hank," Apple called as he made his way to the cab of the truck, hoping as he did that Ike hadn't heard what Sturtz had said.

"Get in boy," Ike said as he turned the key in the ignition. "Time is wasting."

Apple hopped in, putting his guitar case behind the seat.

"If you want to stow that in the back with the canoes," Ike said, "There'll probably be just enough room. I'll wait for ya to do it." Apple shook his head. "No," he said. "That's okay. I like to keep her near me." Ike smiled, nodded and put the truck into gear. "Her," he said. "That's good." He pressed the horn once, and with dust rising from in back of them, they were off.

Ike's truck led the way down 90, the hot August sun blazing through the bug splattered front window. He said nothing, but grunted once when he stopped short to avoid missing a rabbit. He kept the caravan at a steady forty as it made its way down the road.

"Feeling better?"

Apple stared at him. "Excuse me."

"The hay ride," Ike said, never taking his eyes off of the road, a smile curling the corner of his lips. "After you were doing all that singing you should have been on top of the world, but you weren't. I could see it."

Apple shrugged. "I was okay."

Ike Hayes laughed. "So okay that you got so drunk that you upchucked for fifteen minutes?"

"You're wrong I didn't......," Apple started, but Ike Hayes cut him off. "Yeah, you did. I oughta know. I held your head the whole time you were puking."

Apple closed his eyes. "Oh shit," he said. "Was that you?"

Ike nodded. "One in the same."

Apple shook his head. "I'm really sorry."

"For what? You missed me, so no harm done."

"Thanks for not telling Milburn or Lasker."

"Nothing to tell. You just acted like an asshole."

Apple nodded. "You've got *that* right."

"My friend," Ike said, swerving a bit to miss the carcass of what once had been a possum, "everyone is entitled to be an asshole once, twice maybe three times in his life. Beyond that, there is no excuse. The way as I see it, you've got a couple to go."

"Whatever you say. But either way, thanks."

Ike nodded. "You are welcome." He paused, then, "Want to tell me about it?"

Apple muttered a "Nah", and Ike nodded his head. "So be it. None of my bees wax anyway."

They drove in silence for a few minutes.

"So you see your instrument as a woman," Ike said as he shifted into second. "I like that."

Apple nodded, at a loss for what to say.

Ike slowed as he reached the cutoff five miles from Kanuga, signaled, turned onto the Calicoon Road, shifted gears again and half turned to Apple.

"You know, after holding your head and all, I never even got your name."

"Brookman. Andrew."

"Good to know you, Brookman, Andrew."

Apple smiled. "No. It's Andrew Brookman. I just...."

Ike smiled. "Yeah. I got that right off. I was jokin' with you. But thanks for the clarification." He held out his hand to Apple, who looked at it for a minute and then, smiling, shook it. The hand was rough, and powerful.

The truck bounced along the bumpy road and every now and again Sturtz would yell, loud enough that they could hear him in the cab of the truck. "Jesus, man," he howled. "You tryin' to kill us back here?" And Ike would just smile and drive steadily on.

It was hot in the cab even with both windows open and Apple was sweating freely. The red dust from the road made his eyes tear.

Ike looked over at him. "I know this is a special day," he said, "but there's nothin to cry over."

"I'm not crying," Apple said indignantly, "It's just......," he looked over and saw the big grin on Ike's face and chuckled. "Good one."

"Just funnin' you again. Just my way." They drove in silence for a few minutes and when Ike spoke again, it took Apple by surprise.

"You still in high school?"

"Huh? Oh yeah. Starting my senior year in the fall."

Ike Hayes nodded. "These are the good days. Enjoy them."

"Thanks," Apple said. "I plan to."

"You never know when they're gonna end."

"That's cheerful," Apple thought, but he only nodded and said nothing.

"Gotta girl?"

Apple smiled and nodded. "A couple."

Ike barked a laugh. "A couple!"

"Well, one here and sort of one at home."

"Well good for you, boy. Good for you."

Ike glanced out of the rear view mirror to make sure the other trucks were following him, and then looked back at the road. He waved and shouted a greeting to an old man who was walking along side of the road in the opposite direction.

"Mort!"

The old man waved back and then was lost in a cloud of red dust.

"Man's a few months short of a hundred. Been through more shit than I choose to think about, nearer to death than anyone ever oughta be, but he's still kickin.'"

Apple turned in his seat to look at Mort, but all he could see through the rear window was the back of York's head. "One hundred," he said, turning to the road in front of him, "wow."

"Hard to fathom at your age, being old," Ike said, slowing for a bump, "but it does get here for all of us."

"A hundred?," Apple said smiling.

"No....old....," and then Ike caught Apple's grin and laughed. "Now you're funnin' *me*," he said. "Good one." They both laughed.

"Plannin' to be a singer when you grow up?," Ike asked.

"Excuse me?"

Ike jerked his head at the guitar behind the seat.

Apple smiled. "No," he said. "I'm not that good I'm afraid."

Ike shook his head. "You sounded pretty good to me on the hay ride. That *Golden Earrings* thing especially."

Apple thought of what York had said. "I was just hacking around." He looked down at his bare knees. "I'm not good enough to make the big time."

"That's unusual. Seems like ev'ry kid today wants to be a rock and roll player."

Apple shook his head. "Nah. Not me. Wouldn't mind being a comedian though. Stand up. I've thought about that." He laughed. "My parents would not be too happy about that."

Ike shrugged, his eyes fixed on the road. "Not their life, now, is it?" Apple looked at him. "What I mean is, same as they wanting you to be a doctor, if they did of course, only the other way round. Not their life either way. You see what I mean?"

Apple nodded. "I do." He looked at the trees blurring by. "But sometimes it all seems so fucked up." He caught himself. "I'm sorry I didn't mean to….."

Ike's rich laughter caught him by surprise. "Sure you did," the older man said, "and sometimes it *is* all fucked up, but you know what? Someday, if you're lucky, and trust me here, 'cause it doesn't happen to everyone, *someday* when the stars are in alignment or some such thing, on one particular day it all stops being fucked up and all at once it all comes clear."

Gavin smiled at him. "One particular day."

Ike nodded. "One particular day."

Apple looked at the tattooed man driving the truck. "You always want to do this?"

Ike peered over at him. "You jokin' me again?" Apple shook his head. "No. I'm serious. I mean you're so good at doing so many things around camp that I thought…."

Ike shook his head. "Brookman Andrew," he said, "no man is born to be a handyman."

"I didn't mean to…."

Ike waved him away. "No offense taken. Don't worry about it." He was quiet for a moment then he looked over at Apple. "I have been around the street a few times and then a few times more, Brookman Andrew, and like Mort back there I have had my share of ups and downs, and there were things I wanted to do and couldn't for one reason or another and there were things that I *didn't* want to do and had to do, and the result of all that is that I am sitting in this seat next to you driving you to the Delaware River. If you are asking if I always had it in mind to be here in this particular place at this particular time, well, I'd have to say I guess not. The good and the bad, that's what got me here." He snorted. "Now that was a journey."

Apple smiled. "And those stars, or whatever, did they ever line up for you?"

"That, my young friend," Ike said, "I leave up to you to decide."

And Apple knew. "Yeah, they did," he said. "I'm glad."

Ike Hayes nodded.

Apple looked at the scenery going by. "Ed Lasker thinks this is a trip that will make us all men," he said.

Ike Hayes snorted. "Now *that* is bullshit." They both laughed. "Two boys in a boat, having to do for themselves without any modern conveniences and without the help of anyone else does not men make. Discomfort, certainly, making you a man, no. But don't mistake my meaning, I both like and respect Lasker, but a true man is not made because of a canoe trip."

"I don't think that Ed really thinks that...."

Ike shook his head. "Sure he does. In a way he does. It's easier for him to see it that way...to make you boys think that this," and here is spread his hand before him, "clear cut and defined, will make you a man. But fuck, how do you define a man in the first place?" He looked over at Apple who was staring at him and laughed. "Close your mouth or the flies'll get in. What's the matter, you figure a handy man can't be a philosopher cause he sometimes drops his 'g's and has tattoos all over his body? Well, see, then you'd be wrong, and that's my point. I am the *sum* of my parts. Cause yes, I went to college, and yes I graduated, and yes, maybe I wanted more than this, but does that make me more of a man or *less* of a man? Does being a handy man define me?" Apple was about to speak but Ike stopped him with a wave of his hand. "Those were rhetorical questions, Brookman Andrew. They do not need answers. You'll learn about them in college. Rhetorical questions. Right now to you young guys everything is black and white; everything has an answer. But you'll find that most things don't, that there are lots of shades of gray out there. But the idea that one overnight canoe trip can define a boy as a man, in the same way that you fucking up on the hay ride makes you a loser, is just simply ridiculous." He paused. "Okay," he said after a moment, "here comes another one. Rhetorical question, I mean. Ready for it?" Apple nodded. "Okay. Here goes. Do all the women I have had in my life make me a man? Huh?"

"Well, I....."

"I told you it was rhetorical. No answer needed, remember?" Apple smiled as Ike went on. "But, damn boy, if you think the amount of pussy a man has had in his life makes him a man, you got a lot to learn. Shit, the bravest man I ever knew took a bullet in Korea trying to save his buddy and he was the biggest pansy I ever met! Never even *been* with a woman to my knowledge. Does that make him any less of a man? Christ, no!" He leaned over and looked at Apple. "And that's a straight forward answer; not rhetorical at all." He looked back at the road. "The war I fought in, the booze I've drunk? Do *they* make me a man?" Apple was about to speak. "Do not answer, rhetorical again!"

"I had no intention of....," Apple started, and then he stopped, laughed and shook his head. He liked this man.

"But no matter what," Ike went on, " and either way, this is what it all came down to, my life I mean. And no, I didn't plan this for my life, but you know something, I don't resent it for a minute. You're right, I am good at what I do, and more important my young friend, I *like* what I do, and that makes a big difference in how you feel when you wake up in the morning, let me tell you. Maybe *that's* what defines a man. Being happy with his life? Waking up happy. Maybe. Letting go of the bad shit and focusing on every new day that comes along. Probably closer to being truly happy than anything else I can think of."

They rode in silence for a few minutes.

"But if the things that couldn't be helped hadn't been in the way," Apple said, "what *would* you have been?"

"You mean second choice behind handy man philosopher?," Ike said smiling and Apple nodded. "Well, I think I would have been a teacher."

"A teacher!"

"Don't be so surprised, Brookman Andrew, after all what better thing than to share all those things that you said I am good at, and maybe even more? Hell, maybe teaching's not in the same league as cleaning out a stuffed toilet or even being a comedian, but there's something to be said for it. And teachers have to do a hell of a lot of talking, and as you can see, I am not deficient in that department. Anyway, whatever the answer is, we're here."

Apple looked up and saw Calicoon coming up in front of them.

"So," Ike said, maneuvering the truck slowly onto the rickety bridge, "how'd you like driving with Boo Radley?"

Apple was flustered. "I never...."

"Sure you did," Ike said, "you all did, and you know what, I kinda like it. I mean, Boo may have been a little slow, but he did save both Atticus Finch's children. He wasn't trying to do it intentionally like Holden Caulfield, standing on the side of a cliff and saving *all* the children from falling over, that, no one can do, but saving one or two lives every once and again, even by accident, well that suits me just fine."

"An English teacher."

Ike smiled over at him. "Excuse me."

"You would have been an English teacher."

"Maybe. Different set of stars, different day…maybe."

Apple nodded, suddenly very happy.

"Look at you," Ike said, "sittin' there with a big grin like you just figured out what your dick is for."

"You know, Mr. Hayes," Apple said, "maybe I just did."

"Well that's well and good, and I hope that it's true, but just promise me you won't tell anyone about our talk. I wouldn't want to stop being, what is it they call me, 'the enigma of Kanuga?'" He rippled his pectoral muscles and the American flag waved back and forth.

Apple laughed. "I promise."

Ike pulled down the long winding road that led to the river and stopped. "Time to unload."

Apple smiled. "Gee, Ike" he said, "I thought you just did!"

Ike threw back his head and laughed. "Good one," he and Apple said at the same time.

Apple stretched out his hand to Ike, who took it in his. "Thanks," he said. "I…."

"You are welcome Brookman Andrew," Ike said, shaking Apple's hand. "You are very, very welcome."

Truck doors slammed and boys jumped down from flatbeds.

"Come, my young friend," Ike said, "your river is waiting."

CHAPTER NINETEEN:

Hollywood.
March
Present Day

Joey Carter put down the screenplay and closed his eyes.

He had been pouring over the pages from the moment they had arrived and though only half finished he loved the story and the way each of the main characters had been drawn. Apple, Gavin, Dorff, Nicki- strangers before were now a very real part of him. Each had been examined completely, any questions left unanswered solved with interior monologues over the action. He especially loved what the writer had done with Sturtz, keeping him as an ambiguous antagonist. He was one dimensional and vile, but Joey was sure that in the third act, when all the hidden facets of this fascinating character were revealed, there would be more to him than met the eye. He even liked the fact that the writer had used the character's real names in the draft he held in his hand, to be changed, of course, when the film went into production. Big Boss had told him that the piece was loosely based on a true story, but to Joey the line between truth and illusion was no longer there. To him, each character was real and could not have been more real had he been actually present their stories unfolded.

All, that was, but York.

Big Boss had sent him the script with the expressed purpose of his playing York, the central character of the piece, yet after reading and dissecting each line up to the start of the canoe trip, Joey was no closer to understanding the character than he was when he first opened the script.

The frustrating part was that he could see parts of himself in every character but York. He could play Apple with his eyes closed and Dorff, though he didn't like him, he saw being played by his channeling Sean Penn in THE FALCON AND THE SNOWMAN. He immediately fell in love with Nicki, and as for Gavin, well Gavin was the part that Joey longed to play. He had loved him immediately, empathized with every facet of his being, but when he told Big Boss, the man was adamant. "You're not playing gay this early in your career," he said, "no way. Maybe not even later, but then we'll see. For now it is far too dangerous. I envisioned you as York, so you'll play York or no one, and that is final."

But who was York Stewart? Who was this kid who was, seemingly, all things to all these other people? On the surface, Joey had decided, he was simply too good to be true. But if that were so, the character would be dull to the point of distraction. Where was the edge, the thing that made him human? Joey was sure there was something else, something hidden that he could use as a hook to make York playable, but first he had to find it. He glanced back a few pages. Was the fact that York "dissed" Apple's singing on the hayride anything? Maybe, but if it was it was no more than a start, maybe nothing more than an anomaly. And what of the fact that he had ruined the senior group election for Dorff by throwing the prize to him, just when it was within Dorff's own reach. Two anomalies. There had to be more, and if there was something bigger that would make York real, Joey thought, he had to find it before committing to do the project. But, in fact, Joey wondered, could he find it?

Joey stood up and stretched. He had been holed up at the Beverly Hills Hotel since late the night before, telling no one where he was and not answering his voice mail. He needed alone time with the script. That was important. He wanted no distractions as he read. He grabbed a Coke out of the mini bar, cracked it and took a long swig, catching his reflection in the mirror across the room as he did.

The body was good, worked on and in great shape. The face that looked back at him, though unshaven, was intelligent and open, but not, he told himself for the hundredth time, the face of a sixteen year old. "There's no getting around it," he thought, "I'm twenty one and I look twenty one. There's no way I can pull off sixteen, whether I get to the bottom of York or not."

Big Boss had disagreed. "They can do wonders nowadays," he had told him. "Makeup. Special effects. Christ, Streep played an old rabbi in ANGELS IN AMERICA, for God's sake. And besides, you're full of shit. You look sixteen today and you'll look sixteen tomorrow. They'll buy it if you play it right and I know you'll play it right, so what's the problem? Just trust me and don't worry."

But Joey Carter was worried. He had a lot riding on this film. He shook his head. A lot? Everything.

Getting here had been easy, too easy he realized now. Big Boss had brought him along slowly, nothing major, just small kid roles on established television series and low budget movies. He had hit it big at eighteen, playing the misunderstood older son on GUIDING LIGHT, and when that ended when his character was shipped off to a clinic in Switzerland after a year, he segued immediately into GRANDFATHER DAD a popular night time FOX sitcom that, along with his number one single, "Keep Your Eye On Tomorrow," put his face on the cover of every teen magazine in America for the next year.

Then, again through Big Boss's manipulation and shrewd calculation, came the really big one, the one that had made him a star. He had played Randy, the name above the title, young romantic lead in the mega-budget disaster film KISS TOMORROW GOODBYE.

And that was it.

The third largest holiday opening weekend in history secured Joey the position as one of the most bankable new stars in Hollywood. Whatever question there had been on the part of the Hollywood insiders had been quelled. There was no doubt that the good-looking kid from television could open a picture.

Suddenly, his face was everywhere. He was compared to the young Pitt and Damon, to Zac Efron and, in one particularly florid piece, even to James Dean. Scripts poured in, mobs of girls and paparazzi followed him everywhere but in the midst of it all, and though he knew it was a cliché, suddenly none of it seemed real; none of it seemed enough.

Joey Carter finished his Coke, stripped out of his clothes and pulled on a bathing suit. With a towel around his neck and the script in his hand, he made his way poolside and flopped onto a plush chaise lounge. The pool, usually crowded, was, he was grateful to see, fairly empty. That suited him just fine. He ordered an iced tea, signed a few autographs for two giggling girls who came shyly up to him, and lay back and closed his eyes.

None of it was enough. "How ungrateful is that?" he thought, finding the sun with his face and surrendering to it. But no matter how hard he tried to deny it, it was true. There was something missing. He had gotten there too quickly, too easily, and he knew why.

Big Boss.

"I know you've heard it before, but I can do more than this," he told Oprah at the premiere of KISS TOMORROW GOODBYE, a sentiment he went on to echo on all the talk shows he went on to promote the opening of the film.

"Randy was a great part," he told the ladies of THE VIEW, "but I don't want to play second fiddle to tidal waves and earthquakes for the rest of my life."

"I want to do something important," he told a grinning Jay Leno.

"Something like Cruise did with MAGNOLIA," he told Letterman.

"Low budget, but good," he confided to Regis and Kelly.

"Bottom line," he told Conan, "I have to know that I am good. Not the FX. Not my agents, me."

To himself he said, "I have to know that if Big Boss hadn't been there for me that I could have made it on my own."

And then it all hit the fan.

The interviews for KISS TOMORROW GOODBYE that had been set up merely to plug the film, had instead become a confessional, and what the whole country saw was not the next mega star, but rather an ungrateful young man who was bemoaning the fact that he had it all.

In a world not used to unscripted honesty, Joey's words had been taken as fatuous and pretentious. His fervent plea for good roles had become fodder for every comedian on television. Saturday Night Live did a skit about him playing Hamlet, directing, playing concert piano and juggling all at the same time. The Daily Show and Colbert were not far behind. They played him as a punk kid prima donna, ungrateful for what anyone else in the country would have killed for. Almost immediately his Q rating began to slip with the furious and frustrated Big Boss doing all he could in the way of damage control.

So it was that Joey Carter was sent the script for GONE THE SUN.

"Here's a role you were born to play," the attached memo had read. "Trust me, I know. You want important? This is important. It's a small film, low budget, do it and all those schmucks who made fun of you will have to blow it out their ass." It had been written in Big Boss's own hand and signed in his familiar scrawl, with a P.S. "I will not take no for an answer."

But York, dammit, York!

From day one Joey Carter had his own way to find a character. He would not read the entire script, but rather one page again and again until he found what he was looking for. But this time, after reading half of the script that way, again and again Joey found himself lost.

What if he told Big Boss he simply didn't want to play the role? Even as he mulled the possibility over in his mind, he knew there was no way that was going to happen; Big Boss would not let it happen.

York! Fucking York! So handsome and compassionate, York was obviously all things to all people, the golden boy of golden boys, every parent's dream, every boy's best friend, every young girl's ideal, but who the hell was he? There was something missing; something left untold. "If I can't find that," Joey decided, "Big Boss or no Big Boss, I can't do the film."

"What's in the script is who York was," Big Boss had assured him. "Trust me, its all there, and what's not there, well that's what you bring to the party. You are an actor, yes?"

Joey opened his eyes and picked up the script yet again. This time, he decided, he would not stop, but simply read the rest in a gulp, hopefully finding insight to the character of York.

He opened to the place where he had left off, the scene marked, 'Mystery Walk. Exterior. Daytime', and once again began to read.

CHAPTER TWENTY:

MYSTERY WALK: EXTERIOR - DAYTIME 2:30 p.m.

The canoes were put in the water, gear checked and stowed, and then it was time to set out.

Ike Hayes pulled a crumpled slip of paper from his jeans pocket. "Okay," he said, "here's the order in which you and your partner will set off down river. Remember, we have planned this so that you all will be far enough away from other pairs so that you will be totally on your own, but, of course, with your partner whomever that may be."

"That's clear!" Sturtz sniffed to York, so he didn't see the wink Ike gave Apple.

"The older boys will go first. 33, 32, 31...well you get it."

"No, draw a freaking diagram, asshole," Sturtz whispered, and Apple socked him on the arm. "Shut the fuck up, Sturtz," he said. "Listen and learn."

"From Boo Radley? Doubtful."

"So... Leonard Dorff and Gavin Stewart." Two boys raised their hands. "You two gentlemen, will go first and farthest. You all set?" The two nodded, and Ike looked over at Sturtz. "Good. Good to know some people understand me." Sturtz scowled. Ike turned back to Gavin and Lennie. "On your way. Remember, you guys go as far as the blue marker. That's where you make camp."

The other boys watched as Dorff and Gavin pushed off and started paddling down river.

"Aloha, girls," Sturtz called after them, and a few of the boys in Bunk 30 laughed.

When the first canoe was out of sight, Ike checked his paper and yelled, "Brookman, Andrew." Apple smiled and raised his hand. "Ike, yo!", he called back, and Ike barked a laugh. "And York Stewart." York raised his hand, and followed Apple to the canoe. "You boys, green marker." When they had disappeared, Ike called, "The last two members of 33." He checked the list. "Mr. Klinger and Hank Sturtz."

"It's *Henry,*" Sturtz said, scowling.

"Yes, I know." Ike replied smiling. "Yellow marker. Off you go."

Ike Hayes watched the three canoes as they disappeared around a bend in the river. "Safe journey," he called and then went back to his list.

"Bunk 32."

POV: *Apple*:

2:45 p.m.

The river was calm and the sun felt good on my shoulders. I had stripped off my tee shirt though York had warned me against it.

"You're gonna get burned," he said and I shrugged. "Doubtful. Already have a good base tan. Shirt's too confining."

We talked about camp, and friends and home and our plans for college.

"First choice?," York asked. "Still Harvard?" He chuckled.

I laughed. "I wish. Oneonta School of Animal Husbandry is probably where I'll end up."

"Bullshit. Seriously."

"Seriously? Okay. What about Cornell?"

"That's still good with me. Second?"

"B.U."

"What happened to Amherst?"

"B.U. or Amhurst. I'll go with your choice."

"Probably Amhurst and then B.U. We've got to get into one of those."

"We have to be sure we can get a three room."

York nodded. "No question. If we can't, we'll all live off campus. Agreed?"

"Agreed."

For a while the conversation stopped, and I was about to say something when York said, "Best movie?"

I smiled. We had played this game since we saw Robert Redford play it with his buddy in THE WAY WE WERE.

"2001," I said. "You?"

"ON THE WATERFRONT?"

"Still?"

"Always. Best singer?"

I thought for a moment. "Dylan. You?"

"No contest," York said, "Pat Boone."

I laughed. "Get serious. Who?"

"You're telling *me* to get serious. There's a switch."

"Seriously," I said. "Dylan?"

"Dylan."

I nodded. "Best book?"

"CATCHER IN THE RYE. You too?"

"Or A SEPARATE PEACE."

"Really?"

"Uh, huh," I said. "Lotta good stuff in there."

York shrugged. "I don't really like it. That whole tree- shaking thing rings false to me. Best friends don't do things like that."

"Point taken," I said. "Best day"

York paused for a moment, and when he spoke his voice was softer than it had been.

"Today."

I nodded. "Today."

We paddled slowly, looking for the green marker that would tell us where to make camp. From far away we could hear sounds of things we couldn't see; a distant buzz -saw, the incessant caw of a crow, and then, off to our side, a loud splash. We lifted our paddles and looked over at from where the sound had come, but there was nothing there.

"Beaver," York said.

"All you ever think of is sex," I said, and York laughed.

We began paddling again.

"Do you know what 'verguenza' is?"

I looked at York on the crossbar seat in front of me. His tee shirt was stuck to his back with sweat.

"What *what* is?"

"Verguenza."

"Is that a rhetorical question?"

"What? A what?"

"Nothing." I smiled. "Continue."

York was about to say something when he pointed at the riverbank. "Look," he said. An enormous frog sat sunning himself on a rock that jutted out into the water.

"That's a verguenza?" I said. "I would have said that it was a big frog that looked a lot liked Howard."

"You're an idiot. No, really. Answer my question. Verguenza. Hev you ever heard of it? Do you know what it is?"

"'Verg---uenza,'" I said. "Is that 'influe...enza's' sister?"

York chuckled. "Everyone hates a wise ass, Apple," he said for what must have been the hundredth time that summer. Only the sun warmed me more.

The current was with us, and soon we were only using the paddles to keep us on course. It was as if the river knew where we were headed.

In the heat of the day a dog barked in the distance, far enough away that we couldn't see him.

"No," I said, "I have no idea what verguenza means. Enlighten me."

"It means 'shame,' or at least that's as close to a translation as I can come up with."

I wiped the sweat off my chest with a towel. "And you are telling me this because....?"

"I read a book before I came up here and one of the characters told a story about it."

"Verguenza?"

York nodded. "In Spain," he said, staring into the water, "they tell the story of this famous matador."

"His name was Verguenza?"

York shook his head in disgust. "You know...just forget it Apple."

"Oh, come on, lighten up, man. I'm just funning you!"

"You're just *funning* me? Where did that come from?"

"Never mind. Tell me about verguenza."

York shook his head. "No."

I took an oar out of the water, held it above York's head and shook it. As the water fell on him I intoned, "In the name of the father..."

"Jesus, Apple. You can be such a dick!"

I stopped laughing. "Hey, Bro, I was only joking. Don't get all bent out and everything."

"But shit, Apple, everything doesn't have to be a fucking joke. Not everything has to be funny."

"Okay, okay. I'm sorry, okay?" I said. "Tell me the story."

"You fucked it up. Forget about it!"

"Now who's being a dick?"

"It's a serious story. You know...serious? Defined as something that isn't funny!"

"I said I was sorry. Tell the story."

"No."

"Now you're acting like a hurt girl."

"Fuck you."

"You'd love to!"

York turned and gave me a half smile and the butterflies that had started flipping around in my stomach disappeared.

"If I tell you, will you *not* make a joke out of it? I mean, *can* you?"

"Swear to God," I said. "Tell me."

York coughed and spit into the water.

"Eat that, shark, and think you have eaten a man!," I said.

"Shut *up* Apple!"

"It's a line from THE OLD MAN AND THE SEA. The old man has felt something break in his chest and he spits blood into the water and..."

"I know the reference, Apple. Is it at all possible for you to shut up for just one minute?"

I almost answered, then closed my mouth and waited for York to go on.

"In Spain they tell the story of this favorite matador called Rivera," York said. "And if you even *think* Geraldo you are a dead man!"

"I didn't say *anything.* Jesus, York," I grinned. "You have some serious problems."

"Shut up and listen. This Rivera was the darling of the corrida crowd."

"Alliteration. Good."

"Apple!"

"Sorry. Funnin'. Go on."

"Rivera would let the bull pass so close to him that there was hardly any space between them. He would literally dance within inches of the bull's horns. And his kills! His kills were so swift, that the arena would only know that the bull had been pierced when the bull fell, and the bull himself was so stunned by the attack that he would stay on his feet for fifteen seconds, with Rivera's sword in his neck mind you, until finally falling to his knees. And as the bull fell and the crowd regained its voice and roared its approval, Rivera would strut around the Plaza del Toros waving his cap." York waited for me to make an inane comment but I was hooked by the story and only murmured, "Go on."

"One day Rivera misgauged the distance between himself and his adversary and he was badly gored. He completed the kill, but this time, instead of walking around the arena he immediately exited and refused to have his wounds seen to. He said they were minor and went back to his dressing room. No one could believe it when he died a few hours later. 'He didn't seem badly hurt,' they said. 'He looked as he always looked after a fight.' But they were wrong; Rivera had not died of his physical injuries, Apple, he had died of verguenza! He had died of shame." I stared at the back of York's head. There was silence for a moment and then York said, "That's it. That's the whole story. Feel free to make jokes again."

"Don't feel like it," I muttered. "Why'd you tell me that story? I mean now. Today?"

"I don't know," York shrugged. "I've been meaning to. Just forgot until now."

"What the hell does it mean?"

"I don't know exactly. Maybe it means that you shouldn't get too cocky. Maybe that you shouldn't ever get so high up that even a slight fall could kill you. Maybe it's just the whole macho thing. This being the trip that makes us men and all."

I snickered.

"The story stayed with me is all."

"Hubris," I said.

"What?"

"Hubris. My English teacher used the word when we were discussing characters in Shakespeare."

"And it means?"

"Pretty much what you've been saying. Arrogance: too much pride. When you've got a case of hubris and you fall, you fall hard!"

York nodded. "I hope I don't have that," he said.

"You! Jesus," I laughed, "if there is anyone who doesn't suffer from that it's you."

"Thanks," York said, "but I'm not so sure."

"Bullshit. York, answer a question for me."

"Shoot."

"Who is the best athlete in the senior group?"

"I dunno. Probably Sturtz."

"I rest my case."

"What?"

"York," I said, exasperated, "*you* are the best athlete, but do you brag about it and throw it around? No. Does Sturtz, who is second best? You bet your ass. You my friend may have to worry about other things, like terminal ugliness, but never about verguenza."

York shrugged and watched the river as we paddled. "But what if I said it even though I knew I was the best?"

That stopped me. "On purpose?"

"Either way. What if?"

"I don't know!"

We were quiet for a while.

"You mind if I play the guitar?" I asked warily. I still hadn't told him that I had heard what he had said to Sturtz about GOLDEN EARRINGS but something had to rid the day of verguenza.

"And if I did, when has that ever stopped you?"

I laughed. "We'll have to change seats."

"Just don't fall out," York said.

We carefully shifted around as we changed positions in the canoe.

"You tip us over and you're a dead man," York said as I sidled past him.

"Whooooo," I said, making the canoe shake from side to side.

"Apple!"

"Hey," I said, "remember how I shook the chair on the Ferris wheel at Great Adventure? I thought Gavin would shit."

"Hmm," York said, "I wonder if Harvard knows what they're missing by not taking you?"

"Their loss," I said, opening my guitar case. The guitar was warm in my hands.

"Why don't you play the one you played on the hay ride? The one about the gypsies."

I looked at him not comprehending. "The one about the earrings," he said, "it was nice."

My mind whirled. What! If he had liked it, why had he mocked me to Sturtz?

I shook my head. "No," I said. "That was for a different time and a different place."

York shrugged. "Suit yourself, but I liked it."

He liked it? Well, then…. "No. Wrong time," I thought. "Change the subject.

"Dylan?"

"Dylan!"

I tuned the guitar and then leaned back into the canoe.

"How many roads must a man walk down,
Before you call him a man?"

The current moved us forward.

Joey Carter underlined "verguenza", wiped the sweat from his chest, and continued to read.

3:15 p.m.

"Shush," Sturtz said. "Shut up and listen."

Klinger grumbled. "What the hell are you….."

"Shut the fuck up and listen."

"The answer my friend is blowin' in the wind,
The answer is blowin' in the wind."

"The answer is blowing up my ass, " Sturtz said. "Fuckin' Apple." He turned in the direction the singing was coming from and shouted, *"There once was a man from Peru, whose dick was too small to screw."* He stopped and listened as the words echoed down the river. "Now *those* are lyrics, Apple," he yelled and Klinger snickered.

"Klinger, dammit," Sturtz said, looking back over his shoulder at him, "are you going to paddle or what?"

Klinger looked at his friend and shook his head. "Jesus, Henry, when the hell is it your turn?"

Sturtz lay back into the canoe. He had placed his backpack so that he could rest his head on it and was comfortable in the hot sun.

"Klinger, my boy," he said, "it is always my turn." He moved a bit and let his hand trail into the cool river water. "Always."

"Henry," Klinger moaned, "Jesus, man, I fucking packed your gear......"

"Uh uh uh. You *helped* me pack it," Sturtz corrected.

"Yeah, sure," he said. "You stood by supervising while I did it."

"There must always be supervisors as there must always be workers. Kinda like a bee hive."

"Bee hive, my ass," Klinger said, paddling, the sweat making his hair wet and slick, beads of it running down the back of his neck into his soaked Kanuga tee shirt. "I pack your stuff, I get the food, and now I'm fucking paddling."

"Well this is what you're good at, Klinger. This is where you shine. I mean, let's be realistic, on the ball field you are barely competent, and in Hayes Hall, less than that."

"Henry!"

"No wait," Sturtz said. "I'm complimenting you."

"You're....."

"Complimenting you."

"That was a compliment?"

"The compliment is coming. Just wait a minute. Okay, so as I was saying, you are pretty poor as an athlete, and that is not said in any negative way, believe me on that. So you are pretty poor as an athlete..."

"You said that twice."

"I know I did," Sturtz said, "but I am just driving home a point. You see, in things like sports you are pretty ordinary, but at things like *this,* camping and nature and shop, things that *matter,* and will matter later in life, well that's where you really shine."

"You can be such a shit...."

"I can be such a *what*?" Sturtz's voice was indignant. "Here I give you a compliment and you call me a shit? Where do you come off, huh?" He made himself sound angry. "Tell me, huh putz, tell me where!"

Klinger looked confused. "I know what you're doing," he said, but Sturtz knew that he didn't. "Okay," he said calmly, "what am I doing?"

"You're changing things around so that I look wrong."

"What the hell does that mean? That you look *wrong:* wrong at what? Wrong, how? Explain to me what you are talking about."

"No," Klinger said, addled. "You said that I was a poor athlete."

"No. What I said was *pretty* poor, but go on."

"Okay, pretty poor."

"Yes."

"Well, you made it sound like I'm a loser."

"By saying that there are things that you are *good* at! That you *shine* in! How exactly does that make you sound like a loser?"

"Because you said I was a pretty poor athlete."

"But that was a statement of fact. I mean, can you argue it? Jesus man, you make me out to be some sort of shit because I am friend enough to tell you the truth and to praise you for what you do well. Okay then, if that's your definition of a shit, then I guess I'm a shit, though I believe other people might see me as a friend instead of a shit, but hell what do I know, huh?" Sturtz went quiet and then, in a hurt voice, "You know something, up yours Klinger."

"What?"

"Up yours for being a bad friend. Man I wish I hadn't been partnered with you. Even fucking Dorff would have been better."

"Come on, Henry I....."

"No," Sturtz said looking into the water, knowing that Klinger had turned his head a bit sideways so that he could see him, "No, man, no. I was really looking forward to this. It was gonna be fun, you know. But right away you ruin it. You fuck it up and make me the bad guy. You know, maybe it would be best if we didn't fucking talk to each other for the rest of this trip okay? Man, Klinger, you really know how to take the edge off the fun, you really do."

Henry Sturtz stopped talking and looked into the water, waiting to see how long it would be till Klinger said something. He counted to himself, "One....and...two.....and..."

"Hey, Henry...."

What a loser. Never even made it to three. Even fucking Dorff wouldn't have caved that soon. What a total loser.

"Henry, man, I'm sorry. I just thought you were ragging on me when you said I was poor at sports."

"I said *pretty* poor, and let's not talk about it."

"No," Klinger said, and Sturtz could hear the worry in his voice. "I don't want to be the one to ruin this trip. I really am sorry."

Sturtz thought he'd play it out, though he knew he could have left it there. Klinger had turned to him and pitifully searched his eyes for a hint of forgiveness.

But Sturtz wouldn't give an inch. "Damn it, man, I thought you were my friend. That you respected me."

"I do, Henry, really," the miserable Klinger said.

Sturtz shook his head. "No, you don't. Uh- uh, no you don't. You just see me as this really good athlete who is respected by everyone in camp, and you never stop to think that I can also be sensitive, that I can have the same feelings everyone else has."

"Sure I do, Henry."

This was far too easy. Henry shook his head again. "No, no you don't. You see me as an insensitive jerk, just an amazingly good jock who doesn't care about you at all, and that really is untrue and unfair. Don't you know man that the sign of a real friend, a *good* friend, is to tell him the truth no matter the consequences? Well, I told you the truth and you spit in my face to say thanks. Where are you coming from Klinger? Huh? Where are you coming from?"

To Sturtz it looked as though Klinger was close to tears. "Henry, man, I am really sorry," he kind of whispered with his voice shaking. "I really apologize for being such an asshole. I don't want to ruin this trip, man, and I really do appreciate you being honest with me. You're a good friend, Henry. And you're right, I am a pretty poor athlete and I *am* good at this stuff." He paused and then said, his voice brighter, "Tell you what. When we make camp, I'll take care of everything...make the fire, cook...everything. And I won't mind because we're friends."

And at that moment Sturtz half expected Kilinger to ask if he could tend the rabbits!

"Whattaya say, Henry? I'll do all that, and I know you would do the same for me."

"Yeah, right! Not in this life, you loser," Sturtz thought. He waited a few beats before he said anything.

"Would you like to blow me here," Sturtz said, "or wait until it gets dark?"

Klinger looked at him totally lost, totally not sure how to take what he had just said, and then he smiled and Sturtz could see the wave of relief pass over his face. "Er, how about never?," he said, grinning.

"Never would be good for me too," Sturtz said and he reached out his hand. Klinger, beside himself with relief, took it and shook it hard.

Sturtz lay back in the canoe as Klinger turned and continued paddling, humming happily under his breath. He pulled out one of the joints he had bought from one of the waiters, lit it, sucked in and held the warm smoke in his lungs for as long as he could, only exhaling when he had to.

It was a beautiful afternoon.

POV: Dorff

4:30 p.m., on

It's really a shame that you can't wake up in the morning and know what kind of a day you're going to have. Or better yet, know whether the decisions you are going to make during the course of that day are going to turn out good or bad. I suppose while we are wishing for such things, we could throw in a big win in the lottery, perpetual good health and unconditional love for the rest of our lives, but unfortunately for us, things don't work like that.

I guess it was Sturtz that soured the day for me almost as soon as it had begun.

I hadn't been looking forward to this Mystery Walk of Ed's, and after Sturtz' wise -ass comments at the group meeting, I was looking forward to it even less. Back on campus there were always places to escape to, other people to talk to if things weren't going well. On the river, a rustic setting that turned me off from the word go, there was, simply, no place to hide.

The ride to the Delaware was bumpy and hot with Sturtz, as usual, making matters worse with his constant complaining. I would have liked to have ridden in the cab of the car, but I didn't need the 'pansyass' comments from Sturtz that surely would have followed my suggesting it, so I watched as Apple climbed in next to Ike Hayes and then bounced along with Sturtz, York, Gavin, and Klinger in the back. The canoes banged against our legs, Sturtz complained, and we ended up, twenty miles later with sore butts and faces covered with red dust.

"Did all that bumping give you a woody?," Sturtz snickered to me as we climbed down from the truck. "I figure, in the long run, *something* must." This prompted a laugh from Klinger, a shake of the head from York and from me, a weak smile. Sturtz! Of course, I thought at the time, my being paired with him would have made the day even worse.

As it turned out it couldn't possibly have.

Though never very talkative, Gavin had been quieter than usual for a number of days before the trip, so I was not surprised that on the ride to Calicoon he had said almost nothing.

That didn't change once we got into the canoe. He hardly spoke, and then only when necessary as we paddled quietly together down the Delaware, breaking his silence only to warn me against rocks or other hazards in our path. At one point we heard a voice that sounded like Sturtz' yelling something to someone far behind us, but other than that, the chatter of the birds and the constant buzzing of the cicadas, all was still.

"He has to be thinking about what he told Nicki," I thought, and just as I longed to tell him that I knew and that I still thought he was an amazing guy, I knew I couldn't. It was just something you couldn't put into words. "Maybe, I thought if the opportunity arises........."

"Lennie."

I looked over to where Gavin was pointing and saw the blue banner we had been told to look out for. We backstroked, moved the canoe in to the riverbank, hopped out, and pulled the boat onto shore. I looked at my watch. We had been on the river for a little over an hour and a half. Now it was time to make camp.

We quickly divided the chores, and I set out to find wood for the fire, while Gavin started to put up the tent.

As I looked for dry kindling, I kept thinking back to Gavin's conversation with Nicki, playing it over and over in my mind as I had done so many times since hearing it. He had sounded so lost, so confused, so *sad*. And somehow I instinctively knew that if he were to open up to me about it, I could help him. I was certain that he hadn't told York that he was gay, and I wondered now, as I had when I stood listening to him cry to Nicki, if I might be the person he needed to confide in, to share with. I mean, after all, who else was there? At this moment in his life he didn't need the forced bravado of a Sturtz, the wise cracks of an Apple or the indifference of a Klinger. Short of his brother whom he didn't think would understand, who better than I to confide in?

After all, Gavin and I were friends, and though there were not many, we had shared some good talks over the summers. He knew that I was an introspective person, a sensitive person who would never betray a confidence for any reason, *Just Asking*, or no *Just Asking*. As I picked up the dried up twigs, I determined to let Gavin know that I knew his secret. It would help him, and, realistically, I thought, it would make me even closer to him and, through him, to York. It would finally make me one of them, somehow a part of the Stewarts, in a way that even Apple couldn't manage. And to be honest, there was nothing in the world that I could think of that I wanted more than that; to stop being an addendum to their lives, to stop being the last person they thought of to call for a movie in the winter, if, of course, they were to call at all. I was certain that as soon as I told him that I knew his secret and didn't care, Gavin would feel a terrific burden lifted off of his shoulders, and that he would thank me for it. But never really having a best friend, I was a novice at all this. I knew I had to go slow and choose my moment. I went about the task finding dead branches with a strange sense of excitement, but most of the twigs I found were still too green to use and, as I tried to bend them, would not crack.

When I got back to the campsite, the tent was almost up, and, without much discussion, I dropped what firewood I *had* found and helped Gavin finish his job. As we worked neither of us spoke and when we finally were done, we were both drenched in sweat.

"Me for a swim," Gavin said, stripping off his shirt and shorts. He kicked off his dockers and walked to the river's edge in his briefs. "Cold," he said, over his shoulder as he waded in. "Coming?," he called and I shook my head. "Hate cold water," I said, "and besides, I don't think we need buddies out here." He smiled for the first time and moved further in. I watched him until he finally took a deep breath and dove under the water. He emerged and swam with a strong steady stroke until he was lost to me in the bend of the river.

It was too early to make a fire for dinner so I went to my backpack and pulled out my clipboard and the small transistor radio I had brought with me. I sat down, leaned against the side of a massive tree and clicked on the radio. Static. I spun the dial, but other than the voice of someone saying something so faintly and so far away that I could not hear him, there was nothing. "Maybe at night," I thought as I flicked it off and set down to work on the "Farewell 1975" issue of the INQUIRER. I was still working on the issue when Gavin came dripping up to me from the riverbank.

"How was it?" I asked looking up.

He shook the water from his hair as a dog would, while wrapping a towel around his shoulders. "Refreshing. You ought to go in."

I smiled. "I have a rule, Gav. I only swim if forced to or if the temperature goes over 95 degrees. Other than that, it's strictly showers for me."

Gavin nodded and walked over to his tent. "Aren't we supposed to be doing something for this mystery walk thing," he asked slipping off his wet underwear and pulling on his shorts. "I mean, I'm not complaining, but is this all there is to it?" He pulled his Kanuga tee shirt, the one with the sleeves ripped off, over his head.

"Pretty much." I smiled. "Except starting a fire without matches."

"Without matches? Oh, that's right. I remember Ed saying that. But Jesus, why?"

"Indian's didn't know from matches, Gav, so no matches allowed."

"But who would know if we....."

I shook my head. "It's an honor code thing."

He sighed. "Well, I've seen it done in the movies with two rocks and some twigs. Maybe we should get to it before it gets dark?"

"No hurry," I said grinning, pulling out a pack of matches. "So much for honor."

Gavin smiled. "Excellent! And that's it? Nothing else? No identifying birds and plants or anything? Making a bow and arrow? Planting a flag on Iwo Jima?"

I laughed and put down my clipboard. "Nope. I think the whole idea is to commune with nature and get in touch with our inner beings."

Gavin nodded, his face grim. "Oh, yeah," he said. "Let's hear it for inner beings."

I looked at him and was wondering if this was the moment to tell him what I knew, when he changed the subject. "You hungry yet?"

"What time is it?"

Gavin reached into his shorts and produced his watch. "'About six.

"Why don't we wait with eating for a while? I have something to show you that you might like."

"And that is?"

"Uno momento." I got up went to my backpack and pulled out a bunch of tee shirts wrapped together.

"You're gonna do laundry?"

Laughing, I pulled the shirts away. "Voila!," I said, holding up an almost full bottle of vodka.

Gavin laughed for the first time that day. "You sneaky bastard! Where'd you get that?"

"A little something left over from the cabaret. Interested?"

He laughed again and I was delighted that my surprise had pleased him. "Sure," he said, "In fact, I think that is *just* what I need."

"But we are not finished!" I smiled at him. "Once again you forget that this is a mystery walk, and even more important, you are forgetting that Ed said that we can bring along one tool that will be of the most use to us."

Gavin smiled. "And you brought?"

"Well what better tool to make things easier is there than," and here I reached into my back and pulled out a bottle of orange juice, "a screwdriver!"

"Yes!" Gavin said, moving over and flopping down next to me. It warmed me to see that he was happy. He rubbed his hands together. "You, Lennie, are the man!"

I grinned and pulled out two paper cups, put them on a flat rock and poured a healthy amount of vodka and some orange juice in both. We picked up the cups and held them out to one another.

"To the mystery walk," Gavin said, and I added, "and our inner beings." I touched his cup. "L'chaim."

We drank.

"Oh shit," Gavin said, as he took the cup from his lips. "Oh, shit, that freakin' burns."

"But," I said, after expelling some air, "it burns so good."

Gavin nodded and took another sip. "This is going to get me shit-faced," he said. "I hardly had anything to eat for lunch."

"Hey if you're hungry I...."

"No," Gavin said, pointing at the cup. This is what I need. I do not need food."

"Have it your way," I said, holding my cup up to him again. "To absent friends."

"Yeah," Gavin snickered, "like Sturtz."

I smiled weakly. "Oh, yeah. *Just* like Sturtz."

"Jesus, Len," Gavin said, "why do you take all his shit? Like his calling you a tool."

I felt suddenly very hot and I didn't think it was because of the drink. "You heard that?"

Gavin nodded. "Why do you let him get away with it?"

I shrugged. "Dunno. Easier than calling him on it I guess. I know he could kick my ass, and I have to tell you I am not in favor of getting punched." I smiled. "I have a feeling that no matter how cool it looks in the movies, someone's fist in your face hurts really bad." I paused. "That really scares me, being hit. Some people it's heights, or tight places. With me it's getting punched in the face." Gavin looked down and nodded. I could make an opening here. "You know, I've never told that to anyone before."

Again Gavin nodded as I waited to hear what he would say. "It's no big thing," he said, disappointing me. "So someone kicks your ass, so what? At least you'd have stood up for yourself." Gavin shook his head. "Sturtz knows you're not going to fight back. That's why he's always breakin' your chops. You have to confront someone like that."

I smiled. "Well, it's not exactly like he's the schoolyard bully and I can't protect myself."

"It *is* kinda like that."

I shook my head. "What was that thing Gandhi always promoted? Passive resistance."

"Yeah," Gavin said, "but with you, all I see is the passive part. You don't try to stop him at all."

"He's insignificant."

"That's bullshit. I can see the way he gets to you." He sipped from his cup. "You know he, York, Apple and I used to be really tight once upon a time, but now he's even getting to be a little too much for me." He sipped. "His wisecracks are getting a little old."

"Well," I said, "Apple's like that too. Everything you say, he's got a punch line."

Gavin shook his head. "No," he said, "you're reading Apple wrong. Apple is just a wiseass, but he's got a really good heart. I mean if he ever said something in a joke and he realized it hurt someone, he'd be destroyed. He's never put you down, has he?" I shook my head. "You see. He just loves to be the joker, that's all. Sturtz, on the other hand, can be freakin' mean."

I nodded. "You got that right." I looked into my cup. "I guess you heard about the formal party thing he pulled?"

Gavin screwed up his face. "Yeah," he said, "he told us. That was fucking low."

"It was not the best day of my life."

"I only know his version. Tell me yours."

I sighed. "What's to tell? He calls me one day last winter to tell me that he's having a really fancy party at his apartment and that you, York, Klinger, Apple and I are invited. Did I want to go? I say sure and he tells me the only problem is that it's going to be formal, his father's big shot friends from Europe are going to be there and all, so we needed a tux. 'You have a tux, don't you?' he asks me…. I guess he knew that I hadn't… and I say, 'Won't a blue suit do?'"

"Jesus, that's awful."

I nodded. "So he says, no it won't do and that I'd have to buy or rent one or else I couldn't come. Well with my father's salary buying a tux was out of the question, so I took all the money I was saving…."

"Oh, shit, man, no…."

I nodded. "I took the money out of the bank and rented a tux. He called me as I was getting dressed to tell me that it had all been a practical joke."

Gavin shook his head. "Shit, man, I'm sorry. You couldn't get your money back?"

"They wouldn't do it. Big joke, huh?"

"What a dick thing to do."

I shrugged. "I lived."

"I don't know what gets into him," Gavin said. "You weren't there when we went out to smoke some dope and he went ape shit over his stash the other night, were you?"

My blood froze. "No," I managed. "Somehow my name didn't make the guest list. I've heard bits and pieces. What happened?"

Gavin sipped his drink. "We had snuck out after taps… well, hell man, you're part of the bunk…you should have come, whether Sturtz asked you or not"

"*No one* asked me."

Gavin looked down at the ground, obviously embarrassed. "You know how things get, Len. Everyone thought the other person had asked you."

I knew he was lying to make me feel better. "I heard you go. I pretended that I was asleep."

Gavin nodded. "Anyway, we snuck out and went way in back of the archery range where nobody goes. Sturtz had bought some weed and pills from a friend of his at home. You ever meet his friend Bashir?"

I shook my head. "I've heard him mentioned. I've never met him."

"Decent guy. Met him twice when we all got together in the city."

"Guess I mislaid the invitations to those too," I said.

Gavin took a deep breath and blew out some air.

"Sorry."

I nodded.

"Anyway," Gavin said, "we're way the hell up there away from campus and all, and we build a small fire cause it's a little chilly. Sturtz has been carrying this old book with him the whole time and he opens it and he says something like, 'What the fuck?' Turns out his stash is missing."

"He kept it in a book? How is that possible?"

"It was one of those hollowed out jobs. Kinda cool, actually."

I took a deep breath. "So what happened?"

"Now I don't know why he did it, and I have replayed this over in my mind a lot since it happened, but for one reason or another, York reaches over to check out that the book is really empty. Like he knew that it once was in there, ya know? Shit, no one knew the book was hollow. Did you?" I shook my head. "I asked York later and he told me that he had no idea. Anyway, the next thing you know Sturtz goes for York, and he's screaming, 'I'll kill you for this you mother fuckin' cock suckin' bastard,' and stuff like that while he's lunging at him. And Klinger, Apple and I are grabbing Sturtz' arms and legs and trying to restrain him, and York is just sitting there staring at Sturtz as though he's a nut case, which is exactly how he was acting. And Sturtz is pulling against us screaming, 'Five hundred bills, muther -fucker. Five hundred bills the shit cost me and it's gone.' Now, okay, five hundred dollars is a lot of money, even for Sturtz and he has more money than God, enough to buy and sell any of us, but he's still screaming about that five hundred bucks. And this is where it really gets weird. All of a sudden, Sturtz pushes us off him, and we let go cause he seems like he's calmed down, you know, and he points at York, and in this real soft voice he says, 'I'll kill you for this, Stewart. Start making funeral arrangements. I'll kill you for this for sure.' And York is still just sitting there staring at him, shaking his head and saying nothing and Sturtz turns around and heads back to the bunk. A very bizarre scene, Len, very bizarre indeed."

I looked into the woods, almost afraid to move. "Jesus," I said.

Gavin stared at me. "You okay man?"

"Yeah," I said, wondering if I should share a secret that I had been keeping to myself for weeks. "Gav, I fucked up."

"What did you do?"

"If I tell you," I said, "you promise not to tell anyone? Not even York." He nodded at me and I believed him.

I took a deep breath and another pull from my cup. "Back in July when the election thing was going on?" Gavin nodded. "Sturtz was being a real pain in the ass about something. He was on my back all day and I was getting really pissed. And even if he apologized two or three times about the tux thing, I never really believed him. I guess I was still sore."

"You deserved to be." Gavin took another pull from his cup and then looked into it, turned it over, shook it, and held it out to me. "I think I need a refill, my friend."

I poured more vodka and orange juice into his cup and Gavin leaned back against a tree. "Go on."

"It was the day after the hayride. You were all playing softball and I, of course was racing around the campus trying to pull the paper together."

Gavin smiled and held his cup up to me. "To Pulitzer. And," he added, "I mean that in the best sense of the word."

"Thanks." I smiled at him. "I appreciate that. Anyway, I finished everything for the paper, and there was still about a half hour left to the period so I figured I would finish go back to my reading for the A.P. English course. I thought I'd polish off *Macbeth* then I'd only have *Hamlet* left to read."

"Makes sense." His voice was a little thick.

"Okay, so I'm back in the bunk and I can't find my copy of *Macbeth*. I look everywhere for it, but it just isn't there. Then I remember that one day I noticed Sturtz had a complete works of Shakespeare in his locker."

"Oh fuck, Len, you didn't!"

I nodded. "It seems I did. I pulled out the book, opened it and the damned thing is loaded with drugs. My first impulse was to put it back and forget I had seen it, but then I figured this is my chance to get back for the tuxedo and all the other shit things he's done to me over the last two years."

"What did you do?"

"I flushed it; all of it, every joint and every pill. I put the book back and that was that."

"Holy shit," Gavin said, "that would be hilarious except that Sturtz thinks that York was the one who did it to him."

"And now that you told me what happened, I feel terrible about that," I said.

"You have to tell Sturtz, man, or at least York."

I nodded. "I know I do. I can't let York take the blame for something I did." I paused and looked into the fire. "I'll tell York and then the two of us will go to Sturtz together."

"Sturtz is gonna go ballistic."

"What can I do? If York is with me it might not be so bad."

Gavin looked upset. "I don't know man. Maybe Milburn should be there too."

"But if we tell Milburn then he's going to have to tell Lasker that Sturtz had a stash, and that would not be too cool."

"This is fucked up, Len." Gavin took another pull at his cup. "You know what I think you should do?" I shook my head. "Keep your mouth shut."

"But what about York."

"Look, if Sturtz was going to get back at York he would have done it already. I mean it's a while ago and nothing has happened. So, yeah, I'd leave it alone." Gavin paused for a moment and then said, "You know The Luggage King?" I nodded. "He said something to me that stays in my head. 'What is, is,' he told me. So, Sturtz's stash is gone; I think you telling him the truth is going to open a whole can of worms that's gonna hurt everyone. Leave it alone."

"You really think so?" I asked relieved.

"Just say nothing and let's see how this all plays out."

"And you won't say anything either?"

"Not a word. Let sleeping dogs sleep."

"Thanks Gav," I said. "You don't know how relieved that makes me."

"Well," he said, "thank you for being honest about it and telling me. That was impressive, Leonard. Very impressive indeed." He giggled. "I am impressed."

"You hungry yet?" I asked, wanting to get the subject as far away as possible from Sturtz and his missing stash.

Gavin closed his eyes and shook his head. "No. No food. Not yet." He opened his eyes and looked at me. "You know Lennie, I am feeling better than I have felt since I don't know when." His speech was a little slurred. He held his cup up to me. "Thank you, Lennie. You are one of the good guys."

I smiled at him. "Thank *you*, Gav. That means a lot." I got up and moved to where I had dropped the twigs. "You know what I'm gonna do?" I said, bending down and gathering the wood into my hands, and Gavin shook his head. "I am going to start a fire so that when we *are* hungry we will be all ready to cook."

"Want me to help you?" Gavin asked, starting to get up, and I waved him away. "You mellow out and leave the fire to me."

Gavin flopped back down and closed his eyes, and I went about setting up the pile of sticks and twigs. I failed at the first two attempts to get a fire going and for awhile I was afraid I would use up all the matches and the few dry twigs I had found before we had a fire, but the third time was the charm, and soon I had a cheery little fire going in front of the tent.

I looked at Gavin sprawled under the tree, snoring softly, the dappled sunlight highlighting the wine stain on his face, and I felt a warmth for him that I had never known before. He was my friend, and this was good; this was very good.

Fuck Sturtz!

I worked on the INQUIRER while Gavin slept, stopping only when it got too dark for me to see what I was doing. I had also been keeping the fire lit by making a few more trips into the woods to gather what usable twigs I could find. The hamburgers were already made, and I put them on a grill and set it over the fire. I wrapped two large potatoes in aluminum foil and threw them into the embers.

Soon the smell of the cooking burgers roused Gavin out of his nap.

"Something smells good," he said, pushing his hair back from over his eyes. "Hey, Lennie, you should have gotten me up. I would have helped."

"Not much to help with," I said as I flipped the burgers. "Be ready in about five minutes."

"Damn," Gavin said, standing up and stretching, "I haven't slept so well in weeks." He grinned at me. "Still think I have a little buzz on from those screwdrivers."

"There's more where that came from," I said, holding up the vodka bottle. "Help yourself."

"Don't mind if I do," Gavin said as he poured more vodka into his cup. "What time is it anyway?"

"Well," I said, "the sun went down about ten minutes ago, so I make it about twenty after eight."

"Hey," Gavin said, "Lennie Dorff telling the time by the sun. You really are getting into this Indian outdoorsy stuff. I am impressed."

I shrugged. "Don't be too impressed. I had a little help from The New York Times." I laughed. "Sun *rises* tomorrow at 6:15."

Gavin held up his cup. "The New York Times."

"The New York Times!"

We washed our hands and our faces in the cold river water, ate the burgers and potatoes and kept drinking screwdrivers.

And we talked about everything: movies, TV shows, school, color war. At one point, Gavin, now feeling no pain, actually called me York without his realizing it. I didn't correct him.

Joey Carter felt his stomach grumble, but he ignored it. He would eat later. In the script he wrote, "Relationship between Dorff and Gavin. Important? He wasn't sure yet, but something was bothering him about it, and, he thought with a sigh, still no insight into York. Again his stomach groaned. He would order food soon. He put down his pencil, leaned back and began to read the script, with VO Dorff.

V.O. Dorff:

If anyone had asked me, I would have had to say that those hours were the best in my entire life.

At around ten o'clock I remembered the radio and found to my delight that two stations came in fairly well. One was a religious station, the other an NPR station coming in from God only knew where. It was all talk on NPR and I switched to the other station.

"For He is the redeemer, the light and the way," a man's voice said, and then an organ started playing and a tenor started singing about being in the garden.

Gavin smiled. "Only time I go to the garden is to see the Knicks." He shook his head. "You ever wonder how they can believe all that stuff?"

"You mean that the Knicks could win?"

Gavin chuckled. "Uh, oh. I feel a new Apple being born!"

I held up my hands. "Anything but that." We sipped our drinks. "When you're talking about 'they'", I said, "couldn't 'they' say the same thing about us?"

"Yeah," Gavin said considering what I had said, "but in our religion everything is pretty clear cut. It all makes sense. I mean its all written down and everything. Christians have to have all this faith that everything is true."

"But," I said, playing devil's advocate, "if you have faith, then everything makes sense to you because you believe it's true."

"But what I can't get is how you can believe in something that you can't see." He laughed. "And I also can't believe that we are out in the woods somewhere and we are talking about religion! Change the station!"

I did and after we had listened to an unwed mother discussing her take on welfare for no more than three minutes, Gavin yelled, "Change the station!" again. This time there was some quiet string music on the Christian station, and we both nodded our approval.

"You know what gets me," I said, "is not so much about belief, but about feeling left out."

"How do you mean," Gavin asked and I could see that he was having trouble keeping his eyes open.

"You know, being a Jew in a Christian world."

"It never occurred to me. I'm surprised you think about it."

"I guess it's our backgrounds," I said. "My guess is that where you and York live, most of the people in your school are Jews. Upwardly mobile, rich, successful."

Gavin considered this for a moment. "Yeah," he said, nodding. "I guess they are."

"Well, where I live, we are in the minority. We left the really poor ghetto and we haven't made it to the rich one. Kind of being in limbo between ghettos. Not really belonging." I stopped. This, I knew, was my moment. "It's awful being an outsider, being different than everyone else."

Gavin looked into his cup and nodded.

"I've lived with that my whole life," I said. "School, family..."

"Family?"

"My family has always had a pushcart mentality. They may have moved from the lower East Side, but they've taken Rivington Street with them."

"My folks took us in to the lower East Side once on a Sunday morning," Gavin said yawning. "Really different. My mother said it was exotic. Like a market place in Samara or someplace, she said."

"I rest my case. To me it's an every weekend visit to relatives that still live there or to buy stuff from the pushcarts."

"Well," Gavin said, "you're not like that."

I poked at the fire. "That's what I mean. An outsider, even in my own family."

I was getting close and I had to be careful.

"And of course, at camp I have been an outsider since day one."

"Don't put yourself down, man," Gavin said. "Everybody likes you."

I shook my head. "Gavin, everyone sees me as Howard's nephew. That's the definition of Lennie Dorff. The nephew"

"Maybe that was true at first, but when we got to know you that all changed."

"Then why wasn't I invited to the city with you guys? Why was I passed over when you snuck out to the archery range?"

Gavin shook his head, seemingly to clear it so that he could answer intelligently.

"It's not like you think," he said.

"Than how is it?"

"Okay, you *are* a little different. But it's not for the reason you say it is. Look, Kanuga is an athletic camp and, you have to admit yourself that you are not an athlete."

I smiled. "Guilty."

"No," Gavin said, "*not* guilty. There's nothing wrong with not being an athlete. You're a good guy in so many other ways."

"Name one."

Gavin's face clouded over. "Oh shit man, come on. I can't give you examples, for Crissake. You're a good guy and I like you. Leave it at that."

But I couldn't. I was too close.

"It's easy for you to say all that, Gavin, because you have never known the pain of being an outsider."

Gavin stared at me for a minute. "Len," he said. "Ed told me that a few days ago he sent you down to the guest dock looking for me."

I nodded and didn't say anything.

"I was there but I didn't see you," he said.

"I didn't see you either," I lied. "Must have just missed you." I could see a look of relief spread over Gavin's face. Maybe this was the time, and maybe it would be Gavin who told me what I already knew. "Gav," I said, "Ed seemed really upset. What was going on?"

Gavin looked at me for a minute and I think I actually held my breath. Finally, he just took a deep breath and gave me a half smile. It was a messed up day,"he said, "no biggie." He stretched. "You know, I'd like to sit here and talk some more, I really would," he said, "but I'm really wiped. I gotta get some sleep." He drained the last of his drink from the cup, got up and pulled his tee shirt over his head. "'But it was good talking with you, Lennie. You're a good guy." He stepped out of his shorts and stood in front of me in his jockey's. "Night,"he said and made his his way into the tent.

I turned off the radio, made sure there was no way the fire could spread, kicked off my shoes and opened the flap of the tent. He had come so close to telling me. I could feel it. I had to make him know I knew. The right time might never come again.

Gavin was sprawled on top of his sleeping bag, on his back, his arm thrown over his eyes, dressed only in his white jockeys.

"No sleeping bag?" I asked.

"Too hot," he mumbled. I nodded. "You're right."

I dropped the flap of the tent and flopped down on top of my sleeping bag. It was dark in the small enclosure, and though I could barely see Gavin though he was only a foot or so away from me, his steady breathing seemed to be as close to me as my own.

"Gav," I said.

"Mmmm?"

"Thanks for saying...well, what you said."

"'Ssokay."

I hesitated for a moment and then reached out and found Gavin's hand and squeezed it, an act I had seen Apple and York do every night after taps. I couldn't breathe for what seemed to be forever, and then I felt Gavin squeeze my hand back. I felt a feeling in my heart, an expansion: a filling that I never had known existed.

As Gavin took his hand away, I put my hand gently on his cheek so that it covered his birthmark.

I could feel Gavin tense. "What's going on?" he said.

My voice was hoarse. "I just want to feel close to you, Gav. That's all."

"We are close, Len," Gavin said, rolling over so that his back was to me. My hand fell on his bare shoulder and I let it stay there. "Lennie, I want to sleep." Still my hand remained. Gavin swung around knocking my hand from his shoulder as he did. "Quit it, will ya, Lennie," he said. "Quit messing around. Just let me get some rest."

I took a deep breath. "Would it be okay if I put my arm around you, just till you fall sleep. I'd really like that."

"No," he said quickly. "I don't think that would be a good idea. It's too hot, you know."

And then the words!

"It's okay, Gavin," I said softly. "I know. I know and I don't care."

The silence was as thick and as dense as the darkness, and when Gavin finally spoke I could see that he was trying to make sense of what I had said though he was still cloudy from drinking.

"What did you say?" he whispered, and from the tone of his voice, I knew I had gone too far.

"Nothing," I said, taking my hand away from where he lay. "Nothing. You're right. It's late. Let's get some sleep."

I could hear Gavin sit up. "I asked you what you said. Tell me Lennie. Tell me what you meant."

"I told you that it's nothing, just something stupid. Let it go, Gav."

"Let what go? There has to be something to let go of to let go of something. *What* do you know, Lennie? Tell me."

I sat up and put all my weight on my elbow.

"I know...I know that, well, that......."

"Say it," he hissed, and in the darkness I could feel his eyes, only a few inches from mine, glaring at me.

"I know...well...I know that you've been with guys, Gav."

He jumped up, pulled the tent flap open and stormed out. I was right behind him.

"Gav," I said, "please."

He was standing next to the embers of all that was left of the fire.

"You know?" he whispered. "You *know*?" I nodded dumbly, watching as the beautiful evening fell to bits in front of me. "How do you know, Len? Huh? Tell me, how do you know?"

In that moment I knew I had to lie if there was any chance of saving my friendship with Gavin. If he knew I had listened at Athenaeum he would never forgive me. There had to be a way that would put the blame on someone else and let me remain his friend.

My mouth was dry. "Nicki told me," I said, and as the words came out, I saw Gavin Stewart crumble in front of me.

"Nicki?" he said almost to himself. "I don't believe you." He looked at me and I nodded. "She told me Gav, but it doesn't mean..."

"Why?" He looked at me and I could see that he was shaking. "What else did she tell you Lennie?"

I shook my head. "Nothing. Nothing else. I swear."

"But why would she tell you? Why *you*?" Gavin's "you," was filled with such disdain and repugnance that I had to look away. "Tell me Lennie," he said again. "Why did she tell *you*?"

I could feel myself mumbling something about her not meaning to, about her mistakenly saying it and immediately wanting to take it back.

"But she *said* it," he said slowly, wanting somehow to pin it down. "No matter what the reason, Nicki *said* it. She told you."

I nodded, and as his mouth moved as though trying to find words, Gavin Stewart's whole body sagged as he started to cry.

And as he cried I stood, unable to move, wondering how everything had turned out so wrong. I hadn't wanted to bring him pain. On the contrary, I wanted to let him know that I was there for him, that I was his friend, two outsiders against the world. Like blood brothers.

I began to babble, hoping that one of my words might make things right. "But she only told *me*. She didn't tell anyone else. I mean I know she didn't tell York, or anything. She wouldn't do something like that. She even made me promise that *I* wouldn't tell anyone. And I didn't Gavin, I didn't. You have my sacred word, I would never tell another living soul."

Gavin turned away from me, his body shaking, and finally, when I was able to move, all I wanted to do was to make all this right, to let Gavin see that I loved him as a friend, and that I understood. I went to him, put my hands on his arms and turned him to me. I pulled him to me and held him, and for a moment he cried with his face on my chest and then, with a terrible sound, he pushed me away from him.

"And you knew," he blubbered, bubbles of saliva coming from his lips. "You knew and you thought since I was gay, and you're gay that I'd want to sleep with *you*?"

I was stunned. "What are you talking about? I'm not gay," I managed, and Gavin screamed, "The hell you're not. You were all over me in the tent you sick faggot, you mother fucking faggot bastard cunt."

This was not happening. "No," I said, "no. It's not like that at all. I just wanted you to be my friend."

"I *was* your friend, you sick fuck. I *was* your friend and you killed it. You killed it, Lennie. YOU FUCKING KILLED IT."

I moved to hold him again, and he cocked a fist at me. "You come near me again and you are fucking dead. Do you hear me, Lennie, you are fucking dead."

My legs were weak and I could feel bile rise in my throat. "No, Gav, it wasn't supposed to be like this. I just wanted....."

"You just wanted what? Huh? What? To fuck me; to fuck the faggot, to fuck the fairy? Huh? Okay, that's what you want, I'll give you what you want." And he pulled off his shorts and kicked them away, and stood nude before me in the moonlight. "Okay, motherfucker, here I am. Come and fuck me. Take out your limp faggot dick and fuck me! That's all I'm good for, right? SO FUCK ME!"

His voice dissolved into more sobs as I stood in front of trying to find something to say that would make him understand.

"I don't want that, Gavin, I never wanted that." I picked up his shorts and held them out to him. He took them and threw them at me.

"Sure you do," he said as he cried, "that's all I'm fucking good for, didn't you know? All I am is a fucking fag. You fuck fags and then you move on, isn't that how it goes? Huh?"

"Gavin, I........"

"Just leave me alone, okay? Just get away from me and leave me alone."

"Look," I said, "why don't you go back into the tent and get some rest. I'll sleep out here, and I swear that I'll just sleep. Okay? Things will seem different in the morning."

He looked at me as though I were mad. "Go back in there and go to sleep? What are you fucking crazy? And you think things will be better in the morning? What planet are you from anyway? Things will NOT be better in the morning, or the morning after that, or any morning ever again? It's broken, Lennie and it can't be fixed."

And for the first time I felt panic. "What do you mean? What's broken?" I asked, not really wanting to hear his answer.

"What's broken? What's *not* broken? Do you think that I will ever be able to hang with you after tonight? No way? I wish I never had to even see you anymore, Lennie, you know?"

"Gavin," I said and I could hear the pleading in my voice, "you're making too much out of this. I mean what happened? Nothing happened. So I know. So what? No one else knows."

"Fucking Nicki knows and she told you."

"No, Gav, there's more to that than....."

Gavin's crying had stopped and his speech was even and measured. And it frightened me. "It may be broken," he said, "but I can do something to clear the air once and for all."

"What? What are you going to do?"

"What I am going to do, Lennie, is to tell my brother. Shit, it seems that everyone else knows, so why not him? And after I tell him, then I guess I'll see Nicki and tell her what I think about her, and then I will wait out the God damned summer and pray for the day that I can get away from all of you."

"You're being irrational," I said. "It's the vodka. You *will* feel different about all this in the morning, I promise you."

"*You* promise *me*? You know what I promise *you*, Lennie? I promise you that when everyone knows about me, they're gonna know about you too. Huh? Got that, fucker? That's my promise to you. They're all going to know that you wanted my ass tonight, starting with York." He turned and started to the river, stopped, turned and pointed at me. "And you can put that on the front page of your fucking paper for all I care!"

With that, he turned and disappeared into the darkness.

I stood staring after him for a minute, not able to move, and then the bile rose in my throat and all the drinks and the food we had eaten could no longer be kept down. I gagged, and in a rush, the hot remnants of the evening came poring out. Shivers ran through me as I vomited again and again, until there was nothing left to lose. I finally lay back on the ground next to where the fire had been and closed my eyes. My head pounded and chills still ran through my body.

What had I done! My God, it wasn't supposed to have been like this. Why had I pushed it? Why hadn't I been able to settle for the little bit Gavin had given me? What the hell was wrong with me?

But would Gavin really tell York about me? Jesus, what was there to tell? That I wanted to hold him, to be close to him? What harm was there in that? Where the hell was my crime?

But if Gavin *did* tell York, and York misinterpreted it the way Gavin had, then everything was over. Everything. It would spread around camp. Howard would hear about it and he would tell my parents. My God, what was happening? What the hell was happening?" I held myself as I shuddered and rocked back and forth.

"Maybe I should go after him," I thought, "but he could be anywhere out there. Probably better to wait for the morning. He had no other way of getting back to town without the canoe, so he had to come back." I would talk to him then, or at least try.

But what if he didn't listen? What if he didn't calm down by morning? Or worse, what if he seemed to have cooled down to throw me off track, and then went to tell York? There was no way I could take that chance. There must be something I could do that would make York see that everything Gavin would tell him was wrong, misinterpreted.

I sat, leaning up against a tree and tried to think, but all I could see was Gavin's face when I told him that I knew; his surprise, his betrayal. And then I sat up.

All at once, I knew what I had to do.

Midnight:

York Stewart looked at his friend snoring in the sleeping bag next to him.

"Apple."

The snoring continued.

"Apple." He waited. "APPLE!"

"Huh," Apple said, opening his eyes. "What?"

"You're snoring."

"Huh? Oh, sorry man." He snuggled into his sleeping bag and sighed. "'Night."

York smiled and closed his eyes. "'Night."

Klinger had finished washing the dishes and joined Sturtz in the clearing near the fire he had made earlier. He held his hand out and Sturtz handed him the joint. He took a deep drag and handed it back.

The two boys said little as they passed that joint and the next and the next, back and forth between them.

"Good shit," Klinger said.

Sturtz nodded. "Good shit."

Gavin Stewart huddled naked in a copse of trees only a few feet from where Lennie Dorff sat, his mind exploding. Though the night was warm, he shivered as he waited for the morning, trying to understand what had happened and what, if anything, he could do to fix it.

Maybe he had overreacted, maybe not. Either way, Dorff knew that he was gay, and, worse yet, Nicki had told him. My God, Nicki! Nicki had done what she had sworn not to do, but why? Why?

And as he tried to focus, one thing was clear. He had to tell York. Now, to not tell him was no longer an option. His body shook. The thought terrified him but it had to be done. And Dorff. Though in the heat of the moment he knew he had said he would tell everyone about Dorff's coming on to him, he knew that he wouldn't, that he couldn't. This was between York and him and Dorff was inconsequential.

"Oh God, oh God, oh God, oh God, oh God," he chanted to himself as he rocked back and forth. "Please help me."

His eyes wide, his mind whirling, Gavin Stewart sat naked all through the night waiting for an answer that didn't come.

Head Counselor Ed Lasker put his book down, got out of bed and walked barefoot onto his porch. He looked over the campus for one last time that day. All was quiet. He looked into the sky and saw a few clouds over the moon.

"The radio says it's going to rain tomorrow afternoon," he thought. "How lucky the seniors are that they had such a beautiful night."

He went back into the bunk, turned out the light, and went to sleep.

CHAPTER TWENTY- ONE:

Hollywood:
March
Present Day

Joey Carter put down the script and picked up his cell phone. He knew what he would have to do.

He speed dialed Big Boss at his office in New York and heard Ms. Capuzzo's cool, business like voice. "TRANSWORLD PICTURES. Henry Sturtz's line."

"Miss Capuzzo. Joey Carter."

Immediately her voice warmed, as he knew it would.

"Joey! How are you? More to the fact, where are you?"

Joey smiled. "Poolside at the Beverly Hills Hotel, and there is a starlet here who looks so much like you that she could be your double."

Miss Capuzzo chuckled. "Looks like me, huh? What is she, a hundred and ten?"

They both laughed.

"And why are you calling through on this line? Why didn't you call his private number?" Capuzzo asked.

"I didn't want to disturb him in case there was something important going on."

Capuzzo snorted. "With him there's *always* something important going on. And speaking of important," Miss Capuzzo said, "who's more important than you?"

"In the grand scheme of all things, one has to wonder."

"Wonder about other things," Miss Capuzzo said gravely, "but never worry about where you come on his priority list."

Joey smiled. "That's very kind of you. I appreciate it. And speaking of the Big Boss, is he there?" Joey smiled up at the waiter who had brought him his iced tea, signed the bill and shook his head when the young man asked if he wanted anything else.

"Your timing is perfect," Capuzzo said. "He just finished a meeting and is almost out the door to a cocktail thing as soon as he gets off a call from London. How's the weather out there?"

"Warm. Not hot. Tannable."

"Of course. Isn't that why God created Hollywood in the first place? Hold on a second, he's done with the call. I'll connect you to the Big Boss." And then. "We miss you Joey. Get back here soon."

"I miss you too....," he started but realized she was no longer there.

"My favorite client!" Henry Sturtz's voice boomed over the phone, so loud that Joey had to hold the earpiece away from his ear. "Where the hell have you been? I must have left you a hundred voice messages."

"Beverly Hills Hotel," Joey said and Henry Sturtz snorted. "Schmendrick. Why didn't you tell me? I would have gotten you a deal."

Joey smiled. "That's exactly why I didn't tell you." He paused. "I'm halfway through the script."

"All this time and only halfway?"

"I'm going slow. Re-reading, making notes."

Joey heard Henry Sturtz clear his throat. "And?"

"It's amazing."

Henry Strurtz's sigh was audible.

"I love the characters."

"I'm so happy, I'm hard."

Joey Carter smiled and shook his head. "You're all class, Sturtz," he said.

Henry Sturtz laughed. "I invented class."

"I'm glad you're laughing cause you're not going to be crazy about what I'm going to say next."

"Here it comes." Sturtz sighed. "What?"

"I still don't know all there is to know about York, so I....."

"Jesus Christ!" Sturtz yelled. "What the hell is there to know? You play the part, you win an Oscar and you go home. Finished."

"Not finished," Joey said, shaking his head. "Not finished by a long shot. But I do know what I have to do."

There was a slight pause. "And that is?"

"I'm going to finish reading the script and then I have to meet Gavin," Joey said. "The key to understanding York lies with him."

There was another pause on the other end of the line, and from long experience Joey Carter knew that this pause was an important one. In a matter of seconds Henry Sturtz would have weighed every option from every angle and made a final decision; it was what he did, why he was one of the most important and successful people in the entertainment industry.

"You're an asshole, but okay," he said at last, and Joey exhaled.

"Do you know where I can find him?"

"I'm not sure," Henry Sturtz said, "but I can find out in a matter of minutes. The last I heard he was on Fire Island."

"In the winter?"

"Used to be. All year round, maybe he still is. I'll check and see and call you back, if you promise to answer your fucking phone."

Joey laughed. "You have my word."

Henry Sturtz's voice was measured. "You're sure you want to do this?"

Joey nodded even though Sturtz could not see him. "Want to and have to."

"And then you'll do the picture? Either way?"

"And then I'll do the picture. Either way."

Joey heard Henry Sturtz sigh. "You're a pain in the ass, you know that."

Joey smiled. "It runs in the family."

"I'll call you in a few," Henry Sturtz said. "And if you're shtupping everything that moves out there, use a fucking condom for Chrisssakes. Yes?

"I'm not, but I will."

"I want you to play safe. You're a pain in the ass...."

"You already said that."

".....but I love you."

Joey Carter nodded. "I love you too, Dad, and thanks."

Both lines clicked off at the same time.

CHAPTER TWENTY-TWO:

JUST NATURE (August 11, 1975)

One of the most important awards that Camp Kanuga gave out every year was the 'Major K," a chenille letter given to boys from every group who were not only excellent athletes but well rounded in every way. So besides sports, at some point in the summer, every camper who wanted a "K" had to find his way to the shop, archery range and nature shack to do an assigned project. Though some of the Juniors and Inters let their letters go by the boards, in the Upper Senior group, without a 'Major K,' there was no way a boy could be chosen all around camper for the year. Since the 'K' was the highest accolade to be won at Kanuga, every senior's path sooner or later lead to what was known on campus as 'the minor 3.'

And so, at the beginning of August, after putting off their Nature projects for a month, the Upper Seniors began to drift in to Herbie, the Nature counselor's, world. All elbows and raucous laughter, deriding the very essence of anything that had other than to do with athletics, they upset the shack and the safety of Herbie's day. As the upper camp grudgingly came through his door, his usually calm world of lambs and chicks became filled with wall -to -wall testosterone filled, uncontrollable teen-agers.

The Nature Shack had been one of the original structures at the camp and though the rest of the bunks had been rebuilt twice since Kanuga's inception, the Shack always stayed the same. Even a fresh coat of paint every few years could not hide the shabbiness of the building. Hidden in the woods far behind the senior bunks, a short walk from the infirmary that was nearer the main campus, it was the poor relation to the camp, acknowledged, but seldom visited. There was a chicken coop in the back of the building that housed three white chickens, and a pen that held a rather stunted looking lamb and two rabbits.

Herbie looked at his watch. Free play still had forty minutes to go, but if no one had come in by now, he was probably safe to start cleaning up. A wave of relief swept over him as it did at this time every day. He had just fed the animals in the back and had come back into the shack to feed the snakes, when the door to the shack creaked open and two of the older boys came into the room.

"We're here for our Nature project," one of them said, and Herbie's heart sank. Trapped, with forty minutes to go.

He knew these boys by sight and reputation. One, the blonde boy was a twin considered, he knew, to be the most popular boy in camp. The other, Howard's nephew, seemed like someone who might come to the Nature Shack, though, strangely, he never had.

"I'll be with you in just a moment, boys," Herbie said, hoping he wouldn't stutter, as he sometimes did when he was nervous. "You came just when it's feeding time at the zoo." He looked at them for a response, but both remained impassive. He reached into a gray paper carton and pulled out a tiny white mouse. He stroked its head for a moment and then walked over to a large glass tank, took the mesh cover off the top, and placed the mouse in with a large black snake.

"He never eats right away." Herbie said, his back to the boys, "He watches them for awhile and then makes his move."

Herbie turned and noticed that Howard's nephew was looking at his collection of mounted butterflies.

"They're beautiful aren't they?"

Lennie Dorff nodded.

"Would you like your nature project to be mounting butterflies?"

York looked at Dorff and they both shrugged.

"Sure," York said. "That sounds fine."

"Excellent," Herbie said, with a weak smile. "Let me go in the back and get a few. Butterflies, that is. I have them in the back."

York smiled at Dorff as the little man walked away. "There's your next headline Lennie. 'Secret Stash of Butterflies Uncovered!'"

Lennie shook his head. "Actually I kind of like, 'Exclusive: Forgetting Sex with Girls, Seniors Mount Butterflies!'"

The two boys laughed, and Herbie, hearing them as he unscrewed a large butterfly filled jar, was sure they were laughing at him. He closed his eyes, took a deep breath, and reached into the jar with a small net.

York walked over to one of the glass tanks where the large black snake lay watching the panicked tiny white mouse that was trying to find someplace to hide. He looked at the creature's frantic clawing, his tiny pink feet scrabbling at the glass and turned away shaking his head. "Jesus," he said.

Dorff shrugged. "Just nature. Survival of the fittest."

"Maybe," York said, "but there's something wrong about watching it. Death should be a private thing." He laughed. "Whoa! Did I just say that? When did I get philosophical?"

Dorff smiled. "If he didn't eat the mouse, the snake would eventually die. Would you choose the mouse or the snake? And after all, it's only a mouse."

York frowned. "I'm not God. I would hate to have to make that choice."

Lennie nodded. "True," he said, "but someone has to make decisions, good or bad, and after all, as I said, it is only a mouse."

York shrugged. "Still."

Dorff looked at the butterflies lined up behind the glass in the case. "You just can't turn your back on something when it happens to be unpleasant, no matter how hard you want to. Choices have to be made."

"So" York said, "you would be willing to play God?"

Dorff smiled. "I'm only saying that we have to face facts no matter what they are."

York was about to answer when Herbie came back into the main room holding a small net in his hands.

"Here they are," Herbie said. "Two monarchs. Beautiful aren't they?"

The deep orange butterflies were almost identical in size and shape and they thrashed against the mesh pressing in on them.

A noise in back of York made him turn. In the aquarium, the black snake's mouth was filled with the back half of the mouse. As York looked at the mouse's eyes he felt a weakness in his legs. He stood quietly, transfixed, unable to turn away as the snake slowly pulled the mouse in. The mouse didn't make a sound, but its little red eyes were filled with terror. York turned away, his hand steadying him on a table.

"I don't know if you will be able to finish this project this free play, gentlemen," Herbie said, and Dorff stifled a groan. "But we certainly can get a great deal done so that maybe all you will have to do is just come in for a few minutes another night. Does that sound all right to you?"

"To be honest, we were sort of hoping that we could finish up tonight," Dorff said. "You have to understand that there are so many other things that we have to get done before color war."

Herbie gulped. "Of course. Of course," he said. "I tell you what. You get enough done tonight and I'll call the project done. How does that sound?"

Dorff was delighted, but before he could say anything, York broke in. "That's okay. We'll see the project through to the end." Dorff frowned but said nothing.

"Well," Herbie said, disappointed that the boys did not accept his offer, which would have meant one less time of interaction, "here goes." He pulled a wad of cotton from a package. "First be sure that the cotton is saturated with this tincture of ether." Herbie held the wad of cotton to the opening of a large tin can, made sure that it was wet, and then dropped it into a Pyrex jar. "Then," he said, cupping one of the struggling butterflies between his hands, "carefully place the butterfly in the jar with the cotton and close the lid. There."

The butterfly threw itself at the side of the jar; it's wings flapping wildly. Slowly the motion of the wings stopped and the beautiful golden thing that had been a butterfly, lay still on the bottom of the jar.

"Let's wait a few minutes to make sure he's dead," Herbie said. "That will give us a few minutes to get out our mounting pins."

York Stewart thought he might be ill. The smell of the ether was making his dinner churn in his stomach. He closed his eyes and amid the blackness and flashing chains of light he saw the half eaten mouse staring at him.

"I need a little air," he mumbled, and started for the door. On the table the remaining butterfly struggled in the folds of the net. Impulsively, York picked up the net and, as he opened the door, he shook the Monarch into the evening air. He watched as it almost fell and then soared into the darkening sky. Herbie Coles and Lennie Dorff, their mouths open, stared after him.

Finally Dorff spoke. "We'll be back." He pointed at the open door. "He hasn't been feeling well. I'll get you another butterfly. Don't hold this against him. He needs the 'K.'"

"No," Herbie said quietly, "I understand. No problem. I hope he feels better."

Dorff nodded and followed his friend into the woods surrounding the nature shack.

Herbie Coles stood at the open door for a moment watching the retreating boys, and then shook his head, sighed, and with a great sense of relief, hung the CLOSED sign on the door.

"Hey," Dorff yelled. "Wait up."

York stopped, turned and waited for his friend to reach him. From where he stood he could see the porch of the infirmary, with it's rocking chairs sitting empty, waiting for the next day's quota of boys with headaches, bee stings or stomach aches to fill them during inspection. He hated the infirmary. He had been kept there for three nights with a virus when he was thirteen and had never forgotten the hushed silence at night, the sound of the clicking of the nurse's shoes as they went from room to room, and the antiseptic smell that pervaded everything.

During that stay, York had shared a room with a boy called Jamie Cohen who was getting over a bad sore throat. The first day they were both too ill to speak, but over the next two days they swapped comics, talked about batting averages and devised the best possible football teams. Jamie was a few years younger than York, and it was obvious to York that that the younger boy was thrilled to be in the same room with him.

After they were released, Jamie became York's shadow. If York was playing baseball, Jamie was at the game cheering him on. At swim period the younger boy would hold on to a ladder and wave. At line up the two boys would trade light punches as they passed each other. At rest hour, Jamie was in their bunk, massaging York's back while listening to the boys talk about girls and lying about 'doing it.' It was clear to all that Jamie Cohen had found an idol in York Stewart. Apple made jokes, Gavin tolerated him and Sturtz called him a pest, but York liked him and began calling him 'Little Bro,' whenever he would see him, to which Jamie would respond with a smile and a big, "Hey, Big Bro." And York would always go out of his way to say hello to the young boy who adored him.

During color war that year they were on the same side and if he wasn't playing in a game, York would make a point of going to wherever Jamie was playing and cheer him on.

On the last day of color war Jamie disappeared. York asked Ed Lasker where he was and the head counselor told him that the young boy was back in the infirmary. Though he wanted to go up to see him, cleanup was already over and it was only a few minutes before a decisive baseball game was about to start. With glove in hand, York went to play, determined to see his young friend later in the morning. York's team won and as the other boys went off to swim, a sweaty and happy York made his way to the infirmary.

The porch was empty and as he went through the squeaky screen door, he passed the Luggage King who was coming out. They nodded to each other and York proceeded into the room where the Band-Aids and kaopectate were dispensed, and temperatures were taken. The nurse on duty that day was Emma Weiss, an old, gray haired woman who, according to camp lore, had been there since the camp began, seemingly, some said, forever. She was brusque but kind, and York liked her, though he didn't know her all that well. He asked her where Jamie was and was told that the young boy had just been taken by ambulance to the hospital in town. That he was very sick.

A few days later the news was all over camp. Jamie Cohen had died. Though it had been kept a secret and none of the campers and only one or two of the counselors had known it, he had been very sick when he arrived at camp that summer. Leukemia, rumor had it. He had known how ill he was and had wanted to spend what would probably be his last summer at Kanuga with all his friends.

York was devastated. For the remainder of the summer he would wander off without telling even Gavin where he was going, and sit and think of Jamie Cohen and wonder where he was, and if he had known that he was coming to see him after the ball game.

And though York had felt ill from time to time after that, he had never gone back to the infirmary. He promised himself that no matter what he would never go back there again. Now he watched as the camp doctor came through the screen door onto the porch, called goodnight to the nurses still inside and walked off toward his cabin.

As Dorff came up to him, York watched a large hawk circle over the field beyond the trees, and then disappear from sight. "He's got something," he thought and hoped that it wasn't the monarch.

"What happened back there?," Dorff asked as he walked up to York.

York shook his head. "I don't know. Claustrophobia. That smell of the ether. Felt a little wobbly. No biggie. But," he added with a sigh, "so much for my Major K."

"No," Dorff said. "You're okay. I kinda cleared it with Herbie."

"Thanks, Lennie. I appreciate that." Lennie nodded and York chuckled. "What?," Lennie said.

"Trust *you*!"

"Trust me what?"

"Trust you to know the nature guy's name."

Lennie smiled. "That's my job. That's why they call me Pulitzer."

"Pulitzer, yes, and you are a prize! You really are!"

Lennie smiled. "I'll take that as a compliment."

York punched him lightly on the shoulder. "That's the way it was meant." He took a deep breath. "Come on," he said. "Let's get back to campus." He turned and started down the overgrown path to his bunk.

Leonard Dorff didn't move. "York," he said and his friend turned. "I need to talk to you. Give me a minute?"

"We can talk in the bunk," York said. "I have to oil my glove. We still have about half an hour left to free play. I'll have just enough time."

Dorff shook his head. "What I need to talk to you about is private," he said. "Give me a minute here."

York shrugged. "Sure," he said. "I can oil the glove anytime. Next game isn't until day after tomorrow anyway. What's up?"

"Let's sit down over there," Dorff said pointing to the remains of an old wooden merry go round that had once stood in front of a long since demolished 'Little Ones" cabin. Only half of the merry go round still remained. Once propelled by the feet of little children, the ground around it had been so worn away through the years that grass no longer grew there, and only a few hearty weeds had taken root. York sat down on the shaky boards that remained and stretched his long body out in front of him. He was feeling better, the nausea he had felt, finally gone. "You know," he said, "all I needed was some fresh air. I'm back to normal. And really, thanks a lot for the Herbie thing. I owe you."

Dorff laughed. "*You* owe *me*! Now that is funny. Jesus, York all the things that you've done for me over the past few years, and you think you owe *me*! I will owe *you* until I die, and just from what you've done for me already."

"*Congratulations, Mr. President.*"

York smiled. "Lennie," he said, "I didn't do all that much."

Dorff shook his head. "You did, from day one...everything...just being my friend and all. I want you to know that I appreciate it."

York held up his hands. "Okay," he said, "I give. I appreciate that you appreciate all that I have done for you, though I don't think I........"

"You were kind to me." Lennie Dorff's voice started to crack. "You were a friend."

"*Were* a friend? Hey Len, I'm still your friend. Where is this going?"

Dorff took a deep breath. "I just want to make sure that you know that I am telling you what I'm going to tell you out of friendship, and only that. Otherwise I would never mention it."

"Mention what? Come on man, spill! What's up?

Lennie sat down on the merry go round next to York. His mind whirled. He had planned this all day, but now he did not know if he could go through with it.

Leonard Dorff realized that in one minute everything would change, and he was afraid.

Obviously Gavin hadn't said anything about the canoe trip or York wouldn't be acting as friendly as he was. But what if Gavin was waiting for the right moment? What if he were to tell him tonight, or tomorrow? He had to go on the offensive. He took a deep breath. "It's about Gavin."

"What about Gavin? He looked at Dorff's grave, pinched face. "Is he in some kind of trouble?"

Dorff looked at the weeds that grew on the ground around the merry go round. "It's about the canoe trip."

"What about the canoe trip?"

"Oh shit," Lennie said standing up and walking a few paces from where York still stood. "You're going to be mad at me, I know it. It's gonna be one of those kill the messenger kind of things. You're not going to be my friend anymore."

York pulled his body in so that his feet were under the rim of the merry go round. "Lennie, what the hell is going on here? Of course I'll be your friend. I *am* your friend. I'll always be your friend. You're my bud. So just tell me what the hell this is all about."

And again, for one last moment Leonard Dorff had a chance to stop.

And he didn't.

"You know that Gavin and I were partners in the survival thing?" York nodded. "Well it happened after we had eaten. When we were getting ready to go to sleep."

"What? What happened?"

Dorff paused and as he did York knew whatever Dorff was going to say, it wasn't going to be good.

"He came on to me."

"Excuse me, what?"

"Gavin. He came on to me. I was getting into my sleeping bag, and well, he was all over me."

York laughed. "Lennie, please! You've got this all mixed up. You know Gavin. He'll start wrestling out of nowhere. He's been doing that since he was a kid. That's all that was going on. That's all he was doing."

"York!"

"He was fooling around!" York shook his head. "Jesus, Lennie, where's all this coming from? You should know better than to think that Gavin would..."

"He grabbed my dick, York."

A note of exasperation crept into York's voice. "Lennie, you're not listening to me. He was just messing with you; that's all. He and Apple do that to each other all the time. Grab ass. Grab dick. Pinch nipples. That's their idea of a big laugh. It means nothing." York got up. "I'm going back to the bunk. Jesus, Lennie, where the hell did you come up with this shit?"

Dorff's voice shook. "You *are* mad. I knew you would be."

"I'm not mad. I just don't see how after all this time you could possibly think that Gavin could be gay, for Crissake." He started down the path.

Dorff closed his eyes for a moment and then opened them. "He said he wanted to suck my dick."

York stopped and stood very still.

"He said he wanted to sleep with me, to hold me while we slept. He said there was room enough for both of us in his sleeping bag. I'm sorry York. Really. But after everything you've done for me I felt I had to tell you."

York still said nothing.

Dorff went on. "I mean I would never say anything, except to you of course, and only to you because I'm worrying about what might happen if he came on to someone else." Dorff paused and then went on. "I know I took a chance in telling you, but as a friend I felt I had to. I mean what if it gets around camp? What then? What do they say, forearmed is forewarned. I just felt you had to know."

York shook his head, still looking away from Dorff. "It had to be something else. I'll talk to Gav about it. It's probably a mistake."

"He's going to deny it, York. But ask him. Do ask him. All I can tell you is what happened. I mean, shit, why would I lie?"

"Lennie," York said, slowly. "I appreciate what you are trying to do. And I know how hard it was for you to tell me."

"You're mad at me aren't you York? I knew it. I knew I shouldn't have told you."

"No," York said, "no. You were right to tell me. You had to tell me. It's just a lot to take in, you know?"

"You know I still think Gav is great York. What happened on the canoe trip doesn't change anything at all. He's still my friend. I'm just concerned about where this could lead for him and for you if he tries it again."

"I still think he would have told me if..."

"He probably wants to, York, but he's scared to. He doesn't know how you'll take it." Dorff paused and then, with a deep breath, went on. "But he did tell me that he told Nicki."

York turned and stared at Dorff. "He told you what?"

"That he told Nicki he was gay. Maybe he thought she would tell you. Soften the blow and all."

"He told Nicki," York said, almost to himself, "why would he tell Nicki and not me?"

"Like I said, maybe it was to soften....."

The anger in York's voice stopped Dorff in mid sentence. "I'm his brother. We have no secrets from each other."

And at that moment, Leonard Dorff knew that he was safe. York believed him. He looked at his friend. "Is there anything I can do?" he asked, feeling a mixture of relief and sadness. "Name it and it's done."

York looked at Dorff for a moment then tried what could pass for a smile. "There's nothing Lennie. Except." Lennie raised an eyebrow. "I would really appreciate it if this stayed just between us. You haven't told anyone else have you?"

Lennie sounded indignant. "Of course not. This is nobody's business but yours, Gavin's and mine."

"That's great, Len. I appreciate it." York looked squarely at Dorff. "And don't tell Gavin we talked about this okay? I'd kinda like to talk to him about it alone, when the time is right."

"No problem. No problem at all." He paused. "But...."

"But what?"

"I'm just afraid that if Gavin feels cornered he's going to want to lash out at the person who told you."

"I won't ell him it was you, Lennie."

"I don't want him to get so mad that he starts accusing me of things to get you off what I told you."

"That won't happen. Trust me."

Dorff bit his lower lip. "York, I feel so shitty about all this. I mean after all you've done for me over the last few years. If there is anyone I wouldn't want to hurt, you know it's you. I mean, the presidency and all."

"It took a lot for you to tell me. If the positions were reversed I'm not sure I could have." York put out his hand. It was cold to Dorff's touch. "You're a good friend."

"You're my best friend, York." He took a few steps through the brush and stopped when he realized that York was not beside him. "York?"

"You know," York said, sitting back down on the merry go round, "I think I'd kinda like to be alone for a few minutes. You mind?"

Lennie shook his head. "Of course not. As long as I know that we're still friends."

"Of course we're still friends. Thanks for giving me the head's up, Len."

As Lennie Dorff started away from his friend, a small smile formed on his lips. "I didn't want to hurt him like this," he thought, "but there was nothing else I could do." And for the first time, Lennie Dorff felt that he had won the presidency on his own.

York sat and watched Lennie disappear behind the bunks. He leaned back against the broken railing and closed his eyes.

Two red eyes stared out at him, and in the breeze he heard the scrabbling of tiny feet on glass.

CHAPTER TWENTY-THREE:

G-H-O-S-T

He hadn't been able to sleep.

The standing joke had always been that he fell asleep faster than anyone else in the bunk, but now for the first time that he could remember, sleep simply would not come. Taps had blown at ten and after Gavin and Dorff had fallen off, he had lain quietly with his eyes closed as Sturtz, Apple and Klinger argued quietly about whether Maris or Mantle would be remembered longest. When their voices finally droned off and were replaced by soft and steady breathing, York was still awake, his mind ablaze with hundreds of images, sounds and ideas all of them having to do with Gavin. He knew he had to deal with what Dorff had told him, but not now, not now.

But he couldn't sleep! He thought about taking out his flashlight and finishing THE GREAT GATSBY, but decided against it. Though everyone had told him how great it was he couldn't see what all the fuss was about. "Just a bunch of selfish people who cared only for themselves," he thought, "and that Gatsby "what's the deal with him? Big house, but nobody home." What York *did* like was the author's description; the big East Egg houses, the way a summer breeze blew softly through Daisie's hallway. He liked that, but mainly he liked the picture Fitzgerald drew of the old eyeglass sign looking over the valley of ashes on the way to and from the city. That image both frightened and fascinated him so much that he would find himself flipping back to read about it again and again; the story, though, not so much.

York closed his eyes, determined to sleep, and then opened them almost at once as he heard the first, almost tentative, drops of rain on the bunk's tin roof. He pulled his watch from the pocket of his jeans hanging from a nail at the side of his bed.

Just after midnight.

He closed his eyes for what seemed to be the hundredth time, and willed himself to sleep.

It was not to be.

There had to be some other explanation. Dorff had to be wrong. It was Gavin, he was talking about, for Christ's sake. Gavin! *Gavin wasn't gay. He just wasn't! Gavin was seeing Ellen Marcus, wasn't he? Jesus, they had been just a few feet away from them in the bushes the night of the Cabaret! That had to mean something! But wait. Hadn't they gone back to the dance before the others? So? What does that prove? Yes, but Gavin hadn't even spend Carnival Day with her! And what was that about being docked from the hayride? Was it because Gavin hadn't wanted to go at all?*

His eyes snapped open.

Shit!

The bunk was stifling. Maybe that was the problem. Just before taps they had closed the windows in preparation for the storm and now the air was close and still. York considered pulling his blankets off to give himself room to move, but then decided against it. He had always liked the security that being tightly tucked in brought. Gavin had said it came from being a twin because he liked the feeling too. As a compromise, York pulled off his tee shirt, wiped the sweat from his chest and neck and tossed the wet shirt to the foot of his bed.

The bunk was still except for the sound of the rain and Apple who snored softly in the bed next to his.

"Apple," York whispered. "Hey, Apple. You up?"

Apple did not move.

"Apple, man?"

Silence.

York scrunched around the other way and stared at his brother.

Why would Dorff lie? Dorff liked Gavin. There was no bad blood between them. It didn't make any sense. No! No matter what he had said, Dorff was wrong. Gavin was as straight as he was. Hadn't Gavin made it with that hooker Sturtz had told them about in Harlem? Wait! No. Gavin hadn't gone! He had become sick at the last minute. Had that been bullshit, or had he really been sick? What the hell did any of this mean? Was Dorff right?

He looked at Gavin sleeping beside him.

Impossible!

Gavin lay on his side, facing him as he always did, and York wondered as he had so many times in the past if this was how they had lain in the womb, facing each other, snugly fit together yin and yang, waiting to be born. "Hey Gavs," he thought, "Dorff tells me you're gay. Want to fill me in?"

York groaned under the weight of the blankets, his mouth dry and his body soaked.

How could it possibly be? They had shared everything in their sixteen years, every pain: every victory. He would know! Besides, they had no secrets. They never had. But Dorff had sounded so *sure*, so convincing. And, truth be told, York had always had a feeling that Gavin had secrets that even he wasn't privy to.

York plumped his pillow and his hand went to the chain that he wore around his neck. His fingers found the gold and silver mezuzah, wet with sweat, that lay on his chest and he rolled it over and over between his fingers. His grandmother had given it to him for his bar mitzvah three years earlier and there was nothing York prized more.

It had been raining that day too, he remembered, and while their mother finished dressing upstairs and their father sat talking on the phone in another room, their grandmother had taken him and Gavin aside and made them sit on either side of her on the sofa in the living room. "Kinde," she had said, the Eastern European accent still clear in her speech even though she had been in America for years, "before everyone else gives you their presents, I vant my boys to haff mine." She had taken identical jewelry boxes from her ever-present black pocketbook and handed one to York and one to Gavin. The boys looked at each other and then eagerly opened the boxes and pulled out the contents. "A mezuzah for you York," the old woman said. "Inside are *mitzvot*, good deeds, that vill make you a fine and respected person and vill insure your just revards in heaven." She turned to Gavin. "And for you, tatelah, the Star of David, a shield, taken from our past to keep you from all harm." She paused and held both boys to her, and when she spoke again her voice was quiet, almost conspiratorial. "And see what your gifts and the chains they hang on are made of." The boys had turned their presents over in their hands, wondering at their rich color. "Not silver and not gold these are," their grandmother had told them, "but a combination of both. Uncommon, rare, like my two darlink boys." She took their hands and held them, one on top of the other on her lap. "Make these chains a bond that holds you together not only as brothers but also as friends. As long as the chains are not broken, no harm can ever come to you." The boys had nodded gravely and then sat patiently as the old woman slipped the chains over their heads.

From that day on, neither York nor Gavin had ever been without his grandmother's gift hanging securely from around his neck.

York sighed. Besides being his brother, Gavin was his friend, his very best friend. The whole gay thing had to be a mistake. If it were true Gavin would have told him. He was sure of that. They were too close, too tight for him not to. Grandma had known that, and certainly the two of them had always known it though they had never really put it into words.

So why was he buying into what Dorff was saying, and why had he not confronted Gavin with it after getting back to the bunk after Dorff had told him? Confronted! He had never confronted Gavin with anything, ever. How could he do it now? He looked at his brother sleeping peacefully next to him. Gavin had never given any hints of his liking guys, he was sure of that. And yet! There was something gnawing at him that made him believe it might be true.

The heat was so intolerable that York thought he might throw up his dinner. In a fury, he pulled down his covers and lay exposed to the night. Lying on his back, his sheets drenched, he closed his eyes again and listened as the rain grew in intensity, slamming now against the side of the bunk and the roof.

There were distant rumblings of thunder, and York, his hands folded under his head, stared at the ceiling, wondering, not for the first time, if lightning rods really worked.

The night crawled on.

York thought about looking at his watch again but decided against it, thinking that knowing the time would only make the night longer.

He flipped his pillow so that the cool side was against his cheek and closed his eyes.

And if it is true, why did Gav tell Nicki and not me? My God, I'm his brother! His twin! We've shared everything forever. And why the hell didn't she tell me?

And what if it is true and it gets out? What happens then? What do I do then?

"Enough!"

York slipped out of bed, reached on the floor until he found his shorts. He quietly put them on, and with his sneakers under one arm and his basketball under the other, he tiptoed out of the bunk. He stood on the porch and waited for the rain let up a bit, and when he realized that it wasn't going to, he ran barefoot across the black sodden campus, a lone figure amidst the sleeping camp, and into the safety of Hayes Hall.

In the bunk, Gavin Stewart opened his eyes.

York stood in the key and gauged his shot. Then, as though a guard was pressing up against him, he dribbled, feinted, stopped and watched the ball slip easily through the basket.

"Swoosh."

Startled, York turned to see his brother standing at the door, barefoot, shirtless and soaking wet, looking at him.

"I woke up. I saw you were gone."

"How long were you up?"

"Just a few minutes," Gavin lied.

York nodded. "You look like a drowned rat."

"Thanks. You know" Gavin said as he shook the rain from his hair, "this place is off limits after taps."

York smiled. "You gonna tell?"

Gavin snickered. "Nah. I'll let it slide." He studied his brother's face. "You okay?"

York nodded. "Just couldn't sleep."

"You?"

York smiled. "Me. You believe that?"

Gavin shook his head. "First time for everything I guess." He picked up a towel that some camper had left on the benches, wiped the mud off of his feet and walked onto the court.

"Bare feet on the court? That's off limits too."

"You gonna tell?"

York shrugged. "Nah," he said. "I'll let it slide." He unlaced his sneakers and threw them over to the side of the court. "Now there's nothing *to* tell. We're both breaking the rules."

"Maybe that's why I woke up."

"Huh?"

Gavin ran his hands through his hair, squeezed out some more water and wiped his hands on his shorts. "I probably sensed that you weren't there. The shrink we went to when we were little said that kind of thing was possible at a session once. How we know things about each other instinctively."

"Instinctively."

"Yeah, he said that there's some kind of a link between us. You remember?"

York stared at his brother and then nodded. "Kinda."

Gavin held out his hands for the ball and York passed it to him.

"I was watching you from the door. Your form is great," and here he chuckled, "but you are so freaking predictable."

"Excuse me?"

"You always do it just the way you were taught." York looked at him quizzically. "Like this," Gavin said. He dribbled the ball. "Dribble." York, seeing what he was doing, charged him, and Gavin moved easily away. "Feint," he called, smiling. He stopped. "Stop," both brothers said at the same time, and laughed. "And then," Gavin said, lining up the shot. "Shoot." The ball flew through the air. "Swoosh," York called as he watched the ball pass through the hoop.

"Mister Predictability," Gavin said, retrieving the ball and throwing it to York, "that's you."

York nodded. "And what are you; Mister *Un*predictable?" The words had started as a joke, but even York was surprised at the anger he heard in his own voice as he said them.

Gavin took a step back. "Whoa, man" he said. "I was only kidding. You pissed at me about something?"

York shrugged. "Just saying."

"You *are* pissed at me." Gavin felt the butterflies in his belly start.

York shook his head. "No. I'm good."

Gavin nodded, not believing his brother, but to afraid to say more. He moved onto the foul line, looked at the basket, lifted off and watched as the ball hit the rim and flew off to the side of the hall. "No swoosh for me."

"You can't have a swoosh every time."

"Oh, yeah," Gavin said, retrieving the ball and passing it to his brother, "that's easy for you to say. That's easy for the guy that never misses to say."

"Bullshit. Nobody's perfect." York pushed up and let go. The ball slipped through the net. York shrugged. "I guess I must have read that somewhere."

Gavin smiled, glad that what seemed to have been coming had been averted. "Whattaya wanna play?"

"Your call."

"I asked you."

"I don't care!"

Gavin shook his head. "Your call."

York threw up his hands. "Fine. 'Ghost.' I'll spot you the 'G'."

Gavin retrieved the ball. "The fuck you will." He moved over next to the piano that stood next to the stage. "From here. Outside shot." He judged the distance and shot.

"Swoosh." York nodded. "Good one."

Gavin nodded, as York walked up to where he stood. "Thanks." He handed the ball to his brother. "From here."

York shot and made the basket. He passed the ball back to Gavin.

"Same shot." Gavin looked at the basket and pushed the ball into the air. It bounced off the rim. "Fuck."

York picked up the ball and took his brother's place at the side of the old upright piano. The ball slipped easily through the netting.

"Swoosh. I'll take that 'G', thank you very much." York passed the ball to his brother. "Hey Gav," he said, standing off to the side watching his twin move to the foul line, "why did we start calling this 'ghost', when everyone else calls it 'horse?'"

Gavin looked down at his feet, making sure his toes just touched the foul line. "I don't remember *why* we changed it," he said, his eyes narrow as he looked at the basket and shot, watching as the ball bounced off the rim, "but I do remember *who* changed it." The ball dribbled across the floor a few feet and rolled to a stop.

"And that would be?"

Gavin pointed at his brother. "You."

York retrieved the ball and took Gavin's place in the key. "Funny that you can't remember why we changed it, but that you can remember that it was my idea."

"No great mystery there," Gavin said, wiping sweat and water out of his eyes with his forearm. "It's always your idea. You make a decision and the thing is done. You are the man, the man in charge!"

York's shot missed. He looked at Gavin who was going after the ball and decided to ignore the edge in his brother's voice. "Hey, that comes with being older, and three minutes, my friend, is still three minutes."

Gavin nodded and walked back into the key. "You forgot the thirty three seconds. You're three minutes and thirty three seconds older. I always liked the symmetry of that." He lined up his shot. The ball flew through the air. "Major swoosh. 'G' each." He looked over at York. "If, that is, the shot is good enough to meet with………"

"I thought you said I was the one who was pissed. What's *your* problem?"

"No problem," Gavin said and wondered why, perversely, he was bringing them back to a confrontation that he had been avoiding.

York took a shot from left of the key and made it.

Gavin accepted the ball. "I know you well enough to know that you're mad at me about something," he said, "and since your not telling me, that's making *me* mad. Okay?"

York shook his head. "I am not mad about anything, so will you just shut up and shoot?"

Gavin did and missed. He threw the ball to York. "Well, what, then? Something's up! You've hardly said two words to me since you came back from the Nature Shack. You've just been acting really weird."

York laughed. "Me! *I've* been acting weird! Now *that's* funny. Like *you've* been acting normal for the past week or so."

"Okay, here it comes, right on schedule. The turn around thing."

York sighed. "The what?"

"The turn around thing. It's what you always do when you don't want to confront something. You turn it around to me, to make it look like I'm wrong."

"Okay, first of all, I don't do that."

"Yeah, you do."

"And second of all, if there's nothing in what I'm saying about you acting weird, how come even Sturtz has noticed it."

Gavin felt his stomach knot. "Sturtz?"

York nodded and looked at the basket.

"Sturtz has noticed what?"

"That you've been acting weird. That's what we're talking about here, isn't it?"

Gavin nodded. "How do you mean weird?"

"Spending more time in the bunk than on the field. Being moody and irritable a lot. Stuff like that. And you know something, once he said it I knew he was right."

"What else did he say?"

"What do you mean, 'what else did he say?' He said you were acting weird, isn't that enough?"

"And that's all?"

York paused before he spoke, the same gnawing feeling of discomfort he had been feeling rising in him. "Should there be more?"

"What do you mean, 'more? I don't even know what you guys were talking about in the first place. I tell you that *you've* been acting weird and all of a sudden it's all about me."

"Nothing's about you." York looked at the ball. "Look, let's drop the whole thing. This is stupid. You wanna play or quit?"

"Play, but I want to know what you're talking about!"

"Just forget it, okay."

"No. What else did Sturtz *say?*"

York's voice picked up an edge. "I am telling you that *Sturtz* did not say anything else."

Gavin's legs suddenly felt weak. He struggled to keep his voice from shaking. "Meaning that someone else said something."

"Yes. No. Look. Will you let it go, already? I've got a lot of things on my mind."

"Like what?"

"Like what! Got an hour? Like Color War is coming. Nicki's been hinting about us going to the same college again. Mom and Dad are......"

Gavin stared at him. "Bullshit. Tell me."

York felt cornered and he didn't like it. He glared at his brother. "It's everything all at once, okay? It's everything, and to be honest I'm really not ready to deal with this."

"With '*this*'? This? What, this?"

York threw up his hands and stalked over to the side of the hall. "I don't know. You, me...look, it doesn't matter. We'll talk about it some other time. Just take your shot."

"'You...me?'" Gavin was frightened now, and try as he might, he could not keep his voice from shaking. "Just tell me what you're talking about and I'll drop it."

"*Take the fucking shot!*"

"*Screw the fucking shot. Talk to me!*"

York started to say something, then stopped. He nodded his head. "Okay, you want to know? You got it!"

And Gavin knew what York was going to say and he was very afraid.

"Gavin, there's no nice way to say this, so I'm just gonna say it." He looked down at the floor and then up at his brother. "Now don't get nuts about this or anything, but some people are saying that, well, that maybe there's something a little wrong with you. I'm not saying I believe it, but that's why I've been so quiet."

"A little wrong with me."

York looked away. "Jesus, Gav, don't make me say it."

Gavin was adamant, though his legs felt like water. "Don't make you say what?"

York took a deep breath and looked into his brother's eyes. "Some people are saying that you might be into guys."

"Mama, that boy has grape juice on his face."

Gavin turned away from York and moved to the other side of the court. He closed his eyes.

The crystal ball sent out sparks of light across the hall.

"Throw your hands in the air and let me hear you scream."

Ralph's voice rang through the social hall sweat pouring off his hard bronze body.

"Come on everybody, let's party!"

Gavin turned and looked at York. He tried to keep his voice from shaking.

"Who told you that?"

"That's not important."

"Maybe not to you."

"Is it true?"

Though frightened, again Gavin could not stop the anger from creeping into his voice. "Some asshole tells you that your brother is queer and you believe him. Just like that! Can't you see something just a little strange in that, huh, York? Can you see me believing them if they said that about you! Jesus!"

York ran his hand through his hair. "I didn't say I believed them. I just asked you if it's true."

"Just asking! Huh, that tells me that you believe it."

"That's ridiculous."

"No it's not. You're making it sound like I killed someone, for God's sake."

"I just said that someone said something and I wanted to check it out with you. I'm not judging, Gavin, I'm asking."

Gavin looked at the basket. "You shouldn't have to."

"Oh, like I should know instinctively?"

"No, like it shouldn't matter either way so you don't have to say anything at all."

"Oh come on! This is a big thing, Gav."

"A big thing." He paused. "Okay. Since it's such a big thing, let's say that I am gay. Okay?"

"Are you?"

" *Just* say, *dammit!* If I am, then what's it to you?"

York looked incredulous. "What's it to me? Are you out of your mind?" He looked hard at his brother. "Gavin, you're my brother, it's everything to me."

Gavin felt such a great feeling of relief that he thought his legs might buckle. It didn't matter. York was still York. He knew and was okay with it. All the worrying had been for nothing. *Everything is going to be okay.* No matter what happened from here on, York was on his side. York had punched out the little boy in the store who had pointed to the birthmark on his face and he would protect him now. York understood. Fuck Nicki for being a traitor and telling Dorff. York knew and he didn't care.

Gavin looked at his brother standing in front of him and knew that he had never loved another human being as much as he loved him at that moment.

His voice shook. "Hey Bro...York...I....."

York cut him off. "How can you even ask me 'what's it to you?' What's it to me? My God, Gavin, this isn't kid stuff. This is something that will make both of us look really bad if it gets around camp?"

Gavin froze, his smile fading. "What?"

"Focus in here man. This is not only going to reflect just on you, but on me and the whole family too."

"You?"

"And Mom and Dad. How so you think they're gonna take it?"

"There's nothing to take. York it's......"

"Nothing to take? Gavin, if Dorff tells anyone about what happened on the canoe trip...."

"Dorff?" Gavin's feeling of relief shattered into a million pieces. Once again everything was out of kilter, spinning too fast, out of control. A feeling of nausea swept over him. "If Dorff tells everyone what?"

"How you came on to him on the canoe trip."

Gavin shook his head, his voice incredulous. "What? Dorff said *what?*"

York stared at him. "That you came on to him, and until just this minute

I wasn't sure if it was true, but man if you could see your face! It is true, isn't it? Gavin, how the hell could you do it?"

Gavin could hardly speak, but he managed, "It's not true."

York looked at him skeptically. "It's not true? You're telling me that it is not true?" He stared into his brother's eyes. "Really!

Gavin stared back at him and nodded. "Really."

York's face broke into a smile. "Oh man, you don't know how I was hoping you would say that! Talk about relieved!" He laughed. "Whoo! Close one."

Gavin's voice was flat and without emotion. "I think you misunderstood me. It's just not true that I came on to Dorff. That's all I said. That's it. Period."

York's smile faded. "Period? What does that mean, period? Are you telling me that you *are* queer?"

Gavin's frustration was so great that when he replied, his voice was on the brink of screaming. "What the fuck is with you? What do you want me to say?"

"I want an answer."

"An answer, huh? And you won't be happy until you get one. Okay. Here's an answer. I don't know, okay? I just don't know!"

"But you just said that it wasn't true."

"*Do you not listen*? Dorff saying I came on to him wasn't true. And as it happens, it was just the other way around."

"Oh shit man, don't say that."

"Don't say what?"

"He *said* you would say that, Gav. Dorff said you would cover your ass by saying that he came on to you."

"And it never occurred to you that he might have been doing the same thing! That he could be covering what he did by blaming it on me. That he's the one who's lying."

"Then why would he tell me in the first place? That makes no sense."

"York, open your eyes, for God's sake. He was afraid I would tell you and he's trying to cover his own ass before *I* did, can't you see that?"

But York wasn't listening. He shook his head and stared at his brother. "Then just finish this whole thing and tell me you're *not* gay. Forget Dorff. Just say you're not gay. That's all I want to hear."

The two boys stood mid-court, half way between the two baskets.

Gavin felt sick. He stared at York without speaking.

"Answer me Gavin. Are you a fucking homo or not?"

Gavin clenched his hands into fists. "I just told you, I don't know."

York waved him away. "Bullshit. What kind of crap is that? Everyone knows whether he's queer or straight for Christ's sake."

"That's fine for everyone, but *I* don't know. It's not just yes and no. There's more to it than that."

"Like what?"

"Like the thing with Ralph."

York shook his head. "Ralph? Who's Ralph? I don't know any Ralphs." His mind raced, and then he stared wide- eyed at his twin. "Ralph Sanchez?" Gavin nodded. "Oh, Christ Gavin, don't tell me that you came on to *him*."

Gavin's mouth was dry. He snickered. "No, York, once again, and you may find this hard to believe, but he came on to me. Hell, I'm getting so popular *I* might get all around camper."

York put his hands on his brother's arms and spoke very slowly. "Gavin, Ralph Sanchez is as straight as they come. He's had practically every waitress on the girl's side and some of girl's counselors too from what I hear."

"Well maybe he swings both ways."

"Shit, Gav, Ralph Sanchez is as straight as I am, for Christ's sake. If you came on to him you're damn lucky that he didn't break your head or even more important, that he hasn't said anything to anyone about it."

"Now that, that is classic! It's more important that Ralph didn't say anything than that he didn't break my head. At least you got your priorities straight there, bro." He looked away. "You know what? Shit on you!"

"Oh come on Gavin I didn't mean it that way and you know it."

Gavin ignored him. "And what else did you just say, that Ralph is as straight as you are? As straight as *you* are! Hell, you don't have to prove that to me, York. I know you're straight. There's no doubt about that. I mean that's not the issue is it? No question about good old York, being a faggot, it's shaky Gavin we have to worry about, right?"

"Gavin...."

"No, no. Hell, everyone knows you're a stud. *Christ, you've fucking told me! Even when I didn't want to hear, you told me!* But you know York, you're wrong about one thing, hard as that might be to believe. Ralph is not as *straight* as you, at least for one night he wasn't. But you know what, in a lot of ways, he *is* you, and you're him. You know why? Because the two of you are pricks! Cold, self -centered, uncaring pricks. The only difference between the two of you is that he knows he's a prick, and you haven't figured it out yet."

Gavin headed to the door. "Okay, now you're talking crazy," York called after him. "It's late and you're excited. Just stay here and calm down and we can talk this out like always."

Gavin turned back to his brother and York saw that there were tears in his eyes.

"No more like always, York. You just killed like always."

"Oh, come on man, don't get all melodramatic on me. I didn't kill anything. We're just having a disagreement."

Gavin's voice was incredulous. "A disagreement!"

"Yes. I'm just asking you an important question that I think I have the right to ask, and you're not dealing with the issue."

Gavin snickered. "Jesus, York, you make this sound like the fucking Model U.N. or something!"

"And you're standing there like the world has come to an end. Come on Gavs, this is ridiculous. You know how much you mean to me."

"And that would be because....."

"Jesus Christ, Gavin, your my brother...my twin."

"And?"

"And you're important to me. But you have to see that everything you do reflects on me, like everything I do reflects on you."

"But you're perfect, York," Gavin said, his voice dripping with sarcasm. "You have the perfect life. Perfect grades, perfect in sports, perfect girlfriend. You're the all- American boy, the golden boy. Sure you reflect on me, York. Like the fucking sun reflects, that's how you reflect on me. You're a god; everyone knows that. York, the Sun God."

York waved him away. "Oh, don't start that stuff again, please."

"That stuff? What stuff?"

"The 'Poor Gavin' stuff. 'Poor Gavin is not as good as his wonderful brother. York is perfect in every way, but poor Gavin has to be satisfied with living in his shadow. Boo- hoo, nobody loves poor Gavin.'" He turned and smashed the basketball onto the polished floor. " Gimme a break."

"Man, you really *are* a prick. I have never said any of those things in my entire life."

"Well, you know what, you didn't have to Bro. They were always hanging in the air. Always just about to be said."

"So you read minds too. Isn't there anything that you can't do?"

"Well, for one thing, I can't get my brother to tell me if he's a fag."

"Not funny."

"No Gavin, what is not funny is you coming on to Dorff and *Ralph Sanchez* for Chrisake! That's not funny at all. That is potentially deadly. I'm just amazed that you can't see that."

"What I see York, is by not believing me you are just proving that you don't give a shit about me." He walked a few feet and then turned. "Oh, *man*, this has this been a long time coming!"

"Oh Christ, Gavin," York said, "it's a given that I care about you, isn't it?"

"Is it?"

"Of course it is. You're my brother?"

"Again with the brother. And, when you said, 'people are saying that you're a queer,' what was that, a new way of saying, 'Hey Gavs, you mean a lot to me?' Funny you can tell me that, but you can't say, "Hey Gav, people are saying you're gay but just know that it means shit to me 'cause you're my brother and I really love you, no matter what."

"You know I feel that."

"*Then say it!*" Gavin's voice echoed through the empty hall. "Tell me that none of this stuff matters. Tell me that no matter what you really love me."

York looked embarrassed. "We never say that stuff out loud. Damn, Gav that's so...."

"That's so what, queer?"

"I wasn't going to say that."

"Uh, huh."

"That "I love you stuff." We never talk like that. We never have. Why should something like this change that?"

Gavin shook his head. "Well, my brother, if you don't know then I can't explain it to you. But can I count on you? Spoken or unspoken, can I count on you to be on my side."

"Of course you can, but there also comes a time when you have to open your eyes to the potential mess your actions can get us all into."

"*Us*, again! Don't you just mean you? That my horrible actions, as you call it, can really fuck *you* up? Not us, York, you? What are you afraid of, that with a faggot for a brother you might not get Upper Senior Chief?"

"Oh, for God's sake!"

"Huh? Is that it? Or maybe you'll lose all around camper? Huh? And what if you did get it? How would the plaque read, *"York Stewart, All Around Camper, Despite Having A Faggot Brother!"*

"Now you're being ridiculous."

"Am I?"

"Gavs, listen, we'll work this out. Tell me the truth about you and what happened with Dorff and Sanchez and we'll find some way to clear it up. Once I know the facts I can do some damage control."

Gavin's voice was incredulous. "Damage control! Is that what you think we need, damage control? What have I done that has created any damage?"

"Christ, Gav, Ralph Sanchez if nothing else."

Gavin sat down on a bleacher and stared at his brother. "You know what, let me tell you about Ralph Sanchez."

"Damn it, Gavin, I don't want to hear....."

"To hear what? Hell, according to you it never happened, right, so everything I say has got to be a fairy tale, correct? And what harm can a fairy tale do, even coming from a fairy, right?"

"Gavin, you're not a........"

"It was at the Cabaret, York, and I was bombed out of my mind. Everyone had finished cleaning up the hall and I was heading back to the bunk when ol' Ralph stopped me."

"I don't want to hear any of......"

"Sure you do, York, and I'm gonna tell you." He paused for a moment and then went on. "Now a lot of this is a little hazy cause I was shit faced and all."

York pointed his finger. "Well, there you are! That's how we play this. If you were drunk, no matter what happened it doesn't count."

Gavin's laugh was bitter. "How we play this! It doesn't count! No, York, this isn't a game we made up. There are no do-overs. There are no rules about what counts and doesn't count; this was the real thing. Shall I go on?"

"No."

"Good! Anyway, Ralph picks me up just outside those doors and he's all over me, all hot and sweaty and all. I guess you've never noticed being as straight as you are, but Ralph has got one hell of a body. Great chest, big arms, hot ass."

"Jesus!"

"Anyway, he pulls me behind the stage, out to the costume shack back there. It was kinda weird, cause in the middle of all those dresses and tights and uniforms and all, the next thing you know we're both bare-ass."

"Jesus, Gavin, stop."

"Stop? No way."

York turned away and picked up the basketball. He slowly began banging it on the polished wood floor. His head hurt. He wanted nothing more than to dribble, feint, stop, shoot and swoosh. Those were things he understood, was good at. This whole conversation was fucked, out of his frame of reference. "Come on Gav, just stop. We'll forget I said anything."

"You opened whatshername… Pandora's box…my friend, and there's no closing it now,"

" I don't want to hear this. Just stop."

But Gavin went on, and as he did, with everything he said, York slammed the ball down harder and harder, his face crimson, his mouth set. Gavin's voice grew louder, as the sound of the ball grew in intensity. "He was all over me, York." **Bang**. "Kinda like you and Nicki, only the other way around." **Bang**! "And you know what I still can't understand," he shouted over the sound of the echoing ball, "what I can't understand is where the hell he got the lube? Vaseline, for God's sake and it just appeared out of nowhere. Poof, like magic!"

BANG!

The ball rolled away from York. Even with the rain pounding on the doors and roof, his voice boomed across the hall.

"Shut up. Just shut the fuck up!"

"But why, York? You wanted to know if I was gay and I guess that should pretty much answer your question."

York turned away from him, his voice lower and filled with pain. "Just shut up. Please."

But Gavin could not stop. "You know what you *did* forget to ask me York? You forgot to ask me how I feel about all this. Am I scared? Am I confused? Did it hurt? Ya see, York, those are all the questions I kinda wished you had asked but I guess, for you anyway, just asking the big one sort of covers them all, huh? Looks likes Gavin's gay so that's all there is to that."

"I didn't mean to come off like I don't care," York said softly, still turned away from his brother. "I do care. You have to know that I do. I'm just scared. You know, scared."

"Jesus," Gavin growled, "you think I'm not? If you were half the man I thought you were, that would have been the thing you asked me first, 'Are you scared, Gav?' And I would have said yes and you would have said not to worry cause you were there to help me."

York looked at Gavin. "I want to help you, Gav, I really do. I'm your brother." He paused. "I love you."

"Nah. Too little, too late, but, hell, thanks for giving it a shot."

"I *will* help you, Gav, I will. We'll do it together. Just don't give up on me and I won't give up on you. This whole thing took me by surprise, you know?"

"Welcome to the club!" Gavin shook his head, his voice softer. "You think I planned all this? You think I wanted this? You think I asked for this? This whole thing came out of left field."

York's voice became calm, placating

"Look, Gav," he said walking to him. The bottom line here is that you were drunk. I mean those kinda things happen. Ralph took advantage of you. I mean you're probably going through a stage or something and he saw that you were vulnerable. When we get home we'll go back to Kransdorf. We'll get you back into therapy, hell, I'll go to keep you company like before, and before you know it, no doubts and no questions, you'll be fixed up."

"*But you're missing the point, York*. What if I don't *want* to be fixed up? " York stared at him. "You don't listen! You never listen! I don't *know* what I want. I told you I didn't know how I feel and I don't."

"But that's just nuts," York said. "Given the choice you'd want to be straight, right?"

"*Jesus Christ, but what if I'm not!*"

York threw up his hands. "My God, Gavin, what's the matter with you? The next thing you're going to tell me is that you're still doing it with Sanchez."

Gavin's laugh was bitter. "You know, that's pretty funny. I wanted to, but he didn't. He told me to get lost. Wanted to beat the shit out of me, but the Luggage King stopped him."

York's face was a mask. "The fucking Luggage King knows about you! Oh shit, Gavin he's probably telling the story all over camp. Damn. Nice work, Gav."

Gavin looked at his brother and knew at that moment that all hope was gone. There was a feeling of cold in him that he had never known before. He slowly shook his head. "No," he said slowly, "the Luggage King understood. *A fucking stranger understood*! You on the other hand don't understand, and you don't care. You're still only worried about how this will affect *you*. Your still worried about what it might mean to have a homo for a brother."

"Oh shit, don't start that again, Gavin. I didn't say that."

"You didn't have to York."

Gavin's voice was so soft York could hardly hear him. "You know what, we have been around and around on this, and I think I finally know where you stand. And you know what, bro, it's not with me. You're scared of me, and what I might do to embarrass you, but you know, you really don't have to worry. I won't say anything to anyone. I'll go back out to activities and play as if I were straight. I'll do my best not to throw like a girl. Not to skip when I'm rounding the bases."

"Gavin...."

"I won't look at anyone, hell, I won't even talk to anyone if that's what'll make you happy."

"Gavin, stop it."

"But I need to say something that let's you know how I feel about all this. You know what that is York?" Gavin smiled at his brother, his voice low. "Fuck you, York. You know what, just Fuck you."

York's voice was incredulous. "Gavin!"

"Wasn't clear enough? Okay, then let me say it again. I said, 'Fuck you.'"

"Gavin...."

"Jesus, for a minute there I thought you finally got it, but you didn't. It's still only about you, just like it always is."

"I'm not going to lie, sure part of it's about me, but most of it's about you, how you feel."

"Bullshit. It's *all* about you. The sun God wants to stay a god. Doesn't want to be tainted by a little homo dust rubbing off on him."

York moved to his brother, his hand out. "Shake my hand, man. Shake my hand, and we'll take 'em all on together, like we've always done."

Gavin shook his head. "Nah," he said slapping his brother's hand away, "we've never really been together. We just happen to be twins, that's all." His smile was sad. "No, York, it's always just been about you. I've always known it and I'm sure you have too. Grandma's presents were just wishful thinking on her part. They didn't hold us together, they chained us together."

York moved to put his arm around his brother's shoulder, but Gavin pushed him away.

"Just do me one favor, York. Just one. I won't say anything about this to anyone, and I promise not to 'come on' to anyone for the rest of the summer, though God knows it's gonna be hard not to, being as big a homo as I am. I'll do all that, if you'll just promise to do one thing for me."

York's voice was barely audible, hoarse. "What's that?"

"Just stay away from me, okay? No more hoops, no more buddies at swim, no more anything. Just make believe you don't know me and I'll make believe I don't know you."

And York Stewart knew he had lost his brother.

"Gavin, that's ridiculous," he tried, but Gavin kept on talking.

"I know it's gonna be hard because we're at camp and all, but just try to stay as far away from me as possible, and I'll do the same, okay? Deal?"

"Come on, Gav, don't........."

Gavin held his hand up. His voice shook. "I mean it. Stay as far away from me as you can from now on."

"You don't mean that."

"Believe me, I mean it."

"You're the most important person in the world to me."

"You'll live. After all, you're York Stewart."

"Jesus, Gavin, if nothing else, people will notice."

Gavin stared at his brother for a moment and then shook his head in disbelief. "And that makes it perfect." He stared into his brother's eyes. "People will notice! You self centered, Goddamned prick." He bent down and picked up the basketball. "And don't take my things without asking, okay. You have to be careful, York, they might be contaminated." As he moved toward the front door, York's voice stopped him.

"So you're just gonna walk out and that's that. Right? Huh? You never change, do you, bro? Just like when we were little kids. You can't deal with something so you pick up your ball and go home. You said that *I* never change and that it's all about me, well, what about you? Face it Gavin, you've never grown up. You're still the little boy who has to have it all his way or he cries that nobody loves him."

Gavin stopped dead and turned to his brother. "You can stand there and say that to me after all of this? You are fucking amazing! You didn't hear one thing I said to you at all, did you? God, if all the others could have been here to see and hear all this, maybe they would see my wonderful brother as I've come to see him. *You* blew it, York, not me, you." He laughed. "And you know what's so ironic? When it comes down to being there for his brother, when it comes to saying the right things to his brother, York Stewart, the man with the highest verbal scores on the PSAT ends up saying all the wrong things. Mister Perfect, York the Sun God, stands here like a jerk with his foot in his mouth."

And the words were out of York's mouth before he had a chance to think. "Hey Gav," he said, his voice ice, "a foot's better than a cock!"

The fury with which Gavin hurled the ball startled York even more than the pain it caused as it slammed into his side. He stood stunned for a moment then looked down at his bare chest waiting to see if the impact of the ball had broken the skin. When he saw that it had, he looked up at Gavin, his lips quivering.

"You know what, you're right, deal with this one yourself. Just leave me out of it. You want me to leave you alone? You've got it. I'm totally finished with you and your shit. You're a big tough guy and you think you can handle this, well then, go for it. You're on your own little brother." He held his side and watched as Gavin reached the door. "And Gav, while your going, you fucking fag, why don't you go to hell?"

Gavin stopped and turned to his brother. "You know what other question you didn't ask me, York? You didn't ask me if I liked it. Well, you know what, I did! I fucking loved it! Your own twin, part of your own flesh and blood, loved having a dick shoved up his ass."

Gavin pushed open the door and disappeared into the rain.

York stood stock- still and watched as his brother walked off into the night. At any other time, he would have been after him in an instant, but now he stood, unable to move, watching as the rain-swept wind blew the whitewashed door open and shut.

He picked up the basketball. He dribbled a few feet as though in his sleep. He feinted from imaginary attackers; he stopped and stared at the ball. He had taken the most important shot in his life and had missed.

"No swoosh, this time," he thought.

And as York Stewart stood alone in the middle of the deserted court, a pair of empty eyes stared down at him from the valley of his ashes.

"Young man. Young man, are you all right?"

Joey Carter looked over at the elderly woman sitting next to him. "What?"

"I asked you if you were all right."

And Joey Carter, with the open script in his lap, flying somewhere over the mid-West on his way to New York, Joey Carter realized that he had been crying.

CHAPTER TWENTY-FOUR

Frozen In Amber
August 12, 1975
(7:20 a.m.)

The heavy rains of the night before have moved to the East, and the morning air is cool and clear.

Ed Lasker stands on the porch of headquarters and listens to Camp Kanuga sleep. In a few minutes he will put the needle on the scratchy record of bugle calls, as he has done for so many years, and wake the boys with reveille. But this is the moment he savors, that he waits for. The stillness, the peace: the knowledge that within these boundaries all is well.

Ed touches the wooden porch railing and his hand comes away wet. "It never rains in Kanuga," he thinks, "it's only a heavy dew on the ground." He chuckles to himself. "How many times have I said that?" And he thinks back over the thirty years he has been at Kanuga, twenty of them as head counselor, and he shakes his head. Thirty years! "The summer after the war," he thinks. "My God, it was like yesterday."

He walks into the 'On Duty' room, picks up a record and places it on the turntable. He checks his watch. 7:19 a.m. He flips two switches and puts the needle into the spinning grooves. Instead of the crisp sound of reveille that he expects to hear, the last few notes of taps are heard from the speakers around the campus. "Shit! That's a great way to start the day," Ed Lasker thinks as the mournful sound fades and the blare of reveille finally fills the air.

Indignant noises from the quadrangle of bunks; groans mixed with laughter. The sound of wooden shoe lockers slamming shut.

Morning.

As the music stops and the needle is removed from the still spinning record, Ed Lasker picks up the microphone next to him.

"Everybody up. Everybody, up up up. Everybody up up up this bright and sunny morning." The groans from the bunks along the quad are more audible now and Ed smiles. "Long pants and a light sweater. Long pants and a light sweater! Come on you lazy bums, especially the so- called mighty seniors, get your butts outta bed. It's a beautiful day. I'm coming around and I'd better get a "Hey Ed," from every counselor. Everybody up up up! Everybody up up up up up!"

Ed Lasker clicks off the P.A. system and walks onto the porch and then onto one of the large pieces of roughly hewn slate that make up the pathway around the camp.

He walks past the Intermediate Row. "Hey Bunk 21," he calls and a sleepy counselor's voice returns the greeting. "Hey Ed."

"Hey Bunk 20."

"Hey, Ed."

And as Ed Lasker makes his way around the campus, making sure that all are up, that all is well, a ritual he repeats thirty two times, he finally stands in front of the last bunk in the quadrangle.

"Hey Bunk 33!"

No answer.

"Hey Bunk 33!"

Silence.

Frowning, Ed Lasker walks onto the porch and opens the screen door. He is bombarded by noise. Most of the senior group has secretly crammed into the tiny bunk.

"Happy Birthday, Ed," they shout, and he is pounded on the back, hugged, and what is left of his hair is mussed.

He has forgotten his birthday, and though he is pleased, Ed Lasker plays Ed Lasker. "Come on you crumb bums...don't try to get on my good side with this birthday crap. Look at this bunk! What a pigsty." He focuses his attention on a beaming, round faced boy next to him. "Apple, ya bum ya, are you ever gonna learn how to make hospital corners?"

The boy beams! "Probably not Ed!" Lasker swats him lightly on the back of his head. "Ya bum ya!"

The seniors start singing, and Ed Lasker moves quickly to the door. "Gimme a break guys. Anything but that!"

But they are not to be stopped.

"Happy Birthday to you," they sing, and Ed is out the screen door.

"Happy Birthday to you," and he is on the porch, and to his amazement, every boy in every bunk along the entire quad is standing on his porch singing.

"Happy Birthday, dear Ed, happy Birthday to you."

Wild applause and cheering, and the head counselor waves to acknowledge it. "I feel like some ball player standing in the middle of Yankee Stadium getting ready to say goodbye," he thinks and is surprised to find there are tears in his eyes.

The applause continues and as Ed Lasker smiles, an image of Lou Gehrig, his head bowed, standing at a microphone crosses his mind. A chill runs through him. "What the hell was that about," he wonders as he waves to acknowledge the cheers. "Where did that come from? This is a *good* day," he thinks as he heads back to the H.Q. "No, it's a perfect day," and he goes into his office to get ready for breakfast.

FROZEN IN AMBER (2)
August 12, 1975 Lineup and Breakfast (8:00 a.m.)

"One, two, three, four...we want color war!"

The camp is assembled at the flagpole, lined up as bunks, and it is screaming, chanting, cheering.

"One, two, three, four...when the hell is color war?"

"Steady," Ed Lasker says as he stands before them, attempting to restore order, but the noise persists.

"Hold it down," he laughingly implores, as the chants grow louder, faster and more persistent.

"Eddie, Eddie, we are ready," the boys are now shouting.

As he stands on the large rock at the head of the camp, his hands over his head, waving for quiet, seemingly annoyed at the noise, Eddie is secretly delighted. This is exactly the kind of spirit and excitement he had been hoping to engender for the color war only a few days away. "Let it build to a crescendo day after day," he thinks to himself, as he waves for quiet and glares down with love at the camp before him, "and at just the right moment, like a beautiful orgasm, all the energy will explode and I'll declare war with the big 'break.'"

The seniors scream, "What do we want," and the rest of the camp roars back, "Color War," and the seniors yell, "When do we want it?" and as one the camp screams "NOW!"

"Now! Now! Now! Now!" the camp chants.

"Soon! Soon! Soon! Soon!" Ed replies to himself. "It's only days away and you are going to love the 'break' I have planned for you." He thinks of the stunt pilot he has hired to fly over the camp in an ancient Bi-Plane during the rest hour on the following Friday. The way the noise of the engine, unheard of in this part of the country, will draw all the boys out of their bunks, onto their porches and then onto the main campus. And then the shower of mimeographed sheets thrown by the pilot, telling the boys what side they are on, showering down on the campus below, as the traditional cannon shots, officially proclaiming the start of games, goes off behind the Main Office. He thinks of the noise, of the commotion and he himself can hardly wait; can hardly contain his excitement. "It will be the best Color War break ever," he thinks, and though he is frowning at the noise before him, he is filled with the same excitement as the boys.

"Eddie, Eddie, we will not be steady," the cheering continues.

"Let's charge him," Apple says to Klinger.

"Jesus," Sturtz says, shaking his head, "how lame can you get?"

The boys pay no attention to him. It is tradition that when the color war cheering rises to a peak such as this, the seniors and their counselors playfully make a run at Ed, who obliges by letting himself be chased off of his rock some fifteen or twenty feet, before holding up his hands in mock defeat, signifying that the charge was a success and that it is now over.

And all of the Seniors, except for Henry Sturtz who stands watching, the Stewart twins who stand uncharacteristically apart and Leonard Dorff who stares straight ahead as if hypnotized, charge Ed Lasker, and he obliges by running away, and the lower camp laughs and applauds, waiting impatiently for the day when they will be seniors and privy to the charging of the head counselor.

After the charge, the cheering and the laughter slowly fade as the camp realizes that breakfast, and not color war, is now the order of the day.

Now, as he always does at line up, Ed announces the morning activities for each group. When he says that the seniors are scheduled for basketball there is a murmur through the assemblage as the boys realize that the game will be a warm up to the most important game of Color War, the Upper Senior basketball game.

Only the seniors are quiet.

Other announcements are made, and Ed Lasker motions to the members of a sophomore bunk to come forward to raise the flag. Each bunk has a chance to raise and lower the flag and the honor is not taken lightly. There is an air of solemnity over the gathering as two of the young boys take both the American and the Kanuga flags from the chair next to the flagpole and nod at Ed. He in turn motions to Larry Fishman, a chubby senior, who stands next to him, who raises a bugle to his lips and blows the perky tune to which the flags are raised. Many of the boys know the melody so well that they silently hum along with the trumpet.

The flags begin to rise over the young men of Camp Kanuga.

The stars and stripes make it successfully to the top of the pole, but the Kanuga flag below it sticks on it's way up. The young boys, afraid that the bugle call will end before their job is done, yank on the ropes to move it.

"Easy," whispers Ed through clinched teeth, "easy. Don't pull so hard."

But the boys don't hear him and they tug on the ropes and soon the camp groans at the sound of ripping material. Two of the counselors rush to the flagpole and take the ropes from the boys. But the damage has been done. The camp flag has been torn.

The bugle call is over, and as is tradition Ed calls out the name of a group to acknowledge. "Hey Inters!" he calls and the group yells back, "Hey Ed!" Then the head counselor dismisses the boys who move slowly across the red clay road to the mess hall. Still standing at the flagpole, the two boys who ripped the flag, are yelled at by the other members of their bunk and one is smacked in back of the head by one of the older boys. He starts to cry.

As the last of the campers and counselors make their way into the Mess Hall, the Kanuga flag flutters slightly askew in the soft morning breeze, one of it's sides torn away from the stabilizing rope that was holding it.

The talk at breakfast is all about "the war" with speculation rampant on when and how "the break" will occur. The seniors talk mainly about the make up of the sides.

"One thing's for sure," Sturtz says, his mouth filled with scrambled eggs, "if you look at all this logically without all the screaming and yelling, York and Gavin won't be on the same side. They never are. Never." He looks at Gavin and points to him with his knife. "So it's you and me 'Strawberry,' you and me, and we are gonna kill 'em!"

Gavin looks at him and says nothing.

Apple pours a second glass of milk from an aluminum pitcher. "Sturtz," he says, smiling, "I'm pretty sure you'll kill someone someday, but it won't be York."

Sturtz flips him the finger, as York smiles wanly and pushes his eggs around in his plate.

Before Sturtz can answer a roar starts from the lower camp. The boys look up.

"One two three four, we want color war. One two three four, we want color war." The chant is picked up and soon the entire camp is screaming and banging on the tables with their fists.

Only Sturtz, Dorff and the Stewarts continue eating.

Feet stamp on the wooden floor. The building shakes. The roar grows and grows until Ed Lasker gets up on his chair and motions for quiet. This is all part of the game. This is what is expected. And the roar continues. The kitchen staff, mainly from Ivy League schools, comes out into the dining room and watch the commotion with amusement.

Gavin looks around the mess hall hoping for a glimpse of someone who is no longer there. He sees another waiter where Ralph Sanchez used to be, grinning and applauding and stares at him. From the corner of his eye, York sees where his brother is looking and quickly looks away. After a few minutes the counselors get their tables quiet and there is a hush as Ed Lasker clears his throat. Almost to a man, the camp leans forward.

"I am going to say this one time and one time only. If there is anymore of this commotion," and here he pauses for dramatic effect, "there will be no color war this year!"

And the noise explodes again as Ed knew it would, and he waves to the camp that breakfast is over, that they may leave. The boys, still shouting, stand and walk toward the exits.

Sturtz stands and shakes his head. "This is so lame," he says to Klinger as he walks with him on the way to the front door. "Everyone knows this is all bullshit. Everyone knows this is all planned. And yet they still scream the same shit, day after day."

"Jesus, Sturtz," Klinger says, "it's called camp spirit! Get with the program. Lighten up man!"

"Yeah, right," Sturtz yawns. "Klinger," he says, "you are a hopeless, pathetic, lost cause." Shaking his head, he pushes past him into the bright sunlight.

"Hey," Klinger brays, as he pushes him back, "what the hell is your problem?" And as he watches Henry Sturtz bang through the mess hall doors into the bright morning sun, Klinger says a silent prayer that if Sturtz and Stewart are chiefs, he is on York Stewart's side.

FROZEN IN AMBER (3)
August 12, 1975
After Clean Up (9:15)

Ed Lasker looks into the sky and is glad that he had been right about the sun. The rain is definitely gone.

But by nine thirty as the last of the night's clouds move away, the day has become sticky, hot and humid. Jackets have long since been discarded and now, as bunk inspection comes to a close, shirts are coming off as well.

Bunk 33 has been inspected by Larry Caboy who has looked at it hard and long and has come away satisfied that it is nearly as good as it can be. Only a comic book found jammed under York's spare blanket had warranted a point off of a perfect rating.

"Nice going, York," Bob Milburn says as he closes the screen door behind Caboy. "Nice freakin' going."

Henry Sturtz pulls his tee shirt over his head and laughs. "Shit, Milburn," he says to his counselor, "it's only fucking inspection, not the end of the world. Get a life man."

"Watch your mouth, Sturtz." Milburn yanks his whistle and green and white lanyard off of a nail above his bed and puts it around his neck. "And it *is* important ass-wipe. We're the oldest bunk in the camp. We have to set a good example. What we do, the other kids emulate."

Sturtz snickers. "Is that direct from Chairman Ed's Little Red Book?" He pulls off his jeans and underwear. "You are so lame Milburn, you know that?"

"Easy, Henry," York says, "Bobby's right. I was wrong. I messed up. It's no big deal. Just let him do his job, okay?"

"And I don't need you standing up for me, York," Milburn says. "I can take care of things myself without your help."

"Bobby, I was only....."

"Well don't!"

Sturtz, totally naked, looks up at York Stewart and grins. "The golden boy seems to be losing his glow. Maybe that all around camper is not such a shoo in after all."

"Shut up, Sturtz, dammit."

"And he curses too, boys and girls. What stick has gone up your ass this morning, York? Besides which, you look like shit."

York begins to undress. "I didn't sleep well last night."

Sturtz looks shocked. "You?"

"Yes, Henry," York says, his voice tired, "me."

But Sturtz will not be stopped. He takes his dick in his hand, looks down and speaks to it. "Did you hear that, Mister Happy? You weren't the only one who was up all night!"

Bob Milburn is in a bad mood, and he has no idea why. "You guys have lineup in six minutes," he grumbles. "I want you out there on time!" He pauses as he moves to the door. "That means you too, York. You screwed us out of the clean up banner for the week so just be sure you don't screw us again by your being late." He pushes out the screen door which almost immediately swings open again as Apple comes in.

"And what is wrong with Mr. Milburn this morning?"

"It's nothing, Apple," York says, "forget it."

"He's on the rag at York for something."

"Hey, Apple," Klinger calls to him, "Sturtz is doing Mister Happy."

Apple grimaces. "I can do without Mister Happy and any other goodies you might have up your sleeve, Henry.""

"You know Apple, I haven't had any goodies up my sleeve for quite a while now. That book is empty, isn't it York?"

"Whatever you say, Henry." York's voice is tired, flat.

"Yes, there is an emptiness, a void, even in the words of Shakespeare that cannot be filled this summer, because of you, York."

Gavin shoots a look at Dorff who looks away.

"But do I hold a grudge?" Sturtz whispers so softly that only York can hear him. "You bet your ass I do." And he points a finger at York, as he moves back to his bed, smiling.

""What'd we get in inspection?" Apple asks as he pulls off his shirt, tosses it on his bed and unbuckles his belt.

"Just missed a perfect score," Leonard Dorff says. He is lying on his bed, his knees up in front of him, a tootsie pop in his mouth, his clipboard and the column he is editing resting against them. "York had a comic under his blanket."

"*York* did?" He looks over at his friend. "Since when do you read comics?"

York shrugs. "It wasn't mine. Probably someone saw it on the floor as the inspector was coming in and put it there in a hurry. It's no big deal."

"Ah," Sturtz says with a smile, "but we still lost the inspection banner because of you."

"Why don't you tell Milburn that it wasn't yours?" Apple says smelling two pair of shorts to see which is cleaner.

"Because it just doesn't matter."

"Well the inspection banner is just a lot of bullshit anyway," Apple says.

"Not to Milburn," Sturtz says smiling, "and besides, we *so* wanted a ten." He sits on his bed. "But what's really troubling me is that you really are fucking up a lot lately, York. You have to watch that."

"Screw off, Henry."

"Is that anger I hear coming from York Stewart? My word, what next, Dorff throwing like a boy?"

"SHUT THE FUCK UP! FOR ONCE IN YOUR STUPID LIFE, WILL YOU JUST SHUT THE FUCK UP!"

All eyes go to Gavin Stewart who stands in the center of the bunk, glaring at Sturtz and shaking.

Sturtz' smile forms slowly and it is feral. He cranes his head as though uncertain he heard what Gavin has said. "You're not talking to me in that tone of voice are you, Strawberry?"

"Just shut up." Gavin's voice is less certain than it was a moment before.

Sturtz moves toward Gavin slowly, almost gliding. His movement is barely noticeable. And then he is next to him. "Say it again."

"Leave him alone, Henry."

"Mind your business, York," Sturtz says, never taking his eyes off Gavin. He smiles at him again. "Say it again, Gavin. You said it once, so say it again."

And with a quiet fury he did know he had, Gavin Stewart whispers, "Say one more word to me, Henry, and I will fucking beat your head in."

"Come on, Gav," Apple says, and Sturtz waves him away.

"You are going to beat my head in? Fat chance, asshole; fat, fucking chance."

"I said leave him alone, Henry."

"And I said fuck off, York."

"I can stand up for myself, York. Back off."

"Come on guys," Apple says, "this is bullshit. Just cool it."

"Stay out of it, Apple," Sturtz says, standing a breath away form York. "Come on Mr. Perfect, show me what you've got."

Before York can answer, the sound of the bugle calling for morning activity breaks the silence.

"Line up," Bob Milburn yells from the walk in front of the bunk. "Let's go gentlemen. Line up. *Now!*"

Dorff, who has stood watching, breathes for the first time, grabs his clipboard and is the first to move, making a wide arc around Sturtz on his way out the door.

Gavin, pulling on his shorts, gives Sturtz a look as he passes him and falls into step with Dorff. "I need to talk to you," he whispers as they leave the bunk together.

Glaring at York for another moment, Sturtz points a finger at him. "This isn't over, fucker." He moves to his bed, quickly pulls on his basketball gear and leaves, slamming the door behind him.

"You okay?" Apple asks, and York nods.

"Go ahead. I'll catch up to you in a second."

"You sure?"

"I'm sure. Don't be late for lineup."

"Screw lineup."

York smiles. "I'm okay, Bro. Go," and Apple shrugs and leaves the bunk.

York starts to tie his sneaker and then stops and stares down at the floor. He puts his head in his hands.

"York!" Milburn calls from lineup. "Get your ass out here NOW!"

"FUCK," York screams into his hands as he gets up from the bed.

He is surprised to see that he is shaking. He wipes his eyes and nose with the back of his hand, grabs the basketball at the foot of his bed, takes a deep breath, expels it and slams out of the screen door into the sunshine.

In the empty bunk, clean and orderly only a few minutes before, there is total disarray.

August 12, 1975: On the Way to Hayes Hall

"Why'd you lie to him, Lennie? Just tell me why?"

Group lineup is over and as the boys walk to the social hall in small groups, Gavin has fallen into step next to Leonard Dorff.

"What do you mean lie? Lie to whom? What are you talking about?"

"Don't play games with me, Lennie. You know damn well what I mean. You fucking told York that I came on to you on the canoe trip."

Lennie shakes his head. "I never told him that. There must have been some misunderstanding."

"Jesus, cut me a break, man. I'm not a freaking idiot."

"Look, I don't want to talk about it, okay?"

"You don't want to *talk* about it! You're playing with my life here Lennie. What kind of a person are you?"

"What do you want me to say, Gavin?"

"What do you think I want? I want you to tell York the truth. I mean the fucking harm's done, he knows that I'm gay, but Jesus Christ you at least have to tell him that it was you that came on to me."

"What good would that do?"

"It might make my brother not think that I'm some fucked up perv sex maniac that hops on just anyone who's around."

Dorff nods his head. "Just anyone. Like some loser like me you mean."

"I didn't say that."

"You didn't have to. Anyway, I can't do it, Gavin. I won't do it."

"What are you talking about you can't? Why can't you?"

"Because, no matter what you may think, I'm not gay, and if I told York what happened he would think that I was!"

There is exasperation in Gavin's voice. "Lennie, you came on to me. What do you call that?"

Dorff slows his pace. "That wasn't what you thought it was."

"Christ, Lennie, I was there!"

"I just wanted to be accepted by you. To be liked by you."

"Jesus Christ, man, you were!"

"I just wanted to sleep with you like you would with your brother. I wanted to feel close to you. Don't you understand that? I just wanted to sleep having your arms around me. I didn't want to have sex with you, for God's sake. I like girls. I tried to call you back, to explain, but you wouldn't listen. You totally misinterpreted what I meant."

"Then why did you tell York that *I* came on to *you*?"

Dorff stops and looks at Gavin. "Because I didn't want you telling him about me. York has been one of the only people in my life who has ever given a damn about me, Gavin. You hear what I'm saying? In my life! I couldn't endanger that. I *had* to tell him first, so that he wouldn't misunderstand the way you obviously did."

"But you fucking outed me."

"About that, I'm truly sorry. Really, I am. But there was nothing else that I could do." His tone is cold, matter-of-fact.

"Nothing else you could do? You mean nothing else you could do to save your ass. My God, Lennie, you say that York has been good to you and you don't want to fuck that up. Damn man, he's my brother."

"I said I was sorry."

"And that's it?"

Dorff nods. "That's it. I am sorry Gavin."

Gavin takes his finger and pokes it in Dorff's chest. "Well let me tell you something, buddy. If you don't tell my brother the truth about what happened by tonight, I swear to God, I will tell your uncle that you are a screwed up closet case who has come on to me on more than one occasion."

"You wouldn't do that."

"Yeah, I would."

"He wouldn't believe you. You forget, I've got a girlfriend."

"Hello! So have I, numbskull. What the fuck does that prove? And besides, you've been suspect since the day you got here."

The color drains from Dorff's face. "What do you mean, 'suspect.'"

"Non athlete. Bookworm. Not really interested in girls."

"I said I have a........"

"Shit, Lennie, she chased *you*. She's just a pathetic loser who wanted to hook up for a summer. Have you fucked her? Huh? Have you? Shit man, do you even know how?"

"Of course I do, have."

"Bullshit."

"I have."

"Listen to me, Lennie, all that is beside the point. I don't care if you're straight, gay or totally asexual. You know why? Because I no longer give a flying fuck about you! I did, but now as far as I'm concerned you can go screw yourself. All I want is for you to tell York the truth and that's the end of it between us. And as for York, he'll be cool, I know he will, he won't tell anyone."

"You didn't hear me, Gavin. York is my friend. If I tell him, he won't be my friend anymore."

And for the first time in his life, Gavin Stewart wants to hurt another human being, wants to lash out and make someone else feel the pain he has known since he can remember. And as he lies, Gavin finds that this is easier than he ever thought. "Your friend? You think that York is your friend? You pathetic loser! Sturtz has been right about you from the beginning. You can't really believe that York likes you! Not really *likes* you. He pities you Lennie, that's all. We all do. You're a joke and he's just a good -hearted guy who tries to help you out, but your friend? No way. Get this into your head, Lennie. You are nothing to him. Nothing. And you know what, he knew all about that tuxedo gag Sturtz pulled, we all did, for Christ's sake," Gavin lies, "and York laughed about it as much as everyone else."

Leonard Dorff's face has lost all of its color. "But you said, on the canoe trip, you said......"

"Then I guess you weren't the only one lying, Lennie," and as the words come from his mouth Gavin Stewart feels like he is going to be sick.

Bob Milburn comes up behind them. "Move your ass guys." They nod and he walks by.

"And while you're at it, Lennie," Gavin says, turning, "tell Sturtz that it was you that flushed his stash once and for all, or else I will. I'm tired of seeing Sturtz having a hard-on for York because of something that you did." And as Leonard Dorff watches Gavin Stewart move down the long tree lined path to the hall, a thought so unwanted, so uncalled for that it makes him shake, makes it's way, unbidden, into his mind.

"Just asking. What Upper Senior with the initials L.D. has been the biggest joke of the summer unbeknownst to him?"

And Lennie Dorff holds onto the side of a tree for a moment before moving slowly to the hall, and is afraid he is going to cry, afraid he is going to vomit.

August 12, 1975: **Morning Activity (9:40 a.m.)**

Though most of the bunks have been refurbished over the years, Hayes Hall at Kanuga, named for the man who designed it, is almost exactly as it was when it was first built. The floor, where all the major basketball games are played, has been changed twice, the last time five years ago, but other than that, a fresh coat of paint and new nets strung on the basketball hoops, all is the same.

The walls are covered with ancient graffiti, sacred to the campers, that has never been or ever will be painted over. KLEINER '46, CONDON '54, SALEMOWITZ'51 and the rest have taken on almost mythic proportions over the years though almost no one at camp now knows whom the names were. Like the old upright piano that stands to the right of the stage on which the weekly shows are produced, they have seemingly been here forever. They are a link with the past that must never be changed.

And, if the graffiti is sacred, then the plaques that hang on the proscenium of the stage are treated as the holiest of the holies by the hundreds and hundreds of young men who have come to Kanuga over the years. For these are the Color War Plaques, a record in wood, paint and shellac of the teams, the leaders, the members of the Upper Senior Basketball teams and the final scores of every 'war' since the camp began. To have one's name on one of the plaques, whether one has won or lost, is to be part of legend.

At nine forty, the upper seniors walk into the chill of the cool dank social hall, glad for the relief from the blazing sun. The lower group has been sent to the outdoor courts so the hall belongs to them, many of whom will be playing in the most anticipated of all color war games, and who, for good or ill, will be names on a plaque by the end of the summer. Many of them are talking about Gavin and Sturtz.

"I hear he went ballistic, man!"

"Gavin? Unlikely."

"I hear Sturtz really got to him."

"Sturtz's too much of a fuckin' wise guy if you ask me."

"Who asked you?"

"Fuck you."

As a preamble to the actual game, balls whoosh through the air and bounce off wooden backboards. Some swish through the hoops and are retrieved by eager hands. The ping of the rubber balls on the polished wooden floor echoes through the hall.

Then, a whistle!

"Gentlemen," Bob Milburn says when there is quiet, "for all we know, this is the big one, the last big game before the ultimate one."

Sturtz rolls his eyes and whispers to Klinger, "Jesus, enough with the commercials. We get the idea."

"Then you're saying Color War is going to break soon," Sidney Thaner asks.

Sturtz throws him a sour look. "You have a keen sense of the obvious, Thaner. Check the date, for Crissake. August 12? Mean anything to you? The camp season ends in just over two weeks. When do you think we're gonna have Color War, Thanksgiving?"

"That's enough, Henry." Milburn looks at Thaner. "Yes, Sidney, I would say that something big is going to happen around here in the next few days, and since this might be our last basketball period before then, I think it would be wise to take this game seriously; very seriously indeed. Understood?" Thaner nods and Milburn goes on. "This game is also special because it ends our regular season. Today the two A teams, the teams that have won must games throughout the summer will play for the championship with trophies to the winners and Watermelon pits to the losers." Klinger laughs and then stops when he realizes that he is the only one laughing. "So," Milburn goes on, "regular teams. First up, A Team one and A team two. York, Gavin, Klinger, Lishman and Becker on one side, Sturtz, Brookman, Gottlieb, Horowitz and Jacobs on the other."

"Jesus," Sturtz sniffs, "like we don't know what teams we're on by this time."

Milburn ignores him. "Team One: Skins, Team Two: Shirts."

Shirts are stripped off, the boys who were not called, the boys on the second tier teams, sit off on the bleachers, as the two "A" teams slowly make their way to the center of the court.

York Stewart pulls his shirt over his head and flings it to Leonard Dorff who sits on a rickety wooden chair in front of the upright piano, staring at nothing in front of him.

"Hold this for me will you Len?", York asks and smiles as Dorff nods. "You okay?"

"Yeah."

"You look weird."

"Thanks."

York smiles. "You know what I mean, not yourself."

"And who would that be?"

"What?"

"Not important. Forget it."

"You going to play at all?"

Dorff shakes his head. "Not unless there's a "Z" team. What would be the point? Unless, of course you all just want a good laugh."

York looks concerned. "Something *is* up, and it's not just Sturtz. What's going on, Lennie?" York's look of concern is real and Leonard Dorff's mind races. "Was Gavin lying," he thinks, "or is York just playing with me now?" He looks at the handsome boy in front of him and wonders who he is.

"I gotta get in there, but we have to talk. About what you told me last night. I need to hear what happened again. There's something I'm missing. After swim, okay?"

Dorff nods.

"York gestures at Dorff's clipboard.

"Say something nice about me, Lennie."

Again a feeling of nausea, a welling up of anger and sadness that he tries to control, sweeps through Dorff. "I always do York. I always do."

Milburn calls from center court. "Anytime you're ready, Mr. Stewart!"

York shrugs at Lennie. He takes a deep breath, waves at his counselor and moves into his team's huddle.

Milburn points to a large black and blue mark on the side of York's chest, striations of dried blood already scabbing. "Where's that come from?" York shrugs. "Well," Milburn continues, "right after swim I want you up to the infirmary." York sighs. "It's nothing, Bobby," but Milburn is adamant. "Infirmary, right after swim. Understood?" York nods knowing that he will not go. Milburn blows his whistle. York nods at his brother who barely nods back.

Dorff sits staring.

Gavin and Sturtz move into the key, preparing for the opening tap that will start the game.

"Don't crowd the circle," Milburn says, and both boys glance at each other and move back a bit. Milburn steps between them and throws the ball into the air. Sturtz moves so quickly that his action is lost on Milburn as he deliberately steps on Gavin's toe, using this leverage to tip the ball over to Apple.

"You fuck," Gavin yells at him as he guards him going down court. Sturtz smiles. "This is a grown ups game, Gavy," he says as he picks up speed and tears away from the boy guarding him.

The sound of pounding feet echoes through the almost empty hall! Apple, guarded by York, dribbles the ball down court waiting for Sturtz to catch up to the team and assume his position in the pivot. Gavin, still furious that the tip off was stolen from him, is all over Apple, making it impossible for him to find an opening. Finally, frustrated, Apple tries a long jumper from outside the circle, with Gavin almost plastered to him. The shot misses and hits the back rim. Gavin quickly gathers in the rebound with a cursing Sturtz sniping at him from the side. He looks around and passes the ball off to his brother who heads off to his offensive zone.

"What are you, blind, man?" Apple shouts at Milburn as he tries to catch up with York. "Gavin did everything but tackle me. What the hell have you got that whistle in your mouth for anyway?" Milburn pays no attention. "Goddammit, Bobby, blow it when I'm fouled, asshole."

And Milburn does indeed blow his whistle. "Technical on Brookman."

Furious, Apple throws up his hands and storms away as Sturtz comes up to him and smacks him on the head. "Watch your mouth, dickwad," he says. "I don't want to lose this game because of you."

The players mill about just outside the foul circle as York steps up to the line and easily sinks the free throw.

Milburn grabs the ball and flings it back to York for an inbound play. He looks at Apple. "Now how about playing ball and stopping this freaking whining. I feel like I'm at the girls' camp."

Sturtz lifts his tee shirt and wipes the sweat from his face. He looks over at Dorff. "We're playing girl's rules, Pulitzer, wanna play?"

The boys laugh and though he tells Sturtz to shut up, Bob Milburn is smiling too. Lennie Dorff sits, unmoving.

The game continues. Sturtz fronts Gavin, and with a quickly aimed well concealed elbow, he steals a bounce pass aimed at Gavin by his brother. He drives back down the court, moves in under the basket, and sinks a reverse lay up.

"Shirts two, skins one," Milburn yells.

"Didn't you see Sturtz charge me?" Gavin mutters to Milburn as he prepares to go back on offense. Milburn shakes his head, ready to move down the other way. "Jesus, he even deliberately stepped on my toe at the opening tap."

Milburn stops and looks at him. "No, I did not see that. What I did see is your brother throwing to you when there were others in the open. What is this going to be, the York and Gavin show? York and Gavin playing catch?"

"Oh, screw that," Gavin says as he storms off. Milburn, considers calling a technical, decides against it and puts the ball in play. He knows that if he defers to one team or the other there will be no game, just a series of whistles and judgments that he does not want to make. He decides to let the two teams go at each other. He's had enough of the bullshit. He wants to see a game.

York Stewart pauses and then goes for the basket as if driving for a layup. He stops suddenly, his sneakers squeaking on the polished wood, and seeing that his opponent is off balance he backs up and puts up a fade away jumper shot that goes in easily.

The few watching applaud.

As the action moves down to the other side of the court, Sturtz and York are so close together that they can feel each other's breath. Sweat flies from one to the other. As they go up for a rebound under the "shirt's" basket, Sturtz turns and elbows York hard under his ribs. York winces in pain and grabs his side as Sturtz takes the ball and stuffs it in.

"Shirts four. Skins three."

York pulls himself up and looks to Milburn, waiting for a whistle. It does not come. He looks down at the now broken skin on his side and remembers the game of GHOST just hours before. York points a warning finger at a grinning Sturtz, and moves down the court.

Back and forth the two teams go, never more than two points separating them. The pace is fast, and to Milburn's delight, sometimes spectacular. Feet are no sooner pounding down the court one way, than they turn and go back the way they came. The boys are glistening with sweat, their hair plastered to their heads. Milburn hardly blows his whistle, warming to the tension on the court, delighted in how aggressively the two teams are playing. "If this is a preview of the Upper Senior Color War Game," he thinks, "it is going to be one for the books."

The "B" teams realize that their chances of playing this morning are slim, and as some rush out of the hall for a drink or a pee during the rare times out, they pass the word to others in the bunks and on campus and soon the word spreads. "There's a hot game going on in Hayes Hall," and off duty counselors, waiters, stray campers and visitors start drifting in, moving quietly to the seats on the bleachers surrounding the court.

And as they watch the two teams move back and forth across the floor, one lower senior who is supposed to be on the outdoor courts turns to his friend sitting next to him. "There is no way the actual Color War game can be better than this. This is freaking awesome," he says. His friend just nods, not taking his eyes off of the court, then suddenly stands up. "Look," he says.

At the skins end of the court, York, about to go up for a perimeter jumper, spots his brother alone under the basket. Instead of taking his shot, a shot that is clear to all watching he could easily sink, he fires a one handed bullet pass in Gavin's direction. Gavin, convinced along with everyone else that York is going to take the shot, is already looking at the basket, anticipating a rebound. The ball smacks his hand, causing him to cry out in pain and surprise, and then rolls out of bounds.

A shocked expulsion of breath can be heard throughout the hall.

Gavin is furious. "Why didn't you take the fucking shot," he storms at his brother as they go back on defense on the other end of the court. "I told you, I don't want any fucking favors from you. When you've got the fucking shot, fucking take it!"

Before York can say anything, Gavin waves him away and shaking off his hand and wriggling his fingers, moves quickly across the court. He points at Sturtz. "And you fucking watch yourself, Henry. I'm not bullshitting."

Sturtz smiles and fakes a yawn. "If you can't play with the big boys, Gavin, maybe you should sit this one out with Lennie over there."

Gavin cocks a fist. "Listen you prick......."

And Milburn moves between them. "One more word, Gavin, and you are history? Get me?"

Still glaring at Sturtz, Gavin nods, and the game goes on.

By half time, the game is tied and Hayes Hall is almost full, yet the boys on the floor are only aware of the anger that has been building between the two teams and, often, between those on the same side.

The skins, with the Stewart twins, elects to huddle outside the doors of the hall while the shirts agree to remain indoors, sitting on some unused benches they have found backstage.

"God damned Milburn," Apple complains, wiping his face with a towel he has brought from the bunk. "He's like one of those Chinese monkeys. He sees nothing and calls nothing. I haven't been counting, but York must have charged me at least three times."

Sturtz frowns at him. "Then why don't you try using your body to push him away from the ball so that he never gets a pass in the first place, asshole?"

"Hey, muther, you're so great, you guard him."

Outside the hall, under the enormous oak tree, the meeting of the skins is not going well either.

"When are you going take a fucking shot when you're in the clear? You have an open shot and you pass to me? That is such bullshit, York."

Klinger nods. "I've been in the open a lot, York. You're not passing to me or to Lish."

Lishman nods. "I've had a couple of good chances, York."

"I mean you're supposed to be 'the man' when it comes to B Ball, York, and you're playing like you never played the game before."

York shakes his head. "I'm just trying......."

Gavin cuts him off. "Well, maybe you're trying too hard. I told you, forget I'm your brother for one minute. Forget that we've been joined at the hip forever. Make the break, York, make the break and play the game like it's supposed to be played." Gavin pauses, puts his hand on his brother's shoulder and whispers so that the others cannot hear. "It's starting to be embarrassing, York, you know, embarrassing? I know how much you hate to be embarrassed in public, so think how I feel. Think how this could impact on mom and dad, hell, on the whole family. In front of all these people and all."

York shrugs off his brother's hand. "Come on Gav," he whispers, "you've got to get past last night. I was an asshole, okay. I'm sorry."

Gavin holds up his hands. "I don't have to get over anything, you understand me? You, *you* have got to do something. And that is, you have got to leave me the hell alone. Got it? Leave me alone."

York nods. "Got it," he says softly.

"Good," Gavin says, his hands wet with the sweat of York's back. He wipes them on the rear of his shorts, "Just forget I'm your brother and we'll be just fine. I know I have." He turns around and starts for the door of the hall. The other members of the team sit silently for a moment, not understanding, embarrassed, and then follow Gavin back into the hall.

York's legs are numb. He wants to follow the others back into the hall, but instead stands unmoving, feeling a sense of loss so great that it is palpable. He knows that this won't be like the other times they have fought. This time something has been broken and he doesn't know if it can be fixed. And images of not having his brother near him sweep over him and for a few moments he knows the dark, sick feeling of irreparable loss. He stands, holding onto the side of the hall, silently staring down at the lake in the distance below wishing it were this time the day before.

"Oh, Mr. Stewart," Milburn calls from the doorway. "If you are ready?"

York nods and slowly moves back into the hall.

Inside the crowd continues to gather. They are sitting on window ledges, standing in doorways. Sides have been taken, favorites cheered, bets made.

"Do you remember the Upper Senior game in forty nine," one of the parents says to another who sits next to him.

"Forty nine?"

"When Tilson threw from half court and made the basket that won the game. You remember."

"First of all, when Tilson took that shot, it was fifty two."

"Not forty nine?"

The other man shakes his head. "Fifty two. I was an upper Inter. I sat right over there." And he points across the hall. "I'll never forget that game. Now that was a game."

"And this isn't?"

The two men turn to look at the Luggage King who is sitting above them. "*That* was a game? Nonsense. That was a great shot. *This* is a great game. Gentlemen, I have been here forever and believe me I have never seen a game like this." He shakes his head and looks back at the court.

Milburn blows the whistle and both teams gather. The hall is quiet as the two centers glare at each other. The ball is thrown up, the skins win the tap and the hall erupts in chaos once again.

The third period moves quickly, with York taking his own shots and avoiding his brother. Sturtz and Gavin play wary, heads up ball as both teams try to be sure not to foul. Both teams continue to score.

Midway through the fourth period with the shirts ahead by a point, the skins control the ball. Sturtz, his shirt, plastered to him like a second skin, sees Gavin trying to post up in the lane. Making sure Milburn is not looking he takes a gamble and throws his foot out in front of Gavin who goes down hard.

But this time the crowd has seen the move and an "OH," sweeps across the crowd and necks are craned to see what damage has been done. Milburn moves in and there is a hush as he bends down to speak to the writhing Gavin. He kneels beside the boy for a moment and then stands and offers a hand to help Gavin up. The sigh of relief as Gavin gets to his feet becomes a gasp, as seemingly out of nowhere, York flings himself at Henry Sturtz, his fists swinging. Sturtz tries to move away, but York pulls him back by his shirt spins him around to face him and before anyone can stop him, punches Sturtz hard in the mouth.

"Jesus Christ, York, stop it," Gavin cries as he pulls at his brother. "Didn't you hear one word I said out there, for God's sake?"

"That's not just for you, dammit. IT'S NOT JUST FOR YOU," he yells.

"Bullshit, it's all about power and it's all about you and me."

"Get outta my way, Gavin," York yells as he charges Sturtz who pulls away behind Milburn.

Sturtz, his mouth bloody, and shaking with anger, points his finger at York. "You are a dead man, Stewart. You hear me, a dead man."

York charges him yet again, only to be held back by Klinger, Lishman and Thorner.

"York."

"Goddamn it, let me go," York yells as he pulls at the hands that hold him.

"STOP IT!" With a scream, Gavin moves in front of his brother and slaps him hard across the face. His move is so sudden, so unexpected that in a moment the hall is silent.

"Fuck you! Fuck you!" he screams, tears running down his face, his birthmark deep and dark against his skin. "I'm not a friggin cream puff, you bastard, I'm not a freaking faggot. I'm a man, damn you to hell. I am a fucking *man* and I can take care of myself. DO YOU HEAR ME? I DON'T NEED YOU!" With a scream of rage as his words no longer come for his tears, Gavin pulls back and spits full in his brother's face.

In an explosion of anger and frustration that surprises even himself, York pulls away and tackles his brother flinging him down on the floor. The shrill sound of Milburn's whistle cuts through the bedlam in the hall as the two brothers roll around on the court, fists flying, their bodies so intent on hurting the other that the others cannot pull them apart. Finally, with help from some of those on the sidelines, hands reach down and separate them, bringing them up, holding them around their waists and by their arms as the brothers struggle to get free, to get to each other.

Bob Milburn moves in between them. "STOP IT!" he yells. "GODAMMIT, STOP IT!" One of York's arms breaks free and almost connects with Milburn's face. Milburn cocks a fist, which brings a gasp from the crowd. He lowers his hand then stands between the two brothers, a hand on each of their sweating, heaving chests. He can feel the anger pulsating through the boys' skin and muscle and for a moment he feels afraid.

"CALM DOWN," he yells, as the brothers glare at each other. "CALM FUCKING DOWN."

Sturtz, holding his shirt to his bleeding lip, stands a few feet away, staring. Lennie Dorff, his hand to his mouth, eyes wide, tries, but cannot turn away.

And for all there, for all who have witnessed it, the impossible has happened. Like a moment frozen in amber that will always be locked in people's minds and memories, like the graffiti on the walls and the plaques around it, and without anyone knowing it, the world of Kanuga has changed forever.

The silence in the hall is so intense that when the first notes of 'recall' come through the two speakers above the stage, one of the seniors in the bleachers utters a shocked, "uh."

Ed Lasker's voice fills the hall.

"Everybody back to your bunks and get ready for a loooong general swim. Everybody back to your bunks and get ready for general swim."

No one, not a camper or a counselor in the social hall moves. No one knows what to do or what to say.

Finally it is Sturtz who breaks the silence. "Let's get the hell outta here." He moves to the front door, still holding his bloody tee shirt to his mouth, and the others slowly follow. Gavin, hands still holding him, still staring at his twin shakes his head slowly. "It's over York, over!" He turns to the others. "You can let me go," he says calmly. "I'm cool." Hands release him. He stands quietly for a moment then turns to the door.

Milburn nods to those holding York, and he is released. "There's going to be a bunk meeting before swim and we are going to get this straightened out," he says. "Understood?"

"There's nothing to straighten out," York says, his voice resigned.

"Understood?"

The brothers nod their heads.

Gavin starts for the door. "Gav, wait." York calls after him. His twin stops and turns to him. " Please," Gavin says, his voice beginning to quiver, "just leave me alone. Please." He turns, walks a few feet, and disappears into the heat of the morning.

"He didn't mean it, bro," Apple says to York.

"Yeah, he did," York says softly, and Apple sees there are tears in his eyes.

"Come on York, I'll walk you back."

"I'll be there in a few minutes, okay Apple? I kinda need a minute alone."

"You sure?"

York nods and Brookman, putting the ball under a bench for later walks slowly out of the social hall.

And as if by magic, the hall is empty. Campers have gone back to their bunks and the others back to their lives.

York stands alone in the key, and for the first time in his life he has no one to pass to.

CHAPTER TWENTY-FIVE:

FROZEN IN AMBER: AUGUST 12, 1975
THE SWIM

York Stewart waits his turn to dive.

He stands quietly on the float, third in line from the board, and stares silently across the lake. He sees everything, yet nothing; he hears the sounds of the other campers splashing and laughing, but to him all is silence. He looks up and sees a fat, faceless boy leap off the diving board.

Now he is second in line.

As the years go by everyone, whether they were there or not, will, somehow, have been there.

"I was just behind him waiting for the diving board that day," Peter Greenfarb tells his third wife for the fourth time, twenty -five years later. "So close I could have touched him. Can you imagine? So close I could have touched him."

As he moves closer to the aluminum ladder York thinks of the morning and of the basketball game and of his brother's fury, and he shivers under the white-hot sun. He thinks he sees Gavin running on the dock. He squints as he looks, but whoever it was is no longer there.

There had been a quick group meeting under the tree and Milburn had made them shake and the group had sighed a sigh of relief, but nothing had changed. Nothing had been fixed.

And he has never been as sad, or frightened, or alone. "Why wasn't I there for him", he wonders, as he looks down at the broken skin on his side where the basketball Gavin had thrown hit him, and sees that it has become an ugly bruise, discolored, painful to the touch. "He's never going to forgive me," he thinks, "and even if he does, it'll never be the way it was before." And he remembers Gavin walking out into the rain and knows that he will never be able to fix what he has broken.

He thinks of his parents and how this will affect them, how broken hearted they will be, and he knows they will never understand why.

Why? Why had he said what he said? He loved Gavin and he knew that Gavin loved him, so why had he said what he did?

York looks over at the side of the swimming area. He sees Sturtz holding onto one of the ladders. He is talking to Apple who laughs at something he says. Apple's laughter makes York smile, and as he catches his friend's eye he waves at him, a wave that is quickly returned.

"My Uncle Willie was there that day," Steven Hirsch tells Walter Elian as they tread water in the same swimming area twenty years later. He points to the wrong diving board. "It happened right over there."

Splash.

The metal stairs leading to the diving board are clear. The banister is hot to his hands but he doesn't care. He knows what he has to do. The cobwebs of doubt are finally gone and York is at peace.

Finally, York Stewart stands on the hot plank of the diving board, his toes curled under the edge. He looks across the swimming area at the boys laughing with their friends. He does not see his brother. With a large intake of breath, he prepares to dive. The sun radiates into his body and, as he stands waiting for his moment, those who *are* there, those who happen to see him, see perfection. He wears a white Speedo, and against his tan skin the brutal sun makes the material seem to glow. He bounces once, twice and the third time York Stewart takes to the air in a lift that takes him higher than he has ever gone before. He twists and soars, pushing himself ever higher and, as he reaches his highest point, the sun reflecting off the mezuzah he wears around his neck makes those who happen to be looking his way shield their eyes from the sudden sharp glare. In that same moment, York Stewart twists his body away from the swimming area watching the diving board as it comes up below him. There is a splash and the next person in line climbs the stairs and gets ready to dive.

And morning swim goes on.

Boys, only their eyes showing above the water, are stealthily creeping up on unsuspecting other boys as they gurgle, "Dum dum, dum dum, dum dum,

dum dum," for this is the summer of JAWS and everyone in these waters is either a shark or a victim.

Pat Clary, the only Catholic in camp, there because of the athletics, and Jerry Fleishman are arguing about something.

Harold Spitzer holds onto one of the wooden ladders, blows his nose into his fingers then wipes the residue on a wooden piling, sure that no one has seen, but everyone has seen.

There are yells and catcalls, splashing and dunking, and everywhere laughter.

With York gone, Henry Sturtz looks back to Andrew Brookman. "You did, you know."

Andrew Brookman not knowing what he is talking about, stares at him.

"Christ, Apple, fucking pay attention. I said you played a shitty game of basketball this morning." He adjusts his cock in his red speedo. "You realize, of course, that you made me look bad, but to show you the kinda guy I am, I forgive you."

Apple laughs. "You forgive *me*. Thank you and fuck you!" He shakes his head. "He forgives *me*! Henry," he grins, "you are one of a kind."

He will remember this moment for the rest of his life.

Apple rubs his knee. "I got a lump here where Gavin charged me. Maybe I should go to the infirmary after lunch."

"Brookman," Sturtz sniffs, "you are such a girl. He hardly touched you. Look at my *lip*, for God's sake."

"What the hell was the matter with everyone anyway? I mean we've all been out there before. It was only basketball. It wasn't new ground, but it was truly brutal."

"It seems as though the brothers Stewart were on the rag," Sturtz sniffs. "Trouble in paradise. Pay no attention."

"But….."

"What *I* can't believe," Sturtz continues, "is that Gavin told York to screw off in front of the whole group. Gavin told *York*! That he lost it with me, well, chalk it up to his time of the month, but going ballistic with his brother, amazing, fucking amazing." He pauses, considers and adds, "And sad, of course, sad."

"If it was so sad," Andrew says, "why are you smiling?"

"Who's smiling?" Sturtz says, suddenly annoyed. "Jesus, Apple, did you bang your knee or your freaking head? I am not smiling. You do not see me smiling. It fucking hurts to smile."

"Whatever." Andrew Brookman, Apple to his friends, looks for York, but he is nowhere to be seen.

"Damon and fucking Pythias at each other's throats," Sturtz sniffs. "Go figure."

"Anyway," Brookman says as he wipes water from his face. "It'll all blow over by dinner."

Sturtz shakes his head. "I don't think so. No. Not this time. Did you see Gavin's *eyes*? I've never seen him so pissed." He smiles. "Go figure."

The late morning sun is now at its hottest. It bakes into the chipped white wood of the dock, the pith helmet with **HEAD DOCK** on it that covers Larry Caboy's head, the backs of the young men holding bamboo poles around the swimming perimeter and into the heads of all those in the water. It is a stunning heat, a blinding heat and Larry Caboy decides to wait another five minutes before calling for a buddy check.

It is a decision that will haunt him for the rest of his short life.

"Were you there that morning?," people will ask, and even those who were not there will tell them, yes.

In the deep-water area, Gavin Stewart still smarting, his stomach in knots listens to what Gary Klinger is saying as he treads water next to him, and hears nothing. In the middle of whatever it is Klinger is saying, Gavin pushes off from the dock and swims toward the diving raft, Klinger, his mouth open in surprise, looking after him. Leonard Dorff sees Gavin swim past him, and though there is eye contact, there is no acknowledgement. When he gets to the raft, Gavin looks back and does not see who he is looking for. He sees Apple and Sturtz dunking each other and heads to them.

"It's time," Larry Caboy decides, and blows his whistle for a buddy check.

Although it is only mid-day, in the almost sickening heat of that late morning, the day is about to end.

"The whistle," Lou Freedman says to his wife as they prepare for bed forty years later. "I think what I remember most is the whistle."

"Quad one," Caboy yells into his megaphone.

"Clear."

"Quad Two."

"Clear."

"Three."

Caboy waits for a beat. "Three!"

"A little confusion here, Larry." Dickie Gresher, the counselor on post three looks down at Andrew Brookman who is treading water. "Apple, I'm asking you again, who's your buddy and where he is?"

"I told you. It's York, Dickie, and I don't know where he is."

"What do you mean you don't know?" It is Caboy.

"I saw him dive off the diving board, Larry." And as Caboy scowls across the water at him, all at once, a child again, Brookman thinks, "I am in so much trouble."

"York Stewart!" Caboy calls through his megaphone and there is only silence. He is suddenly frightened. "Okay," he calls, "everybody out."

And the counselors echo the words and the boys begin to scramble out of the water. The area churns with the paddling of arms and the kicking of feet. Glistening bodies pull themselves up the crowded ladders until, finally, every camper is either standing on the side of the dock or sitting in the bleachers.

"York Stewart," Ed Lasker, the head counselor calls, praying for a response and knowing, somehow, that there will be none coming.

Larry Caboy, his heart racing, comes down from his tower and stands among the others. He grabs the shoulder of the boy next to him. "Klinger," he orders, "run up to senior row and see if York is up there." Klinger, who usually asks why when told to do something, just speeds off, many of the other boys looking after him.

"We can't wait," Caboy says, and dives into the deep-water area, his second in command, Wes Levy, right behind him.

Ed Lasker tries to keep his voice from shaking and almost succeeds. "Counselors, quickly and quietly, get the boys up to campus." Their faces, some grim and set, others wide mouthed and confused, the counselors begin herding the campers up the path. Looking back over their shoulders, a steady murmur growing amongst them, the boys of Camp Kanuga slowly make their way back, clogs and towels scattered and forgotten on the dock behind them.

"I looked back at the lake from the bridge," a forty-year-old Sol Thorner tells his son who is begging to go to sleep away camp, "and I could see the panic. The swimming back and forth! The panic."

Almost all of the boys are off the dock now, and there is so much anxiety on the part of the counselors left behind that the four boys who remain, the four standing silently out of the way near the boat house, are not even noticed.

The color has drained from Gavin's face as he watches the men in the water, dive and surface, dive and surface and he shivers under the scorching sun. Leonard Dorff, his eyes wide and his mouth open, stares, dumb. Andrew Brookman stands next to Henry Sturtz, his eyes glazed, his mouth moving with no words coming from it.

And the diving down continues. Each time a head breaks the surface the boys lean forward, and each time it is once again only one of the counselors.

The water roils and the diving continues.

And then time stands still.

"Oh, Jesus. Oh, Jesus. Oh, Jesus."

Ed Lasker stands swaying at the side of the dock. The boys crane to see where he is looking and see that now there are three heads bobbing in the water. Larry Caboy and Wes Levy look up at Lasker and begin swimming quickly to the dock, the third head, its neck bent back impossibly, eyes wide, staring unblinking at the blazing sun, being pulled along between them.

Gavin Stewart, who can no longer see nor hear, slips quietly to the ground in front of the boathouse. The sun has disappeared and he has finally reached the dark safety of the bottom.

Leonard Dorff looks over at Gavin then back to the swimming area, wants to scream, and doesn't know how.

Henry Sturtz watches, fascinated, and wonders how this will affect color war.

Ed Lasker leans forward, grabs the inert figure being held by Larry and Wes, and with strength he did not know he had, pulls it onto the blazing hot boards of the dock.

And, as Andrew Brookman watches, seeing and not understanding, yet understanding all too well, there is a frenzy of running feet. Someone pushes past him into the boathouse and sprints back panting, his hands filled with emergency equipment, and Andrew Brookman, Apple to his friends, now Apple no more to the most important person in his life, knows it won't help. Hands pound on an unresponsive chest, warm lips are pressed to blue ones, breath is forced from one mouth to another, and the clear white plastic of an oxygen mask remains unclouded no matter how long it is pressed to the blue gray face of York Stewart.

And Brookman's legs buckle and he has to hold onto the tree next to him to stand. There is a shooting pain in his side, and for a moment he thinks it is his appendix, and then he remembers that his appendix is no longer there, that there is only an empty space inside of him where it used to be. And again he becomes a child, and, for the first time in years, he wants his mother. He is filled with a sadness, a misery, a madness that he has never known before, and he emits a groan that becomes a howl as Ed Lasker, the tears running down his cheeks, gently cradles the lifeless head of York Stewart in his lap.

POV: Apple:

After York's body was brought up from the lake, we staggered through the rest of the morning, the ambulance from town coming and going, plans for moving York discussed, decisions on who would be allowed to leave camp to go to the funeral, phone calls to anxious parents who had somehow heard. The mess hall was open for anyone who wanted to eat.

Only the very youngest went.

The afternoon moved efficiently, yet in slow motion. No one spoke, though the group heads were there to act as grief counselors.

Though they tried, even they couldn't find the words.

There were activities if you wanted them.

No one wanted them.

Things were decided. Things were accomplished.

Yet things, we knew, would never be the same.

CHAPTER TWENTY-SIX:

FIRE ISLAND
March
Present Day

Joey Carter stood, his back to the crashing waves, and watched the house. He pulled his scarf tighter around his neck, but that and even his fur lined leather aviator jacket couldn't stave off the freezing air that swirled off the ocean only a few feet away. It might be a few days shy of spring, but it felt like January. Feeling a bit foolish and glad that there was no one else around to see him, Joey flapped his arms against his sides to keep warm.

Gavin was home, he had seen him returning from a grocery trip, three SHOP AND STOP brown paper bags balanced precariously in his arms, and Joey mentally kicked himself again for not making himself known to him at that moment. He had watched as Gavin fished for his house key. How simple it would have been to just walk up and offer to lend a hand. But the moment had passed, the perfect opportunity to meet Gavin gone. Now, almost an hour later, with the winter wind whistling off the ocean, there was still no movement from the house.

Joey knew that there was no way he could hold out against the cold much longer; he would soon either have to knock on Gavin's door or head back to the ferry, grab a motel room on the mainland, and try again the next day. He had thought he could hold out all afternoon if necessary, but Fire Island in winter, especially after the comparative warmth of Hollywood, was simply too cold.

Just as he was about to give up, the door opened.

Joey moved back toward a pitiful copse of non-descript undergrowth growing poking up from a sand dune, wishing there was a place where he could hide, but also knowing too, that there was simply no way that could happen. One way or another, Gavin would see him. Maybe he had already.

A dog bounded out of the house barking happily, and then, a moment later, Gavin Stewart appeared.

"Willie." Gavin's voice, carried by the cold wind reached Joey. "Willie stay."

And as impossible as it might be, Joey Carter recognized the voice. He had imagined it, no heard it, he thought, as he had read and re-read the script of GONE THE SUN over the last days. He smiled. Gavin sounded like Gavin.

The large dog stopped and looked back at his owner, his tail wagging furiously. Gavin slammed his door shut and clapped his hands.

With that signal the large floppy dog leaped forward, tearing happily away from the house, and, Joey realized with a sudden panic, straight for him.

As Willie bounded toward him, Joey heard Gavin's voice again. "Willie, stay. Willie...dammit." And then, louder, "Don't be afraid. He won't hurt you."

"It's okay," Joey started, "I like...." and then the dog was on him, his tail wagging, a mewling sound coming from his throat, his paws suddenly on Joey's chest and a rough tongue licking his face.

"Willie down," Gavin said, coming up to them. "Bad boy."

But the big dog would have none of it and he continued to bathe Joey's face with his warm tongue.

"I'm really very sorry," Gavin said, gently pulling the dog back by his collar. "I'm afraid he thinks that everyone's his friend."

But Joey's delighted laughter encouraged the dog, and he pulled away from Gavin and once again put his paws up on the younger man and licked.

"He's wonderful," Joey managed, still laughing, as again Gavin pulled the large hound away.

"One thing's sure," Gavin said, with a smile, "he certainly likes you." He grabbed the large, panting dog under its chest and pulled him back. "Sit, Willie," he said. "Be a good boy. Sit."

Willie, his tongue hanging dopily from his mouth, sat.

"Great dog." Joey wiped the dog's saliva off of his face with his glove.

"A little messy perhaps, but really great."

Gavin nodded. "I think so. A little rambunctious, but a good dog all the same."

Joey Carter stared at Gavin Stewart as though seeing a character out of a favorite book that had miraculously come to life. The strange part was, he thought, that like his voice, Gavin was exactly as he had pictured him; older certainly, but amazingly the same. The tousled brown hair, the lanky, almost ungainly body and, of course, the port wine stain on one side of his face. There were lines now, around the eyes and mouth mostly, but Joey looked past them and saw clearly the face of the sixteen year old of 1975.

"You staying out here?"

Gavin's voice pulled Joey back. "Excuse me?" he managed.

"I asked if you were staying out here. Visiting someone?"

Joey shook his head. "Day tripper," he said.

Gavin snorted. "You certainly picked a strange time of year to day trip." He let go of Willie, who proceeded to lift his leg and urinate on a piece of scrub, all the while staring up at Joey, mouth open in what could pass for a smile.

"Well, " Gavin said, after waiting a few seconds for Joey to reply, "it was nice talking to you."

Joey Carter took a deep breath. "You mind if I walk a ways with you?" Before the words were out of his mouth, Joey could not believe he had actually said them.

Gavin looked at him. "Excuse me?"

Joey thought fast. "It's just that I was going to head back, but I thought if I walked a ways with you, you might be able to point out some of the points of, er, points of interest."

Gavin nodded, and then shook his head. "Points of interest!" He smiled. "Look," he said, with a knowing smile, "I'm really flattered. I really am. You're very nice looking and, as far as I can tell, pleasant, but I'm afraid I'm not interested."

"Interested? I'm sorry, I don't……" and then Joey did. "Oh, no," he said, flustered and shaking his head. "It's nothing like that. I didn't mean that I wanted to…I mean, you're very nice looking too, and….. oh shit!"

Gavin Stewart laughed. "No," he said, "I'm sorry. I thought you were…."

"No, I'm….."

"It's just that there's so much of that out here, even off season, that I just assumed….." He pulled off his glove and outstretched his hand. "Gavin Stewart."

Gavin's hand was warm on Joey's. "Joey Carter."

Gavin pulled back a bit and stared at the young man in front of him. "I know that name," he said, pulling on his glove, "and your face is familiar. Television?"

Joey nodded. "And a few movies."

Gavin nodded and started to walk. "I'm sorry if I don't know the things you were in but I'm not much into television and I hardly ever get to a…" He had walked a few steps when he realized that Joey wasn't walking with him. He turned to the younger man, and waved him over. "Points of interest?"

Joey smiled. "Thanks," he said catching up.

Gavin nodded. He pointed to where Willie was chasing three gulls across the beach, frustrated when they took flight, then barking them on their way. Joey laughed for not more than a moment later, the large hound was busily nosing a dead crab that had washed up just above the waterline.

"Attention deficit disorder," Gavin said.

Joey smiled. "Still a great dog, though." There was an awkward silence as the two men walked slowly into the wind.

"Pretty empty," Joey said.

"Excuse me, I didn't….."

"The beach. It's pretty empty."

Gavin looked at the span of sand dotted with sparse beach grass ahead of them. Indeed, the beach was almost totally deserted. An old couple walked briskly past, and a tall man, high above them in the dunes and well bundled against the cold, spoke against the wind into a cell phone.

"That's why I live here."

"Excuse me."

Gavin smiled. "The emptiness. I like it."

"And in the summer?"

"When it gets too crazy I usually sublet and get out of here until...," he waved his hand in front of him,"....until it becomes this again."

With Willie a few feet in front of them, Gavin led the way across the beach.

Joey took a deep breath. "Look......."

Gavin stopped and turned to him.

"I lied about wanting you to point out the points of interest."

"Not really!" Gavin said dryly. "You could have fooled me."

Joey shook his head. "No," he said, "no, I couldn't."

Gavin stopped and looked at him. "No," he said "no you couldn't." He picked up a stick. "Will!" The big dog looked up and when he saw the stick in Gavin's hand leaped up into the air barking furiously. Gavin, reached all the way back and threw the stick down the beach, Willie tearing madly after it." He turned back to Joey. "I saw you watching the house. What's going on?"

Joey Carter shook his head. "Has anyone told you about the movie?"

Gavin looked confused.

Joey took a deep breath. "The one Henry Sturtz is going to make."

Gavin shrugged. "I haven't spoken to Henry Sturtz in years. I read about him, but he doesn't consult me on his projects."

"He's making another movie."

"Good for Henry," Gavin said dryly. He noticed Joey staring at him. "And?"

Joey looked down at the sand, then out at the ocean. "It's about Kanuga."

Gavin could feel himself growing impatient. "I don't understand," he said, but a sick feeling in his stomach told him that he did.

"It takes place in 1975."

Willie had brought the stick back and had dropped it at Gavin's feet, but Gavin did not notice. "He wouldn't dare."

Joey gulped. "Yeah, he would."

"The son of a bitch."

"I've read the script," Joey added quickly, "and although it tells everything that happened that summer, it's done with really good taste."

Gavin's head was spinning. "Everything that happened, I...."

"About you and Nicki and Apple and......"

"He used our real names?"

"No, no," Joey assured him, "only in the rough copy. All names will be changed, you can depend on that."

"Jesus."

Joey pressed quickly on. "I promise you, everything is done in the best of taste. The writer has done an amazing job. His first screenplay too."

Gavin's legs felt like they might buckle. He had to pin down what he had just heard. "You say the screenplay is done."

Joey nodded. "It's finished and ready to go."

"Bullshit it is." Gavin yelled to his dog that was peeing up against a barren dune. "Willie!" he called, "come on boy, we're going home." He turned his back on Joey and started walking off.

Joey followed him, speaking to his back. "I can't show you a script, I'm not allowed to do that, but you have my word it's in the best of...."

Gavin stopped and whirled around. "Taste? Yes? Isn't that what you already said, the best of taste? Well. I don't care if it's got the Good Housekeeping seal, that's one movie that is not going to be made." His eyes narrowed. "Did Sturtz send you?"

"No," Joey said, shaking his head. "It was my idea."

"But he knows about it."

"Yes, but......"

Gavin's voice was hard. "Just exactly what do you want?"

"I wanted to meet you."

"Uh, huh." Gavin's voice was flat. "And again I ask you, why?"

Joey shook his head, frustration creeping into his voice. "I just wanted to meet you for myself."

"You came all the way out here in the dead of fucking winter just to meet me! Please. Give me some credit."

"But I did. I just......"

But before Joey could continue, something clicked in Gavin's mind. "Oh shit," Gavin said, "an actor. You're an actor!"

Joey nodded, and before he could help himself, "I was in......"

Gavin waved him quiet. "And you're going to be in Sturtz's movie aren't you?"

Joey nodded. Enough was enough. No more bullshit. "And there's no way I can play it without talking to you."

Gavin sighed and looked Joey up and down. "Well," he said, "you're too good looking to be playing me."

"No," Joey tried, "I'm not, but I needed to....."

Willie, already back at the house, barked for Gavin to join him.

But in that moment, Gavin Stewart was oblivious to his dog and the freezing cold; oblivious at that moment to everything but the young man standing next to him.

"York," Gavin said softly. "Jesus Christ, you're York."

The tall man in the dunes turned his back to the wind, pulled up the aerial on his cell phone and punched in a number. In his office on Park Avenue, Henry Sturtz picked up his phone on the first ring.

"He's here" the voice from the other end said, the winter wind breaking up his voice. "He's here and he's talking to Stewart."

Henry Sturtz hung up, leaned back in his chair and stared out of the window.

A small smile played across his lips.

CHAPTER TWENTY -SEVEN

POV: Nicki

They told me in the infirmary.

I learned later that when the call came through there had been a quick meeting of the group heads, and it was decided that the best place to tell me was away from the others and at a place where I could be helped if help was needed.

They decided on the infirmary.

They gave me something in a box that they said the doctor needed and asked if I'd bring it up to him. I remember thinking as I walked across campus about how much York hated his infirmary and how he said so many times that no matter how sick he got he would never go there again.

As soon as I saw the look on the nurse's face I knew there was something wrong. Then they took me into a room at the back of the building and told me.

It's a tired cliché, but it *was* a blur.

And there was screaming, so loud and shrill that I wanted it to stop, never realizing that the sound was coming from me, and the nurses holding me, the Head Counselor trying to calm me, the sounds of "There, there," and "Oh. Sweetie," and "I'm so sorry" and the shaking, the terrible shaking: the cold, the injection, and finally, the darkness and the wonderful not knowing.

I slept the rest of that day and all night in the infirmary.

The next day, the day of the funeral, I was numb. I was awake and aware, but I had been so pumped with what I assume were tranquilizers, that I looked out at the world with glazed eyes while my mind still refused to believe what I knew was true.

And though I longed for York, all I wanted was Gavin. If Gavin were with me I would be safe. Where was Gavin? Get me Gavin.

And then the powers that be met to decide if I should be allowed to go to the funeral. They talked and talked, I have been told, and tried to reach my mother, who, of course, was nowhere to be found.

Finally, Moe Feingold put his foot down, said, "She's going," put a blanket around me and bundled me into the back of his Cadillac. He told me to try to sleep and drove just under the speed limit to be sure to get to the Meadows Funeral parlor on time.

I did try to sleep, but it was impossible. With every bump in the road, with every snatch of music coming from a radio in someone else's open car window as we stopped for a light, with every moment that went by, all I could think of was York not being there anymore, not existing, and then all I could do was cry. "York." I repeated his name over and over in my mind as a kind of mantra until it ceased to have any meaning and I forced myself to stop before I became sick. My beautiful, wonderful York was gone. York, whom I loved and who loved me; York who knew me better than I knew myself; York who had left me all alone in the world.

And then I thought of Gavin, and of *his* pain and realized that I was *not* alone, that there *was* someone left and I longed to hold him and cry with him. Once where there were three, now just two remained, and I silently thanked God for Gavin, the one left in my life whom I loved, the one left in my life who understood. I still had him, and he had me, and we would be there for each other, and as I cried softly so that Moe couldn't hear me, I longed to be with him. Gavin was my rock, my safety zone and I wanted nothing more than to have him hold me so that I could feel safe again, so that I could mourn York with someone who loved him as much as I did.

The funeral parlor was jammed and a madhouse. Lots of York's friends and relatives crowded the porches and the hallways outside the chapel. A few of our friends from school nodded at me, not knowing what to say, but the majority of the people there, relatives, friends and associates of the Stewarts didn't know who I was and could not understand the pain that I was feeling. Even though I could see Sturtz, Dorff and Apple seated in different places in the chapel, I knew that for all intents and purposes I was a stranger here no matter how close I had been to York. After all, I still was alive. The feeling added to the surrealism of the last twenty-four hours. Moe had stopped to talk with someone after finding me a seat in the back row, keeping me close to the door, frightened that at any moment I might start to scream and not be able to stop.

I watched, heartbroken, as Gavin was led in with his parents, his eyes dead; his face haggard, his body stooped. I half rose as he almost tripped as he followed his parents to their seats in the front row. And, as we waited for the Rabbi to begin, I longed to be able to hold him as he sobbed with his mother and father so near and yet so far away from me.

The service started and I rocked back and forth in my seat repeating York's name over and over in my mind, and then, amazingly, it was over. I had not heard a word. Only once, when Mrs. Stewart started to scream, was I pulled out of the cocoon I had made for myself and then I jammed my eyes shut and willed myself not to faint.

Gavin and his parents were led out first, and once again there was no way for me to be with him.

I remember nothing of the silent ride to the cemetery, but finally, at the graveside, there was a chance for me to stand next to Gavin and to have him pull me into the heart of his grieving family.

I slowly made my way to just behind where the Stewart's were standing, and then in next to Gavin as the Rabbi prepared to say the words over York's grave. Gavin was holding onto his mother with one hand, the other clenched in a fist at his side. So as not to startle him, I gently pried open the fist and took his hand. He felt warm and safe, and for the first time since I had heard the news of York's death, I felt that I might not die myself. As Gavin turned to see who it was, I managed a smile and squeezed his hand. Instead of the tears and the warm embrace I had expected, a look of such intense hatred crossed his face that I actually gasped. "Gavin," I whispered, "what is it?" He shook off my hand, and thinking that there was some terrible mistake, that he had taken me for someone else, I put my hand on his shoulder. He turned to me again and hissed, "Get away from me, Nicki. Get the hell away from me."

I wanted to throw up. This made no sense; this was insane. For years Gavin had told me how close he felt to me, that a sister could not mean more to him than I did, that we were better than family, and now, all at once, when we should have been consoling one another, he was acting as though he hated me.

"Gavin, please," I whispered to him, "what's wrong?"

He slowly took his arm from around his mother and turned to face me.

In a voice so low that no one else could hear yet so filled with venom that I could not misinterpret what he was saying, he looked squarely into my face and said, "Fuck you, you two faced bitch." And then as he turned back to the coffin in front of him, he looked back at me and muttered, "Why isn't it you who's dead?"

And then there was nothing left in the world and I finally let go, crumpling onto the soft green grass and hard pebbles around the grave, everything slipping away until I cared about nothing anymore.

On the way home, my aunt coming to stay with me, shivering in Moe's car in the warm summer twilight, I willed myself not to start screaming. "What had happened? Had it happened? Had Gavin snapped? Had *I* snapped and imagined it all? But over the next weeks and months when I had called, ten, twenty, thirty times only to be told that Gavin was out or couldn't come to the phone, I knew that it had been real, that the something we once had, the love, the intimacy of two best friends, for some reason had vanished. It was unthinkable, but inescapably true. I had lost the two people dearest to me in the world in two days, and in both cases I didn't know why.

I was totally and miserably alone and I cried for both of the Stewarts.

My mother, when she arrived home from who knows where, was useless as always. "You probably said something to Gavin that he resented," she told me. "You know you *do* have a way of doing that, Nicki. I have told you many times that you are far too outspoken. Boys don't like that." She shook her head at me and started to primp for her date with her latest boy toy.

Our Rabbi smiled benevolently and told me that I would get over York. That it had been puppy love and though it hurt now, time would heal it. "If I needed to talk to an asshole," I thought as I left his study, "I could have called my father."

The girls from camp were no help at all, as they all went hysterical crying as soon as they heard my voice on the phone and I ended up consoling them.

After a while there was only one person left who could possibly even have an idea of what I was feeling.

That's when I called Apple.

But what had I done to Gavin?

As the years passed I grew to accept that I would never speak to him again, and sometimes I actually hated him, but under it all, I always wondered *why*. What had I *done*? What *hadn't* I done? Andrew, people seldom called him Apple after York died, didn't know he said, and early on, after trying to touch base with Gavin a few times himself, said he didn't care. At least Gavin had *talked* to Andrew, though when he had asked, Gavin refused to get together, but when it came to me, for Gavin Stewart I simply didn't exist.

And, God help me, no one could tell me why!

CHAPTER TWENTY-EIGHT:

APPLE GOES TO A FUNERAL –
AUGUST 13, 1975
POV: Apple:

"York Stewart is testing us," I heard Rabbi Flax say as he tried to explain to those staring up at him how such a tragedy could have happened. "He is testing our courage, our strength, our resolve, and yes, our faith in God Almighty. York wants us to be strong. He wants us to continue believing in the creator. He wants us to carry on."

"And he wants you to fuck yourself," I thought as people around me wept. My eyes were so dry they hurt. "You didn't know York Stewart. Your pain is paid pain. You are so totally full of shit! This funeral is totally full of shit." I closed my eyes, and pressed a hand so tightly to them that little chains of light jumped in the blackness behind my eyelids. "Go away," I thought, "all of you people go away. All of you starers and criers, who are you? What are you doing here? Aunts? Uncles? Kids who went to school with York? You didn't know him. You attended his birthday parties and his bar mitzvah. And what is this but just another social gathering to you. So fuck off. Go away!"

But no one would leave until York left, and even then, most of them would follow him back towards the city where cars would stop and the bullshit rabbi would say a few more words before they would all go home, finally leaving York alone, in a place where, finally, he shouldn't have been alone.

The Meadows Funeral Home in Rockport Hills, Long Island was jammed. People were standing in the back, and as I looked over to the side of the chapel in which we sat, I could see that the doors were open so that an overflow crowd could hear the Rabbi's voice and stare at the moaning family that sat in the first row behind the closed, maple casket.

"Hear O Israel, The lord is our God, The Lord is one."

"Who shall ascend the hill of the Lord, and who shall stand in his holy place?"

"I'll bet it's gonna have something to do with clean hands and a clean heart," York whispered to me and Gavin, sitting on the bench directly in front of us, giggled.

The entire camp was crowded into the social hall, all the campers and counselors dressed in whites, the sun shining through the screened windows that looked onto the side campus. Saturday morning services were about over, and in a few minutes weekly awards would be given out. I would probably win senior character, again, which Sturtz said was fitting because, according to him, there was no bigger character in the entire camp than me. "All Around Senior" would go either to York or Sturtz. The other awards, at least to us, no one cared about for they were far from important.

"I think you've got 'all around'," I whispered to York, who shrugged. Gavin nodded then whispered over his shoulder, "You deserve it, but don't forget Sturtz' catch in the game against Arrowpoint." York smiled. "All around is probably Sturtz' this week, and he deserves it. No problema. He's better; he gets it. Simple as that."

Larry Caboy, the head of the waterfront and the counselor who acted as rabbi, was reaching the end of the service.

"Before we conclude, will anyone who has lost a loved one and wishes to say the mourners kaddish please stand and say it along with me." There was a shuffle of feet as a few of the counselors and one or two of the campers stood. The rest of us averted our eyes, somehow embarrassed, somehow not wanting their death to enter our Saturday morning.

"Yisk a dal, yisk a dosh......."

"....shamay rabbo." I opened my eyes. Rabbi Flax moved back and forth almost imperceptibly as he intoned the prayer for the dead. Dead! I said the word over and over in my head until it lost all meaning.

"Dead dead dead dead dead dead dead dead dead dead dead dead........."

The word had spread quickly around the campus and a numbing pall hovered over everything. It was clear that the owners were in shock and didn't know how to proceed, or whether to proceed at all. Some of the younger kids who couldn't fully fathom the enormity of the event still played catch and ran around chasing each other under the glazed eyes of their still disbelieving counselors. But the rest of the camp was quiet, with no one outside the cabins on the upper campus, the senior campus. Most of the older kids were too shocked to move, and they lay on their beds quietly contemplating what had happened to York, and wondering what was going to happen to them.

Gavin was already gone. None of us had had a chance to say anything to him as he had been immediately whisked off to Howard's cabin, and then, under sedation, had been driven back to the city.

In our cabin Dorff was fast asleep, his face to the wall, and Sturtz was lost in a comic book. Klinger had been taken to the infirmary with what they said was a stomach virus, though I knew that it wasn't. I also knew that every time he would lean over the bowl throwing up whatever there was in his stomach, he was ridding himself of a knowledge that he couldn't bear to know was true.

I lay on my bed, stared at a ceiling covered with graffiti and tried to stay sane. I had heard the other kids talking. Was summer really over? Would we be sent home? Would anyone ever swim in the lake again? To me it was all bullshit, trivial. All I wanted to do, *had* to do, was to hold it together.

I finally knew that saying kaddish was no longer a foreign thing.

"Had I killed him?," I thought over and over again as I stared at the place on the ceiling where Sturtz had written, long ago last week, "Mister Happy Rules, 1975." Had it been me? Was it something I had said? What is something that I should have said? Was it something I hadn't noticed that could have avoided all of this? For a moment a wave of nausea so great that I thought I might have to join Klinger in the infirmary swept over me. I sat up quickly, and when the bile did not come up, I lay down again.

They said they would find the cause at the autopsy.

At the *autopsy*!

And the picture of York, cold and nude and alone on a slab at some hospital room in Honesdale, being sliced open by someone without a face, wondering why I was allowing this to happen, calling for me as his insides were taken out and examined, pushed its way into my mind and I barely made it to the ceramic bowl in the back of the bunk.

It seemed that everything I had ever eaten came up, and when there was nothing left to fill the bowl, I dry heaved for another five minutes. I don't think I had ever felt as sick. I stood at the sink, my knees wobbly, and rinsed my mouth with Listerine, yet the taste of my bile remained in my mouth.

Sturtz looked up from his comic as I passed his bed on the way back to mine, but said nothing. When I lay down again and looked over at him, he was once again engrossed in his reading.

And what about Nicki? My God, Nicki! How in God's name was she going to get through this? I had to. I was a guy. But she, she would be destroyed. I wished I could talk with her. I asked Milburn about her and he said he didn't know.

Poor fucking Nicki!

Poor fucking me!

Then, somehow, I slept.

It was agreed late that night that only York's bunkmates would be taken to the funeral the next day, though almost the entire compliment of campers and counselors at Kanuga wanted to go.

So it was that Henry Sturtz, Lennie Dorff and I stood in the blazing sun waiting for Howard Mendelsohn to open the doors of his enormous black Cadillac that would take us from here to where York would be waiting. Klinger, they told us, was too sick to go.

We waited for a few minutes with all four doors of the car open, letting the intense heat inside dissipate into the intense heat outside.

"I hope you used deodorant," Sturtz whispered to Dorff.

"What?" Dorff said, looking confused.

"Get in the back, Lenny," Sturtz hissed, and then looked at me. "Front or back?" It was something York would have offered but it was unexpected coming from Henry. "Doesn't matter," I said. "Less likely for me to heave if I sit in the front though."

Sturtz nodded. "So be it." He slid into the back seat next to Dorff. I got in next to Howard, getting a whiff of his Aqua Velva, so strangely familiar on this surreal day.

The car started, the air conditioning went on and we slowly made our way from the guest house parking lot on the top of the hill that overlooked the camp, down the rutted, red clay road that led to the main road, that eventually, would lead to York.

No one spoke for a long while. Howard finally broke the silence. "You guys okay back there?"

"Yeah," Sturtz and Lenny answered without conviction and in uneven unison.

"Need to stop for anything? A pit-stop? A soda?"

"Nah."

"No, thanks."

"No."

"Maybe something to eat?"

"We're okay, Howard," I said.

"Thanks, though," Lenny said.

"We're good," Sturtz said, and I turned to look at him.

We're good? What was *that* about? Would anything ever be good again? Sturtz mouthed an impatient, "What?" at me, and I turned away and looked at the road through the front window. I stared straight ahead and realized with a sudden jolt that it had only been a matter of days before that I was driving along this same road, anxiously heading for our Mystery Walk. I remembered the old man Ike Hayes had waved to, Mort his name was, and I wondered why he was still alive at one hundred and York Stewart was dead at sixteen.

I took a deep breath afraid I might upchuck again!

"You okay?" Howard asked and I nodded and said nothing.

Rhetorical question.

Ike Hayes and the ride to the river seemed a lifetime ago as I stared at the ramshackle farmhouses that dotted the green countryside; their rooms with people who were blissfully unaware that York had died.

The car kicked up clouds of dust on the rutted road to the city.

"From dust we are formed, to dust do we return, and though dust be our origin, and our end, our spirit dwells on in the house of the Lord."

I stared at Rabbi Flax, hating him. He was a fat bald man, who compensated for the lack of hair on his head by sporting a scraggly goatee under his thick lower lip. The rabbi's black suit was in desperate need of pressing. I stared at it's frayed cuffs. There was what appeared to be egg stains on his shirt.

"Fucking pig. Mother-fucking pig. Cock sucking mother-fucking pig with that typical, 'I'm one of you' bullshit,'" I thought. "Trying to make himself look more like an ordinary person in the middle of one of the richest congregations on Long Island. Horse shit."

"*Does anyone buy this crap,*" *Sturtz whispered through clenched teeth to no one in particular as York strode up to the stage to receive his All Around Senior award.*

"*Clap clap clap, clap clap clap clap clap,*
Clap clap clap clap, Yea York!
Clap clap clap, clap clap clap clap clap,
Clap clap clap, Yea York!"

York beamed as he shook Howard's hand then held the small trophy out so that all could see it.

"*Clap clap clap clap, Yea York.*"

Gavin was standing in front of me clapping for his brother then, unexpectedly he put his fingers to his mouth and whistled so loudly that even Howard and Larry laughed.

York walked off the stage and back into our midst. Gavin clapped him on the back as he headed for his place on the bench. "Look, York," he whispered, "Mom's here." I followed York's gaze as he looked over to where his brother was pointing.

Mrs. Stewart was standing in the doorway to the social hall, the sunlight surrounding her making her even more beautiful than I had remembered. She was holding a large shopping bag in her hand and I knew it was filled with comics for Gavin, candy for the bunk, and the last week's issues of THE NEW YORK POST that York adored. "No better sports pages in the world, Apple," he had told me on more than one occasion." I always took his word for it. Mrs. Stewart waved, the motion of her hand diffusing the light behind her. Then she mouthed, "Way to go, York," and then, with her free hand, she blew her sons a kiss.

Her scream of anguish drew gasps from those sitting around me. At first I couldn't understand what Mrs. Stewart was howling, her words incoherent. Then the words became clear. "My baby," she cried. "My beautiful baby." Gavin, weeping, put his arm around his mother and hugged her as Mr. Stewart put his arm around them both. It seemed impossible, but as Mrs. Stewart fell back into her husband's arms, her head hanging limp on her shoulders, her mouth no longer capable of making any sounds but set in a horrible **O**, she stared directly into my eyes and I knew she didn't see me, and, all at once, I didn't recognize her. The beautiful woman who had stood in the sun had died, and a haggard, unkempt stranger had taken her place.

I looked away, but everywhere I looked there was pain. Nicki, a few rows away, was staring straight ahead, her eyes dry, obviously in shock. Dorff, standing on the side aisle with Howard, looked pale and one step away from falling. Only Sturtz, sitting off to one side with a friend of York's from school, a friend who was sobbing quietly, looked untouched by all that was going on around him. Fucking Sturtz.

And then it was over and the cars were loaded and in the bright sunlight of the day, their headlights were turned on and, seemingly in a heartbeat we stood on a grassy knoll surrounded by granite slabs with small stones on them. Again the Rabbi said words and again people wept, and again York's mother howled her grief.

"Standing in our family plot in Queens, you can see the skyscrapers of Manhattan in the distance."

We were in our beds waiting for lights out. The bunk smelled of toothpaste and Milburn's aftershave. York lay with his hands behind his head. I leaned on one arm looking at him, listening.

"When we buried my grandmother last winter, I just kept staring at those tall buildings and I thought to myself, 'There are millions of people in those buildings, managing their careers, making dinner plans, getting on with their lives, and they don't know we are here.' And then I looked over at the expressway across from where we were standing, and I thought, 'There are people in those cars, going places, meeting appointments, rushing to visit other people, and they don't know we're here, or, for that matter, that my grandma's dead.'"

I looked over at the expressway, the same expressway, and standing where York had stood watching the cars only months before, I suddenly became him and he became me and I began to cry because the two of us were dead. And hands held me as I cried, as I sobbed, and only York, of everyone there, knew that I had died too.

"It's a mitzvah," Rabbi Flax said, as York's casket was lowered into the ground, "to shovel dirt on the coffin of the deceased. Will each of you come forward, scoop up some sand, and throw it on the coffin, before passing the shovel on to the next mourner."

"The sound of the silt and pebbles hitting the coffin was terrible," York said. "They handed me the shovel but I couldn't do it. There was someone I adored in there. I couldn't be a part of closing her off forever, blessing or no blessing."

I yawned. "I guess I've been kind of lucky," I said. "Both my grandparents are still alive. Actually, no one I've ever known is dead."

"That'll change," York said.

"Well, yeah, I smiled. "I know that. I'm just not anxious for it to happen any time real soon."

"Maybe you'll be lucky and it won't." He paused. "You know what else I was thinking while we were burying my grandma?"

"It would have been nice if you had been thinking about her!" I had gone for the joke and I was sorry I said it as soon as the words left my mouth.

York only smiled.

"I was, Apple. Believe me, I was. That's all you think of, the person who is dead. And yourself and what the loss means to you. But on top of that, or maybe because of that, your mind starts wandering, having these thoughts, tying things together that you would never have thought would go together."

"So what else did you think?"

York sighed. "I thought about you."

"Me!"

"Yep. About going to a Knick's game with you and staying over at your place. About going skating at Rockefeller Center the next morning. Remember?" I nodded. "I thought about having fun," he said, "and then of my being dead and of not being able to do things like that anymore." He paused. "Pretty selfish with my grandma dead and all, huh?"

"I don't know," I said, suddenly thrust into a different world. "I don't know."

York was about to say something else, but he was cut off by the mournful sound of the blowing of taps.

Milburn, ready to make a quick exit for his hot date with Iris, clicked off the lights.

Silence.

York and I reached across and found each other's hand in the sudden darkness, and shook them solemnly as we did every night.

"Goodnight, Apple," York whispered, turning away from me and pulling the covers up to his chin.

"Goodnight, York," I said, as the lights all over camp went out.

I could hear Klinger's voice saying the words of TAPS as he did every night.

"Day is done, gone the sun,
From the hills, from the lake, from the sky,
All is well, safely rest,
God is nigh."

"Sleep well, Apple."
"You too, York."
Taps ended.
All was still.
God was nigh.

PART TWO:
THE TIME OF FILM

CHAPTER TWENTY-NINE

October 11th

He had gone to bed thinking about him, and now as he opened his eyes, Leonard Dorff thought about him again. Sturtz.

He fumbled around the night table until he found the clock, picked it up and held it close to his face. Six forty five. Still over nine hours to go! Good.

He clicked the alarm button off so that it wouldn't disturb Elie, and lay back in the semi-darkness of the bedroom.

His wife snored quietly beside him. He watched her for a moment and then silently slipped out of bed. He liked being up before her, the silence.

He peed, splashed water on his face, brushed his teeth and looked at his naked body in the mirror. Not good. He wasn't aging well and he knew it, and what was worse, Sturtz would know it too, and would call him on it. He halfheartedly tried touching his toes, then pulled on his robe that too had seen better days, and started downstairs to make coffee.

The meeting with Henry was set for four, and he was frightened. Where some people thrived on adventure, Leonard Dorff had always consciously avoided the unknown. Danger of any kind terrified him. "So why now?" he thought. "What could Sturtz possibly want?"

Through the years, and though he had tried, Dorff had never been able to successfully put Sturtz out of his mind. How could he? The world was all Sturtz. For years everywhere he looked his early nemesis was there. The cover of ENTERTAINMENT WEEKLY when he took over that film company, the piece on 60 MINUTES on the power he wielded in all parts of the entertainment world, the three interviews with Barbara Walters chronicling his two failed marriages and the son he had with the young Italian starlet who overdosed when he took the child and forbad her from ever seeing him. How she had died and Sturtz had raised his son out of the public eye. (He remembered how Elie had gasped as Sturtz famously walked off the Walters' set when she pushed him too far on the subject of his son.) The Time and Newsweek pieces on his acumen at selecting money- making film projects: everywhere Sturtz. Now, now with just one phone call, Sturtz was back. Sturtz suddenly was no longer someone to read about, but a flesh and blood reality who had entered his life all over again.

Dorff crossed into the kitchen, thinking of what Henry would say if he could see his rag- strewn offices on West 37th Street. And Henry *would* ask him about that, about how he was doing. How could he tell him that month after month business got worse and worse in the rag trade, and that there was always the nagging worry that he might lose everything. He smiled grimly to himself. "THE HOUSE OF REMNANTS," he thought. "I couldn't have chosen a better name for it if I'd tried."

Sturtz! What the hell did he *want*? And, of course, with Sturtz there came Kanuga, a subject about which he never spoke. Even when he visited Howard, now almost ninety but still a strong presence at Kanuga, each Sunday, the subject of camp was off limits. "Too many bad memories," he had told his uncle, " too much pain, and I've put it all behind me." Howard had offered to send the twins, but though Elie pleaded with him, Dorff would not hear of it. He had told her that he wouldn't subject his daughters to the same nightmare he had lived through.

"But they're different from you," Elie had argued.

"But the camp is still the same. The girls are staying home."

"Leonard...."

"Elie, think back. Forget me. We both know how much I hated camp, but think of you. Can you tell me that you were ever happy at Kiunga?"

"You know I wasn't. Every day was a nightmare. But that isn't the point. Leonard."

Dorff sighed sure of what she would say next. She didn't disappoint him.

"It's free, Leonard! What would cost many thousands for others, for us will be for free. The girls, Leonard, the girls can go for free!"

Dorff shook his head. "Not even if they paid *me*."

And though Leonard Dorff didn't win many arguments, the girls stayed home.

And now, out of nowhere, a request, no, a summons from Sturtz.

At first he had adamantly told Elie that he would not go.

He had come home from work that day and she had greeted him at the door with the news.

"You'll never guess who called today?"

Dorff shrugged, took off his coat and undid his tie.

"You'll never guess."

Lennie sighed as he opened the top button of his shirt. "All right, who?"

"Guess."

Sturtz could feel himself grinding his teeth, "Come on, Elie, who?"

"Henry Sturtz. Well, not him really. His secretary."

Dorff's legs went weak. He turned away from his wife and took a deep breath. "What did she want?"

Elie was beside herself with excitement. "He wants to see you in his office on the eleventh. That's next Tuesday."

Lennie worked to make sure his voice wouldn't shake. "Did the secretary say what he *wanted*?"

Elie shook her head. "No, I told you. That was it. Just that he wanted to see you. Oh, and that it was important. You'll wear your blue suit. You can drop it at the cleaners on your way to work tomorrow and it'll be ready when you come home the day after."

Lennie turned to her and shook his head. "No need. I'm not going."

"But….."

Leaving his wife with her mouth open, he walked into the kitchen.

Elie followed him. "Just like that, you're not going?"

"Just like that I'm not going." He opened the refrigerator, took out the hamburgers he had taken from the freezer that morning, pulled back the aluminum foil and put them in the broiler.

"Of course you're going."

"Of course I am *not* going, and that's the end of it."

"But…."

" Again, but. Elie, there is nothing that Henry Sturtz has to say to me that I want to hear." He rinsed four potatoes, took a knife and made small slits in them, wrapped them in paper towels and popped them into the microwave. "What kind of vegetable do you want?"

Elie screwed up her face. "I don't care about vegetables. Forget the vegetables. I want you to go see Henry Sturtz."

Lennie went back to the freezer and took out a package. "Then we'll have peas."

"Leonard, stop ignoring me."

Lennie looked at his wife. "I am not ignoring you. It is impossible to ignore you. But you are not listening to me. I said I am not going to meet with Sturtz and that's final. This is my decision so let's drop it."

"Your decision." Elie snorted. "Typical. *Your* decision; forget about me and the girls as usual."

"This has got nothing to do with you and the girls? Sturtz called *me*."

"But it could affect all of us, don't you see? It could affect all of us and you don't want to go."

Dorff clenched his teeth, pulled a head of iceberg lettuce from the crisper, dug his fingers into it's softness and started pulling it apart. "How could it affect all of us?"

Elie shrugged. "I don't know, but......"

"You just said....."

".....but Goddammit maybe it's something good." His wife's shouting surprised him and Dorff looked over at her for a moment and then away. When she spoke again, her voice was measured, soft. "God knows we could stand something good in our lives couldn't we Lennie?"

He returned to the lettuce. "You don't have it so bad."

"And I have it so good? Oh, I know I'm forgetting how exciting our lives are Leonard. The constant parties, the European trips, the elegant people we rub shoulders with. The fancy cars; the live in help."

Lennie ran cold water on the lettuce. "As long as I'm around you have live in help!"

Elie put her pudgy hand on Lennie's arm, and he pulled away. "Maybe he wants to invite us to a party or something. He knows movie stars, Lennie. At least go and find out."

"I don't need his parties and I don't need his movie stars."

"Then what do you need?"

"I need you to leave me alone, that's what I need."

"Very funny."

"It wasn't meant to be funny. Leave me alone."

"You may not need, but maybe *I* need! Did you ever think of that? That maybe *I* need."

Again, Lennie could feel himself grinding his teeth. "That's *all* I think of, believe me."

"Don't be sarcastic."

He glared at her. "Then don't be ridiculous. You know how much I hate Henry Sturtz, and all of a sudden after almost forty years he calls and I'm expected to jump?" He shook his head. "I don't think so. If you want to find out what this is all about, you go. Have a ball. Maybe he'll take you to Paris or the Riviera on his jet. Maybe Staten Island."

"Staten Island would be at least something. With you, we never go anywhere."

Lennie smacked his hand down on the formica counter top. "Jesus Christ, Elie, you want to go somewhere, fine, I'll give you the money. Go."

Elie's voice was getting teary. "You really are a bastard you know that, Lennie? Do you know how often I ask myself how I ended up with you?"

"I'll tell you how. You asked me to marry you, and I, like a shmuck, said yes."

"I never proposed to you. You proposed to me."

Dorff smirked. "You have selective memory as always. We were in bed in my apartment. I was in you. You tightened up and wouldn't let me out till I agreed to marry you."

"You're a pig, a selfish pig, like always."

"A selfish pig. Now this time you're right. Mister Selfish Pig, that's me. I work my ass off all day long, I come home from work and make your dinner, I wash your dishes, I take out your garbage and on the weekend I wash and dry your clothes, but I'm a selfish pig."

"Lennie....."

"And now you're all over me with this Henry Sturtz thing, and because I don't want to see him, again I'm a selfish pig."

"What about Henry Sturtz?"

Becca, their eldest daughter, was standing in the doorway.

"Your father has a chance to meet with Henry Sturtz next Tuesday and he doesn't want to go."

Becca slumped into a kitchen chair. "That's kinda lame, Pops. Sturtz is big money. He was on *Entertainment Tonight* last week. They said his rise to the top was meteoric."

"Meteoric my ass."

Becca sniffed. "And being in the rag trade is really glamorous?"

Dorff ignored her. "What else did they say?"

Becca shrugged. "Not much. He was at some guy's funeral."

Dorff looked at his daughter. "And?"

"And that was it. He talked about starting a new picture and how much he owed the dead guy. That was all. He's a pretty sharp looking guy, that Sturtz." She picked up a piece of bread and popped it into her mouth. "I'd do him."

"He's my age, Becca."

Becca shrugged. "That's your problem. You look like you could be his father." She looked over at the broiler. "What's for dinner?"

"Hamburgers," Ellie said, using her fingers to fix her daughter's hair. Becca pulled away and looked at her father. "Hamburgers again? Jesus, do you think you could ever spring for a steak once in a while."

Lennie finished slicing two tomatoes and put them in with the lettuce. "When you go out to work, then we'll have steak. Until then, you'll eat what's on the table. "

"That is so lame. I mean sometimes what you say is so fucked up."

"Don't talk to your father like that."

"Why not? You talk to him like that all the time."

"Lennie, say something."

Lennie Dorff pulled two large bottles of salad dressing from the refrigerator. He held them up. "Seven Seas. French or Russian?" When neither responded he shrugged and brought them both to the dining room table.

Elie shook her head and looked at her daughter. "Go wash your hands. Dinner will be ready in a few minutes."

"I'm washed."

"Your hands are filthy."

"Check out Mrs. Clean. They'll do."

"Then go get your sister."

"I'm not walking up those stairs to get the Princess. She knows it's dinner time."

Dorff pointed at the archway leading to the living room. "Go get her."

Becca leaned back in the chair and screamed. "MARGO."

It was answered from a cry almost as loud from above them. "WHAT?"

"DINNER."

"I'M NOT HUNGRY."

Elie moved into the archway. "Margo, you'll come down here and you'll eat. Come now."

"Then wait a minute."

Elie threw up her hands and moved back into the kitchen. "You see what I have all day while you're at the place? And you tell me that you have it hard."

Becca laughed.

"What?"

"Nothing.

Elie's voice shook. "Why were you laughing at me? I don't deserve that Becca. I don't deserve that."

"I wasn't laughing at you. Just chill for once will you?"

"Lennie, you see how she talks to me?"

Becca leaned back in her chair. "I don't know what the big deal is that we all have to sit down together every night anyway. If we didn't see each other we wouldn't have all these fucking arguments. None of my other friends eat with their families."

"You just answered your own question." Lennie handed the silverware and napkins to his daughter. "Set the table."

"Jesus, anything else?"

"*Just do it!*"

Becca shook her head, shrugged and began putting the settings around the table. "You really oughta do it, Pops."

"I'm finishing making dinner. The least you could do is..."

"No, I mean meet with the Sturtz guy. Maybe you could get me a part in his new flick."

Leonard Dorff looked at his daughter as she moved around the table. Kinky black hair framed her round face. White make up on both cheeks highlighted both the black lipstick and purple eye shadow that she wore. Her overweight body was crammed into a low slung pair of black spandex pants and topped with a cut off tee shirt on which there was a smirking picture of some leering singer. Her plump pierced belly jiggled as she leaned forward over each person's place.

Elie took her seat at one end of the table. "I can't believe that you're not the least bit curious to see what he wants with you," she said grabbing a piece of white bread, ripping off a piece and putting into her mouth."

"Really, Pops, it could mean money."

"Who's talking about money?" Margo Dorff strolled into the dining room and flopped down in a chair. She was almost identical to her twin except for the furious acne on her face. "Cause if you have any Pop, you're about a year late with my allowance."

"Your father has a chance to meet with Henry Sturtz and he says he won't go."

"What?," Margo cried. "The rich guy from the camp you went to? That is so phat! Oh Lennie, you have got to be kidding me."

Leonard Dorff's hand shook as he lifted the burgers onto a serving plate. A feeling of such madness swept through him that he thought he might scream. This was his life. This! These women were his family and he hated them with such passion and so completely that he could feel his gorge rise even as he heard them bickering behind him. And he wanted them to be quiet, to be dead, to leave him alone. And Leonard closed his eyes and even as he saw them dead, their lifeless bodies at his feet, he knew that the fault was his. *He* had created them, *he* had nurtured them, *he* had schooled them into being everything he hated. Their voices, their thinking, their very *being* were his doing and they repulsed him and though he wanted to, he knew that he could not kill them, and so, not for the first time did he consider suicide. And as they droned on, unaware that he stood at the stove with their food in his hand, unaware that he thought or he felt, unaware that he *was*, he willed the shaking stopped. And it stopped as it always did, and the feeling of revulsion that coursed through the blood in his veins once again was, because it had to be, sublimated.

"If you want me to go, I'll go," Leonard Dorff said as he placed the dish before them. It would silence them and he knew, as he always did, that he would eventually agree to whatever they wanted at some point, so it was simply easier to do it now.

And for the rest of the meal Leonard Dorff choked down his food as his wife and daughters spent the money they were sure would be coming their way.

Now, while the rest of his family slept, he padded into the kitchen and started the coffee. He sighed when he saw the pile of unwashed dinner dishes in the sink, scraps of food still clinging to them. Margo had forgotten or simply not cared again. On any other day he would insist that she do them before she left for school, but today, he reasoned, the aggravation the subsequent confrontation would bring was far worse than his doing them for her.

He filled the sink with warm water and soap.

If only he could arrive at Sturtz's office having made a success of his life, but he had not. What with Elie and the girls, and his father in the nursing home there was no money saved. He had nothing. Not like Sturtz, not like a high- powered, big mocher millionaire. He knew that as soon as Sturtz saw him he would know that he was a failure and would rip into him as he had when they were kids. And as then, he knew that he still wouldn't know how to defend himself.

He felt nauseated.

Why did Sturtz want to see him in the first place? He went over and over it in his mind. It gnawed at him and made him more and more frightened. Certainly there was nothing that he could do for him. The feeling of inadequacy, the feeling of not fitting in, that he had almost successfully hidden away, now consumed him again.

He heard the toilet flush above him and guessed that it was Becca. She was usually up before Margo, but she would probably pore over *The Star* and *People* before finally leaving the bathroom and emerging for breakfast. He didn't want to see her. He didn't want to see anyone. Not today.

The coffee was ready and he poured himself a cup. He would let it cool while he brought Elie's coffee up to her.

He glanced at the clock as he walked out of the kitchen. 7:15. Just under nine hours before the appointment. Nine hours. He would go into the place and if he left by three he should be to Sturtz in plenty of time.

Yet it still gnawed at him. Sturtz. I am going to see Henry Sturtz. It would be the first time he would see him or speak to him since the year York died. Sturtz, the prick! He remembered all the cruelty, especially the invitation to the party that didn't exist. Could he be doing that again? Could he make an appointment and then not be there? "Maybe," he thought, "knowing Sturtz, maybe."

Then why in God's name are you going?

As he passed the bathroom, from behind the locked door, he could hear Becca humming and the sound of her flipping through a magazine. He tiptoed past.

Elie was still sleeping, so he left the coffee on her night table. She had left her plastic contact lens case opened and two crystal blue lenses stared up at him.

He dressed quietly and, as always, he was out of the house, no goodbyes said, long before any of them even knew that he was gone.

CHAPTER THIRTY:

Andrew:

I had the weirdest dream last night.

I was racing through the halls at school, late for my first period class. I knew I was late, but I had been late before without this panic.

I had made it to the top of the stairs when someone, someone without a face, fell into step running alongside me. "This is yours," he yelled and before I could respond, he had thrown me an oversized aluminum canoe. Though I knew from it's size that it was very heavy, I lifted it easily and swung it over my head as I ran to my class.

The kids, who were milling about when I arrived, broke into laughter when they saw that I could not see them because of the canoe. I turned around and around, from one student to another, telling them to stop laughing, and as I did, the canoe would swing around, striking them on their heads, until, within a few dream moments, all of them were stretched on the cold hallway floor in front of my room bleeding and still. There was no question from their broken, twisted bodies that they were dead. Panicked, I started running, the canoe still held over my head. At the end of the hallway my path was blocked by an enormous man, his body covered with tattoos. "Put it down, Brookman," he whispered. "Put down the canoe." And then he was gone and Nicki was holding a door open for me calling, "This way, Andrew. Drop it, and come this way." I threw off the canoe and headed to where Nicki stood smiling. Just as I reached her she disappeared and all the doors that a moment before were open wide, now were locked and covered with heavy chains.

My eyes flicked open and though I had no idea what the dream meant, I knew it couldn't be good.

I wanted to ask Nicki what she thought, but she, of course, wasn't there.

Nicki:

Agreeing to separate had been easy. To be honest, when I first brought it up, the feeling I had was one of resignation mixed with relief. It had been inevitable anyway, I reasoned, so why not now? I had married Apple all those years ago and he had slowly, and inevitably, become Andrew. He and I talked about it calmly, like adults, and we tried to cover all the bases. We talked about Jess and what it would mean to her, and then we talked to Jess and she nodded as though she had always expected it. She didn't cry. None of us did. Andrew packed his things and left a few weeks later. Jess came down from Ithaca and she and I helped him move into a small apartment just a few streets away as though it were just one more family project to be done together. We helped Andrew unpack, had a huge dinner at Luigi's, Jess went back to college and that, it seemed, was that.

Andrew:

For a while, I must admit, I liked my bachelor life. I had never really had one and the freedom it gave me was heady. I made sure that I graded all my papers and marked all of my tests during my free periods at school so when I got home every evening the time was mine to use as I wished.

And I used it to my heart's content.

I played my music as loud as I wanted, watched my T.V. far into the night, flipped my channels as much as I liked, and I ate when and if I wanted to. Dishes sat in the sink until there were no clean ones left to use, and clothes were worn and re-worn again and again until I would finally force myself to drag them out to a Laundromat. I smoked and I drank at will. I rented porn videos and jerked off. It was as though my parents were out of town for an extended stay and the place was mine!

I avoided mirrors and as long as I did that, it felt great being eighteen at last.

Nicki:

Ours had never been a marriage made in heaven. Andrew and I had never been in love and we both knew it. When we first told our mutual friends, mostly the camp people, of our plans to marry, they were left with their mouths hanging open. Sue actually reminded me that I had always been turned off by Andrew when he had been Apple, and yet, with all that, it seemed strange that she and the rest didn't understand, didn't get it. It certainly was clear enough to Andrew and to me.

There simply was no one else we could have possibly been with.

The first year was hell and, perversely, though it was never discussed, it was exactly what we needed, what we wanted. Passionless sex followed days that were tolerable, and most days were, surprisingly, tolerable. We got through the days that were rough on our own, keeping the conversation general, not needing one another. By the time one year had led to two and then to five, somehow it had gotten easier. There were days, it seemed, when we actually liked each other. Without expecting it, we now could read each other, and through that we devised the kind of shorthand, I was to learn, that couples that *are* in love know very well. Either way, there never was a question of us splitting, we hung on because there was no one else who *knew*, no one else who shared the point of reference that we had in common. And since we had both known that going in, there had never been any hurt feelings or recriminations along the way. The perversity that was our marriage had become a pleasant blandness, and there was a safety in that blandness that our friends, who were still amazed that we had lasted even a full week much less a number of years, perceived as a maturity and devotion that they thought admirable and actually envied. We never argued, we never fought, and, actually, we were as comfortable one on one with friends as we were as a couple. We, to them, were perfect. We, to us, were simply going through the motions.

Then Jessica arrived and though we both loved her to pieces, she too became part of the unwritten scenario.

I was content in the arrangement and, for a long time and I believe Andrew was too.

And then, all at once, it simply wasn't enough.

I had finished my degree in child psychology, opened a practice and it was doing really very well. With two salaries, the money was very good. My mother could travel where and with whom she liked, and anything tangible we wanted we got. Everything could not be better and yet one day I simply woke up and realized things had to change. I wasn't *un*happy, because happiness had never been an option to begin with, I was discontent, edgy, and I wanted more. The strange part, and there was no one more surprised than I, was that the "more" did not necessarily preclude Andrew. There was no way that I wanted to leave him. I just wanted it to be different between us. If we could find a new place in our relationship, I told him, maybe we could stay together, grow together. It was time to try to re-evaluate our marriage. He smiled and wondered why. I suggested going to a shrink together. Andrew suggested we go to Vegas. I suggested we adopt a child; he laughed and said we should join a bowling league. Though we had always had an active sex life, I began to want to make love, and though he didn't verbalize it, every move of Andrew's body said no.

At that point it was inevitable. It had to end.

Andrew:

So when Nicki called it a day, I have to say, I was not heartbroken. It was, I thought, time. And then, after only six months of being separated, it all went sour. Nothing radical, no epiphanies, but all at once I started to be unhappy, detached, dejected. All of the things that at first had given me pleasure now seemed tedious. My shrink said that I had reached a new plateau in our therapy and prescribed an anti depressant. The drug didn't take away my unhappiness, but it did make it a bit more livable; harder to make wood, perhaps, but livable, other than that, zilch. I tried dating a few times, and each time I found myself so bored after only a few minutes that I wanted to scream. I even pulled my guitar out of storage and started playing again, amazed that the first song that came to mind after all those years was WHERE HAVE ALL THE FLOWERS GONE? I actually finished writing the novel I had promised myself I would write, something I had sworn to Nicki that I would do, and then, when it was finally done, and quite good, if I may say so myself, after only one rejection, I perversely, and quite knowingly, put it away in a drawer.

But through all of it, the thing that most amazed me, the thing that seemed totally impossible, was that I could feel such utter pain after feeling so dead inside for so many years.

I missed Nicki, and nothing could have surprised me more.
Go figure.

Nicki:

And through it all, I missed Andrew. Really missed him.
Go figure.

Andrew:

When the evening finally came when Nicki told me she wanted to separate, I hadn't been surprised or upset. To my way of thinking, it was simply the next step in the progression of our lives. That we had lasted nineteen years seemed almost unbelievable.

And now I missed her.

I wondered, at first, if I really did miss *her*, or if the loneliness I was feeling was simply making me feel things that weren't there. Then one night, after we had talked on the phone for half an hour, I felt an ache so great that I knew it was just not my state of mind. I missed my wife, and I missed her as much as I had ever missed York.

I can't believe I just said that.

Nicki:

Andrew once told me that someone had once told him, that someone had told them, that if one was lucky there would come a day when all the stars lined up in the right way and everything would become clear. I laughed at it when he told me, but I am not laughing now.

October 11th.

Andrew:

October 11th. Jesus!

CHAPTER THIRTY-ONE:

October 11th

Nicki Polis Brookman pulled into the parking garage, switched off the ignition and switched on her phone. As she unbuckled her seatbelt and nodded at the attendant she punched in a number. "No more than three hours," she said, her hand held out for the orange parking stub.

"Hello!"

"Hey, baby."

"Mom?"

"Thank you."

"Excuse me?"

Nicki put the stub in her pocketbook and walked up the ramp and out into the chilly sunlight of 33rd Street. She adjusted her earpiece. "I was talking to the parking attendant. I have an appointment with Sue Barrett, so I'm in the city."

Her daughter's voice sounded worried. "With Aunt Sue? You okay?"

"Just a little lady thing."

"Mom!"

Nicki smiled. Jessica always sounded like her mother when she was exasperated. Well, *somebody's* mother, she thought. "Jessica, I have a bladder infection. I need some pills. Sue's my doctor."

Jessica snorted. "And who better to dispense pills than Aunt Sue."

"Not those kind of pills, my love. Antibiotics. And besides, if I've told you

277

once I have told you a thousand times, those other pills are a thing of Sue's and my checkered past. And even then it was a brief moment in time."

"From the song of the same name."

"Exactly something Andrew would say," Nicki thought, but she smiled and said, "Wise ass."

"So you're sure they are just antibiotics, Ms. Woodstock."

"Believe it or not, Woodstock was way before my time." She gasped as a taxi, coming down 33rd Street barely missed an old man with a walker. "Jesus."

"Huh?"

"Nothing, honey. Just traffic. And by the way, my nineteen- year old beauty, speaking of pills and the like, *you* haven't been…?

Jessica's sigh, even all the way from Ithaca, was eloquent. "No, mother, I haven't been! The sins of the mothers, mother, are not always vested upon their progeny."

Nicki laughed out loud and a passing workman looked at her.

"What's funny?"

"You, and the look some guy just gave me."

Jessica chuckled. "Still getting checked out after all these years. Okay, Mom!"

"It wasn't like that," Nicki said, turning to look after the young workman, "though he *was* kind of cute." She waited for the light to change. "He didn't see the ear piece and thought I was just another crazy. The invention of the cell phone has blurred the line."

"And isn't that what you're doing?"

"What am I doing?"

"Blurring the line."

"I know you learned metaphor from your father before you could speak, but I have no idea….."

"Trying to change the subject?"

Now it was Nicki's turn to be exasperated. "What subject?" She excused herself as she bumped into a pregnant woman as she crossed First Avenue. "What are you *talking* about?"

"About the pills Sue is giving you. Tell me the truth, Mom. Are you sure there's nothing wrong?"

"Dear God, I love this child," Nicki thought.

"Mom?"

"I'm here, baby. Just thinking about how much I love you."

"Ditto."

They both laughed. They had watched GHOST together so often that the word had become shorthand between them.

"I'm fine, baby. Cross my heart and, well…. scout's honor."

"Just so I know you're not trying to spare me."

"And you learned drama from your father before you could walk! Jessica, other than burning when I pee….."

"Ewww."

"Well, you asked. Other than that, I am 100 percent."

"Too much information. I am forced to believe you."

Nicki chuckled. "Thank you, your honor."

"Grandma called this morning."

Nicki took a deep breath. She hadn't heard from her mother in almost a month. "Still in Acapulco with Derek?"

"Yes," Jessica said, "but maybe not for long. She says Derek is beginning to bore her."

"Dear God, he's twenty five, she's at least ten times his age and *he's* starting to bore *her*?"

Jessica laughed. "That's Grandma."

"Thank you, my darling, but I know." Nicki paused. "Did she ask you for money?"

"Of course." Jesssica chuckled. "I told her that I didn't have any, but that since your practice was doing so well, she might want to call you."

Nicki smiled. "Turncoat. I'm sure there'll be a message when I get home," she sighed.

"And how's Dad?"

"Nice change of subject."

"Thanks, but really, how is he?"

Nicki cleared her throat. "Teaching."

Again the exasperation in her voice! "I know *what* he's doing, mother, but *how's* he doing? I haven't heard from him since Sunday."

"Last time I looked," Nicki said, "today's only Tuesday."

"True, but we are talking here about the man who would be on a walkie-talkie to me 24/7 if I'd allow it. Is he okay?"

"More than okay. He's doing fine. He does have a little cold, and of course, he's playing that to the hilt, but other than that, he's 100%."

"And the two of you?"

"Not so fine, but we're working on it."

"Getting separated is working on it?"

"Nothing major, my love, just need a little space between us."

"It's been over six months."

Nicki sighed. "Yes."

"And he's still living in that crappy studio apartment."

"Temporarily, yes."

"Mom!"

"Jess!" Nicki smiled. "Give him a call," she said, "he'd appreciate it. Knowing him, he probably took a sick day."

"I've got a class in a few so I'll call him tonight. He'd probably appreciate hearing from you too, Mom." She giggled. "Actually, so would Grandma."

Nicki stood outside the entrance to the hospital and watched the traffic crawl down First Avenue. "Jessie, what's going on between your father and me, well that's something that he and I have to deal with."

"In other words, butt out."

"Words something like that. We'll talk about it soon, you and I, okay?"

"Are you sure *you're* okay?"

"Better than okay. You're my daughter."

"You know Mom, I......."

Nicki frowned. "Jess? Hello?" She held the cell phone away from her ear and saw that there were no power indicator bars to be seen. She sighed, clicked the phone closed and made her way through the revolving doors into the main lobby of the hospital, made a left past the gift shop and headed for the bank of elevators. The doors to one of the cars, a car jammed with people, was just closing as she approached it and though she might have crammed herself in, she let it go. She pressed the call button, and waited patiently for the next one to arrive.

A delivery boy with a vase filled with flowers fell into place beside her. "African violets," she thought, their sickeningly sweet odor, like lilies, repulsive to her. She moved away and stood in front of the next elevator door.

A tall man stood waiting, and even though he was standing with his back to her, she knew him, and for a moment she felt as though she couldn't breathe. Though she stared at him, out of the corner of her eye she could see the numbers of the car's descent on the indicator. Ten – Click- Nine- Click- Eight - click, and afraid that if she didn't do anything before the car got to ground level, he might somehow disappear, Nicki Polis Brookman reached out and, as she had so many years before, gently touched the man's hand.

"Gavin," she said.

CHAPTER THIRTY-TWO:

October 11th

A t least it hadn't rained while he was in the subway. In fact, Lennie noted, the sun had actually come out. He tried to tell himself that was a good sign, but it didn't work. It was cold out but humid, and Dorff could feel sweat dripping from under his arms, and down his back.

He pushed against the crowds of people heading in all directions, and by the time he got to Fifty Ninth Street the crowd had thinned enough so that he found he could walk at his own pace if he wanted to, yet he had to hurry.

Sturtz was waiting.

He got to the next corner and stopped. He looked at his watch. Ten minutes to four. He *would* be on time after all. He reached into his side pocket and pulled out a crumpled piece of paper, just to double check, just to make sure. He looked at the imposing office building towering above him. No mistake. This was it. Sturtz's building.

He took a deep breath and moved to the entrance.

He nodded to the unsmiling gray haired man in livery who opened the huge glass door for him, and walked across the echoing tiled foyer to a bank of polished metal elevators. His hand shook as he pressed the call button.

He waited only a moment and then the thick, shiny doors in front of him pulled open. Dorff entered, pressed another button, the doors closed and in a moment he was pulled skyward as though in a pneumatic tube. No Muzak, no electronic voice announcing the passing floors, no other passengers, just a hushed whoosh breaking the otherwise reverent silence. Dorff stared at the electronic numbers at the side of the gray metal door in front of him as they silently clicked off his ascent. As the floor indicator passed forty, he closed his eyes and took a deep breath. "Be calm. Be calm. Be calm," he whispered to himself, and still he found it hard to breathe. "You knew him at camp," he told himself, "It's only Henry Sturtz." But then he remembered how Henry Sturtz had hated him and he found it hard to catch his breath again. "Picture him naked on the toilet," Elie had advised him the night before, but as a kid he had seen Sturtz naked on the toilet many times and he was still terrified. He was sixteen again and terrified.

He leaned against the back wall of the elevator and the shock of the cold sweat on his shirt hitting his back pushed him forward. *"Be calm*! It's only Henry Sturtz whether he liked you or not," he told himself. "And you are not a kid any more! You are a grown up."

The doors to the elevator whooshed open.

Leonard Dorff closed his eyes and crossed his fingers.

"Mr. Sturtz."

Henry Sturtz looked up as his secretary closed the door behind her.

"There's a Dorff here to see you."

His braying laughed surprised her. "'A' Dorff. What a perfect way to put it. 'A' Dorff."

Miss Capuzzo nodded. "A little man who looks scared." She had been here before. She knew what was coming.

Sturtz took off his glasses and pointed them at her. "He looks scared because he is scared, Carmella. Leonard Dorff was born scared." He smiled, and it was not a pleasant smile. "And we are going to make him scareder."

"No such word."

Sturtz shrugged. "Then there should be. See someone about it." He winked at her. "The missing file, I think."

"How did I know you were going to say that?"

"Because," Sturtz said warmly, "we're like an old married couple, anticipating the other's every thought and whim."

"Uh-huh." She sighed. "You want him now?"

Henry Sturtz considered. "No. Fifteen. Twenty minutes. Let him sweat."

Miss Capuzzo, shook her head. "Have I told you lately that you are a dick."

Sturtz smiled. "Tell me again. It makes me hard."

Carmella Capuzzo rolled her eyes and went back into the outer office.

In Manhattan, if one's West 59th Street office is high enough, one gets an expansive view of Central Park.

Sturtz' office was high enough!

Leonard Dorff stood nervously looking out of a floor to ceiling window. What he saw stopped him cold. In order to see the vast expanse of Central Park he actually had to look down, whereas the Hudson River and the flat expanse of New Jersey were clearly visible straight on. 'Henry Sturtz lives and works in the sky.' Dorff remembered the cover story in *New York Magazine* saying that, and looking out of the huge window, he realized that the article had been correct. A voice brought him back.

"Mr. Dorff?"

Dorff turned and smiled nervously. "I'm afraid Mr.Sturtz is running very late. If you wouldn't mind having a seat over there, I am sure he will be with you just as soon as he is free."

Dorff took a deep breath. "I realize how busy a man like Mr. Sturtz can be," he said "so, if it's a bad day, I certainly understand and can easily re-schedule." He watched her face, hoping that she would find another day for him, hoping that he could avoid the meeting that had been giving him diarrhea for the past two days. He remembered back to his school days and the relief he would feel when one of his weekly dentist appointments would be canceled at the last minute.

But it was not to be.

"Mr. Sturtz did not tell me to re-schedule," the woman said officiously, as she took her place behind her desk, "so therefore, the meeting is still on."

Dorff could feel a thin paper napkin being clipped around his neck. 'The dentist will be with you in just a minute. Just sit back and relax.'

"If you would just sit over there and wait, I am sure that he will be with you just as soon as he can. If, later, he *does* find that his schedule *is* such that he *will* have to reschedule, you will be informed of his decision at that time."

Leonard Dorff smiled weakly and backed away from the woman's desk. He took off his raincoat, folded it neatly and placed it in his lap as he sat down on one of the gray armchairs that were spread across the room.

Phones rang, hushed voices answered, and Leonard Dorff sat staring straight ahead, already feeling the tip of the dentist's drill in his mouth.

Henry Sturtz leaned back in his leather chair and smiled. "Dorff! The nephew. The 'spinmeister.' He hadn't seen the putz in over thirty years, and here he was. "The shmuck," he thought.

Sturtz looked at pile of contracts lying on the desk in front of him and picked up Joey's. "Time for some fun, and a little show for Lennie Dorff." He pushed back his chair, stood up and walked to the door and opened it.

"Miss Capuzzo." he said, "how many times must I ask you for the Carter contract?"

"The Carter contract? The Joey Carter contract?"

"No, the Schlomo Carter contract! Of course the Joey Carter contract. Where is it?"

"I don't understand. I gave it to you this morning."

"Excuse me?"

"The contract. I gave it to you this morning. Right after you came in."

Out of the corner of his eye Sturtz could see Dorff sitting across the room his hands folded in his lap, his eyes wide, taking everything in. "Almost forty years later and he's still a schmuck!"

Sturtz frowned. "I think I would remember if and when someone handed me papers as important and delicate as those, Miss Capuzzo. I have to meet with Joey and his people at Morton's at eight. I need that contract. And since you never gave it to me, I am led to believe that you still have it."

"Well I certainly have the copy. I always file a copy."

"If I wanted a copy I would have asked for a copy," Sturtz said in a voice so even and modulated that he could easily have been speaking to a small child. "I want the original and I want it in the next few minutes, is that understood?"

"But Mr. Sturtz...."

"*Is* that understood?"

The secretary nodded. With a withering glance over his shoulder and never even acknowledging Dorff, Henry Sturtz went back into his office, leaving a thick silence hanging over the reception room. Leonard Dorff, still staring at Henry Sturtz's door felt his bowel spasm. "Oh Jesus," he thought, "Oh Jesus."

As soon as the door closed behind him, Henry Sturtz giggled. "The look on Dorff's face," he thought, " his fucking mouth hanging open like it did at camp. Excellent! Most excellent."

He glanced at the clock as he moved back to his desk and wondered if he had the time to take one of the five minute cat naps that Adolph Bradus had once said defined him. "In the middle of a crisis only you could sleep for five minutes and wake up like you have been sleeping for hours so refreshed you are." Though the old man had smiled when he said it, Sturtz had always thought there was sarcasm in his words. "Fuck, Adolph Bradus," Sturtz thought with a smile. "The motherfucker's in the ground and I've got his company. Fuck 'em all." As he leaned back in his chair he looked at the framed magazine covers on his wall. "Thank you Adolph, and fuck you!"

Sturtz sat down and closed his eyes. He liked the silence.

GONE THE SUN.

He had a title, now all he needed was a script. The picture had to be, was *going* to be the most important thing he had done since he had become president of TRANSWORLD and he had to make sure nothing was going to screw it up, least of all Leonard Dorff. That's why getting him involved was such a fucking brilliant move. Play to his ego, make him feel like a big man, but always make him know who was in charge. Then he would deal with Apple, Gavin and Nicki.

Sturtz opened his eyes, looked at the clock, and shut them again.

"Fifteen more minutes. Enough time for Dorff to work up a good sweat. I just have to play it so he has no idea how much I need him. Fucking loser will probably lick my hand when I tell him I want him on board, and on salary yet. Perfect."

Henry Sturtz felt himself drifting off and went with it.

"The whole thing is a gamble. Maybe opening a can of worms, but it's so perfect that I can't say no. Prestige plus audience appeal; so few have them. The Weinsteins maybe, Zaentz used to. This could be my SHAKESPEARE IN LOVE or THE ENGLISH PATIENT. And it's all for Joey! This is the one that will cement it for him. That cockamamie action picture made him a fucking movie star, and this one will make him an actor to be reckoned with! And it has to be ready for release a year from this Memorial Day weekend."

Memorial Day.

That's another good title. 'Joey Carter, in MEMORIAL DAY! Nah, stay with GONE THE SUN. Joey Carter as York Stewart! No, we'll have to change York's name. But the one's who'll know will know. Joey will kill as York. Okay so he'll be almost twenty- two when we start shooting, and York was what, sixteen? But he plays young and the fucking girls love his ass so much that they'd accept him as a two year old. The golden boy will play the ultimate golden boy and the critics will cream. Sure the usual disclaimers about living and dead and all that shit, but most important is opening on Memorial Day. Go up against the next

Cameron and Bruckheimer, little David against the Goliaths. Even if it makes ten cents, it will be the story that everyone remembers all the way to Oscar time. But it will gross, maybe not Potter business, but big money because every boy who ever went to camp will want to see it, and those who didn't, or don't care will be dragged there by their girlfriends who cum over Joey. It's a lock!

    Calicoon.

    "What?"

    The Harden. What a fucked up name for a movie theater.

    Who called it the Hardon? Apple? Maybe me.

    Do they still go there?

    Rather do bowling and pizza.

    "Find Ike Hayes, will ya, buddy?"

    Ike Hayes?

    What the fuck am I doing near the Archery Range?

    Free play is almost over.

    I gotta move my ass.

    It's still hot.

    I have to find Ike Hayes for before evening activity. What's so Goddamn important, Howard? What's the big deal? It's too fucking hot. It's stifling even though it's after seven. It's even hard to breathe. Can't Dorff look for him? But if I do it, it might mean camper chief? Shit, I'd have it anyway, but what the hell. I'll look for him as a personal favor to you, Howard. I'll check all the diamonds and the tennis courts; maybe the Archery Range. Sun is going down and everything is gold. Like looking through those orange sunglasses. So fucking hot. Trudging up the hill behind the nature house and bending down to avoid the branches on the path to the archery range. Just coming out into the open I can see them. They don't see me. York, Gavin and Apple. They're stretched out near the targets, their backs to me. I recognize them without seeing their faces. York has no shirt on. His body glows in the hot sun. Golden. Gotta get to Ike Hayes before evening activity. I'll ask them if he's been there. Can't move. The trees are holding my arms. What the hell are those three doing up here anyway? They're talking about something. Someone. I can't hear what they are saying: just a mumble. Pulling. Pulling, but I can't get free of these fuckin' trees.

    'What a loser.'

    That was loud and clear. Who said it? York? Gavin? Apple? It doesn't matter because they laugh and the laughter doesn't stop but continues to grow and Gavin laughs so hard that he is holding his stomach and Apple stands up and makes a motion with his hand which brings on more laughter, and I know then that they are talking about me. The laughter is about me. The joke is about me. I am the fucking joke and I can't move. And my face burns and as I turn and finally pull my hands from the trees I look across the wide expanse to the far side of the range and I see Lennie Dorff standing there looking at them too. Maybe they're laughing at him. It is definitely one of us. But they don't see either of us, and as I pull away from the trees, Dorff looks over at me and our eyes meet and we stand that way for a moment and then I break away and move back into the bushes. And I am crying. Why the fuck am I crying?"

Henry Sturtz opened his eyes.

"Huh?"

Under his collar, Sturtz' neck was wet with sweat.

He took a deep breath, glanced at the clock, focused and smiled. Exactly five minutes.

"What the hell was I dreaming?" he thought, as he pressed the intercom.

"Miss Capuzzo."

"I'm still looking sir."

Sturtz smiled. I'm coming back out."

He pushed back from his desk, rolled his neck for a moment until he heard it crack and then stalked over to his door.

"Well?" Henry asked quietly, not moving from his open door.

Miss Capuzzo forced a smile. "May I please come into your office to see if I can find the contract Mr. Sturtz?"

Sturtz' imitation of her was deadly, his voice up two octaves and whiney. "May I please come into your office to see if I can find the contract, Mr. Sturtz?" His voice grew hard. "No, Miss Capuzzo, you may *not* come into my office. What are you intimating, that I'm helpless? That I haven't looked? I've looked. Trust me, I have looked. And you know what, it isn't there!" He snorted. "Shit on you if you can't do your job properly. All the bright *young* kids running around New York who'd give their right tit to have this job and I'm stuck with you."

He half looked at Dorff and waved at him. "Come on in Lennie."

As the shaken Dorff walked past him into his office, Sturtz winked over at his secretary. "Find it!" He turned back to his office and slammed the door.

Carmela Capuzzzo shook her head and went back to work.

CHAPTER THIRTY- THREE:

Andrew
October 11th

"Susie, hey."

I had called the school early, snuffled my excuses for not coming in, and then had gone back to sleep. I got up at the ungodly hour of eight, made some toast and tea and sat watching the guilty pleasures of daytime television, a shit load of unmarked essays from my ten advanced waiting patiently in my lap, when the phone rang. THE VIEW was on and I put the set on mute, delighting in the sudden silence.

"Hey yourself. How have you been?"

I couldn't remember the last time I had spoken to Sue Barrett, but the years hadn't changed the unmistakable upper middle class Brooklyn accent that I had come to love over the two summers at Kanuga when we had dated.

"I'm nursing a cold."

"Perils of being a teacher."

I smiled. "And being a doctor, I suppose."

"Andrew, I'm a gynecologist."

I laughed. "And that's not catching?"

"Most of the time not. No."

"Gotcha." It was good to hear her voice. "And to what do I owe the pleasure of a phone call from my old squeeze at," I looked at the digital readout on my television, just below where Joy Behar was silently bantering with some new young actress, "11:28 in the a.m, and how in the world did you know I would be home. Did you talk to Nicki?" I sneezed.

"Gezundheidt. Just took a chance. I need to get in touch with her and I think her cell is off. She gave me your number as an emergency contact when you guys split."

I smiled knowing that Nicki's phone wasn't off. It was never off. She had once again forgotten to charge it.

Sue raced on. "Another asshole move on your part, that separation, no doubt."

I decided to let it slide. "I'll give her a message. What's the problem?"

I could hear Susie clucking her tongue. "Uh uh. No. That's no good. Shit. She's got an appointment with me in a few minutes, and I'm not going to be there."

"Nice."

" I was trying to head her off before she got into the city. She's probably at the hospital already." She sighed. I guess my receptionist will have to make the apologies and re-schedule."

"Anything wrong?"

"Ahh, my father's raising hell in the nursing home again. He doesn't know who anyone is anymore and he's getting physical. They're close to tossing him out."

"No, I meant with Nicki. I mean, I'm sorry about your father and all, but why is Nicki coming to see you?"

"MOTHER FUCKER!"

I held the phone away from my ear.

"Susie?"

"Fucking Nun cut me off."

I laughed. Some things never changed.

"Because she's wearing a habit she thinks she doesn't have to signal? Bullshit."

I remembered why I had loved her. "No, About Nicki," I said, "anything serious?"

I could hear Sue trying to calm down. I had heard the sounds of Sue Barrett for two years, years ago, and I was still an expert. I thought I had loved her for those two years, and I couldn't, for the life of me, remember why we had broken up. "Bladder infection. Just hurts her when she pees. It's nothing serious so don't start planning the funeral. "

A wave of relief hit me and I expelled the air that I had been saving for what I was sure would be bad news.

"DAMMIT, ANOTHER ONE DID IT!"

"Where are you driving, Vatican City?"

Sue snorted. "That one wasn't a nun, just a civilian asshole. WHO GIVES THESE PEOPLE THEIR LICENSES?" I could picture her, hands tight on the wheel, screaming out of her window.

"That's why God created taxis."

"What?"

"Taxis. You could have taken a taxi."

"Apple, do you have any idea how much a taxi would cost between Manhattan and Bedford Hills."

She probably had no idea that she had called me Apple, but it sounded good, familiar. I sniffled. "Nicki probably won't call," I said, "but if she should happen to call me, I'll tell her you'll call her later. Okay?" Joey Carter, the good- looking young actor my daughter Jess, along with every other girl and woman in the world adored and coveted, had just sat down between Joy Behar and Barbara Walters. I wanted to hear what he had to say.

But Sue wanted to talk.

"So how's teaching?"

"Fulfilling."

Even Barbara Walters looked smitten.

"I gotta tell you, Andrew, that if anyone had told me back then that you would be a teacher I would have told them that they were full of shit."

Joey Carter had said something funny. The women on the sofa around him were laughing heartily.

"And if anyone had told me you would end up a gynecologist, I would have told them the same thing. I would have picked Sturtz."

Sue's laugh was loud and raucous.

"Ah, Andrew," she laughed, "once a pig always a pig."

They were showing a clip from a new movie or T.V. show. Joey Carter had his arms around a girl who was sobbing.

"You keep in touch with Sturtz?" Sue asked and I shook my head. "Not for years. No. You?"

"Nah. And still no Gavin?"

I shrugged even though there was no way Sue could see me. "His choice," I said. "We tried. You?"

"Nope. I see some of the girls, Nicki of course, but nah, none of the guys."

"Not even Dorff?"

"Hah." The way she said it, the word said everything. "Dorff. Jesus, no! You?"

"Never. No."

There was a lull and I watched as the camera pulled in tight on Joey Carter. He *was* a good -looking kid, and now he was talking seriously about something, his eyebrows knit. I'd have to tell Jessica I had seen him.

"What about you Susie, how's the new one? What's this gonna be, number three?"

"Four, and his name is Milton?"

"His name is Milton?"

"Yeah, schmuck," Sue laughed, "and it rhymes with millions."

"Actually it doesn't."

"Fuck you."

"Can't. I tried. What does *Milton* do?"

I could hear Sue's shrug. "Doctor."

" Like I couldn't have guessed!"

She paused. "A proctologist."

I giggled and my nose ran. "So between you, you get them coming and going."

I smiled at her raucous laugh. "Apple, you are such an asshole."

"Which is right up Milton's alley!"

Sue snorted, not ever her most endearing feature. "I do not know how Nicki stayed with you as long as she did."

"My good looks." They were back from commercial and Joey Carter was still talking earnestly about something. Joy Behar looked as though she could eat him right there on the set.

"Or for that matter, how I could have dated you for two summers."

"'Cause I was the best looking kid at Kanuga."

"Yeah, right. Just ahead of York."

And for an awkward moment we both didn't know what to say. Sue broke the silence. "I've got to give you one thing."

"Small blessings," I said, thankful for her filling the void. "And what's that?"

"That you never got pissed about York and me."

Now Joey Carter was laughing, his eyes firmly on the camera, flashing.

"What?"

"About the time York and I made out."

I closed my eyes. Little pieces of light danced in the darkness.

"Apple?"

My mouth was suddenly dry. "What?"

"You okay?"

"When you and York....."

"Fucked. You know the time." There was silence. "Oh, good Christ, you *didn't* know." I shook my head and Sue went on. "I thought you would have known after all these years." She paused. "Actually, I don't know how you *could* have known, but I just assumed......."

"But you and I were....."

Sue's voice was softer. "I know, honey, you were my guy."

My head was spinning. My girl and my best friend? "Then why......" I knew I sounded like a twelve year old and I didn't care.

"We were kids. We did what felt good."

"But York would have never....."

"Honey, sure he would. York was as much of a kid as the rest of us."

With my eyes still closed, and knowing I was going to have to say something, I desperately tried to piece it all together. Okay, that Sue would have cheated on me made some kind of sense. She was wild. I had known that going in. But she and *York*! Why? York loved Nicki. He loved me. It couldn't be true, I thought, but somehow I knew that it was.

"Did Nicki know?"

"Apple, Jesus, no. It would have killed her. And, for God's sake, please don't tell her! I've been sorry about it forever, and believe me when I tell you, it didn't *mean* anything. It just happened." I wanted to ask her when, and where, but I said nothing. To know would be to believe it. There was another awkward pause and then Sue said, "Look, kiddo, I'm sorry that I laid this on you out of nowhere. Shit on me." I could hear her bang her hand against the steering wheel. "Honest to God, honey, I thought you knew."

"I hate to do this," I heard Sue say, "I mean *now* and everything, but I'm here; the nursing home. I gotta go."

"That's okay."

"I'm sorry, Andrew, I really am. I really did love you you know, no matter what happened with him. But I know what he meant to you, and, but I thought you knew and well, I never guessed that; shit, I *am* sorry."

I took a deep breath. "Goodbye, Sue. If Nicki calls I'll tell her I spoke to you."

"Andrew I....."

I hung up. When I opened my eyes and look back at the T.V., Joey Carter was gone.

CHAPTER THIRTY-FOUR:

October 11th

The first thing Leonard Dorff saw when he entered Henry Sturtz's office was a replica of the Kanuga 1975 color war plaque. It was hung on the wall between the TIME cover with Sturtz's smiling face on it and the framed 11x14 of Sturtz being embraced by Bill Clinton. The famous autographed letter from Henry Kissinger, thanking him for the box of cigars, was hung there too.

"You're looking at the plaque. I keep it there to remind me that I was a winner, even though those around me let me down. As you might have noticed from my office staff, it still happens today, Lennie, believe me."

Dorff smiled weakly and sat down in the chair Sturtz pointed to.

"That plaque is an exact duplicate. I asked for the original but they wouldn't budge on it. I have to respect your uncle for that. I'm still pissed at him for it, but I respect him. How is Howard? He's still living, yes?" Sturtz sat down in his chair and stared at Dorff.

Dorff nodded. "He's fine. Very old, but still pretty sharp."

"He must be what, a hundred and ten?"

Dorff smiled. "Not that old. In his late nineties."

"Is that all?" Sturtz shook his head. "He seemed 90 then."

"He was in his sixties."

"He seemed older."

"We were very young."

Sturtz grunted. "And he still owns the camp?

Dorff nodded. "He still has controlling interest. Sold two smaller shares to......."

"Good. Good," Sturtz interrupted. "And you've been well?"

"Well, I had a little scare two years ago. They found a lump under my arm. It was a few bad weeks there, but it turned out that it was...."

"Sebaceous?"

Dorff nodded.

"Not important unless it's the real thing: a walk instead of a run. To my way of thinking, anything, good bad or indifferent has to be the real thing or it's worthless. All my thinking goes in that direction." He pointed to a plaque that hung behind his chair. "See what it says? 'Man who says it cannot be done, should not interrupt man who is doing it.'"

Leonard Dorff coughed. "Actually, I don't see where that...."

"Whatever." Sturtz pulled open a drawer and produced an open bag of tootsie pops. He held it up to Dorff who smiled and shook his head. "Come on, Pulitzer" Sturtz said, shaking the bag at him. "You always liked them at Kanuga. I seem to remember your taking some from my locker when I was in the infirmary."

Dorff felt his bowels spasm. He was sitting with Henry Sturtz and he was terrified. He gulped and shook his head adamantly. "That was Apple's idea of a joke. Remember? He told you that he was only kidding. I never touched anything in your locker."

Sturtz looked at him, a sly grin on his face. "Really." He shook the bag again. "Have one now." Dorff reluctantly reached into the bag and pulled out a lollipop. "Brown!" Sturtz said, "Good. I don't like browns." He gestured with his head. "Eat up, and we'll talk."

Dorff unwrapped the lollipop. "Aren't you having one?"

Sturtz shook his head. "Had one before. One a day is my limit." He smacked his stomach. "Gotta stay tight. I still have that six pack that you always admired." He lifted his shirt. "No fat on this boy, eh, Len?" Lennie nodded. Sturtz frowned, one hand still patting his naked stomach. "You don't like the lollipop? Come on Lenny, eat up." Dorff put the lollipop in his mouth and closed his lips around it. Henry Sturtz nodded, tucked his shirt into his pants and put the bag back in the desk. He reached into the humidor on his desk and pulled out a cigar, bit the tip off and put it in his mouth. He did not light it. "Now, let's talk."

Leonard Dorff, the white stick of the lollipop protruding through his clenched teeth, took a deep breath and waited to hear what was coming.

Sturtz rolled the cigar in his mouth and stared at Dorff. "How would you like to work for me on a project that I have in mind?"

Dorff coughed and Sturtz smiled.

"Right up your alley. A writing job! You still write don't you?"

Dorff shook his head. "Actually I'm really busy at the place and I haven't written in....."

Sturtz grunted. " Bullshit. It's like riding a bike or swimming. Once you've done it...blah, blah, blah. So, sound good?"

Dorff nodded, speechless, and Sturtz went on.

"Here's the pitch. My next picture, *our* picture, is going to be the most important one in my career. We are talking Oscar here. Many Oscars. Get out your tux." He paused and smiled as he saw Dorff's face fall. "Aw, Len, you're not still mad at me about that other tux thing are you?"

Lennie gulped. "Well, I...."

"Good," Dorff said, "because we are going to the ceremonies, Lennie. The fucking Oscars."

"But why me?," Dorff mumbled, sucking his lollipop.

"We'll get to that in a minute. What's important for you to know is that this is going to be a low budget prestige thing. Classy." He paused to drag on his unlit cigar. "You ever see foreign films?" Dorff nodded. "Well, I want this one to have the class of a foreign film. LAST YEAR AT MARIENBAD, THE FOUR HUNDRED BLOWS. He smiled. "What's the matter, Len, didn't think I would know films like that?"

"No," Dorff gulped, "not at all, it's just that...."

Sturtz waved him quiet. "Ordinarily you'd be right. They fucking bore me to tears, but in my business you have to have an encyclopedic knowledge of everything. So, what I'm talking here is Ingmar Bergman, Truffaut, Fellini, that kind of shit, but American." He pointed the cigar at him. "Do you get the point; a small, touching, incisive coming of age story; and cheap. Lennie, I want every Oscar they have a category for." He held a match to his cigar and puffed until his head seemed shrouded in smoke. "Joey Carter is going to star."

"But doesn't he do action films? My daughters have his pictures on their..."

Sturtz frowned. "This will show his serious side. Are you going to let me finish or what?" Dorff nodded. "Good. Okay, here's the real kick in the head." He paused for dramatic effect. "The picture's about Kanuga."

Leonard Dorff choked on the lollipop. He pulled it out of his mouth. "What do you mean it's about Kanuga?"

Sturtz smiled. "I mean it's about Kanuga!" He stared into Dorff's eyes. "And it's about Kanuga in 1975."

Dorff shook his head. His mouth was dry. "No way. There is no way Howard will allow that." Sturtz waved him away, but Dorff was not to be dissuaded. "Henry, you have to understand that after that summer Howard had to be hospitalized. He still thinks that it did kill Moe. There has not been a day in all the years since it happened that he hasn't thought about it, second-guessed it. It was a tragedy, Henry, a terrible tragedy. He's a very old man. He'll never sit still for this. Never."

"There is no such word as never like there is no such word as can't."

Leonard shook his head. "You don't understand, Henry. That day, that moment, defined the rest of Howard's life. I don't think he even felt as bad as he did that day when Phyllis died. You remember Phyllis, his wife?"

Sturtz nodded his head. "Phyllis died?"

"A number of years ago. She had both breasts removed but it had spread."

"Well she was probably glad to be rid of them, being a lez, right?"

Dorff sat and stared at him in disbelief.

"Okay, bad joke. I apologize. But you have to admit she was pretty dyky. Everyone thought so. But back to what's important…. you have to understand something here Lennie, this movie is going to be made whether Howard gives his okay or not. In fact I'm not even looking for his okay. I just thought that out of respect for him I'd……."

Surprised at himself, Dorff cut him off. "Howard will sue, Henry. He will block you at every turn. He may be 'Good-natured Howard,' most of the time, and he may be way up there in years, but when it comes to Kanuga he can be a pit bull. Believe me, Henry, he'll sue."

"Pulitzer," Sturtz said in the same condescending tone that Dorff remembered so well from camp, "with all due respect, your uncle has a lot to atone for."

"Howard has been nothing but….."

"You're right, he *has* been nothing, but without the buts. The way he acted that day, that time. He was in total denial. He wouldn't talk to the press. He wouldn't talk to the counselors."

"Couldn't."

"Wouldn't." Sturtz clucked his tongue. "I choose my words well, though I am possibly not in the same league as a clever wordsmith like you. The fucking guy didn't even talk to the kids. He left that to Lasker and you know what a basket case he was! From what I you're your beloved uncle tried to avoid taking phone calls from parents. It was though nothing had happened, as if no one had seen York's limp body lying on a stretcher, the rubber oxygen thing like a death mask around his face. Like no one saw him being loaded into the fucking ambulance for Christ's sake!"

Dorff avoided Sturtz's eyes.

"Here's a guy, your uncle, who claims to be teaching kids all the important values, the ones he says he lives by. Sure, sure, truth, honesty, decency, fairness, how to be a good winner or a good loser, all the things that sum up your Uncle Howard. A canoe trip that will make a kid a man! I think not! What does he really stand for? Lies, deceit, cover-ups...the fucker could out Nixon Nixon."

"Jersus, Henry, that's not fair!"

"And what does he do it for, nothing more than the almighty buck. We were all commodities to your uncle. To him we represented nothing more than liquidity, cash, good ol' money."

"Henry," Dorff managed, "that simply isn't true, and you know it."

Sturtz laughed. "Not true? Bullshit. He knew what he stood to lose. That he even survived, that the camp survived is a fucking miracle. Getting him involved with this project is doing him a favor, schmendrick. I'm not only offering a chance for him to redeem himself, I'm giving him a platform on which he can affirm that is all is well at Kanuga, and that it always has been, accident or no accident. He'll be able to say, hey, we survived, we're still in business, we're still committed to offering your kid the tools he needs in order to be a success in later life. He can point to me for God's sake. No, my old friend, he won't sue me, he'll fucking *thank* me, for with this picture in theaters and me in PEOPLE magazine with my arm around his old bony shoulders, your uncle will emerge as the ultimate survivor."

Dorff realized that on some level Henry Sturtz was right, and yet he needed to keep him from opening old wounds.

"But what *about* the survivors? The others. Gavin, Apple, Nicki: all of them. They'll never sign waivers."

Sturtz' voice was dismissive. "They won't have to. Pulitzer, have you ever seen the disclaimer at the end of a motion picture about people living and dead. Ever really think about what that meant? Wake up! We aren't going to call the camp Kanuga, for Crissakes, and the story will be *based* on what happened that summer......"

"What happened that summer, Henry, was a tragedy."

"Yes, it was. It was very, very sad." Sturtz made an **O** with his mouth and rolled the cigar around. "Very sad indeed. But things like that happen all over the country, all over the world. It didn't just happen at Kanuga."

Dorff 's voice shook. "But it *did* happen there."

Sturtz leaned forward. "Look, let's say I'm making a film about a plane crash. Does that mean that everyone who ever lost someone in a crash is going to sue? Jesus, Lennie, use your head."

"But this is different. You were there, I was there, this is about Kanuga no matter what you say."

"Prove it."

"Well, all I can tell you is that if you're right, and I don't think you are, and Howard won't sue, don't you think Gavin will? What about Gavin?"

"What about him?"

"Jesus, Henry, don't you think he's been through enough without this being thrown in his face?"

"Well," Sturtz said, puffing on the cigar, "there's always been talk about that day and Gavin."

"What are you saying?"

"Hadn't they fought just before swim period?

"Jesus, Henry."

Sturtz pointed the cigar at Dorff. "Be that as it may. Anyway, that's where you come in."

Leonard felt a wave of nausea sweep over him. "I don't understand."

"Then I'll explain. You have to write a screenplay that reeks with sincerity and class, something that no one could take offense at, not even Gavin, even while you're making a mystery of how York died."

Leonard Dorff shook his head. "I don't really think that anyone...."

Henry Sturtz's voice boomed across the room. "*That's not important, dammit.*"

"The coroner said that it was......"

"Jesus Christ, will you fucking focus here!" Dorff gulped as Sturtz went on. "None of that shit matters. What *does* matter is that you make nice with this so that you tell the story and everyone comes out smelling like a rose."

"You can't really think that I would...."

"Actually, I *do* think that you would, Lennie cause let's face it, you eat this shit up. You always have. Christ Len, I can still see you tear-assing around the campus with your fahcockta clipboard reporting on everything that was going on for that newspaper of yours. You knew everyone, you knew *about* everyone. Who better than you to write this thing, to smooth the way for me, to make sure the production goes well? Remember how well we worked together on getting the booze for the cabaret? It'll be like old times."

Dorff shook his head. "No, Henry, not me."

"Don't be ridiculous: of course you. It's perfect." Again, looking down, Dorff shook his head.

Henry Sturtz got up and sat on the edge of the desk directly in front of him. His eyes were cold. "Listen to me, asshole. You are going to do this for me and you and I both know it. First you are going to write a treatment and then you are going to do the screenplay."

Mustering courage he didn't know he had, Dorff looked up. "You just want me as an insurance policy." Sturtz raised an eyebrow. "You know that Howard would never sue if I were involved in the project."

Sturtz shrugged. "Chalk that up as an added perk." He leaned over and put his hand on Lennie's shoulder, his voice softer. "I *do* want you on this Lennie. You. You know the terrain. You were there. You knew every story, every nuance of what was going on behind the scenes. And you are the spinmeister. Pulitzer."

Dorff shook his head.

"Okay, I admit I broke your balls at Kanuga. You want an apology. Okay, I apologize, but you said it yourself a minute ago, we were kids! But we're not kids anymore my friend. I am offering you a business deal. One that will be lucrative and one, I might add, that could lead to big things for you in the woods of Holly, far away from your farkcokta remnant business. Something that will make you rich and me richer."

"I make a good living."

"Oh fuck you, Lennie. You're barely keeping your head above water, and you know it."

"I........."

"I ran a credit check. You might have been in good shape a few years ago, but lately your business sucks the big one."

"You had no right...."

Sturtz stood up and walked to the window. "I had every right. We always do checks on our employees."

"I didn't say that I would work for you."

"Well, I wanted to see if I wanted to work with *you*, and P.S., you *will* work for me, so stop all of this bullshitting." He turned to Dorff and smirked. "How does that line go, 'Methinks the lady doth protests too much.'"

Dorff started to get up when Sturtz stopped him.

"Sit. Sit. I'm sorry. You just pissed me off that's all." His face softened. "Look, I acknowledge that yes, I was at a camp where someone drowned. But believe me when I tell you that this story is in honor of *all* the kids who drowned, fucking ever!"

"*Someone* drowned? York was more than just someone, Henry."

"Well he wasn't Jesus Christ the way you always made him out to be, for Christ's sake. He was a nice guy who turned out to be a shitty swimmer, correct?"

Dorff just stood staring at him.

"Why me?"

"Why not you?"

"You never liked me at Kanuga, face it. I was always a joke to you."

"Oh shit, here comes Mr.Sensitivity! I was wondering when he would show up. You're not gonna start crying are you? You know something Lennie, you're right. I was *not* crazy about you at Kanuga. You weren't an athlete, and you remember how important *that* was."

Leonard Dorff felt butterflies in his stomach. "Yes, I remember."

"So maybe I rode your ass, but shit, I rode everyone's ass. You just didn't have the balls to stand up to me. You were easy. But you have to know something Lennie, and this is the God's honest truth, though it may be true that I didn't really like you, that doesn't mean that I also didn't respect you!"

"Come on Henry I....."

"No, really. It's true. Look what you did with that cockamamie newspaper you inherited. Everybody read the EXAMINER."

"The INQUIRER."

"The INQUIRER, yeah. People waited for Friday afternoon, for each new issue. I'll be honest; even I wanted to see my name in your little paper. We all did. So I respect you for that."

"But I....."

"Wait, let me finish. You know why else I respected you at camp?" Dorff slowly shook his head. "Because you never used the fact that Howard was your uncle to get special favors. I liked that."

"Thank you."

"You don't have to thank me. It's just a point of fact." Sturtz drew in on his cigar and blew smoke in Dorff's direction. "I respected you for a lot of things and that's why I am asking you to join my team and help me pull off the biggest picture since freaking AVATAR."

"I thought you said it was going to be a little picture."

"*Academy Awards!* It is going to be the biggest picture in terms of Academy Awards, schmendrick! I assumed that was a given, but if your world starts and stops on Seventh Avenue, I....""

There was an edge in Dorff's voice. "Okay, I get it."

"Then sit down and be friendly." Dorff hesitated for a moment and then returned to his chair.

"So, are you on board?"

Dorff looked pained. "Henry, sure I'd like to, but no! It's impossible. Haven't I made myself........."

"Two hundred thou just for the treatment, more for the screenplay, if you can pull that off."

"But I....."

"Not to mention your name up there in forty foot letters. Not, this time, under the banner of the EXAMINER....."

This time Dorf did not correct him.

"....but in the credits for a major motion picture."

"Two hundred thousand dollars?"

Sturtz nodded. "Don't be a pig, Lennie. That's way more than good for a treatment. And there'll be more for the screenplay. This is your first outing. If you do the job that I think you will, offers from the other majors all wanting you to work for them and they'll offer you more."

"Henry, it isn't the money, I have a business to run. Even if I...."

Sturtz smiled. "You must have a second in command. Right?" Dorff nodded slowly, and Sturtz could almost see his mind racing. "So leave the business in his hands for as long as this takes, and the way you write, with your talent, it shouldn't take all that much time at all, and then you get back to the rag trade." He paused. "This is finally your time, Lennie, the break that you always wished for. Don't blow it now."

"How much time do you think it would take to do?"

"To be honest, Lennie, I need it a.s.a.p. We won't get started filming before next August, but I want the script fast".

"But how fast is fast?"

Sturtz thought for a moment. "This is the October 11th, yes?" Dorff nodded. "Okay. I need a treatment by Thanksgiving, so that's the end of next month......"

Dorff's mouth was dry despite the lollipop. "Six weeks?"

Sturtz nodded. "At the most, and if I approve it, you will have to get the shooting script to me a month after that."

"Henry, I don't know anything about this business, but that timetable seems a little rushed."

"Time is of the essence Leonard. Think of it this way. Say you're swimming and you get a cramp. You have to make it to the dock or you'll drown. You're gonna swim your ass off to get there, right?"

"Yes but..."

"No buts. You'll work your ass off to earn the bucks I am giving you. Besides, the picture has to be filmed at the end of the summer. That's the deal. Take it or leave it."

"But the casting, the...."

"Leave all that to me. All I want from you are words. And you could start with three, "Yes, Henry, yes!"

"Henry, it is a wonderful opportunity, yes, but the subject matter and the time restraints. I just don't know."

Sturtz sighed. "A quarter mil and that's my final offer. Take it or leave it, the clock is running, yes or no now!"

Dorff gulped. "Yes, Henry."

Sturtz grinned. "You left out one."

Dorff nodded. "Yes!"

"Excellent." Sturtz looked at his appointment book. "I'll see you here again the Monday after Thanksgiving, 3:00 sharp."

"Henry," Dorff gulped, as Sturtz scribbled into his book, "I don't know. It's...."

Sturtz smiled as he watched Dorff fidget in his chair. "You have kids?"

Dorff nodded. "Two daughters."

"Figures," Sturtz thought and he said, "Well, we'll get Joey Carter to sign pictures for them, to call them on the phone, to come to their fucking school for Christ's sake! We will do annything that will make them happy because you are a valued member of the team. Think they'd like that?"

Leonard Dorff pictured the half naked posters of the young star on his daughter's walls and nodded. "They would like that a lot."

"Excellent." Sturtz said, going through some papers on his desk.

Figuring this was his cue to leave, Dorff stood up.

"Where are you going?" Sturtz asked looking through a drawer.

"I thought that......"

"You're working for me now, Lennie. You can stop thinking. Sit."

Leonard Dorff sat and watched his old bunkmate.

"Henry, I have a question."

"Shoot," Sturtz said, without looking up.

"Can I get someone to help with the screenplay? I don't know the form, the way to,,,,,"

Sturtz sighed. "It's not written in stone, but I think I can get Bob Karmon and Louis Phillips."

"What have they done before?"

Sturtz stopped rummaging around and stared at Dorff. "Lennie," he said, "you need to get out more. They wrote both BATTLESHIP RAIDER I *and* II, and Karmon was up for a Golden Globe for AMBASSADOR WITH A GUN."

"But those were big budget action films. This is going to be a small film."

"Lenny, they are two of the biggest names in Hollywood. Besides, they each owe me a picture. They'll show you the ropes; give you a crash course on how it's done. You're a quick learner, no?"

"Yes, but……"

"Jesus, will you stop with the fucking buts! You'll love them and they'll love you. I promise. They'll teach you everything you need to know about the form. The substance I leave to you."

Leonard Dorff was sweating again. "And the story? What about the story."

Sturtz looked hard at him. "Takes place in camp in 1975. Do I have to draw you a picture?"

"But what do I focus on? Henry, there are so many stories."

Sturtz waved him away. "And you know all of them. And what you don't know, you'll make up. Lennie, this is your chance to make that summer the way you saw it. You'll be just fine."

All of this was going too fast and Lennie knew it. But the money and, he thought, the prestige. Finally, the prestige! He also knew that by being involved in the project he would be able to see that nothing potentially devastating would sneak through unnoticed. And yet……

"No," he told himself, "no more 'and yets'." This would be orthodonture for Margo, paid in full. This meant paying off the house. This was going on the trip to Europe that Elie was always on at him about. This was money in the bank without worry, and maybe, finally, a little respect. It had to be good!

"But," he thought, "it could be trouble too."

A commitment to Sturtz could mean potential pain for Howard and Gavin, and the resurrection of ghosts long dead and to most, completely forgotten. Was it worth the money?

"Do I still have time to back out?" Lennie thought, as Sturtz found what he was looking for, and handed it to him.

"A contract?"

"All made out and ready for you to sign." He held out a pen.

"Shouldn't I take it home and look it over first? Maybe take it to a lawyer?"

"Look it over here," Sturtz said, leaning back in his chair. "Take your time, I'll wait." He looked at his watch. "But don't take all afternoon. I still have work to do."

Leonard Dorff skimmed over the pages. He looked up at Sturtz. "You have $250,000 already filled in."

Sturtz shrugged. "Call me psychic. Besides, that was as far as I was going to go."

Henry read on, his head pounding. Suddenly he stopped and looked up at Sturtz. "Are you insane? I can't sign this with this proviso in it."

Sturtz leaned back into his chair and smiled. It was not a pleasant smile. "Now what proviso would that be, Lennie?"

"You know very well what proviso. The one that says I get Howard to let you use Kanuga for the filming. My God, Henry, you can't be serious."

Sturtz shrugged. "He'll be paid handsomely and, if you'll note, it's for after camp is over. August 24th on. He'll make a bundle. Screen credit too in the final crawl."

Dorff shook his head. "Henry, I....."

"I'm also going to want a complete address and phone number list of all this year's campers before we start. I plan to offer the kids a chance to be in the film as extras. Stay on after the official last day. Pay them of course. Film all their scenes before Labor Day and then focus in on the scenes between the main characters. And speaking of payment." He lifted something off the desk and handed it to Dorff.

Dorff's eyes bulged. "A check for twenty five thousand dollars?"

"Ten percent up front. It's customary. You don't have a problem with....."

"No. No," Dorff managed.

"Good, cause that's the kind of faith I have in you, Lennie."

"Henry, I just don't know....."

Henry Sturtz stood up. He walked around his desk and stood looking down at Leonard Dorff. "I want an answer now, Lennie. No more bullshitting, no more cocking me around. And if you say yes, I want everything. Do you understand? Everything! Truth, what smells like truth, rumor, everything. I want a film script that covers all the bases. And that truth, if the truth is boring and won't play, we add some make believe. You will be paid a great deal of money, but you will earn every single penny. I want the treatment the Monday after Thanksgiving and the finished script by March 15th, latest."

"March 15th? But that's just….."

"That's it Lennie. You come in by those dates and you get me the camp to film at. And I want an answer now. Now! Answer me. Yes or no. Take it or leave it."

And shaking, Leonard Dorff took it.

Sturtz was all smiles. "An excellent decision." He moved back to his desk and flicked the intercom. "Miss Capuzzo. I want you now."

In a moment the office door opened. Dorff noted with a start that the frazzled assistant of only minutes before was now as coolly composed as she had been when he had come in. "Yes, Mr. Sturtz?"

"I want you to witness something." He turned back to Lennie. "Pulitzer, sign here, here and here, and initial here."

And Lennie Dorff did.

Miss Capuzzo took the papers and silently left the office, closing the door behind her.

Sturtz stood and held out his hand. "Time for you to and get to work, Henry. Don't forget, we have an appointment."

Dorff, his shirt wet with sweat, stood again and after wiping his hand on his pants, shook Sturtz' hand.

Sturtz handed Dorff a cigar. "Smoke this later when you tell your wife. It'll turn her on."

As Leonard Dorff, feeling a mixture of excitement, euphoria and terror stood up after signing his contract, he noticed another contract on the desk. "Henry," he said, "here's Joey Carter's contract."

"And?"

"Isn't it the one that your secretary has been looking for?"

The look on Henry Sturtz' face and the laugh that went with it sent a chill through Leonard Dorff that he had only known once before in his life. It followed him though the reception room, down the silent pneumatic elevators and out into the reality of 59th Street.

Leonard Dorff stood in the bright sunlight and could not stop shivering.

"My God," he thought, as people pushed past him, "what have I done?"

And with a cigar in one hand and a half eaten lollipop in the other, Leonard Dorff tried to remember from what direction he had come.

CHAPTER THIRTY- FIVE:

October 11th
Nicki:

couldn't breathe.
All at once, Gavin.

Gavin:

There is a strange disconnected feeling that comes from visiting someone in a hospital, like crossing a border into a new country without passport and with no knowledge of the language. I hated it, but Snyder was sick and I had to be there.

I had met him, Richard, maybe twenty years before, when he had come on to me in Julius'. That dark and somewhat seedy bar was, in those early years before the plague, my bar of choice, and I would stand near the back door observing the entrances and exits. I drank steadily, and very seldom, if ever, spoke to anyone. Richard saw me and somehow found my ignoring him intriguing. He ended up not leaving my side for the rest of the night, and though we had not gone home together, he had made me smile and we had become, and still remained, good friends.

And now he was sick *with* the plague, and I was once again crossing into his country, rehearsing in my mind the words that I would say to the gaunt and shriveled stranger who no longer made me smile.

Nicki:

I had played this scene out in my mind again and again for years, but now that it was real I didn't know what to do.

It was one of those serendipitous things, the kind that make for a good story in years to come. "I was scheduled to be on that plane but my cab was late so I missed the flight that crashed." That sort of thing!

In this case, I simply had an appointment with Sue, ordinary, a minor problem, and all at once there was Gavin. At first my mind would not accept it, but there he was, paler than I remembered and more filled out, but still, unmistakably, Gavin. For the first time in more years than I wanted to remember he was finally *there*, standing next to me, close enough for me to make him look at me so that I could ask him 'why'.

Why!

The "why" had gnawed at me even long after the pain of losing York had passed. "Why?" I had wondered over the years; as I sat in a class at NYU, or held an hours old Jessica in my arms, or started to doze in the midst of a boring play or concert, "Why had Gavin totally cut me out of his life, and so viciously at that? Why had he refused to either see or talk to me over and over again?" The "why" was always there; always.

WHY?

And now Gavin was right next to me, and as I had done so many years before, I took his hand.

Gavin:

"Gavin?"

Her voice came as such a shock that I actually froze. I was turned away from her, but I didn't need to see her to recognize the voice.

And I was sixteen and I didn't know if I could take the pain.

"Gavin?"

And I turned and looked at Nicki Polis for the first time in forever. She stared at me, tentative, the start of a smile on her lips, her eyes shining.

"Hello, Nicki," I said, and turned away. "Hello, and goodbye."

"Gavin, please," I heard Nicki say. "Just give me five minutes."

I closed my eyes and willed the elevator to come. It didn't.

"Please, Gavin," she said, "I think after all of this time, you owe me at least that."

I couldn't look at her.

I took a deep breath. "Either you walk away, or I do, Nicki. However you want it. Either way, in a couple of minutes, one of us is not going to be standing here."

"Jesus, Gavin," she said. "After all this time, just give me five minutes."

"I don't have five minutes."

"You've ruined the last thirty years of my life, Gavin," she said, anger and frustration creeping into her voice. "You can at least give me five minutes."

I looked at her. The pretty girl was gone and a handsome woman had taken her place. There were small wrinkles around her eyes and at the corner of her mouth, but other than that, Nicki Polis looked good.

"I didn't ruin anything, Nicki," I said. "Believe me, it wasn't me who ruined everything. You better than anyone should know that."

Nicki:

I took him by the arm and turned him around to face me. He was still handsome, but as I looked at him I thought that I had ever seen someone look so detached, so blank. His eyes, eyes that once shone with humor, now looked dead.

"But you see, I *don't* know that. Just tell me how I ruined everything."

He shook his head. "I don't want to do this Nicki," he said. "Okay? We're not friends anymore, and we haven't been for a long time. I would have thought that you'd have figured that out by now, but since you haven't, just get used to it because that's the way it is."

The smell of the African Violets was making me sick.

I didn't want to cry, but it welled up inside me, and the next thing I knew I was bawling all over the place! People were staring, but it was a hospital, and people cry in hospitals, so they thought they understood and looked away.

"But *why* aren't we friends anymore, Gav?" I blubbered. "For God's sake at least tell me *why?*"

His face was stone as he looked for a way to get away from me. "Jesus, Nicki, turn off the water works and just get out of my life, okay? *You* want *me* to tell you why? Oh honey, you *know* why. But I'll make a deal with you. You want to talk to me?" I nodded, a glimmer of hope finally coming through. "Okay then," Gavin said, "how about this for a plan? We say good-bye now then meet here again, oh, say twenty- five years from now. How about that? Once every twenty five years we'll have a reunion." He paused. "And if I'm not here, start without me."

Gavin:

And then she slapped me. Hard, right across my face. "Oh, snap," I heard someone say. A young black man was shaking his head and smiling.

"Okay, Nicki," I said rubbing my cheek, "then *you* don't show up."

I expected another swat, but instead Nicki threw her arms around me and pulled me to her. "Nicki," I said, as I watched people walking by watching us, "Nicki, quit it." But she was sobbing into my chest and holding on so tight that I literally could not pull her arms off.

"Youmurmefreen," she sobbed.

"What?" I said, "I didn't get that."

She let go and pulled away.

Nicki:

"I said, 'You were my friend,' dammit," I cried, my nose running. "You were my best friend."

"And you were mine, Nicki and you fucking threw it away without even thinking about it."

I wanted to scream. "What are you *talking* about?" I knew I was shrill and one step away from being hysterical, but I couldn't have cared less. I was finally talking to Gavin. "Why are you so mad at me? Tell me, Gavin because I don't understand it?"

"Oh, please," he said, and turned and started to walk away. "Just let dead things be dead."

I pulled him around and punched him hard on the chest. The young man standing next to us laughed. I turned to him. "This is funny? Well, fuck you, asshole." He held up his hands in mock surrender, and moved back, still watching the crazy lady.

Then I had my face in Gavin's. "God damn it!" I shouted at him, tears running down my face, "if you don't tell me what happened, I will fucking kill you."

He looked at me, his eyes finally alive, filled now with anger. "Oh you already did that, honey. You did that a long time ago."

"*WHAT DID I DO?*"

"What did you do? Dorff, dammit, that's what you did, Dorff."

I didn't get it. "I don't get it," I said. "Dorff what? What Dorff?"

Gavin:

She was really pissing me off. "Will you please stop the act!" I said. "Lennie Dorff. Remember? Pulitzer? Camp Kanuga? Ring a bell?"

She actually stamped her foot in anger. "What about all that? What has that got to do with anything?"

"Nothing," I said, "except you were a fucking traitor and told him that I was gay. Start coming back, does it? Jesus!"

Nicki:

And the world fell apart and sprinkled down on me in little pieces of confetti. What? It didn't make sense. I had to be sure I had heard him correctly. "What?" I said.

Gavin:

"Oh come on Nicki, you told Dorff and he told York. And you know *when* he told him? Huh, do you? You know *when* Dorff told York what you had told him? The night before York died, that's when, and York and I had a fight about it, and you know what, Nicki, York died thinking that I hated him. Nice, huh?" Now I was afraid that I might start to cry. "Maybe it was me, maybe I had made him so upset that he wanted to drown. How about that Nicki?" I grabbed her by both arms. Words poured out of me in a torrent of rage. "And I never understood why, Nicki. I never understood why you had to go and do that, why you couldn't have kept your God damned mouth shut so maybe none of this would have happened. You wanted to know why, Nicki? Well, how's that for an answer?"

Nicki:

I was stunned. My voice was shaking. "Gavin, please." I said, "What in God's name are you talking about?"

Gavin:

"I just told you, as if you needed to be told." The digital readout still read six. "Where in hell are the elevators?" I shouted, and people moved away.

Nicki:

"But I never did that," I said. "It wasn't me."

Gavin:

"Bullshit. Don't fucking lie on top of everything else."

Nicki:

"But why would I do such a terrible thing? At least ask yourself that."

Gavin:

"Like you don't think I haven't for over thirty miserable years. Gimme a break, will you Nicki, and just go away."

Nicki:

Everything was going mad right in front of my eyes, and I couldn't fix it. "But why did Dorff....?"

Gavin frowned at me. "Look, let's get this finished with, okay? Dorff said that you told him. Period. End of story."

"But...."

"Get real, Nicki, why would he lie?"

I shook my head. I pulled his arms from mine and led him away from the bank of elevators. "I don't know," I said. "But he did. He did lie. What I need to know is why you believed him?"

"Because how else could he have known, Nicki?", he said. "Huh? Who else could have told him? Believe me, I was up all that night, huddling in the bushes at the side of the river trying to keep warm...."

I cut him off. "What night? What bushes? What are you talking about?

"The night of the canoe trip, the night that Dorff came on to me and told me that you had told him that I was gay."

"But that's a......"

He wasn't listening to me. "And all I could think of was, if not Nicki, who, and the answer always came back that it *had* to be you."

I tried to be logical, to keep my balance. "But why *couldn't* it have been someone else?"

Gavin shook his head. "Oh, that one's easy." He glared at me. "BECAUSE NO ONE ELSE FUCKING KNEW."

My mind raced. "But couldn't it have been what's his name, for God's sake?" I asked. "That guy you did it with?"

Gavin frowned and shook his head. "Ralph Sanchez didn't know Dorff, and besides Nicki, let me point out the obvious just one more time, Dorff *said* it was you!"

I could feel anger and frustration growing in me. "Fair enough," I said, "but *why* me? What possible reason did I have in telling Dorff? Jesus, Gavin, Dorff? Use your head."

"I'm finished looking for reasons," he said. "I've been looking for reasons all my life. Reason or no reason, you were the only person who knew. Okay? Feel better that you talked to me? Swell, now leave me alone." I shook my head no. "Oh, shit," he said, "I do *not* need this!" and started walking away.

I kept pace with him. "So that's it. Nicki's guilty with no trial."

"Get away from me Nicki," he said, picking up his pace, heading for the main lobby.

I kept up with him, pulling, almost childishly, at his jacket. "But why didn't you ask for *my* side of the story, huh? Why didn't you confront me?" I could feel my heart pounding. "Why didn't you yell at me on the phone when I called you? Why didn't you tell me what a bitch I was for betraying you then so I could have defended myself?"

Gavin sneered and yanked his arm away from me. "Defended yourself!"

"Yes, you asshole, defended myself with the truth. If you had given me that courtesy we could have worked all this out years ago."

Gavin did not break his stride. "I don't see us working this out now," he said. "I just hear you talking to me when all I want is for you to get out of my life again."

"No way that's going to happen until you believe what I am telling you," I shouted at him.

Gavin:

I stopped walking and looked at her. "Don't you think I wanted to believe Dorff was lying, huh? All these years?" I said, "you think I wasn't thinking about you?"

"So if we were both...." She put her hand on my arm again and I shrugged it off.

"You were my dearest friend, Nicki." And oh, shit, my voice was shaking. "Why would you of all people betray me like that? Why would you tell someone when you said you wouldn't, and why Dorff for God's sake?"

Nicki:

"Keep him talking," I thought. None of this made sense, but if maybe if we kept talking it would. "Okay, that's good," I said. "Stay with that. Why *would* I tell anyone, and if I *had* told anyone, which, by the way, I never did, why would I choose Lennie Dorff?"

- - - - - - - -

Gavin:

"Exactly. Why would you?"

Nicki:

"GAVIN," I was yelling now, and from the corner of my eye I saw two security guards looking at us. I didn't care. "Listen to me, *I-never-did*. I have absolutely no idea of what you are talking about." This was a nightmare, something that had come out of left field and was biting me on the ass, something that I never saw coming.

And, crazily, madly, all I could think of was that I needed Andrew.

- - - - - - - -

Gavin:

"Jesus, Nicki," I said, "its ancient history. You don't have to keep lying. You screwed it all up and that's that."

Nicki:

And I knew that whatever I said next was going to determine the course of the rest of my life, of both our lives. "Be smart," I told myself. "Be smarter than you have ever been." And I knew I was on my own, as usual, and I took a chance.

Gavin:

Nicki held on to both my arms, forcing me to face her. "Gavin, look at me." I stared at her. "No, not *through* me, *at* me," she said, and for the first time since she had come up to me, I looked into her eyes. This was Nicki. *Nicki!* And I knew how much I had missed her and I hated her for it.

"Gavin," she said, her voice suddenly just above a whisper, "I can only say this once because in another minute I am going to go hysterical crying and not be able to stop and those two security guards are going to take me next door to Bellevue, so listen to me and try to understand." I turned my face away though she kept a firm hold on my arms. "Gavin...*look* at me, dammit!" I did. "Gavin, I- have- never- told- a- soul. Not one person, ever. No one. Do you understand me? Never." I turned away from her again, feeling, truth be known, just a tad foolish, but she pulled me around to face her. "If you want an explanation that's all I can say, because I never did or said anything to betray your trust, and that is the God's honest truth. You can believe me or not, but I have never told a soul." She paused and I was about to say something when she let go of one of my arms and held up her hand. "Wait," she said, "just one more minute. I think I have a way that I can prove it to you." I just stared at her. "Let's go see Lennie Dorff," she said.

"What the hell are you....?" She didn't let me finish.

"Are you afraid to, or is it that you just don't want to?" I stood silent. "Put me in a room with Lennie Dorff," she said, "and let him tell me in front of you that I was the one who told him."

"Look, Nicki," I began but she waved me quiet.

"If he can convince you that I did it, that I told him, I will step out of your life forever. I swear to that on my daughter's life."

"She has a daughter," I thought. *"Nicki has a daughter."*

"But make him tell us *when* I told him, and *where*, and *why*. That's all I ask you to do, just listen to Dorff. I am willing to bet anything that if you do you'll know that I never told him a thing. He'll either crumble or lie so blatantly that you'll be able to see right through him, but if not," she shrugged, "then I am history. Out of your life forever." She jammed her hand into her pocket and pulled out a cell phone. "Here," she said, and then she grabbed it back. "Shit. I forgot. It's dead."

I almost laughed. "Nicki, I....."

She reached into her pocket, pulled out a quarter and handed it to me. "Here," she said, "I don't know what they cost, but there are pay phones over there. Get his number from information and let's go see him." She paused and looked into my eyes. "I cannot do or say anything else, Gavin. Dorff lied to you, but since you won't believe me, you have to find out for yourself. The ball is in your court."

And all at once, I knew Dorff had lied. All at once, with something as simple as her handing me a quarter, all at once, as I finally held something tangible in my hand, something that could lead me to a truth other than the one I had only assumed, it all became clear; however Dorff knew, it wasn't through Nicki, and it never had been. I had, without thinking, chosen to believe someone whom I had never really trusted, that no one really trusted, instead of the one person both York and I adored. And in that second, like a cheesy flashback sequence in a really bad movie, all of it flashed before me: Ralph, Atheneum, the Luggage King, the Mystery Walk, York's accusations and that terrible basketball game in the hall. Had I been insane? What in God's name had made me write off Nicki without even giving her a chance to defend herself? Did what seemed to be obvious negate all that had come before?

I looked down at the quarter. Nicki wanted me to call Dorff and confront him and suddenly I didn't need to. I knew she was telling me the truth, and everything made sense, and nothing made sense, and the wasted years without her slammed down on me like a ton of bricks.

Nicki:

And I knew he knew I was telling him the truth.

Gavin:

And a sob that had waited inside me for years, found its way out into crowded lobby of a busy hospital. "Oh, fuck, Nicki, fuck," I managed. "Really? You swear to God?" I knew I sounded like a kid and I didn't care. "You swear to God that it wasn't you. That it really wasn't you?" And she nodded her head, fat tears plopping down her face. "I swear to God, Gav," she said, "on my child's life. There's nothing more I know to say." She was crying hard now. "Please, please believe me."

And I threw my arms around her and held her tight, tighter than I had ever held anyone before, and like a last fadeout shot of some made for T.V. movie, we stood crying, holding each other as people going on with their lives stared at us as they went by.

Nicki:

Gavin! I was holding Gavin and he was holding me. What had just happened here? Was it possible?

Gavin:

And as I pressed my face into her hair, a lightness filling my body that I hadn't felt in years, all I could think of was, "She still uses the same shampoo."

Nicki:

I held on tight. There was no way I was going to let go.

Gavin:

Nicki uses the same shampoo! And she has a daughter. And I began to laugh.

Nicki:

And as I felt him laugh, I blubbered even louder into his already wet sports jacket.

Gavin:

I held her away from me, and then pulled her back in a bear hug.

Nicki:

And I knew that people were staring.

Gavin:

And I knew people were staring and I thought, "Fuck them. This is a hospital. People die here, but people are also born here. We can cry or laugh if we want to."

Nicki:

And when I finally pulled away, one hand still holding him to be sure, I snuffled, "My God, there are so many things to tell you, to ask you." And then I remembered. "Oh shit. I have a doctor's appointment. With Sue. Sue's my doctor."

He looked amazed. "Our Sue? Sue Barrett?" I nodded. "From camp?" I nodded again. "A gynecologist," I said, and we both laughed as we had never laughed before. And when he stopped laughing, Gavin said, "Holy shit! Sue's a *doctor*? I laughed and nodded again. "Want one better than that? I'm married to Apple."

God, I wish I could have a picture of the look on his face when I said that, just before he broke out into more peals of laughter.

"Sue's on the fifth floor," I said.

He nodded. "And I have a friend to visit on the ninth."

"Meet you here in a half hour?"

He shook his head, and grabbed onto my hand. "No way," he said. "I'll go with you, then you'll go with me."

Gavin:

Nicki nodded. Her makeup was streaky and her face was wet, and I thought that she had never been more beautiful. Then she smiled and said something that, in its very "Nickiness," told me that she forgave me for everything.

Nicki:

"Now give me back my quarter," I said.

Gavin:

And we both laughed as we cried and held onto each other for dear life.

Nicki and Gavin:

And I was home.

CHAPTER THIRTY-SIX:

MYSTERY WALK (2) –
August

The day was clear and hot, and many of those who crowded the deck of the ferry had stripped off their shirts, exposing their already brown torsos to the August sun.

Andrew Brookman, dressed in a button down plaid shirt and khakis sat on a wooden chair and stared at the water. He had read on the train to Sayville and had considered going below to finish the novel he had brought with him, but the smell of the salt air and the heat of the sun had brought his mother's voice to mind, "It's too nice a day to sit inside and read. Go out and play with the other boys." Andrew smiled as he looked at the firm gym bodies slicked with suntan oil. "I don't think she meant *these* other boys," he thought as the boat made its way to Fire Island.

He was actually on his way to see Gavin!

Of course, he had heard about Gavin from time to time over the years. Some people had seen him; others had heard stories about him. All spoke of him in whispers. It was, "I saw Gavin Stewart a few weeks ago, though he didn't see me. You should have seen the guy he was with!" or "You know that Gavin is notorious out on Fire Island." Or "I hear that Gavin has become a total recluse." They said everything, but they *all* said, "I never knew Gavin Stewart was gay, did you?" From the first, Andrew was neither surprised nor shocked. Gavin's life was Gavin's life.

After Nicki told him about her meeting him again, he had, through her prompting, called him the very next day. His old friend's voice at first had been guarded, even cool, but over the weeks they had talked it had become first more trusting, then even warm and friendly, and soon York could hear traces of the old Gavin creeping through.

They had talked about meeting in the city, but suddenly Gavin had to go to Europe on business. Another date was broken when Gavin's pipes froze in a sudden late March freeze, then this and that, and then, it was suddenly late summer. When Gavin invited him to spend a day on the Island with him, he accepted immediately. He would see for himself what all the rumors were about. Now, sitting on a crowded deck surrounded by half naked men, all of whom seemed to know one another, he began to wonder if it had been a good idea after all.

"Day tripper?"

Andrew looked over at the smiling young man sitting next to him. "I guess so, yes," he said. "How could you tell?"

The young man shrugged. "Just one small bag, and, no harm, you don't look like you're one for the sun."

Andrew smiled. "City pallor, eh? Well, you're right, just the day. Going to make a late ferry back." With nothing else to say, Andrew looked off at the coast of Long Island fading behind them.

"Josh Friedman," the young man said, offering his hand. Andrew smiled and took it. "Brookman, Andrew."

Josh smiled. "Hello, Brookman, Andrew."

And Andrew thought, "Someone else called me that once", and, though he tried to remember who it had been, he couldn't. "No," he said, "it's Andrew Brookman." Josh smiled. "I got that." The young man nodded as if nailing something down. "Just spending one day doesn't give you much time to soak in some sun."

"Actually I'm not going for the sun." He chuckled and pointed as his face. "I guess that's pretty obvious. No, just visiting a friend."

Josh looked at him. "What's his name? Maybe I know him. Fire Island is really nothing more than any small town, except that most of it happens to be gay."

"He's an old friend. Gavin Stewart. He has a house in the Pines."

"Nope, don't know him, but if he's gay, and I assume he is from the address, never call him an 'old' friend to his face." Josh shook his head and clucked his tongue. "Just not a good idea."

Andrew laughed. "Point taken. I will remember that!"

"If you don't mind my asking, what do you do?"

"High School. English."

"English was my favorite subject. But I guess every fag says that."

Andrew's smile faded.

"Oops," Josh said. "What?"

"It's nothing really." Andrew shook his head. "It's just that I have a problem with pejorative terms, no matter who uses them."

"Oh, the 'fag' thing. Sorry. Just out and liberated, nice of you to care though."

A speedboat with four young men in bathing suits zoomed past the ferry, their laughter as bubbly and clear as their wake.

"I must sound very up tight." Andrew watched the speedboat make a wide circle and disappear on the other side of the ferry. " A few years back, one of my students, a black kid, used to call every other black male in the class…well, 'the n' word. I called him on it and he told me that *his* saying it meant nothing and that I should chill. It still made me sick."

Josh nodded. "The, 'It's okay for us to say it, but not you syndrome', huh?"

Andrew smiled. "Exactly. I don't know why it bothers me so much. I guess I hear self loathing in it and that gets to me."

"But isn't it possible that you are hearing self acceptance and not self loathing?"

Andrew frowned. "I don't see self acceptance in using the same negative terms that are used by those who hate you?"

"But in our mouths it's really saying 'fuck you' to those very same people."

"I don't think the bigots see it that way."

"So, using your reasoning" Josh said with a smile, "doesn't that make you a bigot?"

Andrew started to say something, and then stopped.

"I'm sorry," said Josh, "I was just being a wise ass." There was silence for a moment, and Andrew turned to watch those sitting on the other side of the deck wave to the speedboat. "But we were talking about you being an English teacher." Andrew turned back to Josh, holding his hand in front of his eyes to avoid the sun. "English *was* my favorite subject," the young man said. "It's probably a cliché, but it's true. English. I loved Tennessee Williams. But I guess every 'gay' guy says that too."

"Well, I love Williams and I'm not gay, so not *only* gay guys say that."

"Touché." Josh smiled. "And at the same time a not very subtle way to tell me that you are not one of the tribe."

Andrew frowned. "Sorry if I....."

"Andrew," Josh said, "now it's my turn to tell you to chill. You're not gay? You're not gay. It's no big deal. Maybe a little disappointing, but no harm done."

"Disappointing?" Andrew shook his head. "I don't; oh!"

"So much for the pallor!" Josh laughed. "Your face is now beet red. I didn't mean to embarrass you. But truth be told, I like older men and you are a very handsome older man. And since most of the people on this vessel have neither come to Fire Island merely to dance the night away nor to clam, it is in fact, disappointing to find that you are straight. But," he shrugged, "so be it. You still seem to be a very nice man, if a little up tight."

"Older man!" Andrew thought, "Jesus!" and then he looked around and knew that he was.

"Thank you...I think," he said. They both laughed. "It's just that the world seems to be changing so fast, and sometimes I feel as though I never left the seventies."

"'Oh, Brave New World', right?"

"Yes," Andrew nodded, "mixed with a dollop of 'I'm A Stranger Here Myself!'"

"A 'dollop,'" Josh said with a mock sigh. "Who else but an English teacher!"

A few of the young men were standing and adjusting their backpacks and gym bags.

Josh laughed. "Look at them. We don't dock for another ten minutes and they are ready to go. Probably swim to shore if they'd let them. Such, I guess, is the lure of Fire Island."

"You sound jaded."

"Yet another thing," Josh said, "never to say to anyone gay!"

Andrew grinned. "Is there a manual that you can recommend?"

"Touché, once again. I do like you Andrew Brookman. Are you quite sure that you're not even a little bit gay?" Andrew shook his head. "Well then, by any chance, would you have a brother?"

"I did," Andrew said, "but he drowned."

They sat quietly for a while, the ferry slowed, and soon they were there.

Gavin was late. All the people from the ferry had already been met or had found their way down the little paths leading to the beach, and he had not yet appeared.

Andrew leaned against a mooring post, his small bag between his feet, and waited. Josh had said good-bye with a hug that had taken Andrew totally by surprise. "How fast your pallor disappears," Josh laughed, and adjusting the straps of his knapsack and clicking on his Ipod, headed onto the Island. "I'll be looking out for you," he called over his shoulder as he made a right turn and disappeared.

"Why in God's name did I tell him that I had a brother who drowned?" Andrew thought. "What the hell was that about?"

There was music playing at the hotel near where he was standing, and over a fence he could see bronzed bodies gyrating at each other.

"Apple?"

Andrew turned.

For a split second, with the sunlight in back of him, Gavin was York. Tall, rangy, blonde hair flopping over his forehead, York stood smiling at Andrew his hand out in front of him.

Andrew felt like he had been punched in the stomach, the sadness that had been kept welled up for so long now ready to explode into the hot summer's day. Instead he smiled, reached out his own hand and grasped Gavin's.

"Hey Gav," he said.

"Hey, Apple."

The two men stood grinning at one another, their hands clasped for a full minute.

Andrew finally broke the silence.

"After all this time and you're late! Nice!"

Gavin smiled. "I wasn't late. I was standing over there, looking at you and wondering how this was going to go."

"It's going to go fine. Hey, if there's a lull in the conversation, we can always trade comics!"

Gavin laughed as he broke the handshake, pulled out a tissue and blew his nose. "I told myself that I was not going to do this."

Andrew grinned at him. "I'm kinda close myself."

"Apple. Shit. I can't believe you're finally here."

"Well," Andrew said," if you hadn't had to be a drama queen and keep saying that you weren't ready to see me, and then found every excuse in the book to break our dates we could have done this months ago. Frozen water pipes, my ass."

"A drama queen, huh?" Gavin said. "How'd you prepare for this, by watching re-runs of *Will and Grace*?" He broke out into such a big grin that Andrew laughed. "No, actually Apple," Gavin said, "I just was putting off the moment when I would have to look at your ugly face again."

"Ah, Gavin," Andrew said, "nothing changes. You are still a dick!"

Then they had their arms around each other, slapping each other's backs and laughing.

"Damn, man," Andrew said, "it has been too long. Too Goddamned long."

A young man in a green bathing suit that barely fit walked by and grinned at their happy reunion.

Gavin pulled back and with his hands on Andrew's arms stared at him. "It's incredible, but you're still Apple. Okay, maybe a line or two, but Apple all the same. And a little thinner on top."

Andrew laughed. "If not in the middle."

"God, it's good to see you."

"We're both dicks, Gavin. We should have got together long ago."

Gavin nodded. "What's done's done."

"And cannot be undone," they said together laughing. Andrew beamed at his friend. "I'll be damned. You remember!"

"MACBETH? And the fact that you made York and me read the damned thing out loud with you...yes, I remember."

"You know I have taught that play every year since I started teaching and every time we get to that line I always think of the three of us on the archery range."

"It was free play. The sun was setting."

"You remember!" Gavin nodded. " But not *one* free play," Andrew told him, a whole *bunch* of free plays. What did it take us, a week to finish the thing?"

"Somehow I remember just one free play. The light was so rich that it looked gold."

"What I remember is York's comment about MACBETH."

Andrew smiled and furrowed his brow. "What comment?"

"Don't you remember? We had just finished reading the thing and you were going about the symbolism and the hubris...see, I remembered that too....."

"I'm impressed."

"And you are going on about the hubris of this man who had everything but had to have more and more and more. And then you looked at York and said, 'How do *you* see MacBeth?' and York yells out, 'Major loser!' We all fell apart."

Andrew laughed. "You know, I *do* remember that. Damn."

"And wasn't Sturtz there?"

Gavin shook his head. "Nope. Don't you remember, we thought we saw him watching us, but when we called to him he wasn't there?"

"Damn," Andrew said, "your memory is prodigious."

"Why the hell did you want us to read it in the first place? I don't think I ever knew. I mean it destroyed our free play periods."

"It was on the reading list for AP English. We all had to read it, but I was the one who forced the issue."

"Which meant we all had to read it."

"Hey, when D'Artagnan says to read something, Porthos and Aramis damn well better read!"

"And who made you D'Artagnan?"

"Well, maybe I wasn't," Andrew said, "but you sure as hell *were* Aramis! Do you remember how you used to drown yourself in that crap before we went to a dance?"

"So Ellen Marcus would find me irresistible."

Andrew roared. He thought that he hadn't felt so good in years. "Ellen Marcus! Jesus, I haven't heard that name in forever. Whatever happened to Ellen Marcus?"

Gavin smiled. "She and her girlfriend have a place over in Cherry Grove." Gavin laughed at the shocked look on his friend's face. "Take it easy," he said. "I'm bullshitting. I haven't heard about her in years either." He shrugged. "But I wouldn't have been surprised if she had been gay. I mean after dating me, what other man could stack up?"

"You have a Manhattan phone book?" Andrew said, and Gavin punched him on the arm. "And you call *me* a dick!" he said, laughing. "Anyway, let's get out of here, go back to my place, have some lunch and then head out to the beach. Sound good?"

"Sounds great," Andrew said, picking up his gym bag. "Anything's fine as long as I can make the last boat back off the Island. I have a full day tomorrow."

"Don't worry. I will not let you turn into a pumpkin!" He took the gym bag out of Andrew's hand, turned and began walking rapidly down the narrow path Josh had taken earlier. "Come on guest. Follow me. But just remember not to look back. If you do Ellen Marcus turns into a pillar of salt."

"Ellen Marcus, a dyke!" Andrew said, keeping up, "you know, you had me there for a minute."

"Why'd you believe me?"

"I don't know man," Andrew said, "but lately it seems to me that the whole world is gay."

"Almost," Gavin said over his shoulder, "but as long as *you're* still around, the world is safe for democracy! Move your ass paleface. We gotta get some sun on you!"

"They're all gay," Andrew murmured, "and all brown!"

"What was that?" Andrew asked. "I didn't hear you."

"Nothing to hear. Just some uninteresting social commentary."

"All social commentary is uninteresting. Move your ass."

Andrew followed his friend, laughing.

- - - - - - - -

One path led to another, twining and criss-crossing up, down and across reed flecked dunes of sand as the friends walked. Copses of scrawny trees gave way every few feet to wooden houses of different shapes and sizes. There were decks and swimming pools and, everywhere, more brown sturdy bodies. And the sound of muffled laughter and the thumping bass of distant music filled the air.

"We're here," Gavin said as he walked up a path made of wooden planks to a well -weathered white clapboard house. "It's not much," Gavin said, opening the screen door, " but we call it home."

"We?" Andrew asked.

"We," Gavin replied as a huge dog rocketed into the room, skidded on the well -polished wooden floor and leapt on Gavin as though he had just returned from the wars.

"Apple, Willie. Willie, Apple."

The dog, his tail wagging furiously, turned his attention to the amused Andrew who stood in the hallway watching the reunion. He bounded over to him and placed his huge paws on Andrew's chest.

"Bad, Willie. Get down. Down."

"No problem," Andrew sputtered, as the huge dog licked his face. "He's terrific." Willie, still elated, turned back to his owner, skidded over to him and flipped onto his back.

"The dog's a killer," Gavin said, rubbing the animal's belly. "Trained to kill."

"What kind is he? Andrew asked.

"Yes!" Gavin answered.

Andrew laughed. "I had one of the same breed when I was a kid."

Gavin looked over at him. "Don't tell me. Sheba! That was it. Sheba!"

"It's nice that you remember."

"Remember? How could I forget? 'Andrew, did Sheba eat? Andrew, did Sheba go for her walk?' And speaking of your mother, is she......?"

"Still very much with us. Dad died a few years ago."

"I'm sorry."

"About which?"

Gavin laughed. "Still the same old wise ass, eh?"

"No, actually. Not really. It's just seeing you again..."

Gavin nodded. "I know. I feel the same way."

"But what about your parents?"

"Both no longer with us, but let's talk about that later, okay? Not trying to be mysterious or anything, but there are so many things I want to talk to you about and the folks are just one part of it."

Andrew held up his hands. "Not a problem." He looked around the living room. "This place is great. Want to give me the fifty cent tour?"

Gavin stopped petting Willie and stood up. "Sure. But for you it's a buck."

"I can live with that." Andrew swept his arm around the white living room. "What's with all the movie posters? I didn't know you were such a film buff."

"I wasn't," Gavin said, moving to one of the framed 'one sheets' hanging on the wall, "but I sort of became a collector. Remember this one?" He pointed to a huge poster for JAWS.

"You've got to be kidding me. I've seen it about fifty times."

"But do you remember when you saw it the first time?"

Andrew shrugged and looked at another one of the posters. "TOMMY? We didn't see that one in camp did we?"

"No. In the city, you, York and I. A few months before camp."

Andrew looked at the other posters filling the room. DOG DAY AFTERNOON, NASHVILLE, GODFATHER, PART II.

And then he got it.

The beach was crowded, but Gavin led the way to a spot that was empty except for four bronzed, thickly muscled older men who were sharing a huge blanket. As they walked past them, Andrew could smell a mixture of cologne and suntan lotion.

"This good?" Gavin asked and when Andrew nodded yes, he dropped the beach bag he had been carrying and began unpacking it. Soon the two friends were lying on large, oversized bath towels, Gavin dressed in board shorts, lathering himself in baby oil, while Andrew, in a white tee shirt and boxer trunks, applied any exposed part of his body with Coppertone.

Gavin had made a delicious chicken salad that they had eaten on the deck. Willie had lain at Gavin's feet, his head on his master's leg looking plaintively up at him with eyes that cried, 'feed me,' and Gavin did. They made small talk, finished eating, washed the dishes and came down to the beach.

"Too bad you couldn't bring Willie," Andrew said.

"Not a good idea," Gavin said, molding his body into the sand under the towel, "he has a tendency to run away. That's how I got him. I found him at the ASPCA, a few years ago." He was silent for a moment. "Nicki and you!"

Andrew smiled. "There's a non sequitor."

"No, it's just still hard for me to believe that you guys are married."

Andrew snickered. "For awhile there lately it was hard for us to believe it too, but we're working on it."

Gavin nodded into the sun. "I'm glad. From what she tells me, and I don't want to be telling tales out of school here, she'd really like it to work."

"So would I, Gav," Andrew said, "but as I said, it's a work in progress."

Gavin held up his hands in supplication. "Topic closed," he said.

"No. It's okay, really. It's just that we...."

The four men on the blanket in back of them had turned up their boom box and one of them stood and started dancing on the sand, egged on by the others who clapped in time to the music.

Andrew grimaced. "So much for peace and quiet. That's really annoying," he said. "Want to move?"

Gavin shrugged. "If you do, but why don't we give them a few minutes. Maybe they'll lower it."

"We could ask them to."

"Give 'em a few."

"But...."

"Apple, it's really not that bad."

Andrew frowned. "Damn," he said, "am I starting to sound like the old farts at Kanuga who were always complaining about everything we did?"

Gavin smiled. "Maybe a little around the edges. Not so that you'd notice."

Andrew shuddered. "Jesus," he said, "when the hell did that happen?" Gavin smiled as Andrew went on. "I don't want to get old, Gav."

Gavin laughed. "Sorry. Too late."

Andrew squirted a spray of Coppertone at his friend who smeared it into his body. "I assume you figured out what all the posters have in common," he said, closing his eyes and putting his face into the sun.

"Neat change of topic, Gav." Andrew put a spot of lotion on his nose. "Sure I do. They're all from '75. Right?"

Gavin nodded.

"But isn't that just a little strange?"

Gavin smiled. "You needn't worry. I am not living in a dream world, nor have I become a dangerous lunatic. I just needed to have them."

Andrew started to say something, but Gavin's raised hand stopped him.

" And yes, I *have* tried to figure out why! Many, many shrinks and I have tried to figure out why, but none of us has ever come up with anything definitive: theories, yes, hard truths, no. My take on it is that it's nice to see that there was still make believe and fun even in," and his pause was eloquent," *that* year." He shrugged. "Or maybe not."

Andrew realized that this was the first time either of them had mentioned, 'that year.'

Gavin laughed. "And aside from that, some of those one sheets are now worth a fortune. So you see it's not so crazy after all."

The conversation fell into a lull and Andrew lifted himself up onto his elbows and looked across the beach. Yet more toned, tan bodies everywhere, and here he was, the only one on the beach wearing a tee shirt. "And probably the only one on the beach who's straight too," he thought.

Laughter came from behind him. The four men had deserted their blanket and were bounding into the surf. 'Johnny Ride a Pony,' one yelled, and in a moment, two of the men were on the other's shoulders. Andrew watched as they banged into each other, and as one of them was finally forced off his friend's shoulders and disappeared under the water, he lay back and closed his eyes. The sun burned into his eyelids as he remembered a moment years before that he knew he could never forget. He squinted over at Gavin who stared at the laughing men in the water, his face a mask. "I don't usually stay here for the summer. I head somewhere where there's some sanity, but this year, after seeing Nicki again I thought I'd give it a try." Andrew started to say something and decided against it. He closed his eyes again and soon the sounds of the day were far away and those sounds became mixed with other sounds and then other sounds and soon Andrew was asleep.

Something blocked the sun, bringing him back. He squinted up at the smiling young man standing over him.

"I told you that Fire Island was nothing more than a small town! Having fun, Teach?"

Gavin, with one hand blocking the sun, looked up at the stranger. Josh smiled at him and said, "Hi."

Andrew pulled himself up to a sitting position. "Oh, er, Josh, yes?" The young man nodded. "I'm sorry," Andrew said. I was half asleep." Josh smiled. "I'm sorry. I guess I was being insensitive again."

Andrew chuckled now fully awake. "Not at all," he said. Just zoning." He noticed that Josh was looking at Gavin. "Oh, excuse me," he said, "Gavin Stewart, Josh...Friedman, wasn't it?" Josh nodded his head and accepted the hand that Gavin offered. "Josh and I met on the ferry over here."

"It made the trip more pleasant." He grinned at Andrew. "At least for me."

"It was good for me too." Andrew only realized what he had said when Josh and Gavin laughed.

"Actually, I saw you guys hugging good-bye at the dock," Gavin said. "I thought Andrew was going to surprise me and tell me that he was a member of the club."

"No such luck," Josh smiled. "I tried everything I knew but I am afraid he is terminally straight."

Andrew laughed. "And here I thought being straight was a good thing."

"Would you like to sit down?" Gavin asked.

"Sure," Josh grinned, flopping down onto the sand between the two friends. "But only for a minute. I have to get ready for the tea dance. You guys going?"

Gavin laughed. "Look, it took me twenty five years to get Apple out here, I don't think I'll ruin it by taking him to the tea dance."

"Apple?"

"A nickname from olden days. How did we come to call you 'Apple,' anyway, Amdrew?"

Andrew shook his head. "It's not important. Anyway it's better than the first nickname I got tagged with."

"Which was?" Josh asked.

"Trout!"

They all laughed. "Trout. That's right," said Gavin. "Brook-man, Trout. Brook Trout. He snapped his fingers as he remembered. "It was York that changed it to Apple."

"York?"

Gavin smiled. "My brother."

"Well," Josh said, "one thing is for sure, he certainly didn't call you Apple because of your rosy cheeks!"

"Wait," Gavin cried and snapped his fingers. "Yes, he did! That's exactly what he did, because of your big rosy cheeks. Every time you would go out into the sun, your cheeks would get all red." He looked at Andrew. "Whatever happened to those rosy cheeks, Apple?"

Andrew smiled and looked at the water. "Just been a hell of a long winter."

After Josh left with promises to invite Gavin to the next party at his house, Andrew and Gavin lay back on their towels.

"He seems like a nice enough guy," Andrew muttered to the sky. "If he asks you to that party, are you going to go?"

"Probably not," said Gavin, putting more oil on his nose. "For a Fire Islander, I'm not really very social. I actually get a lot of reading done out here." He paused, unsure whether or not to go on. "And besides," he decided, "I'm kind of seeing someone."

Andrew sat up. "Most excellent. Good for you."

"Maybe", Gavin offered, "but it's still new. We'll see."

"Do I get to meet the lucky fellow?"

Gavin shook his head. "He's away. On business."

"Uh, huh!"

Gavin laughed. "No. Really."

"Well in any case, I'm glad for you Gav."

Gavin nodded. "Thanks, but I'm not sending wedding invitations yet."

"Did you meet him out here?"

"Out here, yes last winter."

Andrew looked around, trying to picture the beach in winter. "Ever long for the hustle and bustle of the big city?"

Gavin was silent for a moment and then said, "I don't know. I just feel comfortable here." He paused. "And Willie likes it.

The afternoon wore on, and Andrew looked at his watch.

"It's almost six," he said. "We'd better think about getting back. I have a ferry to catch."

"Five more minutes?"

Andrew grunted a yes. He liked the way the sun felt as it baked into him.

Gavin opened one eye and looked at his friend, started to speak, then said nothing. They lay that way for a minute or two when Gavin said, "When did you know? About me, I mean."

Andrew looked at his friend. "I don't know," he said. "I heard about it over the years."

"Heard about it?"

Andrew laughed. "Not the five o'clock news or anything. Just people from camp I might happen to run into."

"How did they know?"

Andrew shrugged. "I dunno. Just seems they did."

"You didn't know at camp?" Andrew shook his head. "That's funny. I always thought you knew."

"No. It never even occurred to me. I sometimes think that gay people give straight people much too much credit for being perceptive. Dumb as posts most of us. *You* knew at camp?"

"I suppose I'd always known. Didn't want to think about it, that kind of thing," Gavin said with a smile.

"No one at camp knew. Really. Everyone knew about Kirshner of course..."

"Well, *Kirshner*!"

".... and they pretty much guessed about Carlin, but no one ever mentioned you." Andrew looked out over the ocean. "But you never did it up there, did you?"

"Nicki didn't tell you?"

Andrew shook his head.

"Even now", Gavin thought with a smile.

"Get outta here! You did it at camp? Who with? You gotta tell me who."

"It's not important."

"Bullshit it isn't. Okay. Play it your way. I'll figure it out. Someone in the bunk?"

"Apple!"

"Klinger. You did it with Klinger." Gavin laughed and shook his head. "Jesus," Andrew said, "not Sturtz?"

"No, definitely not Sturtz."

"Then who?" He paused. "Oh man, please tell me you didn't do it with Dorff."

Gavin's face clouded over. "It was not Dorff."

"Well then who?"

"I thought you would have guessed. It was you man. You know, you're a real deep sleeper."

Andrew threw some sand at him. "Will you fucking tell me?"

Gavin smiled. "Then Nicki really didn't tell you?"

Andrew's voice was exasperated. "Gavin, would I be going through all this bullshit if she had? No, she didn't tell me. But if you don't tell me, I swear I'm gonna put Ben Gay in your jock again."

"Do you know how much I love your wife, Apple?"

"Fine. You can't have her. WHO WAS IT?"

"Remember cabaret night?"

Andrew nodded. "Of course I remember cabaret night, but I didn't mean did you do it with Ellen, I meant with a guy."

"I didn't do it with Ellen."

"Sure you did. I remember hearing you guys near the trash can behind us on the lawn near the guest dock."

"A lot of sound and fury signifying nothing. No, it was later."

"WITH WHO?"

"Whom, English teacher."

"Gavin!"

"Okay," Gavin said, "You remember the guy Ellen danced with that night?"

"She danced with you."

"Think."

And Andrew thought. "Holy shit," he said after a minute, "that good looking waiter, whatshisname?"

Gavin smiled and nodded.

"Jesus," Andrew said, "you did it with *him*?"

Gavin nodded. "Ralph Sanchez. Him."

"Then, my friend," Andrew said, "I am very impressed. Every girl thought he was the hottest guy at Kanuga."

"Not to mention yours truly."

They lay quietly for a moment, and then Andrew suddenly sat up again. "Did York know?"

Gavin stared at him seeming to consider what to say next. "Apple," he finally said, "how important is what you have to do in the city tomorrow?"

"Now that *is* a non sequitor if I've ever heard one," Andrew said, somehow afraid of what was coming.

"Any chance that you could stay the night? I'd really appreciate it if you could."

"Gavin," Andrew said, "I...."

"There's so much more to talk about. So much more to tell you."

"And I want to hear it man," Andrew said, "but we can get together again. Or you could tell me on the phone."

"It's been twenty five years, Apple. Give me one fucking night."

"It's not that I don't want to," Andrew lied. "I'm having an excellent day. And it's so great to see you that I just, well, I just wouldn't want to spoil anything."

Gavin sat up. "Spoil anything? What are you....?" His face clouded. "Oh, Jesus Christ, Apple, you don't think I'm going to try to get you into bed, do you? Hell man, give me a break will you?"

"No, no, I never thought that you'd......"

"Yeah, you did. Of course you did." Gavin's voice was hard. "I'm a queer aren't I? And that's what queers do, don't they?" He stood up.

"Oh, come on Gavin. You're over reacting. I....."

"No. You're right, Andrew. You caught me. I want to jump your bones. I've been thinking of nothing else for thirty years." He shook out his beach towel. "You know something, fuck you, man. Nicki was wrong. You haven't changed at all."

"What's that supposed to mean?"

"Forget it," Gavin said. "Let's get outta here. You have a boat to catch." He turned away from Andrew and started walking up the beach. "You coming?", he called over his shoulder.

Andrew stood up and shook his towel. "Shit!" he muttered as he slipped his feet into his sneakers and followed close behind his retreating friend.

"Hey wait up, Gav. Come on man, I didn't mean anything. I'm sorry."

The four well- built men sitting on the blanket were watching them and laughing. In a voice, loud enough for Andrew to hear, one said, "Oh, oh. Trouble in paradise."

Andrew stopped and glared at him. "Excuse me?"

"Oh you're excused, honey, but you better run and catch up with that cute number over there or else your dick is gonna be real dry for a long long time."

"Fuck you, asshole."

"Temper, temper dear. Don't be cross with me because you've had a spat with your better half."

Andrew took a step toward the man on the blanket, "You know *dear* not only is your music too loud," he said, "but your mouth is too."

"Is this one butch or what?" the man laughed.

"Fuck you," Andrew said.

"Wonderful comeback, darling. You must be a writer. You have such a way with words."

The other three men stood up and faced Andrew. "Come on faggot," one said. "You want to play? Let's see what you've got."

Without thinking, Andrew lunged at the man nearest to him, tackling him and sending both of them flying to the ground. The others stood laughing, calling support to their friend.

"And now you see the reason I don't socialize!" Gavin said as he waded in between the two combatants wrestling in the sand and started pulling Andrew away. "Not worth it, Apple," he yelled. "Besides, you have a boat to catch."

Andrew, stuck in a headlock, caught his friend's eye. "So what do we do?"

Gavin, struggling to pull the arm away from his friend's neck, grunted, "As soon as I get this muscle queen off of you......"

"Yes?"

The offending arm was pulled away.

"RUN!"

The two old friends took off down the beach, towels flapping in back of them, laughing as they went.

"You *better* run, faggots," Andrew's combatant yelled after them, as his friends laughed and threw their arms around him.

Gavin and Andrew ran to the first path over the dunes and then stopped, their sides aching from running and laughing. They stopped and bent over, their hands on their legs, panting and laughing so much there were tears in their eyes.

"That was amazing," Andrew gasped. "What a rush!"

Gavin shook his head. "Trust you to pick a fight with some muscle queens. Andrew, my friend, those guys live in the gym for God's sake."

"Well," Andrew sputtered, "they started it."

The two stopped laughing for a moment as the realization of what Andrew had said hit them, and then doubled over and roared once again.

When they finally were able to catch their breath, Andrew straightened up and looked at his friend.

"So what's for dinner?" he asked.

CHAPTER THIRTY –SEVEN:

"That was delicious!" Andrew wiped his mouth and groaned contentedly.

"There's more."

"Good grief, Gav. Are you trying to kill me?"

"Yes," Gavin said, picking up the dinner plates, "and after you are dead I am going to have sex with you since I am a gay necrophile."

"I said I was sorry about that about a hundred times. What more can I say?"

"You could make it a hundred and one."

"I'm sorry."

"Apology accepted." Gavin moved to the kitchen with the plates. "We've got apple pie and ice cream for dessert."

Andrew picked up some remaining dishes and handed them to Gavin through the large opening between the dining room and the kitchen. "We can't have apple pie and ice cream," he said. "It's not Sunday night. Apple pie and vanilla ice cream are only on Sunday night."

"Someone at the camp had no imagination," Gavin said, letting the hot water into the sink.

"*No one* at that camp had any imagination, except the three of us, of course."

"Of course."

"You weren't *supposed* to have any imagination. Everything was planned, everything was charted out."

"Monday morning, softball. Monday afternoon handball and tennis."

"Tuesday morning, volleyball and lacrosse. Tuesday afternoon, nature shop and archery."

"I lived for nature, shop and archery," Gavin said washing the dishes.

"Oh sure you did. You were terrified of snakes!"

Gavin snorted. "Which is kind of ironic considering what we know now!"

Andrew laughed. "Okay, what was Wednesday? The morning was basketball and the afternoon......"

They were both silent for a moment.

"Anymore dirty dishes in there?"

"No, you've got 'em all," Andrew said. "Want me to wipe?"

"I'll let the air dry them and put them away later. You want dessert now or later?"

"Later, please. I'm a little full at the moment."

Gavin turned off the water and dried his hands with a dish- towel. "A drink then? A brandy?"

"Gavin, I have not had as much to drink as I have had today since college. Martinis before dinner, two bottles of wine *with* dinner and now brandy." His smile was wicked. "If I didn't know any better I would swear that you were...."

"Say it and I'll sic those muscle queens on you again."

Andrew held his hands up. "I give. Anything but that! A brandy would be fine."

"Go put your behind in one of those chairs over by the fire and I'll bring it to you."

Andrew felt wonderful. Earlier, his shower had been refreshing, and looking at himself in the bathroom mirror, he was strangely pleased to see that there was some color in his face. Along with the excellent dinner there had been stimulating conversation about books, film and music, and now as he sat in the comfort of the armchair in front of the fire, he felt an ease and calm he had not felt in years. He closed his eyes and as the fire warmed him he felt suddenly that York knew that he and Gavin had met again.

"Your brandy, sir."

Andrew opened his eyes and reached for the glass. "Thanks."

"Por nada," Gavin said settling into the other armchair. He held up his glass. "To absent friends."

Andrew lifted his glass. "Absent friends."

The two men sipped from the small glasses.

"Excellent," Andrew said.

"It should be," Gavin replied. "It's over two days old!"

The two friends chuckled and Willie, his toenails clicking on the hardwood floor ambled over and curled himself into a ball between them.

"You finally gonna tell me?" Andrew asked and Gavin nodded. "What do you want to know?" he said.

"Anything. Everything."

Gavin paused. "I don't know if Nicki told you about the film Sturtz is doing."

Andrew nodded. "How'd you find out?"

"Some other time."

"And? How do you feel about it?"

"I had lawyers look into it. According to them at the end of the day there is nothing any of us can do about it. Then I thought more about it and figured, on a scale of one to ten, fuck 'em. It's all bullshit." He looked at his friend. "There were so many other reasons that I wanted to see you, more important ones.

"The first being?"

"That I really wanted to see you...just *see* you. It was finally time and I finally knew it. Apple, we had been inseparable, the three of us, and then... nothing. It was as if when York died we all died."

Andrew nodded and stared into the fire. "I felt that too, but my God, the pain *you* must have felt. He was your brother, your twin."

Gavin smiled. "But he was your brother too, and in many ways, and don't say I'm being too dramatic here because I mean it, your twin as well. The pain was yours too."

Andrew looked at his friend. "Thank you."

Gavin smiled and held his glass up to him in a silent toast. "When we finally spoke on the phone, I knew you were still feeling what I was feeling."

"The loss" Gavin nodded. "The fucking loss."

"But we were kids then," Gavin said. "Kids who had been forced to grow up overnight, and there was no way we could see each other and deal with all that had happened. We weren't prepared. We didn't have the strength to go through with it. So, you see, there was no way we could have gotten together even if we had wanted to."

"No."

"And we both knew it."

"Yes."

"And the months became years and we grew farther and farther apart."

"I tried to call," Andrew said.

Gavin nodded. "I know you did. And I appreciate that. Even then I appreciated it."

"You didn't have to appreciate anything. I was just...."

Gavin held up his hand. "I know. You're right, but I did. But to see you, maybe go to a Knicks game or a movie, that, no." He shook his head. "I couldn't do it. Not then."

"Neither one of us would have known what to say anyway."

"And then it became easier to let each other go. To not communicate at all."

"You're wrong there. It was never easy. I wanted to talk to you...to see you."

"You're right, wrong choice of words. But you know what I mean."

"Yes."

"And as the years went by a numbness set in, at least for me."

Andrew nodded.

"The pain was still there, but there were actually full days when I wouldn't think about what had happened; when I moved through life not feeling anything. And that didn't make it better, just what? Tolerable." He sipped his brandy and reached down to pet Willie's head. "And then I met Nicki again."

Andrew closed his eyes. "Thank God." He looked at Gavin. "I know *that* sounds too dramatic, but I mean it."

Gavin smiled. "Me too."

"And Sturtz's movie, and Dorff writing it for God's sake. Why did Sturtz pick fucking Dorff?"

"Because fucking Dorff was the writer among us, the spinner of tales. Who else but Dorff?"

Andrew grunted. "But a movie! Dorff never wrote a movie!" Gavin shrugged as Andrew went on. "All the faces, the voices, the questions, the pitying looks, the pain, all in the name of some half assed movie about York's death. Pulling him back in, digging him up for the world to see, and for what? So that Sturtz can make another coupla billion. The worst thing is, you know how York would have hated all this if he were still alive."

The two men fell silent and stared into the fire.

"York was always the star wasn't he?" Andrew asked.

"He was supposed to be. That was how it was, but you know," Gavin sighed, and stretched, "we create our lives. Twins. Friends. Relationships. We allow things to happen." He closed his eyes and spoke softly. "I was the quiet one. I liked it that way. Taking stands is a big responsibility and York was good at it. So I let him speak for both of us. And even when I disagreed with what he said I didn't say anything. We had fallen into our roles, you see, and I had allowed York to be the star. It wasn't until many years after he died that I began to speak for myself. To make decisions." He opened his eyes and looked at Andrew. "But before that? It could be frustrating sometimes, but that in itself, the frustration, can define what it's like to be a twin."

"What *was* it like?" Andrew asked quietly. "I've always wondered."

Gavin smiled. "It was awful. It was wonderful." He smiled. "Sounds like the start of A TALE OF TWO CITIES, doesn't it? 'It was the best of times, it was the worst of times.' But you see, it really was."

"What was the awful part?"

"The constant comparisons; my height to his height, my weight to his weight, my hair to his hair. His eyes....." Gavin paused for a moment and then went on. "What he would likely become as compared to what I would become. The comparisons never stopped.

"But I dealt with it because York was my front man. As long as he was there to answer the dumb incessant questions, I didn't have to. And because they knew that York would respond, they directed most of their questions at him. He would answer. All I had to do was nod."

"And the wonderful?"

"All the rest." A log crackled in the fireplace making Willie look up, then groan contentedly as he saw that all was well as he fell back into a deep sleep. "Around him I felt safe. As long as he was around, nobody and nothing could hurt me." Gavin chuckled. "I sometimes think these things are determined in the womb. We probably had long talks in there, getting everything straight before we made our big entrance."

Andrew smiled and stared into his empty glass.

"But you loved him too," Gavin said. "So you know most of what I'm saying."

Andrew nodded. "There is not a day that I don't miss him." He paused. "Warts and all. But going back to the twins thing, as much as you loved him, conversely there must have been times when you....."

"Hated him?"

"No," Andrew said quickly, "Not really. I wasn't suggesting...."

"Sure you were, and I did hate him sometimes, Apple. You see that's part of it. A big part of it."

"Of what? I don't...."

"You remember that last basketball game?" Andrew looked into the fire and nodded. "I never understood what that was all about," he said.

Gavin sighed. "I know."

"But what happened?"

"Just suffice it to say that was one time when I hated him." Gavin's chuckle was without humor. "And yet to most people, he seemed so fucking perfect."

Andrew stared at the fire. "To me he *was* perfect. He could do everything well, he was sensitive before any of the rest of us even knew that others had needs...."

"He was a very special person, Apple, yes, but perfect," Gavin shook his head, "that he was not."

Andrew turned to his friend, and nodded. "I know," he said thinking about his call with Sue. " A couple of months ago I...well, suffice it to say, I know."

Gavin shrugged. "And yet we all thought he was perfect then. But no one is." Gavin rubbed Willie's head, his ears. "Believe me Andrew, no one is."

Andrew looked at his friend. "I think that's the first time I can ever remember you calling me Andrew."

Gavin smiled. "I hadn't realized that I had. But maybe it's time."

Andrew nodded. "God, I wish it could be like it was before with York sitting here and bullshitting with us."

"You wish that, huh. Got a monkey's paw?" They both smiled. "Except in this case he would have stayed the same and we would be the ones who had changed. He'd be sixteen, Andrew. What would we have to talk about?"

Andrew smiled sadly. "Nicki said something like that too."

"Well, then!"

"But why are *you* negating him, Gavin. I don't get it. You of all people."

Gavin sat quiet for a moment. "I adored my brother, Apple. That's why it hurt so much when he fucking killed me."

Andrew looked at his friend. "What are you talking about?"

Gavin stood up and smiled down at his friend. "You into taking a walk?"

The beach was empty, the full moon reflecting as a narrow strip on the ocean below. The pounding bass from one of the dance clubs over near the boat slip could barely be heard over the fall of the waves as the two men walked side by side, Willie, on a long leash, running up in front of them.

"It was a good idea to come out here," Andrew said. "I was getting logy."

"I always try to get Willie out at this time if I can," Gavin said. "That way he lets me sleep later."

"What is it, about one thirty?"

"It was that when we left. I'm guessing about two."

They watched as Willie slowly crept up on a piece of seaweed, pawed it, inspected it and moved on.

"What happened at the basketball game, Gav? Tell me. What did York do to you?"

Gavin nodded. "Okay," he said, "but I'm surprised Nicki didn't tell you. We've been talking non- stop since we met at the hospital. I told her that she was free to tell you anything."

Andrew stopped to pick up a shell, examine it in the moonlight and then skim it into the surf. "I know that," he said, "but she and I agreed that you should tell me what you felt I should know if and when you wanted to."

"That's appreciated, and now is good," Gavin said, "now is fine." He pulled his Topsiders off and walked onto the wet part of the sand, his feet leaving tracks at the water's edge. "It actually started during inspection on the morning of the game.

"So what happened?"

"I'll give you the Reader's Digest version. York confronted me about being gay, I told him that I thought I was, and instead of standing by me, he got all ashamed and worried about how it would affect him if people found out."

Andrew stopped walking. "You have got to be shitting me. York?"

"Bingo."

"I don't believe it."

"Hey," Gavin said, "I was there, think how I felt."

Andrew was stunned, and for a minute wondered if the alcohol had made him mis-hear what his friend had said. "Oh fuck," he finally managed.

"You ready for more?"

Andrew took a deep breath. "I'm not sure." Then. "Yes, please."

"Know how he found out?" Andrew shook his head slowly and Gavin went on. "Dorff told him."

"What?"

"Wait, it gets better. Dorff also told York that Nicki had told *him*, and since Nicki was the only one who knew....?"

"Nicki knew?"

Gavin smiled. "Sorry, Apple, I had to tell someone and I was too ashamed to tell any of you guys."

"Come on........."

Gavin shook his head. "No. It was too heavy for me to lay on you." He paused. "And, as it turned out, to lay on York, too." He took a deep breath. "Anyway, since Nicki was the only one who knew and since she had sworn never to tell anyone......"

"...you thought she had ratted on you. Oh my God, Gavin, that's why you stopped talking to her!"

"Give that man a box of cigars!"

"Oh fuck."

Gavin laughed. "I think you just said that."

"But wait, wait," Andrew said, trying to make sense of what he was hearing, "if Nicki didn't tell Dorff and we know she didn't, right?"

"Right."

"Then how the hell did Dorff find out?"

"I wish I knew, my friend. I only wish I knew."

"It's really late, Andrew. Just say the word and we'll hit the sack."

They had walked back to the house in silence and flopped into their chairs.

As if to answer, Andrew got up and put another log on the fire. "I am so exhausted that there is no way I could ever fall asleep. My head is spinning."

"Too much booze."

"Too much news!"

Gavin chuckled and watched as his friend almost fell back into the armchair. "So now you know about that basketball game!"

"I only wish I had known then."

"What would you have said?"

"What do you mean?"

"If I had told you that I was gay."

Andrew shifted uncomfortably. "I don't know. I guess I would have said that it was cool to be what you were."

Gavin smiled. "That from a man who thought that I asked him here to have sex."

"Oh, come on Gav," Andrew said indignantly, "that's not fair. I didn't think that."

"Really?"

Andrew shrugged. "Okay, maybe a little. But I still came didn't I? I would have been cool with it at camp."

Gavin shook his head. "No, you wouldn't. You couldn't have been. You were just a kid who thought he was sophisticated but who really knew nothing. You would have been upset and probably said all the wrong things. And that's what gets me so crazy."

"That I wouldn't have been understanding?"

"That my brother was only sixteen and I expected him to understand. He broke my heart, Andrew, and it finally hit me only recently, that he couldn't have done anything else. You see, he was a kid and not perfect after all. It was us who had made him perfect. He hadn't wanted to be. It was all our idea." He paused and looked down at his dog sleeping near the fire. "I know there are people out there, especially people from camp, who saw he and I as competitive, even combative and jealous of each other."

"I don't think..."

"Andrew, there are people out there who think I might even have had something to do with York's death."

"Jesus, Gavin, you can't believe that..."

Gavin cut him off. "I know they do. They do. 'Where was Gavin when York needed him? He was his twin, his brother. They were always buddies, why not that day?

Andrew looked down. "He and I were...."

"Where was Andrew? Where was he? Hadn't they fought on the basketball court only a few minutes before?'"

Andrew felt sick. "Gavin, no one ever thought..."

"They think I should have been looking out for him, and Apple I wanted to be, and I would have if he had let me. But I was so hurt and then, you see, those weren't our roles, were they? He was the one in charge. I wasn't supposed to be looking out for him. He was supposed to be looking out for me and he had told me that he was ashamed of me. He fucking left *me*, Apple, and I never had a chance to tell him that I forgave him and that I loved him."

Willie, sensing something wrong, got up and put his head on his owner's knee. Gavin held him close and Andrew realized that his friend was crying into the soft fur of the dog's neck.

Andrew looked down at his hands.

They sat that way for a while until, slowly, Gavin looked up at Andrew with wet eyes and forced a smile.

"I couldn't say all this on the phone, Apple. You see that, don't you?"

"I'm glad you asked me here Gavin. And I'm glad I stayed."

Gavin smiled. "Thanks old friend. Oh fuck, I didn't want to do this." He blew his nose. "But I have missed you!"

Andrew's voice was husky. "I've missed you too, bro. Really."

"And this afternoon? Did you feel anything strange at all? Did it remind you of anything? When we were down at the beach."

"It reminded me that I'd better start working out if I ever intend to win the Mr. Fire Island Contest."

Gavin chuckled and wiped his nose. "Well that's for sure. But I meant the way the day felt. The heat, the sun."

Andrew shrugged.

"Well, maybe it's just me," Gavin said, "but it reminded me...I mean the August heat and all...it reminded me..."

Andrew nodded. "Of the day York died."

Gavin nodded. "For years I kept reliving those last few moments and then, little by little, all of it began to fade. Today it came back with a vengeance."

The fire crackled.

"It was a sunny day. A hot day! A typical August day! Remember?"

Gavin nodded and rubbed his dog's head. "Then it was time for a swim; a cool, refreshing swim on a hot day after a tough game before a good lunch. Could anything be better?" He laughed ironically.

"Gavin, I...."

"Do you remember the day it happened, Apple?"

"Do I remember? My God, Gavin, of course."

"I mean the date?"

"How could I ever forget? August twelfth." Even though the fire was warm, a chill ran through Andrew's body and for a moment he thought he would be ill. "Oh my God," he murmured. "It's today."

"Thirty eight years ago today. I couldn't spend another one alone Apple. I couldn't do it by myself. Not this one." He was crying softly again. "It was just too much. That's why I needed you to stay."

"Oh man, why didn't you say something when you called?"

"I was afraid you wouldn't come. You're not pissed at me are you?"

Andrew turned to him. "Oh no, Gav, no. I just wish I had realized." He slapped his hand against his forehead. "I can't fucking believe it. Every year I remember, and this year I forget! Every year I light a candle, and not this one. The first few years after, I used to actually go to Temple on the day. Me in Temple! Can you picture that?"

Gavin smiled and blew his nose. "It is a little difficult."

"But I did. I went. So you see, I always did remember."

"Apple, there's no need to....."

"I wrote it down in my fucking date book. I write it down every year. As soon as I get my new book for the year, that's the first thing I write down. And when I write it down I always say to myself, 'As if I'd forget.' He snickered. "And I forgot! This year I fucking forgot! Maybe because you called and I knew I didn't have anything else to do today I didn't look at the book. Maybe because......" He looked down at his hands. "Oh Gav, I'm sorry man. I can't fucking believe I forgot!"

"I don't want you to feel bad, Apple. That was not my intention at all." He looked at the fireplace. "Look, the fire's almost out and it's late, but I need to tell you something that I have never told anyone else." Gavin got up. "But I'll need a drink to help me with it."

"Gavin, there's no need to..."

Gavin shook his head. "Yeah, there is. Can I get you another one?"

Andrew nodded yes, afraid to hear what his friend was going to tell him.

Gavin returned with the cut glass decanter and poured a little into his and Andrew's glass. He sat back down.

The small house was so still that the clock on the mantle could be heard ticking.

"You said before that the year after York died you went to Temple." Andrew nodded. "Well, I worshipped in a different way. You've heard of the baths?"

"Yes." All at once Andrew felt beyond tired.

"I found one place on 56th Street, paid my admission and went in."

"Gavin..."

"Men were walking up and down dimly lit corridors, some with towels around their waists, many with nothing on at all. I went to the cubicle they had assigned me, I took off all my clothes, I lay down on the cot they provided and pushed the door to the cubicle wide open. And as the anonymous men came and went throughout the night all I wanted was for one of them to just hold me the way York had, but that was not what they had in mind. That's not what they had come for." The last embers of the fire glowed in the fireplace. "I heard once that someone had interviewed a bunch of homosexual men and asked them what they were looking for when they went to bed with another man. A majority of them answered that they were looking for the other half of themselves." He smiled. "Imagine that." He looked over at Andrew. "That was one I couldn't even tell Nicki."

Andrew nodded. "It's enough Gav. Enough pain, enough humiliation, enough bullshit. York wouldn't have wanted this for you."

"Or for you." Gavin sighed. And for a little while there it looked like things were getting better. And then Sturtz' film and it's all back to the surface again."

Andrew stood up. "And I for one don't want anymore shit to happen to York, you or me. It's time that everyone let him rest in peace, especially Dorff and Sturtz."

Gavin looked up at him. "What do you mean, Andrew?"

"I'll tell you what. First thing Monday morning I am going to call Henry Sturtz and I am going to give him a message."

"Andrew, I told you, you can't stop......."

"And the message will be very simple. I want to serve notice to him that as soon as that fucking film of theirs is finished you, Nicki and I are going to be given a private screening."

"But..."

"No buts Gavin, it's as simple as that. God knows that we've all been through enough and now it's time for it to be over. No more past, only now. We say we want to see the rough cut of the film. They say no, we say lawyers."

Gavin shook his head. "I told you my lawyers said….…."

"Fuck 'em. We'll find other lawyers. Either way I am not going to back down."

"And if Sturtz agrees?"

"Then we go to the screening and we see what they've done and if there is anything in it that demeans York or opens any wounds for either of us, we have it out with Henry right there. While there's still time to cut and edit." He smiled. "Has there ever been a time when you and I couldn't take Sturtz and Dorff in a little pick up game."

"Sturtz is a good player, Andrew."

"Maybe, but look who he's got on his side. We have each other. What do you say, Gav?"

Gavin smiled. "I say we may be in for a battle, but as long as we're in this together, you've got a deal."

And for the first time in years, Andrew Brookman felt like a pressure had been removed from around his chest. "It's the right thing to do, Gav. I know it is." He smiled at his friend. "You know what else I think?" he said.

"I'm almost afraid to ask."

Andrew put his hand on Gavin's shoulder. "I think," he said, "that if I don't get to bed in five minutes I am going to fucking collapse right here on the floor. I am so fucking tired."

Gavin chuckled. "Why so many 'fuckings'?"

Andrew shrugged. "I dunno," he said, "maybe because I feel so fucking good." He looked at Gavin and then suddenly pulled him close and held him.

They stood that way for a long time.

There were two beds in Gavin's room. After using the bathroom and getting into a pair of shorts, Andrew fell into one of them, and, a few minutes later, Gavin the other. Willie lay content at the foot of Gavin's bed.

"Goodnight, Gavin," Andrew whispered. "It's been an amazing day."

"A *fucking* amazing day," Gavin said, and then, "And Ed Lasker thought it was the Mystery Walk that would make us men!"

Andrew chuckled. "Do you have any idea how much I have missed you?"

Gavin nodded. "I have a good idea. "A very good idea." He paused. "Goodnight, Apple," he whispered. "Thanks for being here."

"My dear friend," Andrew answered, "at this moment, there is no place in the world that I would rather be."

Andrew reached up and switched off the light. Instinctively, as he had done with York so many years before, he reached across the darkness to clasp his friend's hand. Gavin's hand was already there.

A small white candle in a glass jar flickered brightly on the windowsill above them.

CHAPTER THIRTY-EIGHT:

AFTER THE SCREENING (2)

Lennie Dorff dabbed the rest of the blood from around his mouth. "I'm going to sue," he whined as Nicki handed him an ice pack and he pressed it to his face.

Henry Sturtz laughed. "You are not going to sue, Lennie," he said. "No one sues when he gets into a fight with a friend."

"It wasn't a fight," Lennie sulked. "He attacked me."

"And I'm not a friend." Gavin put his hand on Nicki's shoulder. "Let's go."

"Jesus! Will you all stop being such pussies!" They looked at him. Sturtz winked at Nicki. "Present company excluded, of course."

Nicki sighed at Sturtz and shook her head wearily. "You never change, do you, Henry?" She swept her hand in front of her. "All this money and fame and you're still, what, twelve?" She looked at Apple and sighed. "I'm ready."

"And as far as suing goes," Gavin said, "if this film is released in its current form, you can count on hearing from all our lawyers."

Sturtz shrugged. "You're welcome to try, but let me remind you that you tried that already and you know you haven't a leg to stand on, so that's crap. Total crap. Nothing is going to be changed and no one is going to be sued." His voice softened. "Look, I'm asking you, for old time's sake if for nothing else, give me ten minutes, twenty. Have a drink with me and we'll talk. There are things we need to talk about. I want you to go away happy. After all, we were once good friends."

They were all standing uncomfortably in the large and beautifully furnished reception area outside of Sturtz' screening room. Thick, overstuffed armchairs and couches were arranged so that those sitting on them would be able to chat easily. A fully stocked bar took up one whole wall and a huge cabinet holding all of Sturtz's awards took up most of another. They had grudgingly come here so that Dorff's already swelling lip could be attended to.

Gavin's voice was even. "What is there left to talk about, Henry? Seriously? What?"

"Ten minutes. Twenty at the most." They all looked blankly at him, and then Henry Sturtz said something he very rarely said. "Please."

Andrew looked at Gavin who shrugged, walked over to the bar and poured himself a shot of Johnny Walker Blue. "Good," Sturtz said, rubbing his hands together, "good. Now we're cooking."

"Ten minutes," Gavin said, pointing at him. He sat down in a soft leather armchair and sipped his drink. He nodded at Dorff. "And the only reason I'm staying is so I can hear this miserable asshole try and justify what he did."

Leonard Dorff, the ice pack still pressed to his mouth, made his way to the bar and poured himself a large glass of Maker's Mark. He started to raise the glass to his lips, then, as he realized the alcohol would cause pain to his open wound, he lowered it. He dropped the ice pack onto the bar.

"Whatever the reason for staying," Sturtz said, "good." He looked at Nicki. "I didn't want to hire a bartender because I thought just us would be better, but I have to tell you, I make a hell of a cosmo. Yes?" Nicki shook her head and wished for the hundredth time that night that she hadn't stopped smoking twenty years earlier. "Apple?" Andrew didn't answer but instead pulled a Stella Artois out of the bar's refrigerator and popped it open himself. He leaned against the side of the awards cabinet. "You want to talk, Henry? So, talk."

Sturtz sat on the armrest of a dark mahogany leather couch. "Okay, since no recording devices seem present," he smiled, "I'll admit to it. Of course the characters were based on you. But, at the same time, they *weren't* you."

Andrew sniffed. "That makes a lot of sense."

"Oh come on, Apple," Sturtz replied, "you're the teacher here, so don't be dense. Most of the incidents actually happened, you'll admit to that, but some of them had to be made up, expanded. All Henry did was report some things and make up others. Sometimes he just put what actually happened in a different setting to make it more dramatic. It's a *drama*, for Crissake, not a documentary."

"From what I remember of that summer," Andrew sniffed, "Dorff made up a lot." He shook his head. "But why did you have him do it in the first place, Henry? I honestly don't see why."

"Why what?"

"Why any of it? What was the point of the film?"

Sturtz held out his hands. "You want honesty?" He paused. "Really? You want me to be honest?"

Andrew nodded. "From you, my friend, it would be novel."

Sturtz didn't smile. "Okay then, I'll be honest." He paused. "I know it won't sound like the Henry you remember and love, but I swear what I'm going to say is true." He looked down at the floor, then up at his friends. "And this is no bullshit. For some reason, and don't ask me what, I needed to get it all of it out of my system."

"Oh, come on," Andrew started, but stopped when Sturtz held up his hand. "That summer, what happened, all of it, one day I just realized that it's been on my mind for far too long." He stopped and seemed to consider. "This actually wasn't the first time. Through the years I had a few writers working on the idea, but none of them worked out. They didn't know the territory. You'll have to admit, that was one helluva summer. Fucking traumatic. I know that all of you thought it didn't affect me, but it did. I just didn't show it the way the rest of you did, but it was digging at me, annoying me." He shrugged. "So, since a little mental house cleaning seemed in order, I decided to revive the idea and finally make the movie."

Andrew clapped slowly. "And the award for best actor goes to...." He threw up his hands. "Come on, Henry," he said, "that's the best you can come up with? 'Had to get it out of your system? Give me a break. You? Yeah, right."

Sturtz looked at him. "You don't believe me," he said, almost sadly, and Andrew shook his head. Sturtz paused for a moment and then grinned. "Okay, you got me." He walked a few feet to the cabinet and lifted an Oscar from a shelf. "Here's the real reason. I wanted to win me another one of these babies."

"Now *that* figures," Andrew snorted, and Sturtz went on, his voice more strident. "Look, see it from my point of view. I have the third CONQUISTADOR sequel ready for release on Memorial Day weekend, and granted that's where the big summer money will be, but I also wanted a small film to get me at least one brother for this guy before the year is over, maybe two if I mount a good campaign." They all looked at him. "You don't get it." He smiled. "But then, you're not in the business." Exasperation crept into his voice. "Really, it's important to me to prove that Harvey and Bob aren't the only ones who can have it both ways."

Nicki looked up. "Harvey and Bob? I don't...."

Sturtz smiled at her. "The Weinsteins?" Blank looks. "First Miramax and now The Weinstein Company? They produced some very classy films that also made a great deal of money. Cash and class, they proved that's what it's all about." He replaced the statuette. "So I needed a prestige film and GONE THE SUN was the answer. CONQUISTADOR 3/ GONE THE SUN. Crap and class. But, as I said, it wasn't the first time I had thought of it. Now, what I needed was someone who was actually *there* to nail it. That's when I thought of Lennie here, and the son of a bitch actually came through. He turned that cockamamie summer into a simple touching coming of age kind of thing, and that was exactly what I had wanted. You know, a little laughter, a little tragedy, and freakin' Lennie hit the bull's eye. Go figure."

Andrew picked up the Oscar, surprised at its weight. "But why Dorff?," he said. " In the two summers you and he were bunkmates you never had a good word to say about him."

"Why not Dorff? I just told you why Dorff!"

"They're talking about me as if I wasn't here," Leonard Dorff thought, "all of them are. To them I'm still invisible." He grimaced as pain shot through his face from where his lip was split. He took a deep breath. "Things don't change." He raised the glass to his mouth, and again thought better of it. He needed a drink, but it wasn't worth the hurt. He was about to put his glass down on the table next to him when he stopped. A pile of flyers advertising the movie had been left there and, as he looked down at them, a wave of self- awareness, almost as foreign to him as had being physically hit by another human being, made his legs feel weak. He stared at the bright colored ads, his name in small print on the bottom just before that of the director, and then looked at the people who sat or stood around the room and realized that the characters in the film were more real than they were. Apple, Gavin, Nicki, he knew the people in the film, but these versions of the characters, he did not know them. The memories he had harbored through the years were not about them, but about whom they had been. These people were strangers. And Lennie Dorff thought, "Who the hell are they anyway?" And then suddenly, it all made sense. None of them mattered. Not one of them. Not then, and certainly not now. A nine to five teacher, a gay recluse and who the hell knew what Nicki did? Even Sturtz, a loudmouth blowhard who had no talent for anything but making money on what other people created, all of them meant

nothing. Nothing. There was no reason to respect or fear these people, so why did he care what they said or did? 'Just asking…who's the most talented person in this room?' No contest, I am, me, Lennie Dorff. I have talent and I used that talent to create something that will last forever. The movie…his movie… was good… no, it was excellent and he had done it. Not Gavin, not Apple, not Nicki, and no, not even Sturtz. He, Leonard Dorff, Isaaz, the failure's grandson, and Schmoil the loser's son was the one who had created something tangible, something that people would see and admire and not walk past without noticing on their way to the next pushcart. Suddenly, a strange and heady feeling of exhilaration and resolve moved through him. Oh yes, he would get through this evening, drink or no drink. He knew that he would. And that wouldn't be all. Later, in the weeks to come, he would get rid of the business once and for all, and then get rid of Ellie and the girls once and for all as well. All of them were what was and he had moved on. Who and what he had been was over, behind him, finished for good. Faltik. He had made a success with this film and he would make another and then another. He was certain of it. He not so gently touched his lip and smiled when the pain hit. No, no one had ever hit him before and 'wonder of wonders,' something he had always dreaded had turned out to be not that bad after all. "An evening of firsts," he thought, and whereas an hour or a day or a lifetime ago the sheer reality of someone hitting him would have paralyzed him with fear, now it didn't matter at all. The pain Gavin had given him wasn't that much after all and, somehow, in the greater scheme of things, it meant, well, nothing. Dorff raised the glass to his lips, hesitated for less than a second knowing what would come, then drank deep, smiling as the pain crashed through his mouth.

"So, why not Dorff?" Sturtz said again. "Who better than Dorff? Not my favorite person of all time true, and, truth be told, he's still not," he looked at Dorff and shrugged, "sorry Lennie, but it's true," he looked back at the others, "but schmuck or no schmuck I figured he knew all of the secrets up there because of that cockamamie newspaper of his, and, as it turns out, he did." He slapped Lennie hard on the back. "And who knew, he's a pretty good writer, too." He looked at Andrew, a sly smile creeping across his lips. "But why do you ask, Apple? Jealous I didn't ask you?" The Oscar suddenly seemed far too heavy in Andrew's hand and he carefully replaced it in the cabinet. As he turned, he shot a middle finger at Sturtz who chuckled as he turned to Nicki. "But seriously, forget all the whys and wherefores and get back to the actual picture. Tell me honestly that Karen Cooper wasn't amazing as, well, you."

Nicki nodded. "She was good, yes."

Sturtz nodded gratefully and then looked hard at Gavin. "And Joey Carter. Was he York or, Luke, or whatever Lennie called him?"

Gavin looked down at his drink and said nothing.

"But the story, the incidents," Andrew persisted. "I'll grant you that a lot of it did happen, but the way he told it was so subjective. I mean this movie is the summer of '75, according to Dorff." He looked at Lennie. "You use real people, us, you change our names and you put the characters we've become into a world that you've created. However good the cast is and however well made the film is, because the story *is* so subjective, it ends up that the whole thing isn't real."

Dorff sipped his drink and looked over at Andrew. "To you," he said. Andrew blinked at him as Dorff went on, his voice steadier and more confident than it had been even moments before. "A lot of that world did exist, Andrew, and not just as I saw it. In some way or another, most all of the things in the film happened. Maybe you don't remember them in the particular way I presented them, but I do, and they happened."

"Oh, please," Andrew sniffed. He straightened up. "They happened? My God, Lennie, if nothing else, York's death! What's wrong with you? Suicide?"

Dorff sniffed. "Well, you'll notice we never come right out and say it."

"Lennie, there was an autopsy."

"Yes, but the common consensus right afterwards was, well, you know this, that he pushed off too high on his dive and smacked his head on the board on the way down. He died of hubris."

"Bullshit," Andrew snarled.

"There was a bruise."

Gavin glared at him. "That bruise was there after our fight in the social hall that morning and you know it. That's not why he died."

Nicki's voice was soft, measured. "York had something wrong with his heart that no one knew about. That's why he died, Lennie. That's what came out in the autopsy. He had something wrong with his heart."

Dorff shrugged as he looked at the others. " Be that as it may, in the context of the story, that explanation certainly wouldn't sell any tickets, so suicide made the most sense." He looked first at Gavin and then back to Andrew. "You know, hurt that he had hurt his brother, not being able to deal with the fact that his brother was a homo and that the whole camp might find out…so the hint of suicide. That made sense." Andrew started to speak and again was immediately cut off. "In fairness," Sturtz interrupted, "Dorff is right. We never actually come out and say anything definitive, *that* would be libelous, but I interrupted you. Go on."

As they saw him take a deep breath, it was obvious to all there that Andrew was trying contain himself. "Okay," he said evenly, "let's take this thing point by point and see where it gets us."

Nicki looked up at him and smiled. She could picture him in front of his classroom, pacing back and forth, a book in his hand, trying to make his class see beyond the written word; to see what was truth and what illusion; to see that *he* saw that there *was* a difference and that it was important, and to make them *know* that it was important, maybe even more important than the story itself. This was the Andrew she loved. And at that moment, she realized that she did.

"Let's examine this carefully, leave the major things for a minute and start with the small ones," Andrew went on, "the things that are *seemingly* inconsequential to the plot and work from there."

Sturtz barked a laugh. "What is this, the last reel of *Murder on the Orient Express*?"

"Look dickwad," Andrew snapped, "I talk or I walk. Which is it? You wanted us to talk this through and now you're acting like an asshole." He glared at Sturtz who nodded. "When you're right, you're right. Sorry. Go on."

Andrew turned to Dorff. " First off, what was that crap about the electioneering and you becoming president of the senior group? I admit it played well, but you were never president, Lennie, York was. He always was, so what was that about? What were you trying to do, make yourself the star and make him a supporting character?" Dorff shook his head, but Andrew went on. "The film you wrote may show you as some kind of half assed hero, the poor kid from the poor area who had to make his way with the entitled kids, but as good as you paint yourself, compared to York, you were nothing." His unspoken, "And you still are", hung in the air.

"What you did was wish fulfillment, Lennie," Nicki added, "and in this case it's very sad. It was a world you wanted but that didn't exist." She paused for a moment, thinking, then went on. "Andrew's right. The whole president thing never happened, but that in its self, isn't important. What *is* important is that the scenario you devised with it demeans York."

Before Dorff could respond, Sturtz jumped in. "Wait, wait *wait*! Back up. Hold the 'demeans York' for a minute. Wish fulfillment? Maybe. Maybe, but aren't there are a lot of things in life that we wish had happened differently?," he offered.

"God, Henry," Andrew groaned, "do anything, but for God's sake, don't get philosophical with us."

Sturtz scowled. "Okay, you win. You want pragmatism? Fine. Pragmatically, *story-wise*, shmuck, it works."

Andrew poked a finger in his direction as he began to pace back and forth. "See, that's my point. That's what I mean. Lennie creates a summer from his point of view….."

"And from things I was told or I overheard" Dorff interrupted. "Like your ride to the canoe trip with Ike Hayes for instance. Remember, Andrew, how you told me about it when we got back to camp? Remember; the 'Brookman, Andrew thing, or the whole thing about rhetorical questions. You told me all of that. Oh yes, there were a lot of factual things like that in that script."

Andrew glared at Dorff. "If I may continue." Dorff shrugged and nodded. "As I was saying,"Andrew went on, "Lennie creates a summer from his point of view and then he bends it and manipulates it until, in the world he's created, he ends up the hero, looking like the injured party, and York, York without being able to defend himself ends up the bad guy." He jabbed a finger at Sturtz. "And you, Henry, you buy all that shit because it works as a piece of fiction that will win you an award? Jesus."

Sturtz chuckled. "Now you're making it sound like a Jewish RASHOMON, and believe me," he said almost as an aside, "if *that* wouldn't get me a best picture, nothing would." His tone became more serious as he looked at Nicki. "Look, you say York is somehow demeaned and I don't believe that for a second, but aside from that, what exactly is wrong with the picture of camp that Dorff came up with?"

Gavin jumped in before Nicki could respond. "Oh, I don't know," he said, "maybe that there are lies inside of lies inside of lies. Maybe that all of what's on the screen came from Lennie's sick mind, maybe that."

Nicki sighed and held up her hand. "Well gentlemen, since it seems that we are not leaving for the foreseeable future," she looked at her husband, "Andrew, would you mind pouring me something strong?"

All remained silent as Andrew nodded, plopped a few ice cubes in a glass, picked a bottle, poured, tossed in a slice of lemon and handed the glass to his wife. "Stoly," he said. "Just the way you like it." Nicki touched his hand as she took the glass. "Thank you."

"So, back to the election," Andrew continued, but Sturtz brushed him quiet. "Screw the election. Jesus, you say the election scenes might have thrown a negative light on York because he threw it to Lennie. I don't see it that way, but okay, I'll give it to you. Okay? But what you're missing is all the *positive* things about York that Lennie added. What about those?"

"For instance?"

"For instance? My God, everything: the scene with the prostitute that you and he visited in Harlem. 'She was ugly but she had beautiful eyes.' That never happened, did it?" Andrew shook his head. "Okay. York's becoming friends with the kid in the infirmary who was dying. Also made up." He looked at Lennie. "And I still think that was a little over the top." He looked at the others. "Didn't that make York look like a hero? Jesus, there were a hundred things." He paused and then snapped his fingers. "My stash." The others looked blank and he went on. "The stash of drugs I had in the hollowed out Shakespeare."

"What about it?" Andrew asked.

"In the movie," Dorff said quietly, "I took the blame for flushing it. In reality it was York who did it. I saw him do it."

Andrew waved him away. "Bullshit."

"You can believe me or not, but he was mad at Henry for something I can't remember, and when he thought no one was looking, he flushed it."

"Something you don't remember," Nicki whispered, "how convenient."

Sturtz went to the bar and put some club soda into a glass. As he was about to put it to his lips, he stopped, put the glass down and pointed at Andrew. "Okay...the Mystery Walk! Perfect example. Great scene, huh? Touching?" Andrew nodded grudgingly. "Okay," Sturtz went on rubbing his hands together and then picking up his drink, "now we all admit that happened, but was Lennie in the canoe with you and York? No. So how could Lennie possibly have known all the things that you and York said in that canoe when he wasn't with you? He couldn't...."

"But......."

"But, and yes there is a but here, *but* he knew how close you and York were, and from that he *created* your dialogue. Maybe, by accident he might have hit on something you might actually have said, but more likely he wrote something he *wished* you had said; maybe that *you* wished you had said."

"I had heard York mention verguenza once and, " Dorff started, but Sturtz waved him quiet. "Where he got the dialogue from, it doesn't matter. The point is that Lennie created the scene, and because of it York comes out of it looking like the golden boy. Demeaning to him? I don't think so."

For a moment Andrew could picture himself, the hot sun beating down on him and York as they paddled down the river, but though he could see their lips move in his mind, all that he could hear was the dialogue Dorff had written for the film, the words he and York had actually spoken gone in the film of time. "But...."

"Again, but. *No*, wait!" Sturtz spoke slowly, making his point. "Go with me here. In that one scene, that scene in the canoe, we see so many parts of York; his kindness, yes?' He paused and went on. " His self doubt coming out, as Lennie says, with that business with 'verguenza'. All those things made him a three dimensional character, and you know why?" His words were spoken very slowly, as to a backward child. "Because-Lennie-made-it-up! And because he did and did it so well, York becomes heroic, lovable, more than just a jock, someone who thinks and feels, and is real. Shit, Apple, Lennie loved York's ass and because of his dialogue it's clear that in that scene *you* love him and, more important, the audience loves him, so what's the harm in that? The canoe trip *happened*. Fact. What was said between you, we don't know. " He paused. "So explain to me how that is demeaning to York? I don't think you can. In fact the dialogue in that scene makes Apple's later loss even greater than it might have been without it." He turned to Dorff. "Right, Lennie?"

Dorff nodded. Somehow, when no one had seen him, he had poured himself another large drink. He pulled at it, and as the pain shot through his mouth, when he spoke, his voice was conciliatory yet strong. "I wasn't trying to hurt anyone or to make anyone look bad. Believe me there were many other things like Henry's stash, what you would call more important things, that I had heard about or knew, that I didn't expound upon."

Sturtz laughed. "'Expound upon'! Am I gonna get an Oscar or what? 'Expound upon.' Who talks like that? I fucking love it."

"Why can't I remember anything we talked about that day?," Andrew wondered to himself, then looked up sharply as Gavin snickered.

"Yeah, it's wonderful. Just wonderful," Gavin said. He looked hard at Dorff. "Okay genius, let's cut to the chase. How about something *I* actually knew, because I was there; something that had nothing to do with York. Why'd you have to lie about that?"

"Like what?" Dorff asked, knowing full well what was coming.

"Oh, I don't know," Gavin, said casually. He snapped his fingers. "Oh, wait. I *do* know." His voice hardened. "How about what happened between you and me on that same canoe trip."

Dorff met Gavin's eyes. "I didn't make anything up. What's in the movie is what happened."

Gavin's tone had grown incredulous. "You fucking sick liar! My God, Dorff, you lied about it to York at the time, and you're still lying about it in the movie. You created a version of what actually happened to save your own ass." He looked at the others. "What's in that movie is not the truth. That is *not* what happened." Nicki nodded and when Dorff didn't say anything, Gavin went on. "Why don't you tell everyone what really happened, huh? It's only us here. For once in your miserable life be a fucking man and try telling the truth."

Dorff shook his head. "What really happened is what's in the movie."

Gavin hit his open palm against his forehead. "Jesus. You really are a sick fucking piece of shit, you know that?" His voice was hard, and Nicki felt a chill run through her as she realized it was the same tone he had used when she had taken his hand at York's funeral. "Oh, no, that's not what happened, not by a long shot and you know it. You don't want to tell everyone, then allow me." He pointed at Dorff. "He told York that *I* came on to *him*? Horseshit. This bastard was all over *me*."

"That's explained in the movie," Dorff said, his voice calm. "I admit I reached out to you, I tried to hold you, to comfort you. I didn't want sex, you were hurt and vulnerable and I wanted you to know I cared, that I was there for you. You misinterpreted my kindness and made it dirty. I had to tell York before you did."

Gavin shook his head. "Bullshit, bullshit, *bullshit*." He looked at Sturtz. "You want to know what really happened? This bastard got me really wasted and when I could hardly see, that was the moment he was waiting for." He looked back at Dorff. "Trust me, Leonard, if I hadn't been drinking you never would have had the balls to do what you did, but there I was, totally out of it, not being able to even see straight, and before I even knew what was happening, you had your hand down my shorts pulling on my dick and jerking me off." Gavin felt all their eyes on him. "I was blitzed okay", he grumbled, "but that's something I do remember?"

Dorff spoke softly as he shook his head. "That's not true. You said it yourself. You were drunk. If you were so drunk, how can you be sure what really happened? What you're saying just isn't true." He pulled at his drink.

"The hell it isn't! You know what you did! And then, and then you have the balls to tell York that it was just the other way around, that I was groping *you*."

Dorff's voice was hard. "He believed me, didn't he?"

"What?" Gavin's voice was incredulous.

"Whoa, whoa, boys and girls, "Sturtz said, "easy, please. Look, it seems that someone is lying and someone is telling the truth and you know what", and he emphasized his next words, "*it-just-doesn't-matter at all!* Get this into your heads. *It's a fucking movie!* That particular scene plays well as written and helps bring the film to its climax, no pun intended, so as far as I'm concerned, that's all the truth we need. And God knows Lennie did not come out as a hero with all that manipulation going on."

"But, my God, Henry," Nicki began, motioning to Gavin, "this is a man's life you're talking about here. You let Lennie create a character based on someone who was once your close friend, and if nothing else, without giving it a second thought you out him to the whole world? That business with Ralph Sanchez, and then York turning his back on his brother."

"It was true, wasn't it? And as I said, it works as a movie too."

'It works as a movie?' What kind of a person are you?"

Sturtz shook his head. "Nicki, you're taking Gavin's side because you're his friend, but what about Lennie?" He looked at Andrew and smiled. "I can't believe I'm standing up for Lennie Dorff. Go figure." He looked back at Gavin. "Don't you see how honest Lennie was in setting the things that led up to York's death in motion? If he's outing you, in another way he's outing himself by admitting he told York that you were gay." He sighed. "And you know, Gav," he said, "there's a statute of limitations on keeping quiet about something everyone's always known about." He looked at Nicki and pointed to Gavin. "There is no way that this is going to hurt him now. Not now. Not by a long shot."

"Henry," Nicki started, but Sturtz continued on. "First of all, anyone from camp who knew Gavin has probably heard that he is gay by this time. We're talking forty years, give or take a year. There have been rumors about him for all those years. I've heard them, you've heard them," he looked at Gavin, "and if you weren't such a freaking recluse, you would have heard them too. So those who know know, and those who weren't at camp will have no frame of reference to base it on, so I ask you, what difference does it make if Lennie tells it his way? What's it going to matter to Gavin now?" He turned to Gavin. "Besides, I did some research about you before any of this started."

Gavin raised an eyebrow. "Why?"

"No matter, not important. What is important is that I found out some very interesting things." Sturtz strolled around the room. "You are a very wealthy man, Gavin. Your business is thriving, though you only go into the office once or twice a millennium. You have a very hefty trust fund and annuity, neither of which depends on your sexual orientation, you donate shit-loads of money to many different causes anonymously, you see practically no one, so, at the end of the day, who gives a shit if you like boys? Explain to me how any of this is going to hurt you."

Gavin stared at him. "So you get to play God? You decide what can or can't be told."

Sturtz frowned at him. "You know, Gavin, you are such a self-righteous prick, you know that? You always were and you always will be. You and your brother both: self-righteous pricks. Your shit never smelled, while I, I was always the bad guy in the scenario. Well, once and for all, fuck that. You say I decide? Okay, I decide. So let me tell you about a decision I made back in 1975, okay? Back then, I decided not to say a word, to keep my mouth shut."

"What are you talking about?" Gavin asked.

"What am I talking about? I'll tell you. You ready, cause here's a news flash that has been a long time in coming. I knew about you, my friend, I knew then, and no one had to tell me."

Gavin's stomach lurched. "What do you mean, then?"

"Then. Back at Kanuga, Gavin, I knew. I knew because I was there. Me. That night. Down at the guest dock. You thought you and Sanchez were alone? Oh no, my good friend, oh no. There were three people there that night, you, Ralph and yours truly." Gavin looked stunned as Sturtz went on. "You had no idea I was there, but I was. I was there for all of it. When I read about it in Lennie's script I was surprised that someone else had known and hadn't said anything until now. And you know what, and here's a twist in the plot, back then, the bad guy, me, I decided to keep it strictly to myself. I never breathed a word to anyone, Gavin, because it wasn't such a big deal. I didn't out you, and oh, boy I could have had a field day, so you can take your moral indignation and, if there is still anymore room in there, you can shove it right up your ass."

No one spoke. Gavin hadn't moved, still staring at Sturtz who went to the bar and poured some scotch into a glass. He handed it to Gavin who silently accepted it, then took the empty one from his old friend's hand. He poured another drink for himself.

"Milburn asked me to check to see where you were. Everyone was back in the bunk except you. He wanted to go himself, but he was afraid Lasker might drop by and not find him there. Of course, first he asked York, but Klinger was puking and your brother was busy holding his head over the toilet and trying to keep Bobby from finding out about the booze." Sturtz slowly sipped while the others waited. "It was after lights out and pretty dark, cloudy, well you remember, few stars, hazy moon. I grabbed a flashlight and headed over to Hayes. The hall was empty, and for some reason I took a chance and headed for the guest dock. That's where I saw what was happening."

Dorff's voice was soft again. "For the film, I thought it would be more symbolic to have it happen backstage in a costume closet." He smiled. "I know most people don't ever notice things like that when they go to a movie, but I do."

"Jesus," Andrew whispered.

Sturtz' voice was placating. Gone was the anger and sadness had taken its place. "So don't go all ape shit on me for being insensitive, okay. In some things, sure I am, I'm known for it and, to tell you the truth, I get off on it, but with something like this, with something that concerns a friend, there was no way that anyone would ever hear about it from me."

Gavin looked at him for a moment trying to pin it down. "You knew."

Sturtz nodded. "From the beginning."

"Then I'm sorry," Gavin finally said, "I had no idea that…" and Sturtz gave him a small smile. "Don't mention it." He chuckled. "I never did." He turned back to the others. "So you see the film was not meant to hurt anyone." Sturtz lit his cigar. "If anything it was meant as a terrific story about a bunch of kids who thought they knew it all at sixteen and ended up knowing shit."

Nicki's voice was quiet as she looked over at Gavin. "How did Lennie know about that game of G-H-O-S-T you and York played? He couldn't have been in Hayes that night too."

Gavin shook his head as Lennie started to speak. "I knew that they called 'Horse' 'Ghost. Well, we all did. But, there was no actual game after taps in Hayes Hall."

Nicki looked at Gavin who shook his head.

"That," Dorff said almost proudly, " I made up."

Nicki looked confused. "But that's what led to their final fight. York's rejection of Gavin."

Gavin answered for him. His voice was low. "York pulled me aside during inspection that morning. We went behind the bunks and he confronted me with what Dorff had told him. I thought no one was there." He looked at Lennie and shook his head sadly. "But obviously I was wrong."

."Just asking," Lennie mumbled and almost giggled, and Sturtz said, "What?"

"Nothing." He paused and when he spoke his voice was a bit louder. "Just Asking.'" That was the name of the gossip column I wrote for the paper." He drank. "Not that any of you would remember." His voice grew harder. "I was watching York that morning, wondering if he had said anything to Gavin about what I had told him. I followed him when he left the bunk."

"And he turned the confrontation into what is probably the best scene in the movie. That one on one game could get Joey a nomination."

Gavin spoke softly. "You are a sick fuck, you know that Lennie, a very, very sick fuck. You manipulated and lied and…"

A stridency crept into Dorff's voice. "Maybe, but you have your story of that time, and I have mine, and mine is up there on the screen for everyone to see. You say I jerked you off and that's not true…."

"I know I was drunk but there are things you don't……"

Dorff had no intention of letting Gavin make his point. "But even if it were true," he said, "who do you think people would believe? You want to bring all this into the open Gavin, fine; then do it. I'm a married man with two children. And what are you, huh, what do you have?"

As Gavin leapt up, Apple moved quickly and pulled him back down. Spittle flew from Gavin's mouth. "You fucking son of a bitch."

Surprisingly Dorff did not pull away, but rather stood his ground and held up his glass in a silent toast to the man who had lunged at him. "Always so high and mighty," Dorff spat. "Always so above it all. York and Gavin, the sons of the holy family. Yeah, right!"

The others stared at Dorff as if seeing him for the first time.

"Okay, Lennie," Sturtz started, but Dorff stopped him. "No," he said, "let me say what I have to say." He looked at Gavin who still sat with Andrew's hand on his shoulder. "You think what I added made York look bad?" His laugh had no humor in it. "Well, my friend, you don't know the half of what I left out."

"Lennie, don't." Andrew's voice was, for the first time that evening, uncertain. "Let it be."

"Let it be? Ooobladee, ooobladah," Dorff giggled.

"I think you've had a bit too much to drink Lennie." Sturtz put his hand on Dorff's shoulder and was surprised at the anger with which it was shaken off.

"I'm *good*. I'm fine," Dorff said, "but it's about time some more ghosts were let out of the closet." He giggled and pointed at Gavin. "And I don't mean *that* kind of closet. No, that's been done. No, this is a het-er-o-sexual secret, one that I could have easily put into the picture, but out of respect for you, Nicki, I didn't."

Nicki's mouth was dry. "What are you talking about, Lennie?"

Dorff finished his drink and went behind the bar to make himself another. "Lennie," Sturtz warned, but Dorff held up a hand, tsked and poured. "*Murder on the Orient Express*," he finally said, "that was good Henry." He drank deep. "And following in that vein, now, as the little detective would say, all will be revealed."

Andrew stood up. "We're leaving. We've heard enough." He turned to Sturtz. "Release your fucking movie. I won't sue, and win your fucking Award, and I hope you choke on it." He looked down at his wife, who sat leaning forward still staring at Dorff. "Come on, Nick, let's go."

Nicki slowly shook her head. "What are you talking about, Lennie? Tell me."

"Wellllllll," Dorff drawled, and for the first time Andrew noticed an effeminancy about him he had never noticed before. Dorff went on, clearly enjoying the spotlight, "it's kind of about your old boyfriend and a girl who wasn't you."

"Lennie, dammit," Andrew demanded, but Dorff sailed on, comfortable in a haze in which he couldn't be sure if he was really talking or not. "I really shouldn't be telling it because it was Henry who told it to me." His eyes sparkled as he looked at Sturtz. "You tell it, Henry. After all, it's your story."

"Damn it, Lennie. Shut the fuck up."

Dorff bowed to Sturtz. "Okay, then I'll tell it."

"What's he talking about, Henry," Nicki asked. Sturtz shook his head. "You don't want to know."

"What," Andrew asked, "was he involved in the Kennedy assassination? Did he kill Jimmy Hoffa and bury him under the mess hall?" Sturtz waved him away, but Apple persisted. "No, really. We're fucking middle aged, Henry. Don't you think it's a little late in the day for 'I know something you don't know'. I think this evening is over."

Nicki shook her head, and put a staying hand on Andrew's. "It's something to do with me, isn't it," Nicki asked, her voice low.

"Oh come on, Nicki," Andrew said, putting his hand on her shoulder, "don't play into his 'gotcha' game. Let it alone."

Sturtz nodded. "I never thought I would say this, but Apple is right, Nicki. Let it alone. There's no point."

Nicki shook her head. "Tell me, Henry, what's Lennie talking about?"

"Yeah, Henry," Dorff slurred, "what's Lennie talking about?"

Sturtz sighed. "At first I told him because I thought it would add to the story, then I realized it wasn't relevant at all."

"Oh, for fuck sake, Henry," Gavin almost yelled, "what?"

Sturtz shrugged. "It seems that York wasn't exactly true to Nicki during that last summer."

There was panic in Andrew's voice. "There's no need, Henry. Leave it alone."

Dorff smiled at him and pointed a finger. "Why, I'll be damned, you know too, don't you Apple? You know, too."

Nicki turned to her husband. "Do you? Tell me. If you know what he's talking about, tell me."

Andrew gulped. "I only heard about it fairly recently, and I didn't think there was any reason to tell you so long after....."

"Tell me."

Andrew sighed. "It was the day you met Gavin in the hospital. The day you had the appointment with Sue."

"Go on."

"Sue called me. She had to break the appointment. Her father or something."

"Her father in the nursing home, yes."

Andrew nodded. "In the nursing home. And while she was talking she let it slip that she and York had......"

The shriek of laughter that came from Dorff made all their heads turn to him. "*She* and York had! Now *that* is hot stuff. Good old saintly York strikes again." He barked another laugh, and spoke his next words into his drink. "Sue Barrett! Nah. He might have *done* Sue Barrett, but it wasn't Sue Barrett, was it Henry? Close, but no cigar." He leered at Nicki. "It was your other buddy, Ellen Marcus."

For a moment no one spoke. Sturtz broke the silence.

"I met Ellen again a few years ago. She called to congratulate me on the Oscar. I took her out to lunch for old times sake." Nicki just stared at him as Sturtz went on. "I know you've kept in touch with her over the years, Nicki: that you, Sue and Ellen are close friends and that she's shared a lot with you." Nicki nodded almost imperceptibly. "Yes," she whispered, "close friends."

Sturtz hesitated. "You're sure you want me to go on?"

"Oh, for Christ's sake, Henry," Andrew answered, "we've heard enough. Just shut up and leave it alone."

Nicki put her hand on his arm. "No," she said, "I want to hear." She nodded at Sturtz. "Tell me, Henry."

Sturtz shrugged. "Ellen kind of drank her lunch, I think she was impressed with the restaurant I took her to, and by dessert she was telling a bunch of tales out of school."

Nicki nodded. "Go on."

"It seems that it happened on the night of the hayride. It seems you were in the infirmary, Nick."

"Stomach flu."

"Whatever. You were in the infirmary and York was by himself."

'There's a story, the gypsies know is true,
That when your love wears Golden Earrings,
Love will come to you.'
The music played in Apple's head.

"Ellen was bummed because you," and Henry pointed at Gavin, "had been docked so she was on her own."

"And...."

Dorff interrupted. "But that wasn't the first time Gavin had let Ellen down." He held an open hand to his face and whispered conspiratorially behind it. "He wasn't with her on Circus Day nor," he said, with a leer, "was he *'with her'* down at the guest dock during the Cabaret. *Later*, of course, as we know he *was* there," he waved an admonishing finger at Gavin, "but not with Ell-en! What a bad, bad boy."

"You are something else, Lennie," Andrew said.

Dorff smiled. "You think?"

"Just amazing. Amazing. You simply don't care who you hurt do you?"

Dorff drank. "Whatever."

"Finish the story, Henry," Nicki said.

Sturtz sighed. "Do I have to?" He watched as Nicki looked down. "It didn't mean anything, Nic," he said. "The way it sounded to me was that it was nothing more than a pity fuck." He chuckled. "Hell, after lunch Ellen and I came back here and *I* fucked her, and, I have no doubt, she went home to her husband and kiddies without the slightest bit of guilt. It meant nothing with me, and it meant nothing with York. Ellen might not be the sharpest knife in the drawer, but one thing you can say for her is that she is a pragmatist." He looked at the four people sitting before him. "Sorry."

Nicki Polis Brookman sat staring at the floor for a moment, Andrew's hand on her shoulder.

Sturtz finally broke the silence. "Again, I'm sorry Nicki, but that's purely and simply the truth." Again, no one spoke, and he went on. "I think that's what the film is all about."

"Henry," Andrew started, but Sturtz held up a hand. "No", he said, "what I have to say is important. Let me finish." He looked first at Nicki and then at his two other old friends who stared at him. "York wasn't the star. He never was. He was a great looking kid who shone at sports and was nice to people. Period. He was not a star and he wasn't a god. You all made him that, then, and for all these years later. He was a kid and he was imperfect, well, shit, we all were, and that's what it's all about, that's why it had to be a small film, an ensemble piece with no big name star above the title. It was about all of us as much and maybe more than it was about York. I know you loved him, and I don't think any of this should change that, I just think that once and for all you, we, should see things as they were. Was he a god, no; was he a dick, no. What he was was sixteen."

Nicki breathed deeply and then looked up. "I'm ready if you are, Andrew." Her husband nodded and got up from his seat. There was so much to be said and nothing to be said. It was time to leave.

"I never meant to hurt you, Nicki," Dorff slurred. She didn't look at him, but rather turned to Sturtz. "Your film as a film is excellent, Henry. I wish you all the luck in the world with it."

Sturtz cockeyed an eyebrow, waiting for more, and then, when no more came, "Why thank you, Nicki."

She nodded. "Andrew?"

Andrew put his arm around his wife. "I'm sorry Nicki. There was no way I wanted to hurt you."

She smiled and took his hand. "I'll be fine. Just take me home," she said.

They opened the door and walked out of the room. "Meet you outside," Andrew called over his shoulder, and Gavin said, "In a minute." He got up from where he had been sitting and looked at Dorff half sitting, half lying on the couch. "Lennie," he said, "you and I know what is the truth. No one else does, and you know what, it's okay. It's over, and, as a wise man once said, 'What is, is.'" Dorff waved him away with a "Blah, blah. Blah." Gavin looked at Sturtz. "As for you, I have to believe you didn't mean any of it to hurt any of us."

Sturtz shook his head. "I didn't, Gavin," he said. "I truly didn't."

Gavin nodded. "Then, goodnight."

Sturtz smiled. "Gavin."

Gavin turned and Henry Sturtz whispered, "Kiss my son for me."

Gavin stood stock- still and looked down at the couch where Dorff lolled. Sturtz shook his head. "He's too out of it to put anything together. Don't worry about him."

"But," Gavin said softly, "Joey said you didn't know, that he hadn't told you."

"That he was gay? That you two were together?" Gavin nodded. "Gavin, I'm in show business. Gimme a break."

"And you didn't care?"

"Should I have?"

Gavin gave a kind of a laugh. "But he's so closeted. We never go anywhere that's public."

Sturtz nodded. "Because he's smart. Let Joey become a star and then come out if he wants to, but not now. Not yet."

Gavin's mind whirled. "And you knew about us and didn't say anything?"

Sturtz smiled. "Seems I do a lot of that."

"Jesus!"

"Gavin, when he went to see you last winter at first I wasn't sure it was a good idea. Then, when I had time to think about it, I realized it was perfect and I encouraged him. I wanted him to get to know you."

"For the picture."

"You're still a schmuck," Sturtz smiled. "No, not for the picture. Okay, maybe a little bit for the picture, but he's my son and I love him and I worry about him." He shrugged. "But there are things that, believe it or not, I am not versed in. Being a homo is one of them. And, I figured, who better to show him the ins and outs, and I won't even make a joke here, than my buddy Gavin, the oldest fagela I know? I didn't know it would become a serious thing, but as long as you're both careful, I'm glad."

"Gav, you coming? " Andrew called from the hall.

"One minute." Gavin turned back to Sturtz, smiled and shook his head. "You just never know do you?" He held out his hand and Sturtz shook it.

"*You* never know because you're a schmuck, but *I* know everything there is to know."

"Maybe you do," Gavin said. "Maybe you just do." He smiled. "Anyway, thank you."

"Go fuck yourself," Sturtz replied, patting him lightly on the cheek. Gavin laughed and went to the door. Sturtz stopped him. "Tell Joey I'll call him next week."

"I'll do that."

"He was good, wasn't he?"

"In the movie? Yeah, he was wonderful."

"Yeah," Sturtz agreed, "he was, wasn't he?'

"Goodnight, Henry," Gavin said and Sturtz nodded in return.

Gavin pushed open the door and joined his friends in the quiet of the night.

Sturtz finished his drink and looked at Dorff who lay on the couch. "You okay to get home, Lennie?" he asked, not unkindly. Dorff's eyes were closed and a bit of drool came from his open mouth. "Maybe a few minutes," he slurred. Sturtz nodded and smiled as he heard Lennie Dorff begin to snore. "You and I are going to make a great deal of money together," Sturtz thought, as he looked at the man sleeping on his couch then clicked off the lights.

Lennie Dorff slept and dreamed of a single blue contact lens. It stared up at him from the top of a pile of dead leaves. The light shone off of it and Lennie Dorff thought he had never seen anything so beautiful. Laughing, he crushed it under his shoe.

CHAPTER THIRTY-NINE:

FINAL CREDITS:

"My God," Nicki said, "it hasn't changed at all." They stood near the head counselor's bunk at the bottom of the quadrangle and looked at the campers getting ready for lunch.

"They're all so young," Andrew said watching as lockers slammed, screen doors squealed open and shut and the raucous sound of boy's voices filled the air.

Gavin stood staring at Bunk 33 and felt Nicki's hand move into his. "Huh," he half laughed, half sighed and Nicki resisted the urge to look at his face. Instead, she increased the pressure on his hand and smiled when she felt him press back.

"Seriously," Andrew asked, "were we ever that young?"

Nicki laughed. "Andrew, that's a cliché, but we were. Only we didn't know it."

"Doesn't matter how old you are, you never know it." They looked up as Howard Portnoy, the head counselor, walked through his screen door, his head still wet from his shower. "So, did you do the grand tour?"

Nicki nodded. "And thanks for letting us. I know it's not visitor's day and it was kind of you break the rules for us."

Portnoy shrugged. "It was okay," he smiled, "Ike Hayes had his eye on you."

"Hello, Brookman, Andrew."

"My God," Andrew almost choked, "is *he* still here?"

Portnoy laughed. "Would there even be a Kanuga without Boo Radley? Sure he's still here and as vibrant as ever. I swear I don't think the man ever ages."

"I would not be surprised," Andrew smiled, "I would not be surprised one little bit." He turned to the head counselor. "Does he still drive the seniors to their Mystery Walk?"

Portnoy nodded. "Would it be a Mystery Walk without him?"

"Ike Hayes," Andrew said, shaking his head "damn!" He laughed. "I don't suppose the Luggage King is still around!"

"My God, Andrew," Nicki smiled, "he must have been 150 when *we* were here."

Portnoy laughed. "Oh, he must have been younger than that, because he was up here for this whole summer. Just left a few days ago."

"Gotta be a different Luggage King," Andrew said, but when the head counselor described him Gavin knew it was the same man who had looked after him after his confrontation with Ralph Sanchez. "I would have liked to have said hello to him," he said.

"Try again next summer," Portnoy said. "He's always here."

"It's really amazing. We were just saying that none of it seems to have changed at all."

"Well," the head counselor said pointing, "the bunks are the same." He nodded towards them. " Well, you can see that. They're painted, though, every four years whether they need it or not." He smiled. "Have you been to Hayes Hall?" They shook their heads. "Last chance to see it before it's totally renovated. New floor, new baskets, new stage, re-built roof," he chuckled, "a lot of us thought it would be cheaper to tear it down and start all over again, but the owner wouldn't hear of it."

"Too much history," Andrew said softly.

Portnoy looked at his watch. "Look, I'm going to blow the bugle for lunch in about ten minutes, you're welcome to eat with us in the mess hall if you'd like."

"One two three four,
We want color war."

The three friends looked at one another and without speaking knew they would decline. Gavin finally spoke for them. "No, but thank you. We'll probably stop for something in at the diner in Monticello if it's still there."

"Oh, it's still there," Portnoy said. "Same owners, I understand. Food's good."

"Great. That or maybe just head straight through to the city."

"Well then, I'd suggest that if you want to get to Hayes without getting run over by a herd of hungry campers, you probably should make your way over there now."

They shook hands all around and headed down the lower pathway to the great wooden social hall. As they turned a corner, Andrew stopped them and pointed. "Look," he said. Behind the upper row of bunks, three trucks waited, the flatbed of each piled high with trunks.

"They'll deliver those to the front of each bunk while the kids are eating," Gavin said. "Another summer over."

The three friends walked without speaking to the doors of Hayes Hall.

They had driven south from Ithaca after they had dropped Jessica at Cornell, and without her constant cheery chatter, the car had seemed empty, too quiet. She had wanted to get a head start on the fall semester and, though it was only the third week in August, they had packed her clothes and books, piled them into the trunk of Gavin's huge black Cadillac and taken the thruway up.

Nicki told them later that as they said their goodbyes, Jessica seemed sadder to leave Gavin than she or Andrew. As soon as the two had been introduced, they had taken to each other immediately and for the whole summer they were inseparable. They were at every play on Broadway and at every movie around the area and found something to like in everything they saw, though they hadn't liked CONQUISADOR 3.

Joey had flown in from Germany where he had just finished his next film, and Jessica had giggled like a three year old when she was introduced to him. Within days she was as close to him as she was to Gavin and they had, for all intents and purposes, to the exclusion of everyone else, become the three musketeers. (Jessica had squealed with delight when a paparazzi picture of her holding hands with Joey appeared on the cover of PEOPLE Magazine with the legend, "Mystery Woman in Joey Carter's Life." Nicki and Andrew framed it and hung it proudly in their living room.)

Weekends were spent all together, with Nicki and Andrew joining them, on Fire Island. Long, languid days were spent on the beach, good food and drink in abundance, Trivial Pursuit into the wee hours of the morning and laughter filling their days. Willie, of course, was beside himself with pleasure.

Earlier, they had thrown open the doors and windows of Gavin's New York apartment and made it ready for the autumn and the New Year to come.

Joey was to have joined them on their trip to Cornell, but at the last minute was called back to Munich for re-takes. He and Jessica had a long goodbye with promises of a week of fun at Christmas.

The idea to take the back roads back to New York had been Gavin's. "Just one more time," he had said, "just to finish it all."

"I thought you never wanted to go back there again," Nicki had argued, but Gavin had persisted and now they stood at the center entrance to the social hall. Andrew pointed at a sign that hung over the door. "The sign's still there. What a rush!"

"I'd like to go in alone for a minute, if you don't mind," Gavin said and both Andrew and Nicki nodded their heads. "To be honest," Andrew said, "I'm fine without ever going back in there at all."

"How about we wait for you over there under the tree," Nicki said, linking her arm through her husband's and walking slowly away.

Gavin stepped through the doors.

The smell of memory was overpowering. Sneakers, sweat and basketballs, age and youth all met here. Wood that had been cut generations before still emitted a fragrance that made Gavin's heart hurt.

As always, it was dark in the hall. Without switching on the fluorescent lights Gavin could see in the dimness that everything was the same; that nothing had changed. He went over to the old upright piano and touched the cracked yellow keys. He turned around at stared at the cavernous hall.

"The last song of the evening will be the senior alma mater."

"And the winner of the camp character award goes to….."
"You and Sturtz definitely will be camper chiefs."
"Shma Yisroel……"
The sound of sneakers skidding on the shellacked floor!
"Here…here….here….I'm open."
"Hey York, look, Mom's here."

Gavin walked slowly, slowly onto the basketball key that faced the stage. He could hear the thunk of the ball, the woosh of the ball, and York's voice yelling, *"Good one Gav. You're the man!"*

And in the shadowy light of the empty hall, Gavin Stewart slipped to his knees, hugged himself and rocked back and forth, his mouth open in a silent O as hot tears ran down his cheeks. "It's okay York," he wept as he rocked, "whatever happened, I loved you so fucking much." And he was aware of the ghosts, aware of the darkness, and as the silent color war plaques that lined the walls stared down at him, he was aware of his life.

He sat rocking for a while, even after the tears had stopped, then looked at the stage where the film ghost of Ralph Sanchez stood beside young actors who stood awaiting their cues for the first time, and he knew it was time to leave.

A recording of a bugle blew through the loud speakers that hung over the stage, startling him. "Everyone out to lunch," Howard Portnoy called after the last sounds of the call faded away. "Everyone directly to the mess hall for your big mid-day meal. Everyone directly to the mess hall! Ira Bayers get those lazy seniors of yours to the mess hall, ya bum, ya." The microphone on the other end of the PA clicked off and Gavin made his way out of the echoing hall.

"You okay," Nicki asked as Gavin walked up behind them. He nodded as he pulled a tissue from his pocket and laughed as he blew his nose. Andrew threw one arm around him and the other around Nicki and led them across campus toward the lake, as boys of all ages, shapes and sizes made their way past them, going in the opposite direction.

The lake was harder than they thought it would be. As soon as they walked onto the quiet dock and looked into the clear, blue water, Nicki began to cry. Andrew wrapped his arm around her, a lump growing in his own throat. Gavin's face was expressionless, his body tense. They stood this way for a moment or two and then, without plan, each moved away from the other and stood looking first into the swimming area and then out to the raft and to the diving board.

And in his mind, Andrew saw:

York climbed out of the water, onto the raft and up onto the diving board. His sleek body glistened in the afternoon sun. He moved to the edge of the board, he tensed and just before he started his dive, he winked at Apple.

The dive was perfection. In slow motion he lifted from the board and rose high, high into the sky. When he could go no farther, his downward arc was so perfect that Apple began to laugh. He entered the water without a ripple, was lost from sight for a moment and then reappeared, shaking water from his hair and giving Apple a wide grin and a big thumbs up.

"How was that Apple?"

"Your best yet, buddy."

"You just bullshitting me?"

"Nope. Swear to God."

"Wish you could come in."

"Wish I could too, and I will sometime, but I can't now. You understand."

"Of course I do."

"See you after swim."

York nodded and started swimming slowly across the lake. Apple called, "York."

York turned, and when he saw that his friend couldn't manage his words, he grinned. "You're not going to get all sappy with me now, are you?"

"I just wanted to tell you," Andrew mouthed, with no sound coming from him. "I just wanted to tell you...," he barely managed.

"No need," York said with a grin. "I know. I do too, my dear friend." He turned and swam slowly away.

Andrew watched him cut slowly through the water. York turned once more, waved and called, "Bye, Apple. See you after swim."

And then he was gone.

And Nicki:

....smiled at the water and said. "Henry says you weren't the hero of our story." And York replied, "I never said I was, Nick. I never said I was."

"I know what happened with Sue and Ellen."

And York replied, "I'm sorry, Nicki. I wouldn't do it now. I was a kid."

"I loved you."

"I loved you too."

And that was enough.

And Gavin.....

...called the others over, and as they came and stood on either side of him, he pulled York's mezuzah and chain from his pocket.

"I'm not sure I know how to do this," he said, and Nicki smiled and said. "There's no right or wrong way." She touched his shoulder. "Go ahead, Gav."

Gavin took a deep breath. "Yiska dah, yiska dah, Shamay, a rabbo," he intoned and then grinned sheepishly at the others. "That's all I know."

Nicki pulled him to her. "That's enough," she said, "he heard you."

Gavin nodded, took a deep breath, drew his arm back and flung the mezuzah as far out into the lake as he could. "I love you, bro," he called into the silence of the day.

"Goodbye, York," Nicki said smiling and wiping her eyes. "Rest in peace."

The three friends stood there for another moment, watching the sunlight twinkle on the water, hearing the first cicadas herald the coming of autumn and then turned and walked back to the car.

They heard the roar of other voices coming from the mess hall.

"Maybe we should have accepted his offer," Andrew offered. "It's Sunday, there's probably pie a la mode."

The friends laughed, Nicki dried her eyes again and got into the car. Andrew pushed the button that opened the gate and they drove through. "Should I close it?," he asked. "No," Gavin said. "Get in. I'm pretty sure Portnoy said it's one of those gates that closes by itself." Andrew got back in the car and as Gavin backed up and then drove through the gate he said, "So the diner in Monticello *is* still open and the food's still good. Whattaya think?"

Nicki shook her head. "No," she said. "Let's try something new." They turned onto the road and headed back to the city.

Ike Hayes walked across the road, closed the gate, and watched them on their way.
